THE DARK
BETWEEN THE STARS

THE DARK
BETWEEN THE STARS

KENNETH C. GARDNER, JR.

iUniverse, Inc.
Bloomington

The Dark Between the Stars

iUniverse books may be ordered through booksellers or by contacting:

iUniverse
1663 Liberty Drive
Bloomington, IN 47403
www.iuniverse.com
1-800-Authors (1-800-288-4677)

ISBN: 978-1-4759-3313-0 (sc)
ISBN: 978-1-4759-3314-7 (ebk)

Printed in the United States of America

iUniverse rev. date: 06/23/2012

DEDICATED TO

MOM, for her faith in me and her love
My DAD and UNCLE ADS, for their inspiration and example
DUDE and DOC, the finest of brothers
ELWOOD and MATTHEW, for reasons they know and
My wife, CAROL, without whom nothing else matters

CHAPTER I

"Y a can learn a lot about America by readin' trains, but ya can learn a lot more about her and about yourself by ridin' 'em."

We'd heard him say it before and would hear him say it again, but each time the meaning was different, as different as the drag freight just passing the Dundee siding southeast of our town was from .the fast freight we'd seen highball through an hour-and-a-half before.

"When I was your age," Twig continued, lifting his stump with his hands as he shifted around, "this country was tight just like a spring or a coiled rattlesnake. It was gettïn' ready to go someplace and in a hurry. I useta read the cars then, too, and I can remember a lot of short dreams: New Jersey Central, Morris & Essex, Michigan Central, Chicago and Alton, Alton and Terre Haute, Hannibal & St. Jo., St. Paul and Omaha. Most of 'em are belly-up or merged now."

The light gray smoke was boiling up closer to our town, tossed up and back like a wooly plume in the breezeless prairie sky.

"Of course, we had our bigger dreams like the Missouri Pacific, the Kansas and Texas, and the Mobile and Ohio, but the country was just gettin' ready to go on its rolly-coaster ride. It'd paid for its ticket and got on board and was strapped in and ready, but was barely movin' yet."

Pearl looked out and said, "She's comin' in."

I looked down the line. From the angle I couldn't tell much about the locomotive except she was big. There was a lot of hurrying on the depot platform, but it didn't look like they would be doing any switching, so it wouldn't be too long and we'd be reading her.

Twig had two spots. Most of the time he'd use the place we were in. It was under an abandoned loading dock on the north side of the

1

tracks. He'd fixed it all up with wood and cardboard and rugs, and if you didn't mind the smell of creosote on warm days, it wasn't bad. On really bright days with the Dakota sun hotter than an N-1's boiler, Twig would be in Spot 2.

Spot 2 was on the south side of the tracks in some tall grass. It was just a piece of white canvas nailed onto some old ties. Twig didn't put any rugs in Spot 2. On the hot days he'd dig up the ground and then lie on it to help keep cool. Before he'd go home, he'd get some marsh water and throw it on the dirt so it would be moist and cool the next day.

No one on the railroad bothered either spot because they all knew Twig.

Merle touched my shoulder and pointed. Heading down-track through the grass on the south side were two tramps. Both carried large kerchiefs bulging with their "possibles."

"Gonna head out," I said.

"Coasters," Twig said from inside.

"Wish I could be one, too," Pearl said, sprawled out on one elbow.

All of us, even Twig probably, wished that.

The tramps were skirting further south through a small marsh and soon disappeared into the reeds. They'd come out near the elevators, scout the situation, and make a run for an open boxcar or maybe a gondola while the train was stopped and the yard bulls weren't looking. Only fools and Easterners caught a train on the fly, Twig said.

We waited, the late morning air full of creosote and dreams.

A large puff of black smoke from the stack and a smaller spurt of white on either side of the wheels and the locomotive inched forward. Then came the sounds—the whistle, the escaping steam, and the metallic "chunk" repeated as each car snapped forward.

The train wasn't rolling very fast when it came by Twig's Spot. We were only a quarter mile or so from the depot. It was easy to read the train.

The locomotive was a big 4-8-2, called a Mountain-type. Twig had told us that steam locomotives were classified by their wheel arrangements. I saw that it had four lead carrying wheels, eight drivers for power, and two trailing wheels supporting the firebox, so it was a 4-8-2. The original type was designed for use in the Alleghenies, out East, so that's where the "Mountain" came in.

I said, "Twig, . . . a Baldwin?"

"No. It's a Lima. Built in '14."

Twig knew everything about the Great Northern.

As usual, most of the cars were Great Northern with "Old Bill," the goat, standing on a mountain and looking straight out at us, telling us to go to Glacier National Park.

But some of the GN cars were older and just had a rectangle with "Great Northern Railway" printed diagonally across it with "See America First" above the rectangle and "Glacier National Park" below it. Twig said that sign had come in just about the time Europe started blowing its brains out.

"Hey, look!" Pearl yelled. He was down the tracks a ways. "A Nickel Plate."

That was a real find, for of the thirty-five cars, I counted twenty-four GN, nine NP, and one Soo, all common. Only Pearl's Nickel Plate was out of the ordinary.

The caboose rolled past, the brakeman tossing a wave, and the clackety-clack hurried down the line to Minot, Big Muddy, Glasgow, Havre, Shelby, Spokane, and Seattle.

We stood up, all except Twig, our eyes watching the red dot heading northwest turn black and the black being lost on the horizon and the gray smoke stretching back from the train lingering over the track and then suddenly it was gone and all we could see was the Hamlein elevator waving five miles up the line, but we'd been there.

"Saw a 'Silker' last week."

"No foolin'?" Pearl sounded jealous.

"Silkers" were the Silk Trains.

"Ever ride one?" I asked.

"Never happen. Ever'thin' is speed with a Silker. The cargo is custom-cleared on board ship between Victoria and Seattle. The baggage cars are inspected, cleared, and are already lined up along the pier. The brakes, wheels, and bushin's have already been checked twice. The bales of silk are off-loaded and loaded onto the Silker as fast as possible. The doors are locked and sealed. The conductor already has his orders, so there's no stoppin'. The Silker heads out off Pier 41 or 89 under steam and high ball. No one's gonna jump that train, especially with its shot gun guards. Sometimes the passengers haven't even gotten off the ship by the time the Silker is gone."

Everything was speed on a Silker. A lot of people thought that was due to the fact that the silk worm cocoons might break open and the silk thread destroyed, but Twig had explained to us that the silk was in bales, not the raw cocoons, and that the speed was due to the volatility of the silk market in New York and the high cost of insurance which was based on each hour the silk was on the railroad.

"Dinner time, boys."

Twig crawled out of Spot 1, pulling his crutches along. Getting them in position, he hopped up on his good leg and pulled a crutch under each armpit. Without waiting for us, he started hobbling home, swinging his stump and leg together.

Twig lived in an old boxcar on the east side of the wye. The wye was a Y-shaped track that extended north off one of the sidings. It went between the brick roundhouse and turntable, which were to the west of it, and a water treatment plant and a water tower to the east. Its base pointed directly at the reservoir the GN built near the river to provide enough water for its steam locomotives. The wye itself could be used when they wanted to turn a locomotive around.

We caught up with Twig, hopping down the wye.

"Not much of a train, huh, Twig?"

"No, but seein' a Plate ain't too bad."

"Did ya ever ride the Plate?"

"Once. Just once. But it ain't nothin' to brag about. It was only from Cleveland to Buffalo and nothin' happened."

He turned off the wye, thumped over a small plank bridge, and followed a hardened narrow path through a clump of willows to his home. We came behind him and soon stood in front of a wooden boxcar, its red paint weathered off, its big doors shut and caulked. A homemade window peered out the west side and a homemade door edged out from the south end where some old pallets with plyboard nailed to them made a porch. The car sat more or less upright on the ground, its trucks having been removed when the car was junked.

"Comin' back this afternoon?"

"Maybe," Merle replied. "But it's our birthday and Maw's givin' us a party."

"How old do ya be?"

"Eighteen. Both of us." We all laughed.

"And you, Lige?"

4

"Eighteen last week," I replied.

"Eighteen," Twig said softly and looked at each of us. "Eighteen," he repeated and turned to his door.

We started down a path that headed out of the willows and ended near Gregory Avenue.

"Happy birthday," Twig called from his doorway.

The twins turned and waved. I yelled "Thanks" even though it wasn't my birthday. Twig went in to his dinner and we headed home to ours.

CHAPTER II

Our town was a creature of the railroads.

Forty years before there had been no town; there was just Old Hugh homesteading a mile or so south of the river. Then some big shots in the Northern Pacific decided to send a branchline north of Kingston to hook up with Sacred Water Lake and the Indian Reservation.

Well, the only place to cross the river was just north of Old Hugh's, so the railroad ran its right-of-way through his farm, let him in on the best townsite blocks and before you knew it, there's a town by the tracks and Old Hugh's the bank's first president and later a millionaire.

But, like I said, the NP only sent a branchline, so the town just got as big as a branchline town gets and then stopped growing. It kind of lingered on the prairie for thirty years and then some big shots in the Great Northern decided that going from Fargo to Minot by way of Grand Forks was too long, so they proposed a mainline directly from Fargo northwest to Minot, and it just so happened that our town was right directly on that line.

When that cut-off came through, our town started jumping. The GN made us a section headquarters. It built a twenty-one stall brick roundhouse, turntable, car repair barns, two water towers, a reservoir, a water treatment plant, coal chutes, stockyards, a two-story depot, and a hotel with a lunchroom. And the wye. The town grew and we became more than just an empty circle in Rand McNally.

I can still remember when the first through-train on the GN came whistling and chugging its way up from Fargo. They put bunting on the cowcatcher, and the mayor made a speech the end of which we all missed because the engineer blew out the steam just then.

From that time on there was only one ambition for the boys in our prairie town on the south side of the river. That was to be a railroadman.

When a rancher from the hill country northwest or northeast of town would drive in a herd of cattle, we'd burn to be cowboys and ride the Wild West and shoot Indians. A big fire like the one that burned the Agnes Hotel and half a block of stores with it, and we'd want to be big city firemen and would start small blazes of our own in Winslow's pasture and put them out with a bucket brigade from the river. And, of course, baseball players. We all would have died to be Ty Cobb or Rogers Hornsby or, if you loved pitching, Grover Cleveland Alexander, Burleigh Grimes, Big Jim Vaughn, Walter "Big Train" Johnson, or the Babe. But all these ambitions came and went. Being a railroadman remained.

Many trains came through on the cut-off each day, but twice a day the mail and passenger trains stopped. Before these events, the day was alive with anticipation; after them, the day was over.

Our town, plowed out of the prairie, sits placidly on the south shoulder of the river, the summer sun lazily climbing the eastern sky. Downtown the ruts in the streets accumulate dust. Inside the stores, clerks are trying to wear out their elbows, leaning on the counters. An old farmer's horse whickers outside the feed and seed store. On the depot platform are two or three freight piles, and the dray wagon is tied up at the rear of the depot, with Hiram, the town drunk fragrantly recalling last night in a dream, sleeping under the wagon.

The steel rails, worn bright, heat up in the sun. Coming from infinity, they stretch off into infinity.

Soon a fleck of smoke appears above one point of infinity. A depot hand, a young Indian from the Lakota Reservation twelve miles north of town, raises the call.

Hiram rolls away from the dray wagon and under the depot platform. The clerks straighten their elbows. Farmers jump to their teams or their Model T's to come to the station to gawk. Small wagons, carts, and trucks pour down from the town to the depot. Jimmy brings the jitney from the Oleson House, hoping for customers. Along the lengthy plank platform stand men, women, and children, looking at the train pulling in.

The engine chuffs by with the engineer only apparently oblivious to the commotion. The engine is long and powerful, a fifty-five inch drivered twelve wheeler (4-8-0). A big stack up front breathes out smoke. Beneath it, the smoke box fronts the steam engine itself, a big black barrel riding the four wheels and the eight huge drivers with a square steam chest above the shiny black cylinders.

Up in the cab, the engineer nonchalantly surveys his domain and drinks in our envy. The fireman flings some coal from the tender into the orange glow of the firebox.

A few passengers disembark and are swept away to family, friends, or to the Oleson. Other passengers get on. The mail is rushed to the post office as other mail pouches are put on board. Freight goes on and the dray wagon is loaded with freight coming off.

Ten minutes later the engineer whistles, the conductor shouts, and the wheels spin and grab. The couplings chunk and slowly the train pulls out. The crowd breaks up and leaves, except for us boys who wait for infinity to absorb the last car.

Hiram rolls out from under the platform and heads north, hoping to find an affluent and congenial ex-passenger, who is not unduly influenced by the prohibition laws, in one of the hotels.

CHAPTER III

It was a downright embarrassing experience going to a birthday party for two eighteen year old boys. Of course, everyone has birthday parties and everybody goes to birthday parties, but Merle and Pearl were the only boys in town whose mother continued to give them parties after they were twelve years old.

She was different and always had been.

She'd come to North Dakota from "Back East" the same year Teddy Roosevelt became president. My Dad, nicknamed Boss, who liked Teddy the cowboy, but distrusted TR the trustbuster, recalled that year by saying "'The Lord giveth and the Lord taketh away,' but sometimes He gives us some strange combinations." Grandpa Bear, who hated Teddy for the way he claimed to have won the Spanish-American War single-handed and doubly hated him for bullying Jim Hill in the Northern Securities case, said it was the year of the three plagues: the grasshoppers, "that infernal cowboy," and Lucretia Inglehoff, as she was known then.

She taught a rural school for one term and then quit. She never said why, but two years later another female teacher who, like her, had boarded at the farm house of the head of the board of education left under what Boss charitably called "mysterious circumstances." No female teachers ever boarded there again.

She moved into town and washed dishes and cleaned rooms at the Woodson Hotel until she met Merle Potman, a farmer with two sections of prime wheat land. They courted on the back steps and in the kitchen of the hotel for two years and then were married.

With their first child on the way, they argued and then fought over a name. Finally, they agreed that he would name it if it was a boy, and she would name it if it was a girl. He chose his own name, and she picked the name of her maternal grandmother, Pearl, the only relative that wrote regularly to her from the East.

Even when one turned out to be two, and two boys at that, she refused to give up the name she had chosen, and despite the rhyming effect, neither would he. So Merle and Pearl it was. After that beginning the twins were used to being embarrassed.

She insisted that with a family, they should live in town, so they bought a three-story house on West Stimson Avenue.

Lucretia Potman became a Georgist single-taxer, a mother again, a vegetarian, a mother again, a suffragette, a mother again, a pacifist, a mother again, a Leaguer, and a mother twice more. Merle, Sr., bought another section, ate pink prime rib and blood-red steaks, opposed woman suffrage, supported the Great War, opposed the ratification of the Treaty of Versailles, was a father eight times, and died of apoplexy on the day Warren G. Harding let Eugene V. Debs walk out of the Atlanta Penitentiary. Mrs. Potman buried his body in Eternal Rest Cemetery, sold the farms, and invested the money in the auto industry, even though she didn't own a car herself.

By the time I was clean and ready, I was already late. The party was set for two o'clock, and I hadn't even started getting ready until a quarter of. I probably would have made it on time anyway, but after I washed with good old Lifebuoy Health Soap and brushed my teeth with Pebeco, I saw Ma's bar of Jap Rose Soap on the stand, so I washed my neck with that. Don't ask me why I did; I just did. I suppose I thought a rose smell was as good as any to bring to a birthday party for two eighteen year old boys who didn't really want one.

Just before I left the bathroom, I checked my beard. There wasn't much there yet, but the blonde hairs were slowly becoming whiskers. I wouldn't have had time to do anything about them anyway, but it gave me a good feeling just to check. I drew the comb straight back through my hair, liberally supplied with Wildroot Tonic, ran downstairs, picked up the presents, and headed down the alley toward the party.

I had five-and-a-half blocks to walk and when I got there I was five minutes late.

The party was going on in both the backyard and the house. I liked the backyard. It was separated from the alley by a white picket fence, and the northwest corner was devoted to a pile of rocks, bushes, and weeds. An old barn had stood there, but just after the family moved into town, Mrs. Potman had it torn down and the rock foundation leveled but left in the corner. It had grown up to gooseberries, currants, wild grapes, and weeds, but she kept it that way for any wild creatures that might want to live there. I suppose she had a couple of cottontails in the bushes and maybe some mice and sparrows, but everything else was bugs and mosquitoes. Except in mid-summer when the gooseberries were good, nobody went in there.

Just east of the tangle, I vaulted the fence and came down inches behind the youngest Potman, Thomas Woodrow.

He turned, a little startled, but seeing who it was, said, "Hello, Elijah."

He was in a little Marmon car, the kind you pedal underneath. I'd seen it before. It was about three feet long, brown with yellow stripes, and had an adjustable windshield, headlights, wheels with corrugated tread tires, nickel-plated hubcaps, a license plate, an adjustable clutch, and an instrument board. The board had "American National Company" written across it and had an on-off switch, oil gauge, meter, speedometer, and a clock.

It had everything, and I wished I had had one when I was Tommy's age, but back then they hardly had any cars in town, much less a little model one.

"Goodbye, Elijah."

He pedaled away, the lucky little kid. It even had a gas control on the steering wheel.

I walked along the garden toward the house. The Potmans' garden was legendary in our town, a garden among gardens. The rows were straight and marked by stakes. Neatly tacked to each stake was a little sign with the name of the corresponding vegetable. No weed dared show its head in the Potman garden, and the younger Potmans had been designated as the weed killers.

Year after year the garden flourished, supplying the Potmans' needs, with much produce left over for the neighbors and friends. The Potman garden was lavish with its crisp radishes, fat carrots, yellow sweet corn, snappy green beans, bushels of blueberries and indigo grapes grown against the "wild corner," and shiny eggplants. Peas, cucumbers, lettuce, pumpkins, squash, beets, tomatoes, turnips, onions, and potatoes completed its staples, but it also contained our town's only kale and kohlrabi.

Mrs. Potman liberally fertilized the garden herself with goat, chicken, rabbit, and cow manure, giving it what she claimed was an incomparable edge over regular gardening practice. She may have been right, based on output and taste, but everyone else in town stuck with straight cow dung.

The garden was protected by a woven wire fence from the depredations of the goat, which was in harness pulling six year old Henry George Potman (Merle, Sr., surrendered early on the children's names) in the little Climax Farm Wagon. Its box was painted green with yellow striping, and the steel gear was red with black striping. The tongue had been removed and a set of hardwood shafts put on so the goat could do the pulling. H.G. had on a big straw hat, a pair of blue denim bib overalls, and he held a whip made out of a sapling and fishline. In the wagon box was a cage of chickens and rabbits, kidnapped from the pen and hutches on the west side of the yard.

"Whoa, there, Old Bill," H.G. called. The goat obeyed.

"Hi, H.G. Sellin' chickens and bunnies?"

"No, I'm takin' 'em for a ride."

I squatted and looked in the cage. The rabbits appeared resigned; the chickens were uneasy.

"Did you come to the party? We get cake and ice cream."

"Yeah, where is everyone?"

"In the house. Boy, Lige, you smell like roses!" I headed for the house. "Giddap, Old Bill."

I rapped at the back door. I could hear someone in the kitchen through the screen. I rapped again, the screen door knocking back and forth on its hinges.

"Coming."

Footsteps and then she appeared, coming around the corner.

"Why, Elijah. Come in. You didn't have to knock."

"Hello, Mrs. Potman. I'm sorry I'm late."

I reached in my pocket and pulled out the two small, neatly wrapped packages. I held them out to her.

"It's all right. The party hasn't really begun yet. No, take them to the boys. They're in the front room with their other guests."

She turned to go back to her work in the kitchen. "Just go on in." As I walked by her into the hallway leading to the front room, she said, "My, Elijah, you certainly smell nice."

A little way down the hall a big oak staircase rose up to my left and wound around above the back of my head to the second floor. Beyond it was a built-in bench, also of oak. Across from the bench were two sliding oak doors leading to the front room. They were part-way open and I stood just outside them looking in.

Across the room by the phonograph were Cecilia and Emily Livingstone. They were cousins and were showing off their differences by alternately selecting records to play. "Margie" by the Ted Lewis Jazz Band was on, so I knew it was Cecilia's turn. Her next would probably be another snappy one like "How Ya Gonna Keep 'Em Down On The Farm?" or "Dark Town Strutters Ball." Emily would choose "My Isle of Golden Dreams" or "I'm Forever Blowing Bubbles" or maybe Al Jolson's "April Showers."

Merle was beside the phonograph, looking pleasantly embarrassed. He liked Cecilia.

I caught his eye and he nodded his head to come over.

There were eleven others in the room, seated on the davenport or armchairs or standing. Elizabeth, Susan, Lucy, and Carrie Potman were seated in the background, too young to join in with the rest and too old to be in the backyard. A chorus of "Hey, Lige!" and "Hi, Elijah" greeted my entrance, with one "Eli" from David Dailey, a boy I hated and the twins were indifferent to, but whose mother was friends with their mother.

I handed the presents over to Merle and he placed them on a table with the others. I stood by Emily. I was right—"My Isle of Golden Dreams" by the Columbia Orchestra came on.

Emily turned. "Lige."

"Hi, Emily." She was an O.K. girl.

"Lige, you're late and you smell like a rose."

David Dailey, who had come up behind me, started to laugh. If it hadn't been a party, there'd have been blood on the floor right then. I'd been waiting for a chance to get him for catching my dog, Ted, and clipping his hair off in patches so he looked like a poodle, though I couldn't prove it was him. "You do; you smell like a rose." He laughed again.

I turned and walked over to Pearl on the davenport. My ears and neck were burning. I hated Jap Rose Soap.

"Pearl, I have to use your bathroom."

"O.K."

We left the room as "My Isle of Golden Dreams" scratched to a halt, and Cecilia and Emily began to argue over which one had jarred the needle.

"Darktown Strutters Ball" followed us up the stairs and down the hall to the right.

Inside the bathroom Pearl gave me a bottle of Bay Rum and I sloshed it on my face and neck.

"What's Dailey doin' here?"

"You know."

"I guess, but I don't like it."

"Whew! Take it easy on that stuff. I use it, too."

"Since when?"

"Since I started shaving."

"Since when was that?"

"About an hour ago."

We laughed and then I looked at him close. There were no cuts.

"Really?"

"Yeah."

I rubbed his face; it was smooth. He really had.

He ran a brush through his dark hair. "Let's go."

As I followed him out, I saw, beside the Madison closet, a movie magazine with Mabel Normand's face on the cover.

"Hey, wait." I picked it up. "She's beautiful."

"Yeah, but ya know what they say about her."

"I don't care. She's still beautiful. And funny."

"Well, she won't be so funny if she keeps monkeyin' around with that dope or whatever."

"I don't believe that anyway. That's just a story Dailey came back with after he visited his grandmother in Pasadena."

"But ya do believe she was mixed up with Taylor. That was in the papers. It was no rumor."

Pearl was right. Mabel Normand and movie director William Desmond Taylor and his murder were not rumor. Everything had been in the papers.

We headed downstairs where everyone else was already at the table.

Mrs. Potman had baked two cakes: a German chocolate for Merle and a yellow cake with chocolate frosting for Pearl. Thirty-six candles blazed as we sang "Happy Birthday," then the cakes were cut and Mrs. Potman brought home-made ice cream out of the ice box. There were also bottles of soda pop from our local bottler—cream soda, root beer, and strawberry.

As the rest of us ate and talked, the younger Potmans went out to their play fort in the backyard, and their mother and Elizabeth brought them plates of cake and ice cream and chilled bottles of pop.

Everyone at the party enjoyed the food, and Dailey made a fat pig out of himself by having three helpings of everything.

When we went back into the front room, Merle sat with Cecilia. I could tell he really liked her because he had even used oxblood Shinola on his shoes, and they looked spit-shined.

I gave each of the twins a Cattle King three-bladed pocketknife. Each knife had a large blade, a small blade, and an awl, which wasn't really a blade.

I didn't notice all of the presents the twins got. Cecilia gave Pearl a Waterman Fountain Pen, but Merle wouldn't show anyone what she gave him.

Mrs. Potman gave each of them a ten karat, solid gold, raised initial ring with a genuine black onyx. They both acted surprised, but I thought they must have known what they were getting because both rings fit perfectly and even a mother can't guess a ring size, so she must have measured and then they would have known.

Dailey gave them a couple of cheap books—*The Man From Bar-20* and *The Sky Pilot in No Man's Land*.

Emily sat beside me while the twins opened their presents, but we didn't say much. She looked nice.

Afterward more records were put on and some couples tried dancing. Merle and Cecilia danced and were a good-looking pair, not at all awkward like Dailey and Emily. It wasn't her fault, though. Dailey danced like a gorilla on roller skates no matter what song was playing. He'd have made even Irene Castle look bad.

Pearl and I don't dance so we played the records. He asked me what I was going to do later.

"Maybe I'll go out to Twig's."

"O.K., but first let's go swimmin' at the res. It's hot enough."

"Good idea. What time is it?"

"A quarter to three."

"What time did we eat?"

"About a half hour ago."

"Start or finish?"

"Start."

"What time did we finish?"

"About two thirty."

"O.K., I'll see you at three thirty."

I knew Ma wouldn't let me go swimming for at least an hour after I'd eaten because she was afraid I'd get a cramp and drown. Her brother Uncle Clem Wheeler had almost drowned when he was ten years old. He had gone on a family picnic to Lake Chautauqua and he went swimming right after he ate. He got a belly cramp and was going down for the third time, my mother said, when Grandpa got to him. My grandfather was a strong swimmer, but even he had trouble with Clem and had to hit him on the jaw to get him to quit struggling and clawing. Ma was on the shore and saw it all. She was only four, but she never forgot it.

I thanked Mrs. Potman for inviting me and said goodbye. I was going to say goodbye to Emily, but I heard Dailey ask if he could walk her home, and she said that would be nice, so I left thinking, *What a creep. Both of them.*

I walked through the laughter and childish chaos of the backyard and leaped the fence. Dailey made me feel low and I needed to get away.

I went down the alley to the east, turned north, and headed toward the river. Most of our town is on the top of a river bluff, but part of it is on the rolling shoulder of the bluff and another part is right along the river itself. That part is mostly shacks for Indians, half-breeds, ne'er-do-wells, and wino bachelors. And one old lady named Gladys Hoar.

Gladys was wrinkly, with a large nose and chin whiskers. She lived in a two-room shack on the north side of the river by herself, but she was supposed to have a sister on the West Coast who sent her money, so she didn't have to make the first-of-the-month rounds of the bachelors' shacks the way the 'breed women did. Besides, she was too old, not too ugly—I'd seen some of the 'breed women.

None of us kids had much to do with the "river rats," especially since most of them kept their small, weedy yards protected by dogs chained outside, summer and winter. Most of us knew Gladys by sight as she shuffled around downtown, but none of us had ever spoken to her, or even thought about her much. Until the previous October.

One Sunday our preacher took as his text Revelation 17:1-6 and brought heavenly fireworks down on the "great whore that sitteth upon many waters," the great whore of Babylon.

A few days later some of us were out hunting the river east of town. We started talking about the great whore and who she was. One of my friends, Emil Mauch, said it had to refer to Gladys. She had the same name and lived by water and maybe she did visit the bachelors' shacks. The more we developed connections, the more we saw that Emil was right.

Because Gladys the Great Whore was an enemy to all true Christians, we decided to do something about it.

On Halloween about a dozen of us boys forsook the usual toilet tipping and gate stealing to gather across the river and battle for the Lord.

We waited in the rushes and willows beside the river just south of Gladys' shack. The road was between us and the shack, but no one used it while we were waiting.

When we saw the light go out, we moved across the road. Emil could make the darndest noises with his voice, so he started imitating ghosts and banshees, wolves and owls. Then the rest of us started calling Gladys' name. Somebody went back to the road, picked up a rock, and bounced it off her roof. Everyone else quickly did the same.

Throwing the rocks seemed to release something in us, and we started yelling, "Whore! Whore!" and "Get out of town if you know what's good for you!"

We stopped the rock throwing long enough for one of us to run forward with a bucket of black paint and splash it on the east side of the shack. Against the grayish-white of the house, it looked like a black octopus or spider as it ran and dripped in the pale light.

I swam on my side. No matter how many times I swam or how much fun I was having, I always swam over the deep water with a tense fear in my brain and belly.

"Lige! C'mon!"

I looked over to where Pearl was angling back toward the south shore with Merle following. They were headed for the western-most shelf and I struggled after them.

The twins had already begun working on the raft we were building by the time I reached the shelf, which was protected by a few willows. The raft itself was two tree trunks which we had pushed into the river upstream and floated down and into the open sluice gate, which was closed only during low water. We were planning on lashing boards across the trunks with a rope. That way if a board loosened up, we could retie it tight while the raft was in use. Nails would work loose in the wet wood and be worthless. Besides, they would rust, and we were all afraid of lockjaw, which we heard you could get from stepping on rusty nails.

We had hunted around town for boards, taken them to my garage, drilled holes in both ends for the rope, and carried them to the res over a spring weekend. When it was completed, we would have a fifteen-foot raft and diving platform.

I rested a minute on shore, then walked back into the water and dropped to my knees.

"Here. Take this rope," Merle said to me.

"O.K."

"Oh, crap! Ya know what we forgot?"

"What?"

"A knife."

"You didn't bring the ones I gave you?"

"Nope," Pearl said.

Merle said, "No," and, after a pause, swam around the end of the raft and walked up on shore.

"Where ya goin'?"

He didn't answer, so Pearl and I held onto the raft and stretched out in the water. I was thinking that when we completed the diving board, we could charge the other boys a dime an afternoon to use it when Merle splashed back with a jagged, clay-covered rock.

"We can use this to cut the rope."

I pulled the rope out of the water, and Merle laid it on the raft and started hitting it with the rock.

"Hey, Lige, I forgot to tell ya. Maw says our cousin from Chicago is comin' out to visit." Pearl was floating.

"What's his name?"

"Axel. Axel Nelson."

"How old is he?"

"About our age. He's a twin, too, but his sister died of typhoid when they were young, two or three."

Merle had been pounding on the rope with no apparent effect. His hands were streaking with wet, clayey mud. "This isn't workin'. Pearl, get around here and pull on this rope. Lige, grab that end and pull it tight across here."

The rope stretched rigid across the board, and Merle grasped the rock in both hands and started hitting it again.

Pearl looked over at me and asked, "Do ya think Gibbons has a chance?"

"Naw. Dempsey is too strong and too good. He'll crowd him and pound him, rough him up in the corners and along the ropes and beat the livin' bejesus out of him. Dempsey's the greatest. Better than Jack Johnson. Tougher than old John L. when he was in his prime."

"Maybe," Pearl said. "But Gibbons can take a punch and he can move, too."

"He'll have to."

"We'll see."

"Yeah, we'll see."

"I wish we could see. Wouldn't it be great to go to Shelby for the fight. I can just see us. We could hop a freight and be out there in a couple days."

Merle continued to hammer at the rope and beads of sweat sprouted on his forehead. He stopped and said, "Yeah, I'd like to go and see them two waltz each other around the ring for fifteen rounds, tryin' to look interested in doin' somethin', at least, for all the money those Montana cowboys shelled out."

He washed his hands in the water and then continued, "Still, it would be great out there, sleepin' under the stars, and eatin' at the Red Onion or maybe the Pup. There are supposed to be 40,000 people in Shelby right now."

He resumed his work on the rope, and Pearl said, "Let's go talk to Twig. He could help us get out there."

The idea was building itself in my mind. We could do it. I looked over at Merle just as he lifted the rock for a mighty swing at the rope. As his hands stopped over his head, it looked like a tiny piece of rock broke off and arced upward, outward, and downward, blipping into the water behind his back.

"My ring! My ring!" He tossed the rock onto the shore and turned around. "Did ya see where it landed?"

"It fell in back of you somewhere," I said. "I thought it was part of the rock."

Merle eased down into the water and felt around with his hand. Pearl and I glided over silently and did the same, the water up to our necks.

After a minute Merle dove under. Then Pearl went. Finally, I did, too.

I couldn't open my eyes, and as I squeezed them tight, comets and clouds appeared behind my eyelids. I touched the bottom and felt gravel, then colder water and more rocky gravel, and then colder water and nothing. I was out to the drop-off, the mouth of the dark water.

I surfaced sputtering and coughing up the water I had swallowed when I cried out. I fought my way back to shore and stood there with my shoulders heaving.

Behind me, I heard Pearl coming out of the water. He said, "It's gone." He looked at his own ring.

Merle came out and looked back. "Yeah," he said, "it's good and gone." He spit into the water. "Let's go to Twig's." Then, "Maw'll be upset."

CHAPTER V

Twig's was a couple hundred yards south of where we were. We let the
sun dry our skin, put on our clothes, and headed up the bank.

On top, we could see the curves of the small river off to our
right as it snaked its way down from the range of low glacial hills beyond
the northwest horizon. To the south of the river, the straight line of the
railroad was marked by snow fences; semaphores; cut banks; copses of
willows, poplars, and cottonwoods; and the dark green of reeds and
sedges where there was water along the right-of-way. Looking to the
left, we saw our town trapped between the river and the tracks.

We moved down the high embankment and picked our way through
some marshy ground which may have been the old river bottom, then
up a little rise onto solid ground and the base of the railroad wye.

I tried to step on the ties, but since they were designed to support
tracks and trains and not as human stepping stones, I'd have to use a
short-step rhythm if I wanted to step on every tie. I soon tired of that
and got off on the ballast.

Merle and Pearl were arguing boxing. All of us loved the sport, but
they had been sparring with each other and with a big Swede named
Gust Hammerback for a couple of years, so they were better at it than I
was. They were talking about the Criqui-Kilbane fight earlier that June
in the Polo Grounds, New York City.

The previous fall our new school superintendent, Mr. Colton, had
decided to give the high school boys some lessons in the manly art
of self-defense. He had the janitor fix up a make-shift ring in a large
hallway between the lavatories and the furnace room of the school
basement. It had three strands of rope, ring posts, and turnbuckles,

but it had just a piece of canvas stretched over the concrete floor with no padding.

Later, the janitor told me all about Mr. Colton coming down to check it out. He pushed on the posts and pulled on the ropes and smiled. When the janitor mentioned putting something soft under the canvas, Mr. Colton stopped smiling.

"No, Mr. Thompson," he said, "padding won't be necessary under the canvas. No one is going to be knocked down. I'll only spar a little with the boys and teach them how to defend themselves with their gloves. No padding is necessary. In fact, padding might impair our footwork. I assure you, the ring is satisfactory, highly satisfactory. Thank you."

The next day, instead of going outside for calisthenics with our athletic coach, Mr. Brown, we were told to report to Mr. Colton in the basement.

Mr. Colton was already in the ring, dressed in long trunks, some black canvas shoes and white socks, and a little whisper of reddish chest hair. He had on a pair of wine-colored Fitzsimmons seven-ounce gloves. He looked at us and smiled. Down in one corner were two other sets of gloves—a pair of eleven-and-a-half ounce Corbetts and a pair of five-ounce tan youth trainers.

Graduated from the University that spring, Colton fancied himself a historian and a fighter, akin to Julius Caesar, I suppose, though Caesar just ordered the fighting and didn't take part in it himself. A few weeks in our school showed Mr. Colton that he was not about to change the world through the application of historical lessons which his students were to learn and put into practice. Instead, he saw girls who smiled a lot and learned enough to pass the tests, and he saw boys who snickered about "Baldy" or "Chrome-Dome" (which he wasn't—his hair was only prematurely thin) and barely learned anything.

He seemed to think if his history teaching was a failure, at least he would put into effect some of the boxing techniques he had learned at the U. and make some kind of impression on the thick male skulls that sat before him in daily defiant array.

"Boys, I know all of you want to be men some day."

Merle nudged me from behind. Pearl and I were in the front row. The three of us were as big as any of the seniors because our mothers had held us back a year from first grade.

"Well, men know several things that boys do not, and one of those things is how to defend themselves in a scrap."

Merle stuck a knuckle into the small of my back.

"Today I want to show you boys a lesson in self-defense and we'll use those gloves." He pointed awkwardly to the gloves in the corner.

"But first I need a volunteer." He peered at us. No one moved.

"Come, come, boys, I won't hurt you. I'm wearing gloves, too." No one spoke.

"Well, then, I'll just have to pick one of you."

Suddenly, Pearl shot forward a step, turning his head around slightly, his right hand on the back of his thigh where Merle had pinched him.

"Splendid. Splendid. Come in here, Mr. Potman, and put on those dark green gloves over there."

Merle grabbed me by the arm and said, "We'll help him."

"All right, but hurry up."

We climbed into the ring while Mr. Colton was explaining various stances and punches to the others.

At home Merle and Pearl had all three types of gloves Colton had plus Corbett eleven-ounce and Corbett eight-ounce styles. It was easy to see what Colton with seven-ounce gloves was going to try to do to the kid wearing eleven-and-a-half ounce balloons. Merle and I each put a five-ouncer on Pearl and laced them up tight.

When Colton finished, he called Pearl to the ring center. The rest of the boys formed a square outside the ropes, but Merle and I acted as seconds in the corner.

"Wait a minute. I told you the green gloves, not the tan ones."

Pearl stood there, looking sheepish in his street clothes. Mr. Colton studied his face for malevolence, but failed to find any.

"All right. I guess it's all right. Now, here's what we'll do. Put up your gloves like this. There. A little higher. That's right. Now extend your left arm like this. There, that's right. Pull your right down here. O.K. Angle your body like this. Good. Now, Mr. Potman, I want you to throw what we boxers call a left jab. Here. You punch out like this."

Pearl waved a jab into the air.

"Splendid. That's it. Now, boys, when Mr. Potman jabs at me with his left, I will block his left, like this, and then I will throw a hook at his chin, like this."

He looked around and Pearl winked at the boys behind Colton's back. They grinned and some of them choked off laughter.

"Well, you may think it funny now," Colton said, "but you will see that it is most effective. Mr. Potman, shall we begin the lesson?"

"O.K."

"Splendid. Now, then, stand as I showed you. There. Now let's move closer. There. When I say 'jab,' you throw out your left jab at my head."

"O.K."

"Splendid."

Pearl and Colton stood toe-to-toe.

"Remember to defend yourself at all times."

"O.K."

"Jab."

At the command Pearl stomped his left foot on top of Colton's left foot and ripped a right hook into the man's left side, punishing the wind out of his body and forcing his guard down. Then Pearl shot a solid left cross to the jaw and released his foot. Colton fell to the canvas-covered concrete. Momentarily dazed, he tried to sit up, but instead rolled over on his face.

Pearl backed off and put up his guard, while Merle and I rushed over and helped Colton struggle to his feet. He stood in the center of the ring and felt the egg on the back of his head as Merle and I moved away.

Colton wobbled slightly and then saw Pearl in front of him.

No one breathed.

One of Colton's gloves came up and touched the right side of his jaw. Blinking his eyes, he managed to gasp, "Class dismissed," and then silently crawled out between the ropes and into the boys' lavatory.

When I went down the next day, the ring was gone. From then on Mr. Colton stuck to trying to teach history.

The twins were arguing about Criqui and his sheep bone, but I could hear music coming from Twig's place. We'd bought him a Cecilian phonograph and a pile of records. He liked to have the phonograph out on his porch and listen to music day or night.

Behind Twig's place was probably the only one-holer in our town that had never been tipped on Halloween and behind the one-holer was a little mound. We turned off and crossed the bridge. Twig was sitting in a wooden chair reading a two-day old newspaper. He looked up. "'lo, boys."

"Hi, Twig. Whatcha readin'?"

He turned down the volume and "Dardanella" faded away. "*Bringin' Up Father*. That Jiggs kills me. How was your party?"

"All right," Pearl answered.

"I got somethin' for ya." He pointed over at a bench against his house. On it were two wooden decoys that Twig had whittled and painted, both mallards, a greenhead and a hen. The twins picked up the decoys and stroked the wing cuts and the smooth roundness of the heads.

Their almost inaudible "Thanks" told me they already had the two out on Long Pond or Cliff Pond east of town with a gray fall wind driving the waterfowl out of Canada.

They seemed kind of embarrassed, so I said, "Say, Twig, on the way over here, we were talkin' about Criqui and Kilbane. Merle says Criqui won because he was younger and stronger, but Pearl claims Kilbane would have won if Criqui didn't have that sheep bone put in his jaw because of his war injury. What do you say?"

The twins moved over, one on either side of Twig. I sat down in front of his chair.

"Well," Twig began, "as I see it, ya can't overlook that sheep jaw. Animal jaws can take a lot more punishment than a human jaw can. Look what Samson did to the Philistines with the jawbone of an ass, and that Frog was four or five years younger, and that can make a difference, too. But I think the main reason that Johnny Kilbane lost is because he hadn't fought in two years. In that time your body forgets how to take a punch. It gets soft, not just physically, which can be built up by trainin', but mentally, which takes steady ring work to keep sharp. Two years of lay-off and Kilbane lost that kind of toughness. Round Six and the Frog nails him on the button and it's all over."

I thought over what Twig said and it made sense, as usual.

Pearl spoke. "If you were us, would you go to Shelby?"

Twig looked over at him. "I would, but not so much for the fight, if that's why ya want to go. Dempsey will K.O. Gibbons, there's not much doubt about it. But just the goin' and the comin' and the bein' there, that's what I'd like." He looked toward where the GN ran, hidden by the willow grove. "Why don't you boys go?"

"We were just talkin' about that at the res," Merle said.

"What'd ya decide?"

"Nothin'."

"We wanted to ask you," I put in.

"Well, I'd go," Twig answered.

"What's a ticket cost?" Pearl asked.

"Wouldn't buy one. Where's the adventure in that? Ya might as well wear a suit and tie and drag your Sunday School teacher along, too. No, I'd hitch. Ship my clothes ahead to Havre, and then a couple days later I'd hitch the fast mail. Get off at Havre, get a hotel room and clean up, then hitch a freight to Shelby, get a fight ticket, and just walk around waitin' for somethin' to happen. With 40,000 men in town, somethin's bound to happen. Then I'd watch the fight, ship my clothes to Minot, and catch the fast mail out, clean up in Minot, and freight train it home."

"But a fast mail with no open cars," Merle said. "Isn't that dangerous?"

"Ya buy a big leather belt. They have 'em at Wiltons' uptown. When the mail's stopped, ya climb on top of a car, lay down, and buckle your belt around the line that runs along the top or anything else that sticks up. That way when ya fall asleep, ya won't roll off the car. From here to Havre, ya'll fall asleep."

"But what about our parents?" It was Pearl's question.

"What about 'em?"

"What if they say we can't go?"

Twig looked at Pearl. "Well, then, either don't go or don't ask 'em."

We all glanced at each other. I stood up. Merle walked over and picked up the decoys and slowly came back. I tried to fill up a crack in Twig's path with dirt I scuffed up with my shoe. The crack must have been pretty deep.

Finally, Pearl said, "Our cousin from Chicago is comin' to visit. We can't go anyhow."

Twig didn't say anything.

Merle moved off, carrying the decoys.

Pearl started after him, turned and said, "Thanks again for the decoys."

Twig nodded and looked at me.

I stared down at the crack. It looked bigger. I said, "It's gettin' toward suppertime, Twig. I gotta go." I walked down the path and looked back just before I started through the trees. Twig was staring toward the railroad, as if he were listening for the Fast Mail.

"We'd like to go just as much as you, but what with Axel comin' we can't, and even if he wasn't comin', Maw wouldn't let us go. We'll read about the fight in the papers and probably see some pictures, too. They'll have motion pictures of it and we can see those."

"I know."

"Besides, your Maw won't let you go, either, so you don't have to put all the blame on us."

"I know."

The bat had gone. The twins turned to go north across Lamborn. On the other side Pearl looked back. "C'mon over tomorrow night. I've got my radio workin' and we'll see what we can hear. When Axel comes, who knows what we'll have to do to entertain him, and maybe we won't be together much."

"O.K., I'll try. Thanks."

"O.K., good night." He quickly caught up to Merle.

I headed east, up a slight, gently rising hill that would take me home. My shoes sounded on the sidewalk. The movie had gotten out late and the town was quiet.

It was a good town, but most of the time it was too quiet.

CHAPTER VII

The next day it rained. I stayed in and played awhile with Ted. His coat was almost recovered from the shaving Dailey had given him.

Ma had bought some new records. "Barney Google" by Jones and Hare and "Yes, We Have No Bananas" by Furman and Trout were funny and I played them a lot. So was "Old King Tut," also by Jones and Hare. Ma liked "The World Is Waiting For The Sunrise" and "Roses of Picardy" played by the Paul Specht Orchestra, but "Roses" was too melancholy for me. I could only play it once and then I went back to Jones and Hare.

The rain quit shortly before supper. After eating and waiting around fifteen minutes because Ma had a rule against eating and running, I went to the Potmans'. I had to use the sidewalk because the alley was all puddles and mud.

The house looked much bigger from the front than it did from the rear. I was always much more impressed with it when I walked up the sidewalk than when I jumped over the back fence. But I rarely used the sidewalk. Each window in the front of the three-story house gleamed from the inside as clouds blocked off the late-June sun.

Tommy answered my knock and ran to get his mother. She came down the hall from the kitchen. "Why, Elijah, come on in. Pearl said you would be coming over." She sent Tommy upstairs to get him.

"It was a good rain, wasn't it."

"Yes, it was, Elijah. The crops needed a good drenching and they could use another one next week. Then some good July sunshine and we'll all be happy in September."

"I hope so."

It evidently took Pearl longer than she thought it would. "Pearl will be right down. You can wait for him here. I have something on the stove."

"All right." I sat on the built-in oak bench as she went to the kitchen. I could hear noise and laughter coming from the other side of the sliding oak doors opposite the bench. The little Potmans were cowboys and Indians.

Just after the Great Northern had built through our town, the bench became a major topic of conversation. I overheard Mr. Potman telling Boss about it when I was seven or eight.

Even though the Italian workers lived on the work train (every evening their music drifted into our town from the west), the railroad had difficulty finding rooms for all of its workers and crews, so it put out a call for help to anyone in town who could possibly take in even one railroad man for a few weeks. Out of civic duty Mr. and Mrs. Potman agreed to rent a room, and two men were assigned to it by the GN.

George McDowell was as neat as the Lewis Stone-mustache he wore. The Potman twins played Hide and Seek and I Spy with him after he told them he had twin boys in Minot who would be going into first grade, too.

George Kemnitz was from nobody knew where and nobody cared. He let the twins feel his biceps and liked to hear them say how strong he was, but, other than that, Kemnitz avoided them. He also avoided Mrs. Potman. He talked to McDowell and Mr. Potman, but only about the railroad and women. He featured himself a real ladies' man.

His stories about the way women found him irresistible, and the crude way he talked about the women that loved him in Fargo and Minot, and what they did together, angered both McDowell and Mr. Potman. They began avoiding Kemnitz and started looking for a way to put him in his place.

A few weeks after McDowell and Kemnitz moved in, Mr. Potman went into the Oleson House dining room for lunch. As he was finishing his coffee, he saw the swinging doors to the dining room open and a face glance around and disappear back into the kitchen.

He called the waiter over and asked, "Who's the new girl working in the kitchen?"

"That's not a girl. That's some boy from up Overton way. He just started here yesterday. Why?"

"Oh, no reason. I just saw this face I didn't know, that's all."

"And you thought it was a girl, huh? Well, that's an easy mistake to make. He's got real fine features."

"Yes, he does. What's his name?"

"Alfred."

"Where's he staying?"

"He's got a room at the top of the back stairs."

That evening Mr. Potman paid a little visit to Alfred's room and then hurried home.

McDowell was wrestling with the twins in the living room, so Mr. Potman looked in, said "Hello," and kept going down the hall and then up the stairs. He knocked at a door on the second floor.

"Who's there?"

Mr. Potman took that as an invitation and opened the door. "Hello, George. How are you?"

Kenmitz had just finished rolling a cigarette from some Bull Durham. He tugged the bag shut with the string between his teeth. "Hello, yourself. What d'ya want?"

"I was just coming up to see if you were dressed to go out."

"Go out? What for?"

"What for? Why, I thought for sure that you'd already have a date with that new kitchen help at the Oleson. I know she just got in yesterday, but, what with your reputation, I thought you'd be going to the movies or to dinner or doing, well, you know, something else."

"What kitchen help? Last time I ate at the Oleson there was some big ugly farm boy droppin' dishes back there."

"George, I ate there today, and there was this real pretty young girl working in the kitchen. I talked to her awhile. Her name's Alfreda."

"Alfreda? My Gawd, whatta name!"

"It's different, all right, but she's a peach. And she told me she's awful lonesome, what with just being off the farm and all."

Kemnitz blew some smoke out of his nose and sat up straight, "Oh, yeah?"

"She said she wouldn't mind being escorted around the town or to a movie show by some trustworthy gentleman. Fact is, she'd appreciate it very much."

"Oh, she would, would she?"

"Yes, she would. I couldn't think right off of any single men in town I'd trust her with, a delicate creature like Alfreda, but then you popped into my head, and so I told her about you."

"What?"

"I told her about you, about your job and that you're a single man, and that you would be about the only gentleman that she could trust herself with in this town."

"And what'd she say then?"

"At first she just didn't know, but after I vouched for you as a man of honor, she said that she would be gratified if you would call on her tomorrow night."

Kemnitz jumped up. "Tomorrow night! My Gawd! Where?"

"She has a room at the Oleson. She can meet you about seven by the back stairs. She would enjoy attending a movie and then going for a stroll around the town before retiring. What shall I tell her?"

"Tell her 'Yes,' Potman; for Gawd's sake, tell her 'Yes'."

The next evening, precisely at seven, Kemnitz, freshly bathed and shaved, came up the alley behind the Oleson and saw one of the loveliest young ladies he had ever seen standing at the foot of the stairs.

Dozens of people saw them walking arm-in-arm down Villard Avenue, then turn north on Chicago Street. Dozens more saw them enter the movie theater together. And still dozens more saw them leave, strolling north along Chicago.

Somewhere along the walk, Alfreda suggested that perhaps they could stop to rest, if only there were a bench around, and she affectionately squeezed Kemnitz's hand, which had been holding hers ever since they had turned off Chicago onto dimly lit Stimson.

His mind must have raced. There were benches back in the Railroad Park, but that was over two blocks away and lacked privacy. "C'mon," he said, leading her across the street and heading west. "I know where there's a bench."

Soon they were going up the Potmans' walk. Kemnitz opened the front door and peered inside. The sliding doors were closed as were the two doors leading off the hall and the door at the end of the hall. Only one bulb was burning in the hall, instead of the usual three, and that bulb was the one by the staircase, making the hallway a shadowland. Except for the bulb, the house was dead.

"After you, my dear," whispered Kemnitz. "There's a bench just to your right."

"Oh, my goodness, there is," tittered Alfreda. She sat down, and then slid over, putting her body in line with the sliding doors. They were slightly open, but the living room behind them was pitch dark.

Kemnitz sat down and put his left arm around her shoulders. He whispered something to her and she shook her head.

He kissed her on the cheek and she protested, telling him to stop.

His left arm hugged her tighter and he whispered at length into her ear. His right hand dropped onto her knee.

She picked his hand up and put it in his lap. It came back up, heading for her breast. She slapped it hard and put it back in his lap. It went to her knee again and she left it there.

Kemnitz hugged her tight and tried to kiss her, but she turned her head, so he kissed her cheek again. His hand went under her skirt. She squirmed on the bench and her legs parted. He held her tight with his left arm, his head pushing into her cheek, his right hand coming up, up, up her leg.

Until it felt something that shouldn't have been there, but which, incredibly, was.

Kemnitz's head and arm jerked back just as the sliding doors roared open, and a flood of light revealed Mr. Potman, George McDowell, and a half dozen rails as spies and "Peeping Toms."

Kemnitz leaped to his feet, shot a terrible glare into the grinning faces, and ran out the front door, followed by the hoots and laughter of the men. He never came back to our town, not even for his clothes or shaving kit, which the Potmans gave to the Salvation Army after a year.

Alfreda/Alfred went back to Overton, a richer person in both experience and wealth.

She/he was killed at Belleau Wood on June 6, 1918, cut apart by a Maxim gun, they said.

Pearl and Tommy came down the stairs. I stood up. "Hi, ya, Lige. C'mon up. You go play, runt."

"Aw, Pearl, lemme listen, too."

"Not tonight. Maybe some other night."

Tommy ran down the hall. We went up the curving stairs, turned to our right, and went the full length of the hall, turned up a short flight of stairs to a landing and went up another flight to the third floor. We walked down a hall to the front of the house and entered the radio room.

Pearl was a radio nut. He first caught the bug the previous year when he read in the paper that a fifty-watt transmitter in Fargo was broadcasting under the letters WDAY. He sent in three dollars for a subscription to *Radio Merchandising* and a little later for *Radio Broadcast* and started reading everything he could about radio, or wireless telegraphy as it was called then. When school resumed in the fall, he tried to organize a radio club, but nobody would join, except for Merle and me, and the only reason we said we would was because it was Pearl, not because of the radio part.

He got a crystal set, but was disappointed in it, so for Christmas his mother bought him a radio outfit.

The outfit was sitting on a table just in front of the window. It was called a Tuska Combined Tuner and Detector. It looked like a black rectangular box with a lid that lifted up revealing a tube. On the front of the box were two large dials, a couple switches, and some wires that led to four places: the head set, a small "B" battery, a large "A" battery in its own maple case on a bench, and the aerial and the ground. Pearl had strung up the wire aerial outside the window and between the peaks of the roof. The ground was attached to the hot water radiator by the window. A crock was on the floor.

"Sit down. I'll turn it on for you. I turned it off to save the battery."

I sat down on a wooden chair beside him. He put on the headphones and worked the dials. The tube glowed orange.

He whispered, "Ya know, I was ready to give up on this thing. A lot of the time there was just howlin' and squealin' and all kinds of static, and if ya got a station, pretty soon another one horned right in, and ya couldn't figure out who was sayin' what."

He dialed some more.

"Than about a month ago it cleared up. Not the static, but the stations. You'd get just one station at a time on your dial." He pushed the headset tight around his ears, then took it off and handed it to me. "Listen."

I put it on. Some man was reciting "Blow, Blow, Thou Winter Wind." Suddenly, the voice faded away. I gave the headset back. "It's gone," I said.

Pearl listened awhile, then handed the headset to me. "It's back."

I put the headset on. An announcer said, ". . . speech from William Shakespeare's *As You Like It*. And now singing an aria from Puccini's *La Boheme* . . ." I gave it back.

"It's Hoover," Pearl said.

"What? Singing?"

"No. It's Hoover that cleared up the air. He should be president."

"That's not what Boss says. He says Hoover should be horsewhipped for helpin' feed all those Bolsheviks over in Russia."

"He wasn't feedin' Bolsheviks; he was feedin' Russians—people. And he did a good job of it, too. Just like he did with radio. Some nights I can hear Dallas, Texas, or Denver, Colorado. A few nights ago I heard them talkin' on KSD in St. Louis, Missouri, about President Harding's speech. I didn't hear the speech, but these fellas said it was about the World Court. If it wasn't for Hoover, I probably wouldn't have heard 'em talkin'."

"So what? You're not gonna get us in the World Court and I don't think Harding will, either."

"O.K., but who told you that Pancho Villa kayoed Jimmy Wilde in the seventh for the flyweight title the morning after it happened, and you wouldn't believe me until the paper came in that evening. You can thank Hoover for that bit of information, too."

Pearl had me there. And just a month before, Pearl was also the first to know that Jess Smith, a big shot friend of Harding and of his Attorney-General Harry Daugherty, had committed suicide, and some of the Republican politicians at the court house had been considering a slander suit against Pearl for spreading malicious gossip when the fast mail came in with the *Fargo Forum*, and there it was on page one:

"OHIO POLITICAL LEADER
KILLS HIMSELF IN HOTEL"

I didn't want to argue. I took a pack of Yucatan out of my shirt pocket and handed him a stick.

"Thanks."

I put one in my mouth, too. I put the pack and the empty wrapper back in my pocket; I didn't see a wastebasket.

Pearl turned a dial and put the headset inside the crock. "I can't listen and chew at the same time."

The crock reverberated the sound coming out of the headset, and if you got right above it, it sounded pretty good.

Pearl and I sat chewing Yucatan and listening to the sound of the Pomona College Choir coming out of the crock.

CHAPTER VIII

The next day Axel arrived and I didn't see the twins for a few days. I had already bought a bunch of fireworks for the Fourth, so I decided to set some firecrackers off early.

I found some Campbell's Soup cans and some others about that size in the garbage and washed them out. I took them to the garage and pounded a nail through the closed end of one of the cans. I forced a screwdriver into the hole and wiggled and pushed it back and forth, widening it. I kept stopping to measure it against a Cannon Cracker because if the hole got too big, it wouldn't work.

When the Cannon Cracker fit snuggly in the hole, I got a small scrub bucket and put in a couple inches of water. I carried the pail, can, firecrackers, and matches to the alley. Ted stayed in the garage. He didn't like firecrackers.

In the alley I checked both ways to make sure there were no cops around. Because of what had happened two years before, the judge said that the twins and I could only shoot off fireworks in our own yards, and, technically, the alley wasn't my yard.

In 1921 they'd brought an addition into the city limits and put in a sewer and water system. Something was wrong with the sewer, and a terrible smell came out of the drains on each corner. On Independence Day the twins and I walked over to the new addition, and I dropped a large firecracker down one of the drains. The explosion blew the drain grate out, missing us by inches. It hit the graveled street thirty feet away. A large trench appeared in the street where the sewer had caved in. That part of the system was ruined. Even though we had run away as fast as we could, someone had seen us and we got taken to court. Bear paid for all the damage.

The next year Pearl had stayed up until three o'clock in the morning on July Fourth, working on and listening to his crystal set. At eleven o'clock he was still asleep, so Merle and I sneaked into his room with a five-gallon cream can, which we put right beside his head. Merle dropped a firecracker in the can and we took off. The rest of the Fourth wasn't much fun because we spent all our time avoiding Pearl, who was looking for us with a baseball bat and a headache.

I put the bucket down in the middle of the alley and put the soup can and firecracker inside. I lit the fuse and ran back. When the Cannon Cracker went off, the soup can shot straight up into the air much higher than the telephone and electric lines. It looked like about forty feet, but it was hard to judge.

I gathered up my stuff. Most of the water was gone, and what remained was smoking and had pieces of Cannon Cracker floating in it. I went back to the garage, pounded a hole in another can, put more water in the bucket, and walked back to the alley. That time the can flew about thirty-five feet.

I did another three cans, but none of them topped the first one. It was too bad the Cannon Crackers blasted the holes too wide to use again. It was slow going, having to make a new can each time.

After the fifth can I went out to Twig's and we watched some trains. At first we talked politics, but Twig got all worked up, saying the two major parties were busy stealing the country blind of both money and freedom. He had nicknames for the presidents. Harding was the "Editor," Wilson was the "Professor," Taft was "Tubby," McKinley was "Macaroni," and I knew it was time to quit on politics when Twig started calling TR "that goddam cowboy."

I changed the subject to the railroad. Twig told me about the old timber trestle the GN had built across the Gassman Coulee three miles west of Minot. The coulee was about a mile-and-a-half wide and a hundred feet deep, so the trestle was a gigantic piece of work. Twig wasn't on the GN when it went up, but he was when it came down. In August of 1898, a windstorm knocked down part of it and weakened the rest, so the railroad decided to replace it with a steel bridge. The Gassman Trestle couldn't compare in height to something like Two

Medicine Bridge out in Montana near Marias Pass, but it meant something to the men who had built it back in '86 and '87. Twig said Knob Walsh, who had helped build the trestle with Shepard-Winston & Company and who was living in Minot, came out the day after the storm, walked right out on the trestle to where it had fallen away and, with tears running down his cheeks, took off his derby and sailed it out and down into the coulee. He stood there with the timbers creaking, and Twig thought he was going to follow his hat, but after a minute or so, he spit a big brown cud of Spear Head off the trestle, took out his handkerchief, wiped his chin and blew his nose, and walked back off the trestle. He went across a field to his son-in-law's phaeton and rode back to town without saying a word to anyone.

The GN ran a track down into the coulee and up the other side. They used that until the steel bridge was completed the next year.

Twig said, "That coulee was the jumpin' off place for the teamsters and track layers to head west until they bumped into the Pacific. A'course, they did hit a slight inconvenience called the Rockies, and the Cascades were a sticky problem in the winter, but nothin' could stop Hill's boys. On one of those days back in '87, out on the plains, they laid over eight miles of track, a world record then and a world record now. I got to know a lot of those men in Minot later: Knob Walsh and Roy Tanner, Al Wangen and John Hayter, and a full-blooded Sioux Indian from Minnesota named St. John Little Wind, who we called 'Johnny.' Some of 'em were old and some young, but all of 'em worked those tracks clean across Montana. That was pretty wild country then, but none of my friends quit and look what they done."

He straightened out his stump and looked at me a long time. "It's not every boy what can say he seen a heavyweight champeenship fight."

"I know."

"Did ya ask your folks?"

"Not yet."

"Ya gonna?"

"Yeah . . . maybe."

"Ya don't need to go with anyone else. I traveled plenty by myself and I preferred it that way."

"Merle and Pearl are my friends."

"Friends or no friends, you're gonna be the one that lives your life. Ya hafta do the choosin' yourself."

"I'll ask."

"That's a start."

"I'll ask," I said again, a little mad.

"I heard ya and I said that's a start."

Twig was the kind of person who, once he bit on something, wouldn't let go until it went his way. I crawled out and stood up.

"I'll ask."

He scooted out and got up on his crutches. "I gotta go rest up a little, Lige. I'm gonna set pins tonight at the bowlin' alley. I need a little cash money."

"I might come by."

"That'd be fine. I'll set for ya some free games."

"Naw, if I bowl, I'll pay full price."

"Suit yourself."

He headed down the wye and I walked the mainline toward the depot. The platform was deserted and I sat down on it, careful to avoid any splinters.

I looked up and down the tracks at nothing.

The sun was melting what was left of the morning from almost directly overhead. It felt good. I looked into it, leaning back on my arms. I closed my eyes and a pink-red ball sailed around in a red-orange sea.

I started thinking about my Aunt Esther, Boss' younger sister who had stayed in Minnesota until Bear and Boss got settled in Dakota. She had married the wood shop teacher in our town some six years before and left from the same platform for her honeymoon in Glacier National Park. I had watched her in an all-white traveling outfit with a big white hat and white skin. I thought she looked like an angel, and I was sorry she had married the teacher who stood off to one side, accepting congratulations and tugging at his collar. His new haircut accented his large ears, and I could see that his black shoes already had scuff marks on them.

Then it was time to go, and he tried to help her on board, but she turned and saw me and came off the train and over to me and put her arms around me, and, smelling of lilacs, said "Goodbye, Elijah. Take care of this old town for me. I love you."

"I will," I said, but I couldn't tell her I loved her, even though I did, and I started to cry, so I ran off the platform and was halfway home by the time the train headed west. I'd only seen her twice since then.

I opened my eyes just as something grabbed me by the ankle. I tried to jerk free, but I couldn't. I sat up and looked over the edge of the platform into the dirty face of Hiram.

"Gotcha, Lige," he cackled and let go of my leg. He rolled out from under the platform where he had been sleeping, slapped at his clothing a little, and smiled his three-toothed smile at me. "Ain't got anythin' fer me, do ya, Lige?"

"No, ya know I don't."

"I knowed it, but I thought I'd ast anyway. What were ya doin'? Waitin' fer a train?"

"No, just waitin' to go home to dinner."

"Lemme walk with ya up to the Oleson. Mehbee they got somethin' fer me there."

"All right, but I'm goin' now."

"Jack Johnson! Jack Johnson! C'mon, JJ!"

A massive black Labrador with a huge head crawled out from under the platform and fell in behind Hiram. Most people in town agreed that JJ not only looked and smelled better than Hiram, he also had better manners. JJ was fiercely loyal, so those people who would have liked to straighten Hiram up or even boot him out of town never dared try anything in JJ's presence. And wherever Hiram was, there was JJ.

Hiram wasn't so bad if you walked on his windward side. We went east on the platform past the two-and-a-half story Great Northern Hotel. Through the windows I saw the Beanery with its long lunch counter, one table and its chairs, and the menu written in white across the mirror on the north wall.

We started up the slight, gravelly incline called Dakota Street that crossed the marshy land just north of the depot toward the business section of town.

"I wonder if that old hop-head has anythin' fer me?"

"No, he doesn't. He's sick so just leave him alone."

I walked faster. The "old hop-head" was Doc Blanchard, who had a small room on the top floor of the Oleson. Everyone in town knew that he was a morphine addict, and that it was killing him, but no respectable person ever mentioned the fact in public. To do so would have been like parading an idiot son or an unmarried, eight-months-pregnant daughter down Chicago Street on Market Day. Though our town had its share of idiots and pregnant single girls, they were always kept out of sight. So was Doc Blanchard. But there was Hiram, boldly figuring a way to finagle a drink or two off the man who wasn't really there.

I took a crumpled dollar bill out of my pocket, and when Hiram caught up to me behind the Oleson, I handed it to him. "Here. Take this and buy what ya need. And leave Doc Blanchard alone."

"Thank 'ee, thank 'ee, Lige. I knowed ya was a good boy. C'mon, Jack Johnson, we've got to see a man about a mule."

Hiram and JJ moved down the alley ahead of me, then turned left and entered a small brick building. Even with Prohibition, the people who wanted to drink knew where to go.

I walked home, using the alleys wherever I could. I didn't feel like seeing people.

CHAPTER IX

Dinner was fine and I helped with the dishes after Boss went back to the Bank. At the table my stomach had been all knotted as I tried to explain what a chance to see Dempsey and Gibbons would mean to me and about the experience of riding there "up top" and about the belts and about how I already had more than enough money for a fight ticket, but Ma looked over at Boss with her lips in a tight line, and when he saw that, he said, "No," though I could tell he would have said, "Yes," if it had been up to him alone.

So, that was that. In a way I felt relieved. As I washed the dishes, my hands got pink and wrinkled, but they felt good. I started thinking that I'd like to talk to someone, Emily or the twins, or maybe I'd go out the east road to Jimmy Pound's farm and ride horses with him.

"Elijah."

"Yes, Ma."

"As soon as you're done with the dishes, I have something else I want you to do."

"I'm almost done. What is it?"

"Your father and I both have some sweaters that need repair. I want you to take them down to Miss Hoar and see what she can do with them. I've talked with her already and she says she has to see them first."

"Miss Hoar?"

"Yes. Actually, we could buy new ones, but we were talking about her the other day. She's so proud that she would never think of taking charity, but she does need money. Your father is well aware of that fact. So we thought that if we gave her some business and paid her, it wouldn't be charity. We think it will work out very satisfactorily for all concerned."

"Miss Hoar?"

"Yes, you know where she lives, down on the river road across from the ice house pond, or just this side of it. Take your bicycle and it won't be such a long trip."

After I had finished the dishes and the mandatory fifteen minutes had passed, Ma gave me the sweaters, and I went out to the garage for my bike.

It was a swell bike. It was a Hawthorne De Luxe Motorbike. I don't know why they called it a Motorbike because it didn't have a motor, but it did have a coaster brake, mud guards, combination electric headlight and tail light attached to the front hub, and a wire mesh basket.

I put the sweaters in the basket and pedaled out of the driveway onto Lamborn. I couldn't believe that I was going to the Great Whore of Babylon's house, but I was. I turned at the corner and headed north, coasting down Salem Street, a track of dirt and gravel that sloped toward the river.

In the winter boys used Salem Street for their sleds, defying any cross traffic on the avenues. I went across Stimson, where three winters before Joe Richardson broke his arm when his sled ran into the lumber yard's coal wagon. As the hill leveled off in the river valley, I pedaled across Gregory, beyond which I marked a spot where I had seen my older brother Josh set a record for distance after he came home on furlough in 1919 and borrowed my Shooting Star sled.

I built up speed as I came to the last avenue, Mill, and the sharp left turn onto it. Normally, you'd slow down for a corner, but Kaiser, a black shepherd, terrorized everyone who rounded Salem and Mill. Kaiser attacked through the honeysuckle bushes, pounding terribly beside my bike, his yellowish eyes feverish to see his teeth sink into my ankle. His barking was deep and punctuated after half a block by spumes of white from his mouth. My legs pumped faster and faster, but Kaiser didn't bite. Soon he slowed, stopped, and then trotted back home. Actually, no one had ever been bitten by Kaiser, but all of us knew that if our legs slowed down, even a little, he would grab us by the ankle or calf, yank us off the bike, and chew us to pieces.

I turned north at the next corner and pedaled to the old bridge on Glen Haven. I got off my bike and walked it across, hoping to see a turtle or a duck or anything that I could watch for awhile, but the river flowed undisturbed. I hopped on my bike and slowly pedaled to the river road and followed it off to the left. I went up and over the NP tracks and rounded a slight curve before I saw Gladys' little house.

After coasting into her brief front yard, I stopped and backed the bike up onto its stand. Holding the sweaters over my arm, I knocked quietly on the front door. There was no answer so I knocked again, louder. With no answer to my third attempt, I decided that no one was home. I was turning to leave when suddenly Gladys came around the corner with a hoe pointed right at my heart.

I yelled.

Gladys started. "What's wrong, boy?"

I felt stupid. "I'm . . . I'm Elijah Cockburn. My mother sent me down with these." I held out the sweaters.

"Oh, yes. Yes. Well, I've been out in the garden and my hands are too dirty to handle those sweaters. Carry them into the house, please." She opened the door and held it for me, leaning the hoe against the house. "Go in, Elijah."

"Thank you."

The room was dark. Gladys pulled aside a curtain, and I saw her bed made up in one corner, a spinning wheel, a Damascus sewing machine and some neat piles of cloth and clothing against a wall, two wooden chairs, a small table with a book on it, a wood stove in the middle of the room, and what I took to be a family picture on one wall. And that was it. There was no rug or carpet, just a worn, but clean, wooden floor.

Gladys went into the kitchen where she washed her hands with water she poured from a pitcher. The part of the kitchen I could see was neat and had a tiny table and two chairs. The walls had been painted yellow once.

She came into the front room. "Let me see those." She walked over to the window with the sweaters. "Sit down, please. I have to check on these."

I sat down by the table. The book was the *Holy Bible* with a cover worn smooth.

She turned from the window. "Yes, I can do these. All of them." She folded each and piled them together.

I got up.

"Wait a moment and I'll get you something to drink. Do you like milk?"

"Yes, Ma'am, but I have to go."

"Nonsense, boy, I won't have you leave without a little refreshment."

She was gone a short while and I heard her at the ice box and then at the cupboard. She came back with a glass of water, a glass of milk, and some cookies, all on a plate.

"I have a cow in the summertime."

I wondered what happened to it in the winter, but I didn't say anything.

She put the plate down on the table and pulled up the other chair. "It's nice to have company."

"Yes, Ma'am."

I reached for a cookie, but stopped in mid-reach. Gladys was praying a short grace. I withdrew my hand. After the "Amen" she lifted the plate to me.

"Take the milk. It's for you. And some cookies. Don't be bashful."

"Thank you, Ma'am."

The cookies were molasses, and the milk was cold and creamier than what we got from our milkman, Tom Pound.

Gladys asked about each member of my family, including Josh, who was still in San Francisco. She said she had known him quite well before the War.

I put my empty glass back on the plate and stood up. A couple large crumbs fell on the floor. I looked down.

"Don't worry; I'll get that." She went to the kitchen and came back with a broom and dustpan.

I moved out of the way and she swept up the crumbs. She left the broom and dustpan and walked me to the door, not a very long walk. "I suppose it's baseball or swimming for you today."

"Yes, Ma'am. Thank you for the cookies and milk."

"That's perfectly all right. I enjoyed your company. Come down and see me again."

"I will."

"Wait a minute."

She went back to the kitchen and I heard her getting something down from a high shelf. She came back smiling. "I don't know if this is any good. I bought it last Halloween, but no children came by—only some hooligans."

She held out some gum—Black Jack, California Fruit, and Beeman's Pepsin. "If it isn't, you can throw it away. I don't chew gum."

I took a Black Jack. "Thank you."

"Go on; take another."

I took a California Fruit. "Thank you."

"You're welcome. Now get along to your fun and God bless you, Elijah."

CHAPTER X

Ted was after a jackrabbit, dodging through a snag of buckbrush. I could see him jumping, trying to keep the jack in sight, his ears bobbing like small floppy wings.

I felt the afternoon sun on my shoulders, and I saw it sparkle the river where a couple of mud hens were running on the water.

I'd been walking the river with Ted for almost an hour, out past the Pound farm to where I hunted each fall.

Ted went splashing into the river. It was good to see him enjoying himself.

A mile north, beyond the shoulder of the river valley, I could see a green spot of trees and bushes. I couldn't see it, but inside the green was Sam Larkin's house. The Haunted House.

Sam Larkin had been a farmer. His wife died giving birth to their son Raymond, right there in the bedroom of that house. Sam raised Raymond himself; he never remarried.

Ray Larkin was drafted in 1917 and killed in France in 1918. Sam received a telegram from the War Department, the only telegram he ever got in his life.

After the news of Raymond's death got around town, several church women drove out to Larkin's with some food. They found the cows in the barn, needing to be milked. They knocked, but got no answer, so they walked in. Sam Larkin's body was hanging from a rope.

He'd driven a spike as high as he could into the studding of the bedroom where his wife had died. He made a noose, stood on a chair, tied the rope around the spike, and put the noose around his neck. He kicked the chair away and strangled to death. The wallpaper behind his body was torn by his fingernails. I heard Boss say Sam did it to keep from grabbing the rope to try and save himself.

Raymond had sent Sam three pictures of himself in uniform. They were good-sized, showing him from the chest up. In two he was wearing his soldier hat.

Before Sam hanged himself, he had put his wedding picture on his bed and beside it he had the three pictures of Ray, but he just had the faces there because he'd cut the uniform part off. Boss went out with the chief of police, the sheriff, the coroner, and some others, and I heard him telling Ma that it was an eerie feeling being in that room with Sam, Raymond's pictures with the top of his head cut off in two of them, the bed where Mrs. Larkin had died, and a big pot of beef stew all over the floor where Mrs. Clark had dropped it.

They cut Sam down, but left most of the rope on the spike. I'd looked into the bedroom when I was hunting gophers in the summer of 1921 and the spike, rope, and scratches were still there.

No one had ever moved into the Larkin place. Sam's brother lived in Minnesota and he rented the land out. People swore they could see lights in the house at night, moving bluish lights, and some even said you could hear a baby crying or someone screaming or laughter out there when there was a full moon.

No one I knew dared go out to Larkin's after dark.

Off to the south, I saw another grove of trees that marked the Hepburn place.

Joe Hepburn had homesteaded 160 acres back in the '80s and raised his family there. He built a small frame house south of his claim shack, which he never tore down.

Joe, Jr., started helping his Dad farm and soon began buying more land. He bought land to the east right up to the river and to the south and to the west. When TR was hunting lions in Africa, Joe, Jr., was celebrating a land purchase that gave him two full sections. He added onto the farm house, tripling its size, and built a huge barn and silo.

When the Carver Cut-off was built, the tracks had to cross Hepburn land, and Joe, Jr., collected a bundle of money which he used to expand even more. Joe, Sr., didn't like what was happening, but by then Joe, Jr., was in charge.

One day, Joe, Jr., his wife, their three kids, and his mother Margaret drove into town for Market Day. When they got back, they couldn't find Joe, Sr. They searched around and discovered that he'd taken all his clothes and moved into the claim shack.

He'd been acting strange so they let it go. That was in 1916, and seven years later he was still living in the shack. He refused to drive a tractor, truck, or car and began working the original 160 acres with a team. He refused even to walk on the new Hepburn land. He started doing his own cooking, washing, and mending just like he had done back in 1885. He stopped speaking to anyone except to some store clerks, the feed and seed man, the elevator man, and Karl Knudsvig, our town's last blacksmith.

Margaret used to worry about him, especially in the long nights of January and February, but Joe, Jr., began sending her to California every winter, so she worried less and less. In 1922 she moved to Pasadena permanently.

Joe, Jr., continued buying acreage. He survived 1920-21 and the poor wheat prices better than most.

The last time I saw Joe, Sr., in our town, he had a long white beard and was laughing and jawing with Knudsvig.

The bluff I was walking had never been plowed, and no one had ever run cattle or sheep on it, either. It was scrub land with alkali soil. Every so often I'd come to a small gulley that ran down to my left toward the river. Both Bear and Boss told me the gullies were what was left of the old buffalo trails that had been cut into the bluff hundreds, maybe thousands of years before.

Ted came loping up a gulley and over to me. He shook the water off, some of it hitting my pants.

I sat down, careful to avoid any thistles, and scratched Ted between the ears. Way off to the north and then getting larger to the northeast I could see the darkness of the Divide. Everyone seems to know the east-west Continental Divide follows the Rocky Mountains, but not many people could tell you the north-south Continental Divide runs just a few miles north of our town. Mr. Pomeroy, our science teacher, told us those hills were formed when the glaciers melted off thousands of years before. When Mr. Pomeroy first came to teach in our town, he would go weekend camping in the glacial hills far out in the east end of the county.

Mr. Pomeroy said the hills were built from the gravel, rocks, and debris released from the glaciers as they melted. Water was also released and formed glacial lakes far to the northwest. When the lakes drained, the glacial river gouged out the wide valley our little river was in. From where I sat, I could see that our river could never have made that wide trench. The top of the north bluff was a mile away, and our river was barely thirty yards wide at its widest and in most places below me was about ten yards wide.

First the glaciers, then the hills, then the river, then the buffalo. I got up and crossed another gulley before working south, going up a slight incline, then down, then up a higher incline and down, and then up the highest one around.

The hill rose gently above the prairie so it wasn't hard going up. At the top you could see a wide depression in the center of the hill, littered by thousands of bones.

I walked into the depression and pulled away some brush. Hidden in a little cave I had dug was a buffalo skull, the only one left in the depression. I took it out by the horns and looked at it. Ted looked at it, too, and then started after a meadowlark.

The skull was grayish-white and brittle.

After the buffalo came the Indians, and after the Indians came the whites. The white men had slaughtered the buffalo on the surrounding prairies, taking the tongues and the hides.

Bear said that some buffalo hunters must have gotten a small herd in a stand in the depression and killed most all of them. Later the bone pickers never found the place because it looked just like any other hill on the prairie.

The bone pickers were making plenty of money when Bear and Boss came out to Dakota from Minnesota.

Grandpa Bear had big shoulders and a barrel chest, and once he almost broke a man's back by using a "bear hug" when they got into a fight. After that, he was "Bearhug" Cockburn, until it was shortened.

Dad got his nickname because of the way he ordered two of his younger friends around when he was seven and eight. (They both died of scarlet fever when Boss was ten.) After Grandpa and he moved into town, Dad became president of the County Fair Association, chairman of the Merchants' Association, served a term as mayor, and became bank president when Bear retired, so the nickname was appropriate.

They had homesteaded eleven miles east of the "depression hill" in 1883. Back in Minnesota the year before, Grandma Anna had died giving birth to twins—my Uncle Josh, who died, too, and Aunt Esther—and Bear got so lonesome that the next spring he left Esther with his mother, packed up Boss, and came out to Dakota Territory.

They made a 160-acre claim and built a sod shanty with a big room and a little room. Bear and Boss lived in the little room, and the horse, cow, and two oxen shared the big room. The shanty had a mud-chinked pole roof and a stove in which they burned cow chips, road apples, and a little wood.

Their first crop wasn't much because they got a late start what with breaking the sod and all, but they decided to stick it out, especially when the hunting was good that fall. Geese aplenty were out on the lakes to the east: Big Sam, Little Sam, Chokecherry, and the two Finger Lakes, and deer were thick up in the hills.

They were snowed in pretty good by December, but they had plenty of fuel stacked outside their door and more than enough to eat.

Just after New Year's, Bear went over to the neighbors three miles away. He wasn't going to be gone long so he left Boss at home.

Boss was tired of the smell of the dung when it was burning, so he decided to make a change while Bear was away. He found and cut some buckbrush, brought it back, and started feeding it into the stove. Some of the sparks must have fallen on the roof because when Bear came out of the neighbor's house, he saw a mess of smoke coming from his shanty, and he high-tailed it for home on the horse.

When he got home, Boss had the cow and the oxen out. He'd also saved their clothes, blankets, tools, guns, and most of the food. The fire was out, but the roof and the door were gone.

Bear figured that if they didn't live on the claim, they could lose it, so they hitched the oxen to the wagon, put their things and the stove (after it had cooled down) in it, and drove a couple hundred yards south to where the soldiers on the old Ft. Sully Trail had dug a breastworks for protection against the Sioux. It was a large hole which narrowed down to a trench on the north side.

They unhitched the oxen, unloaded the wagon, and then tipped it upside down over the trench. They dug the snow out of the trench, put all their food and gear under the wagon, attached the stove pipe to the stove and shunted it between the wagon box and the north trench wall. They nailed a couple blankets up for a door and lived there until spring. Of course, they had to keep the animals at the neighbor's place, but they paid for the feed.

In the spring they rebuilt.

After Boss told Bear what had happened, I don't think Bear ever said anything about it. He did say that after they piled snow over the wagon box, it was just as warm as the shanty.

I put the skull back into its hiding place and heaped brush around it. The buffalo had been part of the land, the hills and the river were part of the land, and I felt that I was part of it, too.

I took off my shirt, tucked it into my belt, and went whooping and yelling down the hill.

Charging through buckbrush and snake berry bushes, I killed hundreds of buffalo and dozens of Chippewa. The Sioux nation was awed by the exploits of their great chief.

At the edge of the bluff, I dropped down on all fours and crawled forward to scout my enemies. I could hear my heart pounding in my ears, and my breath was wheezing in and out of my lungs. Ted came barking, left behind in the great Sioux charge.

Below, I saw no whites, no Chippewas, no buffalo, only two blue-winged teal on the river and several painted turtles on a rock. As I edged toward the river, the turtles plopped into the water, and the teal flew away quacking.

I hopped across the narrows on some rocks. Halfway across I squatted and drank some water from my cupped hand, then I headed into some brush, well back from the river.

To the north was an ox-bow, completely cut off from the rest of the river. Boss told me it was spring-fed and that's why it didn't dry up. We called it Long Pond. Halfway between Long Pond and the river was a large pinkish boulder with lines of gray and white. It sat in the middle of a small depression, and its sides were smooth and squared off. It had been used by the buffalo to rub against, to remove winter hair or insects, or to get rid of a plain old itch.

I climbed up Buffalo Rock and lay down on its pink and white surface, warm in the sun. It felt good against my sweaty back. Ted whimpered a little below and then ran off to the ox-bow.

Stretching out with my hands behind my head, I watched a whole herd of white buffalo stampede across a blue prairie. Then I sat up and I was crying—for the hills and the river, the buffalo and the Indians, the great Sioux chief, and for all the mistakes there were in the world.

CHAPTER XI

"**C**'mon swimmin' with us this afternoon. We're goin' about two, so stop by then."

"O.K."

"Don't forget."

"I won't."

"See ya then. Bye."

"Bye." I hung up the phone.

"Who was that, dear?" Ma asked.

"Merle. He wants me to go swimmin' with him and Pearl and Axel."

"That'll be nice. You haven't seen much of the twins since Axel came. You go rest as soon as you finish the dishes, then I won't have to worry about you."

At ten of two I was heading down the street to the Potmans' place and at two I was being introduced to Axel.

"Cockburn, huh?" He had to look up at me and I could see that he didn't like it. I stuck out my hand, but he had already turned away. "Let's go swimmin' then."

He and Pearl walked ahead; Merle and I trailed behind. Merle said, "Don't call him 'Axel'. He wants to be called 'Ax'."

"O.K."

"Maw says he's been in some scrapes in Chicago, so Aunt Ethel sent him away for the summer. She wrote Maw that she can't feature him gettin' into any trouble in North Dakota."

"Well, she's probably right."

"Another thing. Don't rile him up. He carries a knife. I've seen it."

"So what? I carry a knife, too."

"Not like his. The blade's over six inches long."

"I don't think he likes me."

"He don't like too many people, but I guess he's had it pretty rough in Chicago."

Soon we were at the base of the south side of the res, and we all walked Indian-file along a well-worn path that worked its way to the west end where we swam. Near the top Pearl broke into a labored run up the trail. Axel didn't run, so Merle and I raced past him, already stripping off our clothes and throwing our caps in the air.

Near the water Pearl was talking to Eddie Barton, who was drying off in the sun. Just as Merle and I sat down to work on our shoes, Pearl hit the water. Merle went in next, and after I folded my clothes around my shoes and put the bundle against an old driftwood log, I splashed in. The water was chilly and I didn't go out too far.

I bobbed up and turned onto my side, running my hand back over my forehead and hair to clear the water. Axel was sitting on the log. There were fifteen or so boys swimming, and he only knew two or three to talk to, so I guessed that he was nervous, but I wasn't going to go up to him by myself and ask him in. He wasn't my cousin. I swam out a ways and waited. Soon Merle came by.

"Where's Ax?"

"On the log."

"Let's go get him." Merle splashed toward the shore and I followed slowly.

Axel had taken off his jacket. It was a dark brown one with two big pockets. It was spread across the log and on it was a small black-and-white package.

I climbed out and ran my hands over my belly and legs, scraping the water off so I'd dry faster. Merle was sitting with his back against the log. Axel had just taken a big puff on a cigarette and was blowing out a cloud of smoke and masking a cough.

I came up to the log and Axel picked up the cigarette pack and asked, "Want one, kid?"

I dried my hands on my jacket and took the pack.

"Merle's too chicken."

The pack was one I'd never seen. In our town cigarette smokers usually chose Camels or Lucky Strike or Chesterfields or they rolled their own.

"Brought along a couple o' packs of Nails from Chicago. They just come out."

The pack was a black-and-white checkerboard with a large black rectangle in the middle. Near one side of the rectangle was a skeleton with a burning cigarette in its left hand. The smoke drifted up to the top of the rectangle, and under the smoke were the words "Wooden-Kimona Nails."

I turned the pack over. On the back it read:

"Stop here a moment and cast an eye

As you were once so once was I

As I am now so you will be

Smoke up before you follow me."

The air got a little chilly. I tossed the pack down to Axel. He started to say "Chicken," then thought better of it and just took another puff and blew the smoke in my general direction. I turned and walked into the water. Pearl and Eddie were over by the raft so I made for them.

Merle finally got Axel into the water, but he only stayed a couple of minutes. Merle swam over to us and said that Axel was smoking again. He was the only boy we knew who had ever smoked at the res, and he was already on his second one.

We were trying to figure something out about the raft when Pearl asked where Axel was.

No one knew; he wasn't on the log.

Pearl swam over and walked up to the log. He shouted back, "His clothes are still here."

"What if he drowned?" Merle sounded scared.

I felt hollow in my stomach as Merle dove off the raft and struck out toward Pearl. What if he was dead? It would be partly our fault. Eddie and I got out near the log. Merle was still in the water, talking to some other boys, but I could see that they didn't know where Axel was, either.

Pearl said, "I'm goin' up. Maybe I can spot him from there." He started up, but just as he did, Axel appeared on the ridge to the east, the forbidden ridge.

Axel cupped his hands around his mouth and yelled, "Hey, fellas! C'mon! There's girls over here. Naked!"

He disappeared from sight.

I shouted to Merle and motioned him in. I felt my cheeks getting hot, a sure sign of anger. I went running toward the forbidden ridge with Eddie beside me. Pearl was already at the top, but he had stopped and was just standing there. Eddie and I stood beside him and looked.

From where we were, the banks of the res curved to the north, then east a little, and then back to the south. Axel was on his belly on the south swing-back, peering through some bushes. He looked across at us, grinned, motioned us over with his arm, and then brought his forefinger up to his lips. He turned and went back to his peephole in the bushes.

Eddie swore and took off running with Pearl and me right behind. The bank went downhill as it curved north, and we had to stay under control so we wouldn't run right off the top. There was no real trail, just weeds and a few bushes, gravel, and clay.

The reason there was no trail was because no one ever walked on that part of the bank. The top bulge of the S-shaped res was where the boys swam; the girls swam at the bottom of the "S," safe behind the huge bank and the honor of us boys. When any girls were swimming, they put a white cloth on a stake pegged into the top of the bank. Seeing the cloth, every boy would stay away from "Girls' Cove." Both sexes swam naked, but no one had ever spied, until Axel.

Eddie followed the curve around to the south and tried to add more speed to overcome the increasing steepness of the bank. Axel looked at Eddie and I could see that he was mad that Eddie wasn't trying to be quiet. He rolled over on his side, getting ready to tell Eddie something, when Eddie threw himself onto Axel.

Pearl and I pulled Eddie off. He had been sitting on Axel, hitting him in the head, though Axel had caught most of the punches on his arms which were wrapped around his head in defense.

Axel was swearing. He had a very foul mouth. Blood from an early punch on the nose was splashing down on his chest as Pearl led him past Merle, who had just arrived. Axel's back was red and welty from Eddie's weight pushing him against the weeds and gravel.

"What happened?" Merle asked.

"He was spyin' on the girls," I answered.

"Damn him. My sister is down there," Eddie said.

"I'm sorry, Eddie." I could tell Merle felt really bad.

"That's all right, Merle. It's not your fault, even if he is a relative."

"Do ya think the girls heard us?" I asked. We were on the outside of the bank and couldn't see them.

"No, they're too far down and I don't think they saw us 'cause the bank's too wide." Eddie sounded certain.

"Well, I hope they didn't. He's got a filthy mouth."

Eddie started walking downhill toward the curve. I looked at Merle, but he just stood there with his head down, so I followed Eddie, catching him at the curve. Around the curve and heading south, I could see that Merle hadn't moved.

Eddie was saying how much he hated Axel and how he wished he had broken his nose instead of just bloodying it. We reached the top of the bank and headed down to where Pearl was helping Axel get dressed.

I picked up my bundle by the log and started dressing, too. Axel put on his jacket and reached in his pocket for a smoke.

Pearl and Eddie went over to get their clothes. They were standing ten feet away and talking low. I was rubbing my feet, getting the dirt off, when I saw Axel head toward Eddie, pulling his hand out of his pocket as he came around the log. His knife was in it.

I jumped up. Axel and I were like two legs of a triangle with Eddie the point. I yelled, "Eddie!"

Axel lunged, Eddie turned, and I leaped, all at the same time. I caught Axel by the right wrist and the knife blade just nicked Eddie's shoulder. Axel had a small wrist, and I bent his hand back against it until he cursed and opened his fingers. I shook the knife loose onto the ground.

Eddie was trying to see the scratch, but couldn't. Pearl had caught hold of Axel and held him as I picked up the knife and heaved it out into the res as far as I could. The small Hayes boy thought it was a fish jumping and yelled that to his brother.

Eddie felt the nick, but didn't get much blood on his fingers, so he didn't hit Axel. He just stared at him while he was getting dressed.

Pearl wouldn't release Axel, so Axel stopped struggling, but he had spit dribbling down his chin he was so mad. His breath came in gulps and his nose was wet-red again. When Eddie left, Pearl let go and Axel sat down.

Pearl got dressed and then Merle came down the hill. Pearl went over to him as he dressed and started whispering. Merle stood up and looked at Axel on the ground. He started for him, but Pearl held him back. Finally, Merle gave up and got dressed.

We all sat there as other boys came and went. They saw how we were and left us alone.

Eventually, Axel said, "I'm sorry," to no one in particular.

No one spoke.

"I'm sorry," he said again.

We knew he didn't mean it. Pearl stood up and said, "Let's go."

CHAPTER XII

We were walking down the wye and three of us felt dirty. Merle acted really low.

"Hey, who's the vet?" Axel had seen Twig down the wye.

"He's no vet," Pearl said. He was walking with Axel. "And just shut up about his leg."

"I wasn't gonna say nothin'."

Twig turned as we came up to him. "Afternoon, boys."

Pearl said, "Hi," and then I said, "Hello, Twig," but I said it kind of soft because I felt bad about not going to the bowling alley the night before. Merle was trudging up from behind.

"Who's your friend?"

"He's our cousin. Twig, this is Axel Nelson, Ax. He's from Chicago. Ax, this is Twig."

Axel nodded his head toward Twig, but didn't say anything. His nose was clean.

"Chi-town, huh? The Big Junction. Lotsa railroads." Twig put out his hand.

"Yeah, I guess." Axel hesitated and then shook Twig's hand.

"There's a freight due in. I'm goin' over and read it. Wanta come?"

"Sure," I said.

We walked to Spot 1 and Merle kept up.

All of us, except Axel, got as comfortable as we could, which wasn't all that comfortable. Axel said he was going to walk around a little and ambled toward the roundhouse. A few minutes later the freight started moving away from the water tank. As it got closer to us, Twig said, "Somethin's wrong."

"What?" I asked.

"I don't know. It's just goin' too slow."

When the engine was directly opposite Spot 1, the head shack dropped off the other side, ran forward, and threw the switch. "That's it," Twig said. "She's goin' in the hole. Somethin's comin'." He crawled out of Spot 1 and looked down the tracks. "Prob'ly comin' up behind."

The freight went into the siding and the hind shack threw the switch. We looked east down the tracks and could see a gray plume and under it a black dot that steadily grew into a locomotive. As it passed the depot, we could see some of the platform loafers take off their hats and wave them.

"Judas Priest!" Merle yelled. "It's Harding! It's President Harding!"

"No, no," Twig said. "He went way south of here."

"St. Louis," Pearl said.

At first I thought maybe Merle was right. Harding was heading west, and I could see bunting tight across the cowcatcher and small American flags whipping above the marker lights, so it could have been the President. Then it went roaring by and I knew Merle was wrong.

Along the side of the tender was a banner that read "Powder River Bill's Wild West Show and Circus."

It wasn't a long train, but it was the most colorful one I'd ever seen. The cars were orange, blue, and white, and so were the circus wagons, full of animals, on some of the flat cars. We couldn't see the animals in their cages because the wooden sides were in place on the wagons, but we could read names like "African Lion," "Leopard," "Bengal Tiger," "American Black Bear," and "Bongo the Gorilla."

There were flat cars with covered wagons and stagecoaches, and the cattle cars were filled with horses, zebras, and camels. Merle said one car had elephants and Twig agreed, but Pearl and I didn't see any. I guess we probably just missed that car because you can't have a circus without elephants.

The canvas and tent poles were on a couple of flat cars, and then some passenger and sleeping cars, followed by a red caboose that looked strange after all the orange we'd seen, and then it was gone.

I was thinking how funny it was for a Wild West Show to be heading out toward Montana, which was the West, and how people out there saw horses and cowboys all the time, and even if the Indians were all on reservations, people could still see them, so why would they pay money to watch things Montana had anyway when Twig asked, "Where's Axel?"

All of us turned around, trying to see where he'd gone, but Twig was already yelling at the shack to hold the train because Axel was about fifty yards up the siding, and he'd just ducked down to crawl under a boxcar.

"What the Sam Hill! Your cousin is dumber than a load of bowling balls, Merle. Get around there and bring the brainless wonder back."

Merle ran across to the siding and then around the caboose and up the far side of the tracks toward Axel, just like Twig had taught us. Twig always showed us how to be safe around railroads because the one time he wasn't cost him his leg. Whenever he got reminded of losing it, he said his stump would start to tingle and itch as though a thousand dwarfs were trying to hammer little rubber spikes into it.

Twig sat down and started rubbing his stump. The shack gave a signal and the train lurched forward. The siding connected to the mainline about a quarter mile up. Twig waved his thanks to the shack, who waved back. Then Twig rubbed and waited.

Merle and Axel came into view as the train passed. Merle hopped over the siding and the mainline, looked back at Axel, and said something. Axel stepped over the tracks and together they came down to Twig. Merle looked upset, but didn't say anything, while Axel had an egg-sucking grin on his face.

"Whatta ya tryin' to do, boy? Get yourself one of these, or worse?" Twig swung his stump around as he spoke and hopped up on his crutches. "You boys can stay or go, as ya please, but I want a little private talk with Axel here. C'mon, son, and walk with me."

Twig and Axel headed northwest along the mainline, kind of slow and deliberate. Ten minutes later they were sitting on a stack of ties talking. The sun started bringing out wet in my armpits.

A small freight came hustling by, only twelve cars and all of them common, either GN or NP.

Just as the twins and I were talking about leaving, Twig and Axel got up and started back toward us. As they got closer, I heard Axel laughing. Twig said something and Axel laughed louder. When they got up to us, Twig said, "You boys can go home now. Ax can take care of himself. Right, Ax?"

"Right, Mr. Terwilliger . . . I mean, Twig."

Twig looked up and down the mainline and then said, "I guess I'll mosey on home and listen to some music before the fast mail comes through. I'm gonna set pins again tonight."

"O.K.," I said. "Be seein' ya, Twig."

The twins said their goodbyes.

Ax watched Twig work his crutches over the ballast and then said, "So long, Twig," and, after a pause, added, "Thanks."

Twig half-turned, nodded at Ax, and then he continued on while we four (because Ax had become one of us) headed down the mainline to where Villard Avenue intersected it, and we could walk the street toward home.

At first the only sound was of eight shoes walking on and kicking ballast. The sun was slowly dropping behind us, but its warmth wasn't diminished. Finally, Merle spoke. "What'd ya talk about?"

Ax took out his Nails, hesitated, and then put them back in his pocket. "Lotsa things."

"Such as?" Pearl asked.

"Well, Mr. Ter . . . Twig told me a lot about trains and what ya can and can't do around 'em."

I said, "We figured that much. What else?"

Ax glanced at me, then said, "Lotsa stuff, some of it personal. He told me how he lost his leg."

"Twig told you that," I blurted out.

Ax smiled. "Yeah, he did."

Ax was really one of us. He'd heard the story from Twig's own lips—how Twig became Twig. Ax didn't say any more, but we knew the details by heart.

Twig had been working for the GN a long time. He was single, so he had transferred to most of the divisions between St. Paul and Seattle. During the War he was in our town.

One day a storm turned into a blizzard which continued into the night. Twig was living in a three-room house in the west end of our town on a street nicknamed "Railroad Row."

Twig hated to be cooped up, so he decided to get out and visit some friends at the roundhouse, despite the snow and wind. It was only a four-block hike.

The government was running the railroads and there were round-the-clock shifts in the roundhouse and car barns in an effort to help defeat Kaiser Bill. After Twig battled his way through the drifts and wind, he entered the repair shops during an unauthorized lunch and rest break. The winning of the War would have to wait. Men were dozing, eating, playing cards, or talking quietly. Even the foremen were off in a little group by themselves.

Twig was looking for his best friend, Swede Hedbom, but no one knew where he was. After a search of the car barns and roundhouse failed to find him, Twig, Harry Anderson, and Walter Patterson headed for the turntable.

When Twig walked out the door, he saw the giant turntable with one locomotive on it slowly revolving. It shouldn't have been: there was no one around.

Twig stopped and nearly fell. His boots, which were frozen in the blizzard, had partly thawed during his search inside and were very slippery.

As the locomotive swept by, Twig saw Swede, or what was left of Swede, down in the pit, lying on the outer circular track over which the turntable was running. Why Swede had started the turntable moving, and how he got caught under it, no one would ever know, but anyone, including Twig, could see that Swede was dead.

That didn't stop Twig, though. Swede was his friend. Twig jumped into the pit and ran toward Swede. At intervals beside the track were small drain holes covered by gratings. When Twig came up to Swede, he couldn't stop with his frozen boots, and his right leg slipped down and wedged in a drain where one of the grate ribs had broken off. The turntable came around and Twig grabbed it, and without even a lurch, it sheared off his leg just below the knee. A second or so later Patterson shut down the turntable.

At first it didn't hurt much, and Twig told us he was saying to himself, *What a dumb stunt to pull,* when he swung his stump up and saw it squirt out a jet of blood into the snow. Then the pain hit and he passed out.

Patterson went for help while Anderson used his belt and a wrench to make a tourniquet.

A short freight was dropping off cars on a siding, so a foreman went out and talked to the engineer, who knew Twig. Some of the men wrapped Twig up in coats and put him in the cab. They uncoupled the rest of the train and the engineer started for the mainline.

The GN runs through our town at an angle to the east-west avenues. Out on the west side Villard intersects the mainline, but on the east side Garringe Avenue is just south of where Salem Street crosses the tracks north and south.

Our hospital, which was really just a large three-and-a-half story, green and white frame house where Doc Lee lived, was on Tilden Avenue, three blocks north and two blocks east of Garringe. One of the foremen telephoned Doc Lee, explained about Twig, and told him to hitch up his cutter and meet the locomotive at the Salem Street crossing.

Doc arrived two minutes after the locomotive did. Twig was pretty white when they got him to the hospital, but Doc Lee saved his life. The Doc said Twig's leg was one the cleanest amputations he'd ever seen.

Back at the roundhouse they cleaned up Twig's blood and carried away what was left of Swede, but somehow they forgot to get Twig's leg out of the hole.

After the storm let up, one of the men on the next shift went into the pit to clear some snow. He noticed something in a hole and bent down to pick it up. When he saw what it was, he rose up with a jerk, conked his head on the turntable, and knocked himself out. He was an old Russian who didn't speak any English, so they couldn't understand what he was yelling about when he came to in the roundhouse.

When someone did bring Twig's leg in, no one knew what to do with it, so they wrapped it in some old newspapers and put it in a snow bank. Later that winter, after Twig got out of the hospital, they gave it to him—boot, sock, pants leg, and leg.

Now Ax knew all about it.

We were walking slightly uphill, Merle, Pearl, and I beside each other and Ax a step or two back. "What else did ya talk about?" Merle asked.

"Well, it's so easy to talk with Twig, and after he told me about losin' his leg, I told him how I lost my Pa."

The twins glanced at each other and then quickly looked away. We kicked up dust on Villard awhile, then I spoke. "How did you?"

Out of the corner of my eye, I saw Ax pick up a long stem of quack grass and start taking the seeds off one at a time and dropping them on the street as we walked.

"When I was ten, my Pa worked for an electric company in Cicero. The workers chartered four steamers for a summer lake cruise. Pa and I went aboard the *Eastland* and worked our way to the front. The morning was drizzly and I was cold so Pa put his coat around me.

"All of a sudden the ship tilted toward the dock, and a bunch of people crushed me against the rail, and I started to cry. Pa was tryin' to push people away from me when the ship straightened up.

"Then it went over the other way and Pa was gone while I held tight to the rail. I was hangin' on way up in the air and screamin' 'cause I could see the water down below and hundreds of people thrashin' around in it. But I never saw Pa in the water.

"Just when I couldn't hang on no more, a policeman reached over and grabbed me by Pa's coat and hauled me up over the rail and onto the side of the ship. He said, 'I've got a live one, Tommy,' and handed me to some young guy who passed me down a human chain to safety. I didn't want to leave Pa, but no one would listen. Pa drowned."

No one else said anything.

We were coming into the business section of our town. I could see the Bank on our left where Boss would be working in his office with his coat hung across his high-back chair, and the dome of the courthouse three blocks up the street where Bear probably was, chinning with his friends.

The brick Bank was two stories high, and the courthouse was two-and-half, and both were solidly built. The Bank had never been robbed, and the worst thing that happened to the courthouse was when I was hunting pigeons with a broom in the big silver dome. I was jumping from joist to joist and I missed. My leg went through the courtroom ceiling while court was in session, and the judge looked up so fast that his toupee fell off. Everybody just about split a gut and the defense lawyer called for a mistrial. Bear got me out of that one.

"Ya know," Ax said, "Twig and now you guys are the first people I've ever really talked to about Pa. Twig is just like Pa."

I dropped off two steps and began walking with Ax. When we passed the drug store, he took out his Nails and dropped the pack into a refuse barrel. A block later we crossed the NP tracks.

Ax said, "Twig told me somethin' else."

"What?" I asked.

"He said you guys are plannin' to hop a train and go see Dempsey kill Gibbons on the Fourth of July."

"No, we're not," Merle said.

"Maybe we are," I countered.

"He said it would be easy as pie if we're careful. He wished he could be doin' it . . . We could do it."

I knew we could, too, and I knew that if we just went ahead and did it and got back safely, Ma wouldn't care so much. She was just worried about what might happen and had it all built up in her mind. But if the twins didn't go, it wouldn't be an adventure in the same way it would be with them, so I didn't say anything more.

"We could do it," Ax implored.

We turned left on St. Paul, and Ax said, "Let's do it. Let's go for Twig."

No one else spoke until we got to Lamborn. While we waited, a farm wagon drawn by a black team went by headed east, followed closely by a Durant Six and an Overland Red Bird.

"Most traffic in years," Pearl commented.

We all crossed the avenue.

Ax wouldn't give up. "Let's go to Shelby."

I said, "See you guys later," and turned east. Ax was their problem.

CHAPTER XIII

After supper I was too tired to go bowling; I went to bed early. Before I went to sleep, I thought about a lot of things—Miss Hoar, Uncle Clem, the *Eastland*, Ax, the twins, Twig.

I thought about what it meant to lose someone you really loved, someone like your Dad. But I had never lost anyone that close. I had lost Grandma Ruth, though.

Ruth had been Bear's second wife. I tried to remember her, but I was only seven when she died of what they called "quick" cancer. She was a big woman and talked in a way I thought was funny. She was from Arkansas and had bought a restaurant in our town. Bear's first wife, Grandma Anna, had been dead seven years, and within a year of the day he started eating in Ruth's Restaurant, they were married.

I couldn't remember her funeral because I hadn't been allowed to go. Our neighbor, Mrs. Denning, watched me while the others were at the funeral.

I was riding my tricycle when they came back from the cemetery and stopped in front of our place, three black cars.

Boss, Ma, and Josh got out of one car. They were all in black. Bear, Aunt Esther, and Ruth's sister got out of the car right in front of me. I looked up and there was Bear, all black, including his hat and tie, except for a white shirt. His face and eyes were red from crying. When I saw him standing there, I started to bawl.

Bear reached down and cupped a hand around the back of my head. "There, there, Elijah," he said, "Grandma Ruth's gone to a better place and she doesn't feel pain anymore."

I couldn't tell Bear that I wasn't crying just for Grandma; I was scared of him and his blackness.

The only thing I could recall about Grandma Ruth, except for her size and voice, was her fried chicken. Just before I fell asleep, I remembered a picnic in Bear's backyard with Grandma's fried chicken. I'd never tasted any so good since then.

It was the summer before she died and everyone was eating and talking. I was next to Boss, and Grandma was right across the wooden table from us.

She said, "Ya'll know where the mos' painful place is to get a mosquito bite?"

Boss looked up and said, "Now, Ruth, remember, you're in mixed company."

Everyone laughed and I was so proud of Boss because he could get everyone to laugh.

Then Grandma said, "Right on the knuckle of yo' han'. It jus' bothers me somethin' awful."

And then I was asleep.

Ma woke me up. "Merle's on the phone."

I got up. It was eight o'clock and I wiped a little drool off my chin and went down to the telephone.

"Hello."

"Hello, Lige?"

"Yeah."

"Twig's been hurt."

"What! How?"

"Last night at the bowling alley. Maw just found out from the owner's wife, Mrs. Weiser. He's up in Doc Lee's hospital."

"How is he?"

"Mrs. Weiser didn't know. Doc thought at first his leg was broken, but he doesn't know for sure. Visiting hours start at ten, and Ax, Pearl and I are goin' up. D'ya wanna come?"

"Yeah. Stop by on the way."

"O.K."

"Thanks for callin', Merle."

"That's O.K. Goodbye, Lige."

"G'bye."

My mouth was dry so I drank some orange juice Ma had on the table. Then I told Boss and Ma about Twig. I washed, dressed, and had just started to eat breakfast when Boss kissed Ma goodbye. He usually spent a couple hours at the Bank on Saturday mornings. As he started for the door, he said, "I'm sorry about Twig."

Ma said it would be nice if I brought Twig some fruit. She had a basket I could use, and I could go to the fruit and confectionary store to get some apples, oranges, and bananas before I went to the hospital.

It was only ten minutes of nine when I finished helping with the dishes—too long to wait without doing something. I rubbed my face and decided to shave.

In the bathroom I took out my shaving cup. It was white glass set in a silver frame with a handle. Bear had given it to me as a present, and he had a large, fancy "E" engraved on the frame.

I opened a package of Witch Hazel Cream Shaving Soap and dropped a round cake into my cup. I ran a little hot water on the soap.

I took out my shaving brush. It had a smooth white ivory handle and a head made of badger hair and French bristles. Boss had given it to me.

The soap lathered quickly and I brushed it on my face. It was warm, but it soon cooled off.

I took a deep breath and reached for my shaving kit. I took out my Ever-Ready Safety Razor and opened it. Boss had given me the kit. He said it was a cheap one, but after I learned how to use it, I could get a better one. Or maybe I'd want to get a straight razor. Both Bear and Boss used Mandarins with genuine English steel. Unlike the razor, the cup and brush were top-notch.

I unwrapped a single-edged Ever-Ready Radio Blade and put it in the razor. I closed the razor and looked in the mirror.

Where should I start?

Not too near the throat or the jugular veins.

I decided—right in front of my left ear. I turned my head slightly to the right and leaned a little closer to the mirror. I pulled the skin tight around my chin with my left hand, raised the razor, and tried not to think of what our art teacher, Miss Samuels, had said about Van Gogh.

The first stroke was smooth. I looked in the lather and saw some blonde whiskers. Smiling, I rinsed the razor and went back to work.

Ten minutes later I was done, and I'd only needed the Climax Styptic Pencil on three spots.

I cleaned the razor, brush, cup, and sink and splashed on some Bay Rum. My skin felt cool, but the three spots shot fire. I had to use the styptic on the biggest one again.

I had shaved for the first time and it wasn't that hard.

When I went downstairs, Ma smelled the Bay Rum. She came over to me and looked close, then she smiled and gave me a hug. She was going to say something, but didn't.

I rode my bike to Villard and got the fruit. I was certain that Twig was all right.

Ma made up a nice basket, not too big so it would be hard to carry, and a few minutes after she had finished, the twins and Ax stopped by.

As soon as we were on the sidewalk, I said, "How did it happen?"

All three knew and all three helped each other give me the low down.

Just north of the Blackstone Theater, our town had a three-lane bowling alley beneath a recreation parlor which had pool, billiards, and cards, and which sold only soft drinks, unless you knew a guy who knew a guy who knew, what Boss called, "visually impaired swine."

Twig would earn a few dollars by setting pins. One pin setter could work all three lanes just by being quick and careful. Somebody would bowl on one lane. You'd give the ball a push down the return channel and throw the downed pins in the rack. By that time a bowler on another lane had rolled, so you'd use a small catwalk over to that lane, jump down, and take care of the ball and pins the same way. Then up on the catwalk to repeat the same steps again, with the only variation being when you lowered the rack of pins to start a new frame.

Pete Weiser, the owner, let Twig put a rope above the catwalk so he could move along it without his crutch.

Twig had been setting pins for a couple of hours when Pete Wilson came in. Pete had once owned a tavern somewhere called "Pete's Place," but prohibition had shut him down. He still had a taste for his former goods and was able to obtain a steady supply. In our town he worked in the meat market, and his shoulders and biceps were rock hard, built up by the sides of beef he lifted.

Pete began bowling with P.V. Larson, the elevator man, and Hank Hankinson, the tinsmith. About halfway through the game, Pete decided to have a little fun. He was behind anyway, and in his condition, it didn't seem likely he could catch up.

Hank spared, and Twig sent his ball down the return channel, set the rack of pins down, and released them. Neither of the other two lanes was occupied.

Pete took a big drag off one of his smelly Pollock Stogies and puffed the smoke out. Then he turned to P.V. and Hank, winked, and said, "Watch this."

He picked up his ball and bowled it down the alley, but immediately after he released it, he reached over, took Hank's ball, and sent it down the same alley.

When Pete's ball hit the pins, Twig jumped down from the catwalk to pick up the eight downed ones. It appeared he heard Hank's ball a little too late. He had just started to turn to get his hands on the catwalk and jump to safety when the ball smashed into his ankle, knocking him flat.

P.V. and Hank ran right down the alley and crawled in to Twig. They carried him upstairs while Pete sat in a chair and laughed. "The little crip's all right. I was jus' havin' some fun."

They drove Twig to the hospital in P.V.'s car. And told anyone who would listen that they had nothing to do with it.

My face got hot when I heard what Pete had done, but when I heard about the laughing and what he called Twig, I thought my head would explode. I knew deep inside, though, that part of my anger was due to the fact that I hadn't been there when Twig needed me.

It was six blocks from my place to the hospital. I had lost a lot of my anger by the time we asked the nurse what room Twig was in, but when I saw him, the anger came rushing back.

He wasn't a big man anyway, but lying in the bed, he looked so tiny and white. He lifted his hand when he saw us. "Hello, boys. C'mon in."

We all said something.

Twig looked over at the man in the next bed, then back at us. "This is Jens Nilsen. Useta be a farmer."

Jens nodded at us and went back to looking out the window.

I didn't know what to do so I walked over and shook Twig's hand. The others did the same. It looked like they didn't know what to do, either.

I held up the fruit basket.

"Fine, fine," Twig said. "It looks real good. I'll save it 'til after dinner, then Jens and me'll have a reg'lar fruit feast. Right, Jens?"

Jens grunted.

We stood near the bed looking at Twig. Finally, I asked, "Does it hurt?"

"Well, yeah, it hurts considerable, but Doc says it ain't busted, so I'll be out in a coupla days."

No one spoke. Ax was clenching and unclenching his fists and I was still feeling hot. A minute went by and Twig motioned us closer. He whispered, "Jens tried to cut his throat with a razor, but Doc ain't gonna report it. Figures Jens is better off outside the nuthouse in Kingston."

I looked over and saw the white dressing on Jens's neck.

And then Twig was crying.

Tears rolled down his cheeks and streaked his white gown with little gray blotches where they fell. He held the sleeve of his gown against his eyes for awhile, and after he had stopped crying, he wiped his cheeks. "I'm sorry, boys, but since I lost my leg, anythin' that happens to my other leg really scares me."

We were all standing on one foot and then the other, trying to avoid Twig's eyes. I had my hands in my back pockets. Ax had his arms crossed in front of him and appeared to be examining a water spot on the ceiling.

Merle said, "You'll be O.K. as soon as you get out of here."

"Yeah, we'll come and see you when you get home," Pearl said. "Is there anything you'd like?"

Twig laughed a couple short laughs. "Yeah, I'd like to have two good legs, a baseball bat, and Pete Wilson."

Jens rolled over and got out of bed. He poured and drank a glass of water from the pitcher on the night stand and then trotted out of the room. His throat couldn't have been too bad.

I figured that was a good time to leave so I told Twig that I had to be going. I added, "I hope you like the fruit."

"It looks good. I'll give some to Jens."

"That would be fine."

The others said their goodbyes and quickly we were out in the sun. The temperature was going up and it felt like it would be in the 70s again that day.

A west-bound freight went by three blocks south of the hospital. It was slowing down for some switching.

"I wonder if Twig feels funny," Merle said.

"About what?" I asked.

"About him bein' in the same building where he lost his leg. Maybe in the same room."

"He didn't lose his leg in the hospital," I said.

"In a way he'll never lose it," Pearl said.

"Yeah, in a way." I pictured the little mound in back of Twig's place. It always gave me the creeps to think about what was in there so I didn't very often.

"I just think he was nervous about Jens," Merle said.

"Hey, where ya goin'?" Pearl shouted to Ax, who had been walking behind us, but when we turned the corner onto Fifth Street East, he had gone straight on Tilden. We ran across the street and the postmaster's lawn to catch up to him.

Ax wouldn't say anything at first. He just kept walking fast, breathing loudly through his nose.

"Whatsa matter?" Merle asked.

"What's the matter?" Ax's voice was loud. "What's the matter?" He was even louder.

I looked around, hoping that no one I knew was listening.

Ax's voice toned down. "Are ya a bunch of girls? All ya can talk about is the leg Twig lost, and how he's feelin', when what he wants us to do is get some revenge on Pete Wilson."

"What?" My voice started loud, but it cracked at the end.

"Twig didn't say that," Merle insisted.

"No, he didn't," Pearl added. "He was only sayin' what he'd do if he was healthy, not what we should do."

"Of course he's not gonna come out and ask us to fight his battles for him, but the way he looked and sounded when he said it, I know he wants us to do what he'd do for us if the tables were turned."

I tried to think back to the hospital room. It didn't seem to me that Twig's voice had been so different, but then I saw him again, a little man all red-eyed from crying, and I didn't care if Ax was right or wrong. Twig was my friend and someone had hurt him deliberately. Pete would have to pay.

Also, I felt guilty.

"All right. I'm with you, Ax."

"Good."

The twins looked at me. They glanced at each other, and then Pearl reached over to a caragana bush and pulled off a stem. He began plucking each leaf and rolling it into a little green ball which he'd flick away using his forefinger and thumb. Merle pulled a little cross out of his pocket and polished it on his shirt.

When Pearl flicked away the last ball, he said, "I'm game."

Merle said, "It's all right by me, too." He put the cross away.

We all started walking, Ax and Pearl in front. The sunlight through the elms and box elders straggled over us in patches of bright and shadow.

CHAPTER XIV

On Saturday nights everyone knew where Pete Wilson was.

There was a blind pig under the general store west of the Bank run by Tillie Mortensen. Tillie weighed two hundred and fifty pounds, was married to a man half her weight, and had five children. Boss said that with her reputation, it was a good thing they all looked like her.

It was rumored that in her younger days Tillie had been involved in opium and prostitution in Minot, but no one knew if she had been on the buying or the selling end.

One thing we knew for a fact was that before the War, Tillie would drive her Packard "Twin Six" Coupe out to Montana and play poker with the cowboys in saloons, bunkhouses, wherever there was a game. She wore green eyeshades, smoked cigars, and placed a loaded .45 on the table near her right hand. We knew it was true because when one of our mayors, Mint Oliver, and his wife were driving back from Glacier National Park, their car broke down outside Glasgow, Montana. It was dark before Mint made it to town so he headed for a saloon which was still lit up. While the barkeep was trying to get him some help, Mint wandered into a backroom (looking for a restroom, he said), and there sat Tillie—eyeshades, cigar, Colt Peacemaker, and the biggest stack of chips on the table.

No one in Montana broke up Tillie's games, and no one in our town touched her blind pig. Anyone who needed a belt in safety on a Saturday night went down the basement stairs to Tillie's.

Men like Pete Wilson, Odin Sundahl, Ed O'Connell, Heinz Troftgruben and others with the thirst would be there whether they could afford it or not. Hiram would be there, too, "cleaning up" behind their backs. Jimmie Pike, a friend of my brother Josh, had been to Tillie's and told me all about it.

It was getting late. The four of us were up on the Bank's fire escape, outside the second floor door which led to a hallway and four apartments. The escape was a series of grated steps and a long landing of painted-black steel, and I had to change positions every few minutes or my feet would start to fall asleep.

The basement door banged shut and a figure moved up the stairs.

"Is that him?" Ax asked.

"I don't know," Pearl answered. "Wait'll he gets near the light."

Ax was acting nervous. He wouldn't stand still like the rest of us, just kept pacing the landing and sometimes took a few steps down the fire escape and back. Finally, Pearl told him to stay put because he was afraid someone inside would hear him and call the cops or, worse yet, Boss. Ax kept holding the left side of his coat, a long one even though the temperature was still in the 60s. The rest of us wore jackets.

Merle was also acting strange, but in a different way. He sat off by himself and didn't say much. He told us he was looking at the stars.

"Naw, it's not him," Pearl said as the man walked under the light in the alley. "It looks like Sundahl."

The big farmer wandered out of the light.

The basement door slammed again. Two figures came up the stairs.

"Hiram and JJ," Pearl said.

"Tillie must be closin' up." I said. "Pete must not be in there tonight."

"He's got to be in there." Ax's voice was desperate.

Merle stood up. "Let's go."

The door banged again. Someone was talking in the basement stairwell. A woman laughed.

Tillie came up the stairs, then turned and looked back down. "C'mon, Pete."

"Yah, yah."

"There's two of 'em," Pearl said. "What are we gonna do now?"

"I don't know," I said.

"Goddam it; goddam it." Ax was mad, but not too loud.

Merle whispered, "Let's go home."

Tillie and Pete walked out to the light. He said something and she laughed. I heard her say goodnight and she headed down the alley.

Ax said, "Let's get him."

I grabbed him by the shoulder and said, "Quietly. Get down the steps quietly."

We started down.

Pete was still under the light. He was trying to get a cigarette out of its package. It wouldn't come.

We were all down and standing in the dark against the Bank. Pete turned and looked right at us, but then kept turning.

The alley in that block was different. It formed a "T," with the back ends of buildings on all sides. The Bank was on the right side of the "T's" stem, just below where the top crossed it. Across the alley to the left of the stem stood the small brick jailhouse where in mild weather you could sometimes see the hands and arms of a prisoner hanging outside between the bars of one of the windows. The buildings that fronted on Chicago Street ran their back ends across the top of the "T." Most of those buildings butted right on the alley, but there were two indentations. Pete stopped turning when he saw the smaller and darker one.

He shoved the cigarette pack into his pocket and started weaving his way to the niche. After he disappeared into it, we ran up the alley and carefully approached the opening.

I peeked around the corner. Pete was halfway down the dead end, facing the wall of the Blackstone Theater. A dark, wet streak was on the wall. I moved into the niche and the others followed.

Pete buttoned up and turned toward us. "Who're you?"

I walked up close to him. He wasn't so tall, but he had broad shoulders and a big chest.

"Who're you?"

"Do you know a man named Twig?" My voice was shaking.

"Wha . . . ?"

"Do you know a man named Twig?" Pearl and Merle moved up, one on either side of me.

"Bull shit," Pete said and tried to push between Pearl and me.

I grabbed him by his right arm, but he shook loose and threw a fist that hit me smack in the mouth. I tasted salt.

Pearl had Pete's left arm and Pete was trying to hit him in the back of the head. Merle grabbed Pete's right arm and I hit him in the stomach.

The breath went out of him and I hit him again, harder. His knees buckled and whatever he had to drink at Tillie's came gushing out of him. I dodged back and the twins let him fall in his puke.

He was on his hands and knees, swaying and coughing.

Axel stepped forward, pulled a baseball bat from under his coat, and hit Pete just above the left ear. Pete went down on his left arm.

Pearl grabbed Axel and pushed him up against the wall. "What the hell did ya do that for?" Pearl was mad.

Merle and I kneeled down on either side of Pete. I picked up his right arm and felt for a pulse. I couldn't find one. I was kneeling near some puke and it stunk.

"I can't find his pulse, Merle. You try."

Merle couldn't find it, either.

Pearl came over and we rolled Pete on his back. Pearl put his ear close to Pete's mouth and whispered, "Quiet."

No one moved.

I heard the cry of a solitary nighthawk above the alley light near the jail.

Pearl looked up. "He's dead."

CHAPTER XV

"**Y**ou killed him, but we're all accomplices. We'll all go to prison."

Pearl was the first one to recover enough breath to talk after we had quietly walked out of the alley and then run down to the railroad yards and Spot 1.

"What are we gonna do?" Merle asked.

No one said anything, then Axel spoke. "We avenged Twig."

"Shut up, Axel," I said. "As far as I'm concerned, you just keep your mouth shut. And leave Twig out of this."

Axel opened his mouth, looked at me, then closed it again.

Some clouds drifted in front of the full moon. No one spoke. I watched the clouds wisp out to nothing.

"All right," I said, "either we turn ourselves in or we don't. That's the first choice we have to make and we have to make it right now."

"I'm not givin' myself up."

"Shut up, Axel," I said. "You don't have a vote here."

Axel got up and stomped off, kicking ballast as he went. Up the tracks a ways, I saw he hadn't thrown away all his Nails when a match flamed to life and then went out. A little red dot told us where Axel was and what he was doing. I didn't think anyone in town would see it, and there were no more night shifts at the roundhouse, so I let it go.

"Do ya wanna go to the cops?" I asked.

"No."

"No."

"O.K., we don't. Now what?"

"People will know it was us," Merle said. "What with it bein' Twig in the hospital, and Pete Wilson put him there, people will put two and two together, and it will come up us."

"We can make up a story," Pearl offered. "About where we were tonight."

"You got any alibis, any witnesses? And once they start questioning us, well, I trust you guys, but Axel is gonna break for sure."

"So what do you think, Lige?" Pearl sounded hopeful.

"We've got to get out of town; we've got to run away."

"Where?"

"Out west."

"How?"

"Hop a freight—tonight."

"We can't," Merle said.

"Why not? What else can we do?"

Merle didn't answer.

"We've got to go home; get some clothes, boots, and gear; and meet back here. And you can't tell your mother. If you tell her, she'll be an accomplice, too, because she won't tell on us."

Merle started to sob a little. I looked up the track and wished I had a rifle sighted on that little red dot. Suddenly, the dot went spinning and crashed with a shower of sparks.

My stomach hurt. I took a deep breath and said, "You guys take Axel, get your stuff, and we'll meet back here at two-thirty. There's a freight due about three; I've heard it before."

The twins stood up.

"One more thing. We've got to get rid of the bat."

After a moment Pearl said, "I'll do it. I know what to do." He headed uptrack to get Axel.

I looked at Merle. "It'll all work out. We'll be back some day."

That didn't help. Merle's shoulders were shaking and he was trying to keep from crying out loud.

I waited until Pearl and Axel came up, then I said, "Two-thirty and don't talk to anyone."

The three of them headed down the wye. I walked home in the shadows.

CHAPTER XVI

Boss and Ma didn't care what time I got in during the summer. They were heavy sleepers so they never knew when I did get in and never asked.

After I reached home, I didn't want to take any chances, so I climbed a big box elder, shinnied out on a large limb, and got onto the roof of the front porch. I took off my shoes, walked over to the window, opened it, and climbed into my room.

The moonlight was enough for me to find everything I needed. I packed it all in a suitcase, except for my canteen. When I was done, I sat down on my bed.

As I sat there and looked around the room that had been mine for seven years in a house I'd lived in all my life, I felt my throat getting tight. I had to swallow hard.

I wanted not to have gone out that night. I wanted to be asleep. I wanted to go down and tell Boss and Ma where I was going and not to worry. I wanted at least to write them a note. But I knew I couldn't.

I wiped at my eyes and stood up. I began to walk around the room, but the creaking made me stop. The moonlight on the floor made me realize I should do something before I left.

I took a piece of rope out of my closet. I picked up the suitcase and the canteen and kicked my shoes under the bed. They thunked against the wall and I regretted it. I listened, but I heard nothing downstairs. I sat down and put on my elk leather boots.

Once outside the window, I closed it. I looped the rope through the canteen strap and the suitcase handle, tied it, lowered them to the ground, and took the tree down. I undid the rope and hid the gear by the spirea bush near the front gate. I threw the rope on the porch roof.

I walked around to the garage and opened the door. Inside was the smell of gasoline and dog. Ted came up and lashed my legs with his tail. I kneeled down and patted and hugged him, then I stood up and went to the paint shelf. I pulled off several cans of paint and held them up to the window until I found one marked "White." I shook it and there was plenty. I took a brush, a screwdriver, and a stirring stick; wheeled my bike out; shut the door; and rode away.

The night air was cold on my face and it was colder still going over the river. A few dogs barked as I passed and then quickly fell silent.

I put the bike down in the ditch and sneaked up on the house. I opened and stirred the paint, put the screwdriver in my pocket, and started.

It took longer than I had figured to finish. I had to get an old stump that was used as a chopping block and roll it from in back up to the wall, stand on it, and put it back when I didn't need it anymore.

By the time I finished, I was sweating. I closed the can and left it and the brush in the ditch while I walked down to the river. I scooped up some water and splashed my forehead, cheeks, and neck. Finally, I washed my hands.

When I went back to my bike, the moon was off to the east still giving good light. Everything looked white and I felt better.

Back home, I put everything away, but I didn't clean the brush. I just put it in turpentine. I petted and hugged Ted for the last time, shut the door, picked up my gear, and began walking the life of an outlaw.

I was filling my canteen at the public fountain at the north end of the Railroad Park and keeping an eye on the empty police car on Lamborn in front of the City Hall, when suddenly a freight came clackety-clacking its way in on the GN. I should have heard it before; I should have been listening for it, but I hadn't been, and as I looked down the NP tracks I could see it heading west, but slowing. I wondered if it would stop and if it did, for how long.

I crossed the park and almost headed down Villard before I realized that I would pass within half a block of Pete Wilson's body. I cut left, went down two blocks, then turned right on a lonely Tilden until I came to the marsh by the GN. I skirted the marsh, causing the red winged blackbirds to fly up, scolding.

Across the marsh, I saw the freight locomotive taking on water at the tank east of the Great Northern Hotel. I linked up with Villard again and told myself we shouldn't have agreed on Spot 1. It was too far out. We should have met at the coal dock near the depot. That way we would have been right next to the stopped train.

I hurried on, the gear getting heavier.

The train whistle sounded, shrill in the night, and I heard the metallic clank-clank-clank as the engine started moving, the cars tugging at their couplings.

The train was coming, but I could see Spot 1. The engineer whistled for the Villard crossing, and Pearl was yelling at me about being late.

Everything was wrong. Twig said never to jump on a moving train, but if we waited, we might never get another chance.

Glancing back, I thought the freight was long enough to hop on after the engine went by. I yelled, "Duck down in the shadows so the engine crew won't see us, then we'll make a run for it."

The locomotive was building up speed. The big headlight cutting a slice out of the black, an orange glow from the firebox, a deep puffing growl, a heavy rumble of metal rolling over metal, and the engine was by.

"C'mon," I yelled. "Let's go."

I had my canteen flopping around my neck and a ton of suitcase in my right hand. The others each had either a suitcase or a large leather bag, but no canteens. We were moving with the train, looking for an open car.

Box car—shut. Box car—shut. Box car—shut. Gondola. Flat car. Flat car. Box car—shut.

"We might have to hop a flat car," I yelled.

"What?" Pearl yelled back.

I saved my breath.

More cars went by. Half the train went by, then a box car—open. All of us began to run closer to the train. I looked back and it was a whole string of empties.

I picked out the fourth one. I was running and the canteen was bouncing on my back. I was watching the train on my left and where I was going to run straight ahead, and then I thought, *Cripes, I hope there wasn't anybody at the roundhouse or car barns*, but it was too late for that. The train was picking up speed, and if we missed the car, we'd never make one further back.

The wheels were cutting a metallic song near my feet. The fourth empty box car was on my shoulder. *Why did I pack so much stuff?* I heaved the suitcase in with both hands and just about fell, but didn't. I moved over, put my hands on the lip of the doorway, and kicked myself halfway into the car. I swung a leg up and I was in.

Quickly I turned and grabbed Pearl's leather bag. I tried to give him a hand, but he came up the same way I had.

Merle's suitcase came flying, then Merle was up and in.

Axel's suitcase was next, but he was too short and the train was pulling away.

"Run!" Merle yelled. "Run!"

Pearl and I began yelling, too, but Axel was slowly losing ground. He slid over closer to the box car, and I hung out because I thought he'd gone under the wheels.

He hadn't. He'd grabbed the ladder and was trying to push himself up with his feet. One bounce. Two bounces. Finally, he was on.

We sat down and breathed. Pretty soon we heard some pounding overhead, and Axel's feet and then his legs came into the top of the doorway.

We jerked the door closed a little more. I grabbed the door, Merle grabbed the car, and we both held Pearl with our hands as he guided Axel down into the box car.

Each of us chose a spot to sit and I passed the canteen around. Pearl and I were sitting close together. He drank and passed the canteen back to me. I drank without wiping it off and screwed the top on.

I looked back at our town, already just a dim blob of light and dark. I tried not to think of Boss and Ma or Bear or Twig or even Ted, so I ended up with Pete Wilson.

I turned to Pearl. "Did ya get rid of the bat?"

"Yeah."

"What'd ya do with it?"

"I haven't told Merle or Axel and I'm not gonna tell you, Lige. The cops might beat it out of you. But it's some place no one will ever look."

CHAPTER XVII

The car we were in was completely empty, except for us. It rocked and swayed, and the floor was hard and rough, but soon the others were asleep, all in jackets with various items of clothing rolled up under their heads as pillows. They'd dug their caps out and put them over their faces.

I was sitting on the north side of the car. Mr. Pomeroy had told me once if I wanted to see God, I should look at the stars. I was looking at God.

Up to the northwest the Big Dipper burned white with distant fire. I followed its pointers to the North Star and saw the Little Dipper circle down from it. To the northeast was one of my favorite constellations, Cassiopeia. One reason I liked it was because it was easy to find, but another was because it looked so elegant. Underneath it, closer to the horizon, was the star Capella, hard to see because of the moon.

I stood up and leaned out, the wind strong in my face. Almost overhead I could see the star Vega and off a ways to the east Deneb. I leaned out further and twisted my neck to see Altair to the southeast. The three formed a large "V" in the night.

Sometimes when I was looking at stars and saw the "V" or Cassiopeia or Orion in the winter, I wondered why God didn't spell His Name out in stars so that people could believe more easily.

Off to the west, I saw Arcturus, which was mentioned in the Bible, but I couldn't recall where. It looked reddish in the western sky.

I walked across to the south side of the car to look for Antares in the Scorpion. My brother Josh was a Scorpion, but no one said that around Ma. Ma hated astrology; it was sinful. I was too late; Antares was gone, but I did see the red planet Mars and Jupiter, two of our solar system's eight planets, over to the east.

I'd seen enough of Mr. Pomeroy's God, so I rolled up some pants for a pillow, lay down away from the doors, and pulled my cap over my face. It didn't feel right going to sleep without brushing my teeth, but no one had remembered toothbrushes or tooth paste.

I couldn't say the "Now I lay me . . .," although I'd been starting my prayers with it for years out of habit, but I was as good as a murderer, so I just asked God to bless Boss, Ma, Bear, Twig, and Ted and to help things work out for the best and said "Amen." I didn't mention any of us in the car.

The box car's rocking kept up, and a minute or so later I felt a splinter against my rear end. I moved over and prayed again, asking Him to forgive us for killing Pete Wilson. I squeezed my eyes tight and said, "Amen." Then I was asleep.

When the car jerked, I woke up. So did the others. I crawled to the door. God was gone; it was starting to get light out.

From further back in the car came "What's goin' on?" and "Where are we?"

We were in a little town, a village really, and they were doing some switching. I couldn't see the depot sign. The car jerked to a halt.

"Where are we?" Pearl had come up beside me.

"I don't know? Heil or Sanders, maybe."

The car jerked forward.

Pearl said, "I have to take a leak."

"So do I, but we'll have to wait 'til we get goin'. If we drop off now, they'll see us and might report it."

Merle and Axel came up.

"I'm gettin' off," Axel said.

"Why?"

"To go."

"You wait 'til we get goin', then go out the door."

The train was pulling away from the siding, and the village was still asleep in its white houses.

Even if you stand close to the edge of the doorway when you go, the wind will whip around and get you wet anyway. After each of us had finished his business, a hand was sneakily wiped on a pants leg.

All of us had some money, but no one had brought any food. It didn't look like we'd be able to eat until we got to Minot.

We all took a drink from the canteen and tried to get back to sleep. That wasn't so easy. Although my body was tired, with daylight, the swaying and clacking of the car, the hard floor, and the whistle giving a warning at every crossing, I couldn't sleep.

Then just as I started dozing, the train slowed and we came to another village.

More cars were switched, but no one got up to watch. I was closest to the door so I told the others it was Sanders. That made the last one Heil.

It seemed we just got up a good head of steam again when we made another switching stop. I was getting angry. I knew that while we were asleep we'd passed through four stops without switching, but since then we'd been switched three times in a row, and each stop brought us closer to the time when Pete's body would be found.

Then I thought that maybe we'd switched at the other places, too, but that everyone had slept through it. But if that were true, why did we all wake up at Heil and not at any earlier switching? I didn't know and "I don't care."

"What?' Pearl asked.

"Nothin'."

I was hungry, but all I could do was look out the door. The first part of June had been dry, but rain in the second half had greened things up considerably. Green fringed the tracks with weeds and grass, or reeds and cattails if it was wet, and green covered the earth with wheat, barley, or oats stretching away to the north and south, and then a whistle and a section road, brown and dry-looking, came and went, and then more green.

The train was slowing down again. All of us got up by the doors. A crossing, an elevator, a depot, and back from the depot, a village, Schazville.

We were jerked backward and forward as cars were added or left. Then we were stationary on a siding for awhile as a hot shot freight ripped by. The force of the train blasted a wind right into our car.

When the highball rattler was gone, I walked across to the other door. A block away I saw a man and a woman walking. He was using two canes to get around in a jerky walk. They came to a building and stopped. The man took an American flag down from a pole, unlocked the front door, and hobbled inside. He came out, locked the door, and the couple went back the way they had come. I guessed it was the Schazville Post Office, and the man had forgotten to take the flag in the night before.

I looked around for a restaurant or café or an "Eat" sign, but I didn't see any. In fact, I didn't see much in Schazville for there wasn't much to see—a postmaster and his wife, some dried-out buildings, and dust when the wind came down Main Street.

The train jerked and we were off again toward Minot and food.

We starved for another ten or twelve miles and then the freight slowed and stopped at Baden. We had been traveling through German and Russian German territory, and the town names reflected it. The switching was done while I tortured myself with thoughts of a short stack with butter and syrup dripping down the sides. Four strips of rasher bacon. Fresh-squeezed orange juice.

"Hey, look!" Merle called out.

I came over to his door. He pointed to the left and I saw a half dozen or so men running from some bushes to the train. The last one clambered aboard the freight car three in front of ours just as the train started moving.

Northwest of Baden we headed through some hilly country. The sun was warming up the day and we sat in the south doorway, talking about Minot.

About ten minutes or so out of Baden, Gaultier shot by and then we clattered over the Mouse River, the same river that went through Minot further upstream.

The only things we really had to worry about in Minot were the cops and the fact that it was Sunday so no stores would be open. Despite these worries, we were relaxing as much as our empty stomachs would allow when the tiny village of Graves whizzed by.

Just out of Graves, Pearl nudged my shoulder and said, "I think there's someone on the roof."

I listened and there was some kind of noise up there.

Axel sat up. "There's someone on the roof."

A thick rope with some knots came swinging down through the north doorway, and a man climbed down and dropped onto the floor.

As he straightened up, he said, "Hello, boys."

I said, "Hello" and the others responded, too.

"Nice day for travelin'. Where ya headed?"

No one said anything, so I said, "Just to Minot . . . to see my brother."

The man walked over to the rope and gave it a pull. Then he leaned on the door with his hands in his overall pockets.

"Minot, huh? Tough town. I hope your brother takes good care of you boys."

Another man climbed down the rope, swung inside, and dropped.

The first man said, "These boys are headed for Minot."

The second man said, "Do tell." He gave a tug on the rope and walked to the opposite side of the doorway from the first man.

"I was just tellin' the boys here that Minot is a tough town, especially for four youngsters."

"I said we were goin' to see my brother."

"Well, so you did. I forgot about that."

"And he's a policeman."

The two men grinned.

A third man came down the rope and into the car. He pulled on the rope and went over by the first man.

"Yessiree," the first man said. "Minot can be a tough town. Show 'em, Case."

The man called Case held up his right hand. The last two fingers were missing.

The first man said, "Now that happened in Minot just a coupla years ago. Right, Case?"

"Right."

"Just a coupla years ago Case was chasin' a pussy up on High Third Street, and it snapped those fingers off as clean as a whistle. Right, Case?"

"Right."

"I think it was a black pussy, too."

The second man snorted a laugh and a fourth man hung on the rope and dropped inside. He gave the rope a jerk.

I didn't like what was happening one bit and I could tell the twins and Axel didn't, either. Pearl was clenching and unclenching his fists, and Axel was standing shoulder-to-shoulder with Merle and me. I wanted to do something—grab the men one at a time and throw them out of the car, but they hadn't done anything threatening. We were hitching a ride and so were they. What could I do?

"Now, boys, I have a little proposition for you." The first man pushed himself away from the door and walked toward us. He was about forty; the other three were younger. "Let's just say that your policeman brother is on vacation, so there you are in Minot without a place to stay and without a lot of money. You need a job."

A fifth man dropped into the car and tugged on the rope. He pulled a length of two-by-four out of his belt.

"Like I said, you need a job. There aren't any in town so you go out to a farm and ask for work. And the farmer hires you because you're a likely lookin' young man, and besides, you'll work cheap. Right?"

No one spoke.

"Right?" he said louder.

Merle and I both said, "Yes."

"Now you have a job, but you know what you've done? You've taken Case's job. He wanted that job, but didn't get it 'cause he wouldn't work as cheap as you."

A sixth man came off the rope and into the car.

"Now Case doesn't like losin' his job to you. Right, Case?"

"Right."

"So what me and the boys here are thinkin' is that you shouldn't work so cheap. Everybody demands the same wages, but higher than cheap. Case wants four dollars a day and that's just what you boys want, too. Right?"

Merle and I again answered, "Right."

"Fine, fine. Ya know, I said to myself when I first laid eyes on you, I said, 'There's four smart boys.' Now the way to show us that you won't be stealin' Case's job is for you to join our organization. It just so happens I have some membership cards right here, and each of you can join for only a dollar."

He pulled out a small stack of red cards. He held one up. Near the top it read "Membership Card," and below was a black seal with part of a globe and some words, but all I could read were "I.W.W. GENERAL."

Pearl turned and whispered, but too loudly, "They're Wobblies."

The first man said, "Yes, boys, we're Wobblies. At least that's what the plutocrats and their journalist henchmen call us. We prefer to be known as Industrial Workers or citizens of industry, but Wob or Wobbly, it's still gonna cost each of you a dollar to be a bundle tosser on the farms around Minot. Who's gonna be first?"

None of us moved. The first man said, "Boys, either you ante up a frogskin each or you're gonna hit the grit off this Jim Hill goat."

The other five advanced around their leader. The four of us moved away from "two-by-four."

"Last chance."

We spread out a little. Axel felt for his knife, then shot me a dirty look. The twins and I never went for ours.

"And here I thought we had four smart boys. I guess it's true—they don't grow nothin' smart in North Dakota." He glanced at his men. "Let's teach 'em a lesson."

All six of them rushed us.

Two of them slammed into me and I went down. I was struggling up when a fist nailed my jaw shut. I went back down and rough hands grabbed me and pulled me up. One pair of the hands put my left arm behind my back and, pulling up, forced me over to the doorway.

On my way out, Harold Lloyd flashed into my mind, but I didn't have a clock arm to grab. I hit and rolled and lay where I stopped. I thought my back was broken.

A few seconds later I realized it wasn't because if it had been, I wouldn't be feeling the pain I felt in my knees, ankles, and feet. My hip, side, back, shoulder, arms, hands, and head hurt, too.

The noise in my head was just the train, for when the caboose was gone, so was the noise.

Carefully, I got up and climbed the embankment to the tracks. Looking up the line, I saw Merle standing on the embankment, and as I was watching, Pearl went flying out of the car and rolled down into the weeds.

I started up the tracks toward Merle, and Axel came out of the car. They must have picked him up by the arms and legs and pitched him out because he landed square on his back. He didn't move.

"Are you O.K., Merle?"

"I think so, but we'd better get over to Pearl. I saw the guy with the two-by-four after him."

As we went half-running to Pearl, we saw our bag, suitcases, and caps come sailing out of the car one by one. A suitcase burst open like a large cloth flower when it landed.

Pearl was sitting in the weeds, trying to rub his lower back. "Son of a bitch! Son of a bitch!"

"What's wrong?" Merle asked.

"I might have a broken rib or somethin'. Back here."

Merle kneeled down and put his hand up under Pearl's jacket and shirt. He pushed.

"Ouch!"

He pushed again.

"Ow!"

"It's not broken. What happened?"

"I hit two guys. I think I broke one guy's nose. When they saw that, four of 'em tackled me, and when they got me up, old 'two-by-four' gave it to me in the back. Then they pushed me off. Goddam Wobblies . . . Where's Axel?"

"He's up the track," Merle said. "We'd better get movin' 'cause he's still layin' there."

We headed for Axel, Pearl the slowest.

Merle spoke to Axel, but there was no response. He slapped his check lightly and then grabbed his chin and moved his head side to side. A little blood showed on the rocks beneath Axel's head.

Merle listened for his breath, and when he heard it, he turned Axel's head to the side and put his own jacket under it.

"See if they threw out your canteen."

I walked the tracks until I found it. It was dented, but still held water. I brought it back and gave it to Merle. He took out his handkerchief, wet it, and then cleaned some of the blood out of Axel's hair.

"I'll get our stuff," I said.

"I'll help." Pearl walked with me.

The latches on my suitcase were sprung. I put all my clothes and gear back inside, but I couldn't carry it by the handle or everything would fall out again. I cursed the rope I had tossed on the porch roof. I put my cap on, tucked the suitcase under my arm, and picked up Merle's suitcase.

Pearl found his leather bag and Axel's suitcase.

Axel was sitting up. When he saw us, he said, "Those dirty bastards. Those goddam dirty bastards. They chased me down into the end of the car, and then they carried me back spread eagled and said they were gonna see if I could fly."

I could see a large egg under his hair.

"When we get to Minot," Axel continued, "I'm gonna report those guys to the cops. Those goddam bastards."

He stood up. He could walk all right.

"We're not goin' to the police," I said.

Axel turned. "Why the hell not?"

"Because we're wanted for murder."

CHAPTER XVIII

Maybe fifteen miles to Minot. Fifteen miles of carrying a suitcase under my arm. Fifteen miles with bruises, bumps, and abused muscles crying out "Stop!"

The sky was blue, like Ma's eyes. Bear also had blue eyes, a darker shade. Boss and I had brown eyes; so did Josh, dark brown like molasses.

It was sunny and we were sweating, but it wasn't unbearable.

A hawk went wheeling around, searching a field for a mouse or a gopher. Just a slight flap or two of its wings sent it gliding like a living kite. My feet were getting sore, and I thought if I had a rifle I could being that flier down, but then I knew I wouldn't—I'd given my heart to the hawks a long time ago.

Crops and rangeland stretched north and south, but weeds and short grass crowded the embankment. Western meadowlarks, boasting their black ties over yellow vests, called from fence posts, and when we passed sloughs or marshes, red-winged blackbirds chipped or whistled at our passing, while yellow-headed blackbirds squawked and grated and rasped at us as they flew up.

Merle, who took the lead, scared up a covey of partridges. Bear called them "patridges" and Boss called them "Huns." They flew off to the south, their wings going flit-flit-flit-glide, flit-flit-flit-glide, until they all sat down, and then I really wished I had a gun—a shotgun—and Ted. Partridge had just been introduced into the state, and I was glad to see these had survived the winter.

Merle also scared up a fox, and it flashed off to a tree claim a hundred yards north of the tracks, its brush showing white all the way.

We saw a doe killed by a train, and off the embankment lay her dead fawn, which didn't look like it had even been hit. Both of them stunk so bad that we didn't get too close. Axel started retching when he saw the maggots working in the doe's eye sockets.

Trains came and went in both directions. We'd move off the embankment and wait for each one to pass, but they were going so fast that there was no chance to hitch one.

"Hey, what animal is that?" Axel asked, pointing at the Great Northern logo on a passing boxcar.

"A Rocky Mountain goat," Pearl answered.

The Great Northern had been changing its logo over the past couple years from "GREAT NORTHERN RAILWAY" written diagonally inside a rectangle to a circle with a Rocky Mountain goat standing inside and "GREAT NORTHERN RAILWAY" written on the edge of the circle.

"Oh, that's it. I was wondering what that Wobbly meant by 'Jim Hill goat'."

The rails, the ties, and the ballast went on and on. The rails gleamed in the heat. The newer the tie, the stronger the smell of creosote. Our boots continually crunched the ballast.

We filled our canteen at the village pump in Carver, but there wasn't any place where we could buy food. The streets were so dead that we didn't take any precautions about not being seen.

Just beyond the village we came to the junction of the Carver Cut-off that we'd been on and the other GN mainline which went east to Sacred Water and Grand Forks, then south to Fargo. The train traffic increased. Six miles to Minot.

About a mile outside Carver we stopped to relieve ourselves and rest. We looked at Pearl's back which was purpling up. It was hard for him to keep up, but he had to, so he did.

Following the tracks would take us right into Minot, which we could see in the distance white and dark on the hills on either side of the Mouse River.

None of us said much while we were walking. Pearl was too far back. Merle seemed like he was turning something over in his mind and didn't want to be disturbed. I didn't want to talk to Axel.

Minot grew larger and larger and then we were there.

Even though we were in the city, the tracks had places beside them choked with weeds, tall grass, bushes, and trees, just like in our town.

We came to the railroad yards. I saw some car barns, a roundhouse, a water tower, a gigantic coal dock, and other railroad buildings, most of them weather-worn, but the car barns looked almost brand new.

"Hey, you boys! Hold it!"

"Yeah, where the hell d'ya think you're goin'?"

Two railroad bulls came up to us. The insides of my stomach and chest told me we were going to be arrested.

"I said, 'Where the hell d'ya think you're goin'?'" The bull who spoke had an average build. His partner was hugely fat.

"To my brother's," I said.

Pearl came up and we were all together.

"Who's your brother?"

I thought for a second. "Harold Lloyd."

"Oh, a wisenheimer, huh?"

"No, that's his real name, honest."

"Never heard of 'im. Where's he live?"

"Down the tracks a ways and then north three blocks."

"Did ya jump train?"

"No."

"Then how 'dya get here with all them suitcases? What 'dya think this is, a hotel?" The average guy moved his left foot forward and got himself balanced. He carried a club in his right hand.

The fat man, who hadn't spoken since he'd told us to "hold it," moved over in front of his partner. "Boys, have you seen any Wobblies? We're lookin' for Wobblies and we mean to clean 'em out of these yards. Have any talked to you?"

We all looked at each other, then Pearl said, "No."

I said, "Nope, nobody has."

"Well, if any of 'em try, get away from 'em. They can be dangerous, especially if you don't do what they want. Most of 'em are Bolsheviks, Reds, and we want 'em out of Minot."

The average guy came around the fat man. "This is private property. Find your way to your brother's place by some other route and get the hell outta here!"

"Sure, Mister," Merle said. "We're goin'."

"C'mon," I said.

We started walking north to an opening between two buildings. Mr. Average Guy began hitting his left palm with the club. "Don't ever let me catch you train chasers in my yard again!"

When we were almost to the buildings, Axel turned and started to yell something, but Merle pushed him ahead, saying, "Don't, Axel. He might turn us in to the cops."

On the other side of the buildings, there was a small grove of box elders and ash trees with a lot of thick quack grass around them.

"Let's stop here," I said.

After a brief discussion we decided that it was as good a place as any to hide our stuff, so we pulled up grass and covered our bag, suitcases, and canteen.

Bear had been camping once and almost lost an eye when he came out of his tent at night to visit the latrine. A sharp twig got him. He had taught me always to check a campsite and remove all low-hanging branches, so I did what Bear had taught me and then we started looking for a place to eat.

The two railroads in Minot, the GN and the Soo, were right down along the Mouse. We walked over a couple of blocks to a public crossing, went across the tracks, and headed for downtown. We went uphill, searching the store fronts and passed by several restaurants that we agreed were too fancy.

On a corner we saw a place. It had a big L-shaped lunch counter with wooden stools and five booths along the window sides.

We walked in, not too fast, not too slow, and took the last booth. Someone dropped a platter in the kitchen. The counterman, dressed in white, looked up, but didn't say anything.

We studied the menu, but didn't see what we wanted.

A waitress came over. "What'll it be?"

"A stack of cakes, a side order of bacon, cottage fries, milk, and lots of syrup." Pearl was hungry.

"Ya missed breakfast."

"Huh?"

"Most of that's on the breakfast menu. Ya can't order it now."

She was right. At the top of the card were the words "Evening Lunch Menu." There were no pancakes listed.

Pearl studied the menu.

"Next."

I ordered a t-bone steak (sixty cents), three fried eggs (thirty-five cents), a piece of homemade blueberry pie a la mode (twenty cents), and a glass of milk (ten cents). Potatoes, bread, butter, and coffee came with the order.

Merle had the same.

Axel took two pork chops (forty cents), two fried eggs (thirty cents), an extra order of French fried potatoes (fifteen cents), and cherry pie a la mode (twenty cents).

Pearl had a double order of ham and eggs (eighty cents), cottage fries (twenty cents), and plain apple pie (ten cents).

After the waitress left, we went to the restroom one at a time. Washing my face never felt so good before.

When our food came, I asked if I could buy a newspaper.

"The *Minot Daily* don't publish on Sundays."

"What time do you open in the morning?"

She looked down at me. "Six. We got customers."

I looked at my food. "Thank you."

The food was delicious.

I poured a little milk in my coffee and stirred in two teaspoonfuls of sugar. "I think we'd better order a sandwich each to take with us."

"Why?" Merle asked.

"In case they don't have any on their morning menu."

It felt good in the café. I liked hearing the kitchen noises and smelling the kitchen smells. Customers came and went and didn't look twice. It was nice to be there if you didn't think about why.

Pearl straightened up and a little burp came out. He put his hand up to his mouth and excused himself. Then his head jerked and he whispered, "Cops."

The door was in back of me. "How many?"

"Two."

The waitress came over with our ham sandwiches.

The cops sat on stools and began kidding the counterman. Each got a cup of coffee. They began laughing with the waitress.

Pretty soon she came back to us. "Are you boys wantin' anything else?"

"No, Ma'am."

"Well, ya can't just sit here all evening."

"No, Ma'am."

"What d'ya want then?"

No one spoke.

"Well?"

Axel picked up a menu. Quickly, he said, "Oyster stew."

"Four oyster stews, right?"

I looked at the others, then at the reflection of the cops in the mirror behind the counter. They had started their second cups of coffee. "Yes, Ma'am."

The stew came in a large bowl. I dipped my spoon in and turned over an oyster. The other three were dropping little round crackers in their bowls and slurping the liquid. No one dared try an oyster.

I chased the oyster around with my spoon and pinned it to the bottom. I forced the spoon into it and cut a piece out. The oyster bobbed up and revealed something black inside. I put my spoon down and covered the bowl with my napkin.

Soon the others were finished. Dead oysters lay in the bottoms of their bowls.

The cops left.

We got up, not too fast, not too slow, and walked to the register. We each left a dime tip.

"Let's see. Steak, eggs, pie a la mode, milk, and an oyster stew. That'll be a dollar thirty-five. Oops. Plus one ham sandwich, makes it a dollar forty-five."

I paid, picked up a toothpick, and walked outside. The cops weren't around.

Pearl came out. "Ahh, that was good."

Merle and Axel came out.

"Why d'ya order oyster stew?" I asked.

"I looked at the menu and it caught my eye 'cause they'd written it in ink. Somebody had to say somethin'."

"Yeah, you're right. Somebody did."

"Anyway, the cops are gone," Pearl said.

We walked down toward the railroad, laughing a little. We'd beaten the railroad bulls and the Minot cops. Axel said he didn't think it was so tough being on the run, being wanted.

I didn't want to hear that kind of talk, so when we crossed the tracks, I wasn't happy listening to the details of Axel telling about Big Jim Colosimo and how he had run Chicago and how Axel had met him personally and began doing errands for him and how Big Jim had got bumped off in 1920 and Johnny Torrio took over, putting Axel back to square one, but some day Axel was going to meet Torrio, too, and start doing him errands.

There was still some daylight, but it was cooling off. Back in camp, my teeth and tongue felt pretty scummy, so I rinsed out my mouth with water and rubbed my teeth with my finger.

The mosquitoes were bad in the grass so near the river. We had to put shirts over our faces and our hands in our jacket pockets in order to sleep.

From under my shirt, I could tell it was getting darker. I listened to the trains in the yard, the switch engines, and locomotives on the mainline.

I was over a hundred miles from home, sleeping on the ground. I'd been thrown off a train and my body was sore. But I was with two good friends and an acquaintance and I had a full belly.

A passenger train pulled into the station to the west of us. I heard the sounds of human arrivals and departures. The whistle sounded and the locomotive began chuffing. Since we were in the bottom of a valley, the sounds came easily to us.

The train was heading west.

I said a prayer to God, asking the usual blessings and, for the second time, forgiveness.

It kept stabbing at me that it had been less than twenty-four hours since I had helped kill a man.

CHAPTER XIX

I woke up cold and stiff.

It was no longer dawn; the sun was up. I had to urinate bad. I walked over to the railroad buildings and found a pelican pond, where they dumped the boiler sludge. I used it as a toilet and wiped my fingers on my pants.

I looked around for a long piece of wire or rope to tie up my suitcase. I couldn't keep carrying it, with it trying to come open every time I shifted position. I walked around the buildings into the yard, but had no luck.

When I got back, the twins were getting up. I told them where I'd been and they went over to the pond.

We got Axel up and then hid our stuff.

I discovered a couple of big mosquito bites on my neck.

Axel leaked on an ash instead of going to the pond.

I told the others I had to have a wire or some rope.

Pearl said, "It's not five yet. We can look in a few alleys for some." The fall hadn't broken his watch.

Mist was rising off the Mouse. No trains were coming, so we used the public crossing and headed for an alley behind the Leland Hotel. A street clock chimed five times. I looked through the hotel's garbage, but there wasn't anything I could use.

We entered the alley in the next block. We saw a Ford truck halfway up the alley with a heavy canvas covering its load. Two guys were looking at the motor. A lot of steam was escaping from the radiator and both front tires were flat.

We walked to the other side of the alley. One of the guys was swearing about someone named Jake letting the water get low and not checking the tires.

The other guy was wearing a loose-fitting coat. He was just listening when he saw us and said something low to the swearing man, who turned and looked us over.

They started toward us and we moved away fast. The swearing man held up his hand and said, "Wait a minute, boys. We're not after you. We want to hire you for a little bit."

His name was Matt; the loose-fitting coat was Joe. Matt explained that they had to get a load of boxes from the truck to a building half-way up the next block, and it had to be done quickly. When he said he'd pay us well, we agreed.

Matt set us up in a chain. I'd carry a box from the truck a fourth of the way up the alley where Pearl would take it to Joe at the end of the block. Joe would carry the box across the street to Axel, who would carry it a fourth of the way up the next alley, and then Merle would take it another fourth of a block and stack it inside a wooden shed attached to the back of a brown brick building.

Matt said if Joe gave us the word we were to stop work and hide inside a doorway or behind something until the "all clear" was given. He said it was for our own protection, that there were other people after his goods.

He took me over to the truck and threw the canvas back a little. I saw cases marked "Canadian Whiskey. Product of Canada." Matt waited to see how the chain worked and then went over to Joe, said something, and walked out of the alley and up to the next block.

With no traffic to slow us down, the work went smoothly. In a little while I was sweating and Pearl was, too. He said his back hurt some, but not as much as he thought it would.

On one exchange Pearl asked, "Lige, do ya think we should be doin' this?"

I shrugged and went back for another box. I was thinking bootlegging was nothing compared to murder.

It got to be an automatic routine: truck, box, walk, Pearl, walk, truck, box, walk, Pearl, walk—just automatic, except when I had to get up and flip the canvas further back.

The truck's radiator kept spitting steam and water.

We were about two-third's unloaded when Matt whistled and Joe said, "Get outta sight."

I kept my box with me as I squatted behind a row of garbage cans. Looking between two of them, I could watch the street. I didn't see anyone, but a big brown rat came out from under some wooden steps, scurried across the alley, and wriggled into a hole about the size of a half dollar. Its naked tail gave me the creeps.

Everything was quiet and I was getting ready to stand up when a car drove slowly by the alley. There were some markings on the car, and the two men inside wore visored caps and uniforms. I stayed hidden.

A minute later another whistle came down the alley. Joe appeared and said, "O.K., let's get back to work."

And work we did. All of us moved a little faster. I was wiping the sweat off my forehead, and I hated to have to stop and flip the canvas back a little instead of taking the whole thing off at once, but that's the way Matt had said to do it.

Finally, I handed the last box to Pearl and followed him to Joe, who took the box across to Axel and whistled to Matt. Matt came down from the corner and we all went up the alley to the wooden shed.

Matt and Joe counted a hundred cases while we stood near the door, which Joe closed and locked. After the count Matt and Joe talked quietly and then Matt came over. "Boys, you did good work. Now I need a little more of your help movin' these cases. I know it's hard work, but I'll pay each of you five dollars when you finish."

Five dollars! The soreness in my muscles melted away. It seemed to me that Pearl's back got better, too; he stood a lot straighter.

All of us agreed to help. Joe pushed a door open and each of us carried a box down the basement. It had a concrete floor, a sewer drain, and lots of wooden boxes. It smelled musty.

There were stairs leading up the left-hand side, but Joe passed them and walked up to the west wall. He stood in front of two huge packing crates.

He turned and faced us. "Boys, I don't even know your names."

We introduced ourselves. I went first, then Merle, then Axel, and Pearl was last.

Joe's eyes squinted. He walked over to Pearl and said, "D'ya think I'm stupid? What's your real name?"

Merle spoke up. "That is his real name. We're twins."

"That's right," I said.

Axel chimed in. "And I'm their cousin."

I didn't know what that had to do with anything, but at least Axel had said something. Joe stepped back and appeared to be trying to understand.

He turned to the packing crates and then came back around with a pistol in his hand. I almost dropped my box.

"All right, Elijah, Axel, Merle, and . . . and . . ."

"Pearl."

"Yeah, Pearl. Matt and I are takin' a big chance lettin' ya down here, but we're payin' ya good, and we're gonna demand loyalty in return. What you're doin' ain't exactly legal. I suppose ya figured that out. But if ya go to the cops . . ."

"We won't go to the cops," I said.

"No, we won't," Merle agreed.

"Or if ya tell anybody about what ya see here, I'll find ya and give ya a free swimmin' lesson in the Mouse. O'course, you'll probably drown from all the lead that'll be in ya."

He waved his gun just in case any of us had missed it, then he opened his coat and put it back in a shoulder holster.

I tried to see if he had any notches on it, but I couldn't tell.

He put his hands between two crates and pushed them apart. They moved easily; they must have been on hidden wheels.

A large steel-reinforced door was in the wall behind them. Joe took a key and unlocked it, then he slid it open and said, "C'mon."

I was the first in line. A breath of cold, damp air met me as I entered a short, dark tunnel. At the end of it, Joe lit a kerosene lantern. In the glow of the lantern, a large room opened up. The room must have been located right underneath the street.

I carried my box of whiskey into the room and put it down where Joe said. There were other boxes in the room, all labeled with different names of liquor, but mostly whiskey. At one time the room must have extended to the north and south under the street, but it had been blocked off with what looked like very thick wooden walls with steel reinforcements.

Joe waited in the room until he counted a hundred cases. He blew out the lantern, locked the door, and pushed back the crates. "C'mon," he said.

We followed him back to the wooden shed.

"Wait here."

He went through a door into a brick building.

"What's he gonna do?" Axel asked.

"I don't know," I said.

"He's either gonna pay us or kill us," Pearl said, "and I'll be the first to go—he doesn't like me."

"Shut up," Merle said.

Matt and Joe came through the door. Matt was talking about somebody not being able to make a delivery because he'd gotten himself cut up in a knife fight at a gambling joint on Third Street. He stopped talking and looked at us.

"Well, boys, Joe here tells me you did a swell job for us, and that we can count on you to keep it on the QT. Is that right?"

We nodded our agreement.

"Then here's your jack."

He handed each of us a five dollar gold certificate, to which we all said, "Thank you."

"In the alley you told me you were just passin' through. Any idea when you'll be leavin'?"

I looked at the others. Pearl's eyes were on the door and Merle and Axel were studying their boots.

I said, "Maybe tonight. Maybe tomorrow. Soon."

Matt said, "If you could use some extra dough, I've got a job for you that just opened up. It's along the same line of what you've been doin', and if you take it, I'll turn that five-spot into a sawbuck. Are you interested?"

No one answered so I asked if we could talk it over in private.

"Sure."

Pearl was for getting out, but the promise of a "saw" was too much for the rest of us, although I didn't really need the money.

"When do we start?" I asked.

Matt looked at his watch. "It's seven thirty now. Why don't you go get breakfast and come back here at nine and I'll put you to work."

"For how long?"

"Three, four hours tops."

"O.K., we'll be there."

Joe unlocked the door; Pearl was the first to squeeze by him.

In the alley Pearl was upset. "Joe don't like me. He looked at me funny again."

We were going to the café we'd eaten in the night before.

"You'll be all right." I tried to reassure him.

I had my hand in my pocket. The fiver felt good because I'd earned it myself. Bear and Boss had had nothing to do with it.

CHAPTER XX

Both the counterman and the waitress were new. I couldn't tell about the cook and his flunkey because I hadn't noticed them the night before, but the food was still good.

I had French toast (a quarter), fried ham (fifteen cents), and a glass of milk for a dime. The others ate well, too.

As I was paying, I asked for a paper, but the counterman told me it wouldn't be out until later in the afternoon.

We loafed around the warehouse district awhile and then took our time walking the couple blocks to the wooden shed. When we got there, it was exactly nine o'clock.

Merle banged on the door. Joe must have been waiting because on the second bang, he let us in. He flicked a cigarette butt into the alley, looked around, and locked the door.

"Me and Matt might be nuts trustin' you guys like this, but I don't think we'll have any problems, do you?" He patted his left armpit.

"No, sir," Merle agreed.

"C'mon."

We went down the basement, but Joe walked over to a different crate and pushed on it. An old door was in back of it. Joe unlocked and opened it and we followed him inside.

He lit a kerosene lamp, and it looked like we were in a trench with a series of shelves cut into its sides. We followed Joe to the end and came to a long tunnel that went at right angles in both directions, paralleling the street above.

When Pearl caught up, Joe asked, "D'ya know what that used to be back there?"

No one did. We followed him down the tunnel.

"When the Great Northern came through here, some of the heavy labor was done by Chinese coolies. Minot started growin' and their money spent just as good as a white man's, so some of 'em headquartered out of here, and some of 'em quit the railroad and lived here. Two things ya can't separate are a Chink and his opium, so Minot became the opium center of Dakota Territory. Back there was an opium den, years ago."

We turned a couple of corners. I figured we were at least four blocks from where we started. We came to a large wooden door. Joe pounded on it three times, then waited and hit it three more times. Someone on the other side opened it and we walked into a warehouse.

We rode a freight elevator up to the first floor, and Joe took us over to an REO Speed Wagon with the name of a dray and cartage company on the side.

"Who's the best driver here?" Joe asked.

I had driven automobiles a little, but always with Bear or Boss supervising. I knew neither of the twins had even been behind a wheel. We looked at the Speed Wagon.

"I am," Axel said.

"O.K., ya drive this rig up to Third Street. It's a short street, only a few blocks long, but we do a lot of business there. You guys do the haulin' and I'll do the collectin'. You other three get in the back there. Let's move."

I heard Axel tell Merle that this would put him in jake with Torrio when he got home.

The back was filled with cases and kegs. I was just sitting down when Axel put it in gear and the truck leaped forward. I fell back and hit my head on a keg. By the time I got up, we were outside the warehouse. After two blocks we were climbing a hill and Axel was doing all right. We could peek out the back and see the valley to the north and the crest of the hill to the south. We leveled off and came to a stop sign. Axel did a good job stopping. The intersection was a busy one, and it took a couple of false starts before Axel got us across. A block later we took a right onto Third Street.

The truck ground to a halt. Joe came back and told us what to do: pick up what he said and take it where he said.

It was a sunny morning; the temperature felt about sixty. There were people on the sidewalks and in the yards of the few residences on the street.

I asked, "What about the cops? What if someone reports us?"

Joe looked at me and said, "Don't worry; the fix is in. Nobody'll bother us."

I felt better and we started carrying booze, putting it where the new owners wanted it. Joe seemed friendly with everyone, but he collected on the spot in cash.

We worked our way north down the street. At the smaller places Axel stayed behind the wheel, but when there was a lot to carry, Joe made him get out and help.

The largest building of all was at the end of the street on the west side. It was two stories high and stretched half a block west. We started carrying the booze in and Joe took the manager out to the truck to count the boxes. They came back in and Joe collected a huge wad of bills.

"I'm leavin'," Joe said. "When ya get done, take the truck back to the warehouse and then scram until four o'clock. Come to the alley, knock twice—no more, no less—and I'll pay ya."

We were just finishing when the phone rang. The manager answered it. After listening for several seconds, he said, "Damnit. They weren't supposed to come 'til after the Fourth. I'm too goddamned overstocked . . . Thanks . . . G'bye."

We were just at the front door when he yelled, "Hey, wait! I need some help!"

All four of us walked up to the bar.

"Wait right here."

He came around the end of the bar and went over to a door leading further back. He opened it and yelled, "Shorty, come here. And bring Ben."

Shorty was about four-and-a-half feet high and had brownish skin, but he was white. Ben was a huge colored man.

The manager said, "I just got a call that the Minot Police Department will be payin' us a visit at one this afternoon. We've got to break this place down and make it respectable. Shorty and Ben, you get back there and hide that gamblin' stuff. Get those books and magazines and that other junk in there. I'll have these fellas help me with the hooch."

Shorty and Ben left, and the manager, who said his name was Archie, told us what to do. All the bottles and glasses had to be hidden in secret compartments in the wall behind the bar. The kegs had to be taken to a closet filled with cleaning supplies and placed behind a false wall. The liquor still in cases had to be taken upstairs to Room 25.

The bottles, glasses, and kegs were first, then each of us grabbed a case and headed upstairs.

Archie was getting soft drink bottles and putting them in the ice box. He looked up and said, "Tell the girls about the raid. Tell 'em to go shoppin'."

The second floor had just one long hallway from the front to the back of the building. The stairway came up in the middle of the hall. The number of the room right across from it was 14. Next to it were 12 and 16, and next to the staircase were 11 and 15. There was no Room 13. I saw a couple dozen door handles, but no girls.

We walked down the hall toward the bigger numbers. I could smell different perfume-like smells as we passed each door, and, underneath it all, something else.

"Lysol," Axel said, when I asked him what it was. We were in front of Room 25.

I put my box down and knocked.

No answer.

I knocked again.

No answer.

Axel kicked the door.

A sleepy voice said, "Go 'way. We ain't open yet."

Axel kicked the door again.

"Jus' a minute. Jus' a minute."

I heard someone moving around and then the door swung open. In the doorway stood a tall colored woman wearing only bloomers and a button-up camisole, except it wasn't buttoned up. One of her breasts was uncovered.

"Now what y'all nice young white boys want with ol' Black Betty anyhow?"

She ran her hand up the door frame and her breast went with it. It was the first real breast I could remember seeing, even if it was dark brown. I could feel my face heat up, and my voice cracked when I said,

"We don't . . . we . . . we're supposed to tell you there's gonna be a police raid at one o'clock."

"Oh, shit!"

No woman I knew ever said that word—it sounded awful.

Betty went into her room. "Bring that juice in heah." She pulled back some curtains and opened a door behind them. She turned on a light and pointed. "In theah."

While we were storing the booze, Betty went down the hall knocking on doors and yelling, "Raid's a-comin'! Everbody up! Raid's a-comin'! Everbody up!"

We went down the stairs, got another box each, and headed back up. The hallway was alive with women talking, laughing, cursing, and many of them were still getting dressed right there in their doorways. Most of them were colored, but six or so were white. I tried to keep my eyes straight ahead.

As we walked down the hall, some of the women said things to us or whistled at us. It was embarrassing to have to listen to them.

On our third trip there were fewer of them in the hall, and by our sixth trip all of them were gone.

"I never saw so many women with no men around, except for Ladies' Aid night at the church," Pearl said.

"Yeah," I agreed. "And some didn't have any clothes on."

Merle didn't say a word.

Pearl said, "And so many colored women—ya'd think we were in New Orleans or Atlanta some place."

"Boy, can they cuss!" I said.

"Yeah," Pearl said. "I wonder what kind of hotel this is anyway?"

"You dumb hayseeds," Axel said. "This ain't no hotel. It's a goddam whorehouse."

CHAPTER XXI

Archie told us the truck would be all right out front—the cops wouldn't touch it—but we decided it would be a lot safer for us up the street. Axel drove the truck a block south and we got back in and waited.

A little before one, two police cars parked at the end of Third Street, and six policemen got out and stood on the sidewalk, looking at their watches. At precisely one o'clock they all walked in Archie's front door.

Ten minutes went by and then the six came out, started their cars, and drove toward us. We ducked as they went past. After they turned the corner, Axel started the Speed Wagon, cut a U-turn at the corner, and parked on the east side of the street across from Archie's.

We crossed the street and went inside.

The main room looked like any recreation hall with its pool tables, card tables, and chairs. Six empty soft drink bottles lined the bar.

I asked Archie about the raid.

"Don't worry about it," he said. "The cops pick out a place here on High Third or one downtown and stage a raid about once a month. I'm just the manager, but the owner, Mr. Duffy—who never comes within a mile of the place—has some people on the take, and we get a phone call which gives us time to clean up and make everything legal. The coppers don't look too close, but they will nail us if they see somethin' out in the open that ain't up to snuff. Anyway, they come, look around, and leave. They've done their duty for another month and we can get back to work—so let's get back to work."

While Archie was working behind the bar, we went up to Room 25 and began hauling the booze downstairs. As we worked, some of the women came back to their rooms. Most of them went to sleep.

Black Betty talked a little to us each time we came in for a case, so when we had finished, we went back to her room just to be friendly.

Two other women were in Room 25. The colored one turned as we came in and said, "Hey, Betty, yo' sure is lucky. Yo' gots four nice white boys callin' on yo' and it's still daylight."

Betty and the white woman laughed, then the white woman began coughing.

The colored woman came up to Pearl and walked around him, looking him all over. She said, "Yo' sure is big and strong. Lemme feel your muscle."

Pearl flicked his eyes at us. He looked embarrassed, but pleased, too. It's true he was the tallest of us four, but there wasn't half an inch difference between Pearl, Merle, and me. He unbuttoned and took off his shirt. He had no undershirt, but his back was to us, so the women didn't see the purplish bruise there.

Pearl pumped his right forearm up and down a few times and then locked it, making the bicep hard. The colored woman stepped forward and grabbed him in the crotch. "Uhumm! My-oh-my!"

Pearl recoiled backwards.

I couldn't believe it. Merle's and Axel's mouths dropped open, the white woman laughed and coughed, but Black Betty got mad. She kicked the two women out of her room and pulled the door shut, then she apologized while Pearl pulled his shirt on, fumbling with the buttons.

When he'd finished, she asked, "Are y'all Minot boys?"

"No, Ma'am," I answered.

"Ah'm not from here, eithah. Just passin' through. Come up from the Windy City, but that ain't mah home . . . . Hmm, been passin' through 'most a year now; maybe time to move on."

In the next room a woman started playing a phonograph, some blues—Bear and Boss didn't care for that type of music, and Ma thought it "sinful," but Twig liked it, especially when he was feeling down, and I liked it, too.

Betty poured herself a drink from a bottle on the dresser. "Drink?"

Each of us said "No" or "No, thanks," but Axel's voice sounded empty.

"Are yo' boys gonna stay in Minot?"

Merle answered. "No, we're movin' on."

"Me, too. Just as soon as Ah can. Just as soon as Ah get 'nough money saved. A little mo' and Ah've got enough to go back home agin."

The blues kept working their way in from next door.

Betty put her empty glass on the dresser. "Boys, Ah've worked aroun' people mos' of mah life, and Ah don't think yo' have, so Ah'm gonna give yo' some free advice that Ah hope will help yo' when yo' leave heah."

Each of us looked at her.

"If y'all gonna be aroun' people, yo' havta smell good, and, frankly, yo' boys don't. Now theah's a bathtub through that doah. Ah'm gonna go downtown for awhile and Ah want each of yo' to take a bath. Theah's soap and towels a-plenty in the cupboard and when yo' get done, it wouldn't hurt to try this." She took a small jar out of the dresser and put it on top. "And change yo' clothes once in awhile."

She left.

I was embarrassed and I knew the others felt bad, too.

"Goddam whore," Axel said.

Merle opened the bathroom door, but didn't go in. He looked doubtfully at us.

Axel said, "I'm not first. There's no tellin' what's in that tub."

I said, "I'll go first." I got some towels and a washcloth, picked up the jar, and walked into the bathroom. It was a jar of Mum. I ran a tub of water and got in. It felt good.

Next door the phonograph had a woman with a voice I'd never heard before singing the blues. She sang about the three men she had loved—her father, her brother, and the man that wrecked her life.

I loved Boss and Josh, but I sure didn't love Pete Wilson.

I settled back in the warmth while she sang, "I got the world in a jug, the stopper's in my hand." Lucky her.

My eyes closed and she sang, "Beale Street Papa, come back home," and later, "Baby, won't you please come home."

It wasn't really like Ma calling to me because the woman was supposed to be someone's wife. She sang about sadness and hurt in a voice that was strong underneath all the pain, a voice that wouldn't break and neither could we.

I opened my eyes and stood up. The water and suds ran off me into the tub and I felt good.

After I dried off, I cleaned the tub. I rubbed some of the white cream in my armpits and got dressed. I didn't like putting my old clothes back on, especially my socks, but my other clothes were down near the railroad.

Two of us sat in chairs and one of us sat on the floor while the other one was in the tub. There wasn't much furniture in the room and no one dared lie on the bed.

Axel waited until last. With him splashing in the tub, Merle said, "Somethin' sure is strange."

"What is?" I asked.

"Well, I've always heard that colored people have a funny smell, but Betty didn't smell any different from a white woman, and she wasn't wearin' any perfume, neither."

I thought about it and agreed with Merle.

Pearl said, "When I was carryin' boxes in the hall, I didn't notice any different smell if I passed a white lady or a colored lady, just a whole lot of lady smells."

"That's true," I said. "I can't wait'll we get home, so I can tell David Dailey and some of those other know-it-all's a thing or two."

I stopped—the twins stared at me. We didn't speak again until Axel came out of the bathroom, then Merle stood up and said, "Let's get our money and get outta here."

CHAPTER XXII

Archie paid us two dollars apiece for helping him out of a jam. He told us we could have permanent jobs there if we wanted them after we got older.

Axel drove the truck to the warehouse and we walked back to our suitcases. After I changed clothes, I bound my suitcase with a piece of wire I'd picked up at the warehouse.

The ants had found our sandwiches so we had to go to the café to eat.

After we had ordered, I bought a paper and read through it carefully. There was a murder in it—a sheriff had been killed on a train near Moorhead, Minnesota, by a twenty-one year old prisoner who had escaped. The paper also said President Harding was crossing into Washington State on his way to Spokane, and the sports page claimed the Dempsey-Gibbons fight was on the ropes financially. There was no story about Pete Wilson.

"What d'ya mean, no story!" Pearl exclaimed. "They had to have found his body by now. Lemme see that paper!" He began paging through it.

Axel spoke up. "Maybe the cops aren't gonna say anything until they've notified his relatives. They do that sometimes."

"But Pete's got no relatives," I responded. "He was hatched."

No one laughed.

"Maybe Axel's right," Merle said. "Yeah, that must be it."

We ate in silence. Pearl folded the paper and gave it to me. "There's nothin' in it."

I opened the paper to the sports.

"Maybe that Moorhead killing and the two posses bein' out will take the heat off us," Pearl offered.

"Maybe," I said and went back to the sports.

Pearl explained his new theory to Merle and Axel, who received it unenthusiastically.

I saw that the Giants were four-and-a-half games up on the Pirates, and the Yankees were nine ahead of the Athletics. That was fine by me. I was a Yankee fan.

There was a picture of Jack Dempsey and his parents and another one of Tommy Gibbons eating. He weighed 178 lbs.

"Hey, listen," I said. "The Dempsey fight might be off. They haven't made the final payment of a hundred thousand dollars to Kearns yet."

"They'll come through," Merle said. "If they called it off now, the people there would tar and feather 'em and then tear down the town."

"Kearns better get it while the gettin's good 'cause his meal ticket's comin' to an end," Pearl said. "Gibbons has been in eighty-eight fights and never been off his feet, and he ain't gonna be now. Dempsey's been down at least six times."

"Shoot," I said. "Look what Dempsey did to Willard and to Miske and to Carpentier. Those fights didn't last no time."

"We've got to get out of here."

"What're ya talkin' about, Axel?" He looked scared and it worried me.

"I just figured out why there's no story about Wilson in the paper."

"Why?" I asked.

"Because they're onto us and probably got men here in Minot, in Fargo, Kingston, Sacred Water, all your big towns, lookin' for us and don't want to tip their hand. They'll figure there was no way we could have left, except by train."

"But how do they know it was us?" Merle asked.

"We told 'em."

"How?"

"By runnin' away. A dead body shows up in an alley, and four guys who had somethin' against the dead man are missin' the next day. Does two plus two equal four?"

"Damn!" Pearl exploded.

I had to admit Axel had it figured, but we couldn't have stayed, either. I looked around the café. No one appeared interested in us.

"O.K.," I said. "Axel's right. It all makes sense so now we've got to keep movin'. There'll be a couple of trains through tonight. We'll catch one of 'em, but no freights, not right now."

Axel asked why not.

"Too slow. We've got to get some distance between us and the cops, and a fast mail or a passenger train will do it."

"But how are we gonna ride one of those? There aren't any open cars. You gonna buy a ticket? That'd be real smart."

"Twig told the twins and me how. We'll do it his way. But first we've got to make plans. If we can get to Shelby, we can get lost in the crowd. Fight or no fight, there'll be a crowd. Pearl, you go to a store and buy four big leather belts, the kind Twig talked about. And better get another canteen. And some toothbrushes and toothpaste. Merle, you go see Joe about our money. Axel and I will take care of the gear."

We paid our bill and went our different ways.

Axel and I walked down to the railroad, crossed over, and picked up the suitcases, bag, and canteen. We didn't want to go back downtown, and we didn't want any trouble with the bulls, so we climbed up the stairs of a covered foot bridge and walked across it to the north side of the Mouse. We climbed down and headed west. A couple blocks later we came to a large bridge. We crossed it and walked to the GN depot.

We found the express office and paid shipping for our baggage to Havre, Montana. We used the names of Tom and Jim Johnson. The agent asked if we were brothers. I answered, "Yes." He said we didn't look like brothers. I was glad to get out of there.

As we were walking back, the train that would carry our gear came in. There was no stopping after that: we had to go to Havre.

Pearl came back with the stuff we needed. He said he had gone to two different stores for the toothbrushes so the clerk wouldn't be suspicious.

A little while later Merle came in and divvied up the money.

I'd checked the time on the two trains. Both came in much later. We lay on the grass. Our suitcases and bag pulled out. It was a long wait.

An ant got under my shirt and ran on my stomach. I sat up and my shirt tightened down on her. In class Mr. Pomeroy had said most ants were female. Pearl said he thought all his were female and all his uncles were male. Mr. Pomeroy laughed. That was one of the reasons I liked him. You could have some fun in his class and he didn't get mad.

The ant bit me. I unbuttoned my shirt and flicked her off my stomach. There was a small welt, pinkish-white, with a red area around it. I was lucky it had been only a black ant. They were small, not as small as a red or an orange ant, but at least it wasn't a pissant. They were red and black giants with big jaws that could cause a really painful bite.

I spread out my jacket and lay on it with my hands behind my head. I remembered reading Thoreau's description of an ant war. After I had read that, I got the twins and we caught dozens of ants, both reds and blacks, and had them fight a war.

You'd get one of each kind and put their heads together. They'd lock their jaws around each other and fight to the death. We had dozens of battles going on at the same time. The red ants were smaller, but they seemed to win most of the fights.

We tried to find a champion ant, but after an ant won a battle, it never seemed to be the same and generally tried to run, or more often, hobble away. If one of us kept pressing the jaws of two winners together, they'd lock jaws, but after they were put down, they'd break and try to escape, or they'd just hang onto each other until one died of exhaustion. Second battles were never as exciting as first ones.

Some ants just would never fight. They'd break and run as soon as they were put down. That's why I invented the Punishment.

The Punishment was a magnifying glass,

When we found two coward ants, we figured they were disgraces to the ant world. I'd take my magnifying glass and train a ray of sunlight onto a coward ant's abdomen. In a little while there was a puff of smoke—the ant was burning. It was somewhat hard to see because the magnified sunray made you see spots, but when the spots went away, there was a burned-out ant carcass. We'd give the other coward a chance. One of us would drop her on the carcass, and after she'd had time to rethink her cowardice, we'd give her another opponent. If she ran again, she was torched. Black ants were the easiest to burn—they were the biggest.

I'd read somewhere that bears ate ants. They'd bust open a log and lick them up with their tongues. After I read that, I decided to see what ants tasted like. I caught a black, a red, and an orange. One at a time I crunched them between my teeth. The black one was sharp and acid like a pickle. The red tasted like pepper. The little orange one was sweet. I never ate a pissant; they were too big.

Suddenly, I realized that I had never torched a pissant. I thought that I'd have to try that since there were big nests of them in Winslow's pasture back home . . .

I stopped thinking. I opened my eyes and tried to sit up, but my hands and arms were asleep. I waited in a funny kind of pain for the needles to start. They did and after a bit they went away.

I leaned against a tree and didn't think anymore.

When it was time to eat, we went to a different place in case somebody had been asking questions at the corner café. After our meal we bought sandwiches and had them wrapped in wax paper. We put them in our jacket pockets.

We asked if we could fill our canteens and got a funny look and an "I guess so" from the waitress. It was a good thing we wouldn't be coming back—she'd remember us.

We used the toilet, washed up, paid our bill, and left.

We killed time by walking uphill to the Normal School in north Minot. It must have been overcrowded that summer because there were several tents set up as classrooms north of the huge Main Building. While we were on campus, a cop car went by, so we decided to head back.

It was dusk when the train we wanted stopped at the depot. We were in some weeds north of the tracks with the train between us and the platform. One at a time we checked up and down the tracks for bulls and then ran over to a coach.

I clambered up between two passenger coaches, used a short ladder, a hand-hold, a window sill, another hand-hold, and I was on the roof. I kept low so no one on the platform would see me.

Ours was the seventh car, if you counted the engine and tender as cars, or the fifth if you didn't.

Pearl, with a canteen, and Axel were near the middle of the car. Merle and I, with the other canteen, stayed near the rear. I lay on my back, unbuckled my big leather belt, looped it around the line, and buckled it. Twig had said you could ride "up top" without the belt, but there was no way you should sleep up there without one.

The conductor shouted, "'board!" The whistle sounded and the train began moving.

People on the platform behind us were waving goodbyes.

The train picked up speed. We were on our way to the Great West and Jack Dempsey.

CHAPTER XXIII

Riding on top was a lot different than riding inside. The wind was always pushing on us, except when we stopped at a station, which wasn't as often as it had been on the freight.

We were closer to the locomotive so there was more noise. The engine sounds, the swaying-car noises, the wheels singing over the rails, and the wind in our ears were a lot louder than the more muffled sounds inside a boxcar. Also, on top we were at the mercy of smoke, soot, and an occasional cinder when the wind was wrong.

The lights of Minot disappeared quicker than the lights of our town because of the hills. The train went around a curve and Minot was gone.

Being on top took some getting used to, but once I had checked the strength of the belt and saw that it held even when I put all my power against it, I felt better. I switched over to my stomach and lay with my face on my arms and tried to relax.

The car really started swaying side-to-side as we hit top speed. I took off my cap and stuck it inside my jacket. The others did the same.

It was hard to believe that only two days had passed since . . . but I wouldn't let myself think about that, or about anyone in our town.

I did think about Twig once—when we thundered across the Gassman Coulee trestle—and what he would say if he knew what we were doing. Otherwise I tried to keep my mind on Shelby and the fight. When would we get there? Would there still be tickets? Who would win? What would Dempsey be like in person? I hoped the hundred thousand dollars would be paid.

After I got into the rhythm of the swaying car and the sounds of the train, I went to sleep.

I didn't notice any of the small towns we passed through, except one when I woke up in a feathery rain. Coming up were the lights of the town, misted and indistinct. We didn't even slow down and soon the lights were washed out.

The rain wasn't heavy, but it still soaked us. I was cold, but the wind started drying my clothes as soon as the rain stopped, and I went back to sleep, not really aware of the dampness.

We must have hit Big Muddy around midnight—my watch hadn't been acting right since the Wobbly incident. It was our first stop, and as we sat beside the brick station with its platform, also of brick, the engineer got out with an oil can and checked the running gear. I could see him in the light of the station platform lamps.

I hugged the roof when I heard footsteps on the ballast and then some metallic pings. Two men were alongside, tapping the wheels with hammers, listening for metal fractures. They moved on.

After the trainmen finished their inspection, we got down and hightailed it into the darkness opposite the station to relieve ourselves.

We climbed back up, and I ate half my sandwich and washed it down with a drink from my canteen. Merle did the same.

The train started and I buckled myself down. I was on my back, but the night sky was cloudy. After awhile I turned over on my stomach; it was easier to sleep that way. I said a prayer in which I mentioned my family and Twig.

I was asleep when we entered Montana, but soon we were in Culbertson; I raised my head and read the station sign. I was asleep again before we pulled out.

During the night we came to towns with stations and waiting rooms, passengers ready to head west, Poplar and Glasgow, but they were hazy through my sleep.

Once when I woke up, I looked back to the northeast. The horizon was a pale yellow with horizontal stripes of orange and a few blotches of purple which were clouds. Above the horizon purple faded into black and darkness. I went back to sleep.

I woke up again in Malta. It was daylight. I ate the rest of my sandwich and drank some water, which was still cold. Everyone else was asleep.

As we left Malta, the sun was burning away the clouds. It was going to be a hot day. I lay on my back and watched a large white cloud grow smaller and smaller as the sun got higher in the eastern sky. Finally, it was tiny and gray and then gone.

While I was watching the cloud, we clattered over a bridge. I didn't think the river was the Missouri.

We passed through a small town without stopping, but we did stop at the next town, which didn't appear any bigger. Maybe it was a flag stop, not a regular one.

While we were there, the other three woke up. One at a time we crawled to the back of the car, climbed down, and got relief standing on the coupling. Twig would have been mad.

When we left the little town, Dodson, it was a cloudless sky. We were running along the valley of the river. It was close on our left side and the valley swaled out to our right, ending in a line of bluffs. Beyond the bluffs the Montana plains swept on and on into Canada.

Every so often I could see a herd of cattle standing out brown and white against the lighter brown and green. This had been buffalo country, and I tried to imagine huge herds of buffalo coming over the bluffs, through the green-turning-to-brown high plains grass, and splashing into the river.

I thought I heard something and looked around. Merle was crying.

I unbuckled, crawled over, turned around to face him, and buckled up again. The wind was pushing at my pants legs.

"What's wrong, Merle? Are you sick?"

"No."

"What's wrong, then?"

He looked at me. There was some dirt in the tear marks on his cheeks. He asked, "Do you think there's a Hell?"

"Yes, I do. The Bible talks about it."

He lowered his head.

"But if you're sorry for your sins you won't go there. Just ask Jesus to forgive you for helpin' kill Wilson. All you did was grab his arm. I did more than that and it was Axel that did the killing."

"I know. I'm not worried about that."

"What then?"

"When we were at the res that day with Axel, I saw her."

"You saw who?"

"Cecilia."

"So?"

"I saw her naked."

"So?"

"I saw her naked, and after you guys left, I stayed and watched her until she went in the water."

"O.K., so?"

"So I'm not sorry. It's a sin and I'm not sorry. I'm not sorry and I'm goin' to hell for it."

I didn't know what to say. He was the one who said he wasn't sorry.

The train was slowing down. I looked over my shoulder and saw we were coming into a town. I started unbuckling my belt.

"Lige?"

"What?"

"After awhile, after a coupla years, I'm goin' back."

"Home?"

"Yeah, I'm goin' back home and marry her."

I turned around, slid over, and redid my belt. I hunkered down, waiting for the inspection to get over. Merle was an all-right guy. He'd help kill a man, and there was no way you could make that right, so he'd come with us, but he'd seen Cecilia naked, and he'd make that up to her by marrying her.

Still he's going to Hell. He's not sorry he saw her.

131

CHAPTER XXIV

We drank plenty of water from Chinook to Havre. The day was hot and sunny.

My canteen was empty by the time we were rounding the curve heading into Havre with bluffs south of the tracks and the town spread out to the north.

We waited on top until the coast was clear and then sprinted south, away from the station. We waited in a weed patch until the train pulled out, then went to the office and got our baggage.

Merle bought a newspaper from a news butcher and went into the station to check on the local freights, ones that would go to Shelby. When he came back, he told us our watches were off because we had crossed over into Mountain Time. We set our watches back an hour, but I had to go back another ten minutes—my watch was really getting out of whack.

We went looking for a hotel and found a cheap one a couple blocks from the station. We asked for a room with two beds. After we had registered and paid for one night, the clerk had a boy watch the desk while he took us up to the second floor.

He unlocked the door, opened the window, and showed us the bathroom. We weren't too interested.

He stood by the door, apparently waiting.

"Where you boys from?"

I didn't think it was any of his business. No one else spoke, either. He waited. Finally, I said, "Glasgow."

"Goin' over to the fight?"

"Maybe."

"Not too many of us here are, but then I guess you don't have much excitement in Glasgow."

"Enough." I looked around for help, but no one gave me any.

The clerk handed me the key. "If there's anything you fellas want, just ask. Or if it's later tonight, my brother works the night shift. Ask him."

"O.K., we will," I said. He was still near the door, so I reached in my pocket, felt for a small coin, and handed it to him. He looked at it, hesitated without saying anything, and left.

We went through the paper. Harding in Meacham, Oregon; Yanks Win; Heavy Rain Raises Missouri, Yellowstone. Nothing about a murder in North Dakota. But it was a Montana newspaper. We argued among ourselves on that point, but no two of us agreed on where we stood.

The fight, however, was on. Jack Kearns had agreed to it and was trusting that the final hundred thousand would be made good. Jack Dempsey stared out of the newspaper at me in street clothes. I could feel tiny jumps in my stomach as I thought about the next day.

Merle gave up the paper and walked around the room. In a drawer he found a Bible. He sat on the bed for awhile holding it and then announced he was going to "Ask For Guidance."

"Asking For Guidance" was something the twins and I did when we couldn't make up our own minds. Sometimes it worked. Axel asked what Merle meant. After we explained it, he said it was nuts, but that he'd try it, too. Pearl and I had already decided to.

We all sat on the bed and prayed. My prayer was short; I just asked God to help me do the right thing. When everybody had finished praying, Axel said he wanted to go first.

He picked up the Bible and, closing his eyes, opened it. The Bible lay on his left hand, and he put his right forefinger down on a page and read the verse his finger was on.

"And Tamar his daughter-in-law bare him Pharez and Zerah. All the sons of Judah were five." It was from First Chronicles.

"See," Axel said, "I told you it was nuts." He dropped the Bible on the bed.

"It was nuts 'cause you didn't believe to begin with," Merle said. "You had no faith."

Axel got off the bed and went into the bathroom.

I picked up the Bible. My verse was Ephesians 4:14—"That we henceforth be no more children, tossed to and fro, and carried about with every word of doctrine, by the sleight of men, and cunning craftiness, whereby they lie in wait to deceive."

After I read that, I started to agree with Axel, but I didn't say anything. The twins didn't know what to make of it, either.

Merle went for the New Testament, too. We had "Asked For Guidance" enough times to know that you stood a better chance of good news in the New than in the Old.

He got Luke 21:36—"Watch ye therefore, and pray always, that ye may be accounted worthy to escape all these things that shall come to pass, and to stand before the Son of Man."

Merle put the Bible down. "I've been prayin'—a lot."

"So have I," Pearl said.

"Me, too," I said. "Read that again, Merle."

He did and I could see a flicker of hope for all of us. All we had to do was keep praying.

I thought Pearl would be sure to pick from the New Testament, but his finger landed on Deuteronomy 22:5—"The woman shall not wear that which pertaineth unto a man, neither shall a man put on a woman's garment: for all that do so are abomination unto the Lord thy God."

That didn't have anything to do with us and Pearl was disappointed. I wondered, with the world the way it was, why God was interested in something little like clothes. It seemed to me that He'd have more important things on His Mind. I vowed to continue to avoid the Old Testament.

Axel came back in, all cleaned up. "You guys better wash before we go eat."

He was right. Riding on top had left us with dirty faces and gritty hands. Merle was the dirtiest so he went in first.

After everyone had finished, we went across the street to a café, where we sat at a table—there were no booths, just tables and a counter. There weren't too many customers at that time of day. The waitress came over and took our orders. She was the largest woman I had ever seen. In our town I thought Mary Wagner, who ran the Golden Day Bakery, was big. She was supposed to weigh 280 lbs., and the twins and

I joked that she made her dresses by sewing together old flour sacks. Our waitress topped Mary easily.

We heard a customer at the counter call her "Tiny" and Axel started to laugh. She looked over at us and I could tell she knew why he was laughing. Sometimes I wished that Pete Wilson had killed Axel.

When Tiny brought our food, I looked at her close. She had a real nice face with a big friendly smile, and she smelled nice, too—real clean-like.

I said, "Thank you," as she put my plate down and she smiled. She had really white teeth.

I'd seen steaks in North Dakota, but my first Montana steak put them to shame. It was a huge slab thicker than my thumb was wide and squeezed my American fries right off the plate. It was done just the way I liked it—dark brown with no blood. And it cost me the same as it would have in Minot.

When we got up, I put fifty cents under my plate for Tiny. She was clearing our dishes while we were paying. She looked right at me and smiled again, then she walked to the kitchen.

She had really small feet for a woman her size.

We had talked about how dangerous it was for all four of us to be on the street together at the same time, so we went across the street to the hotel in pairs—Merle and Axel, Pearl and I.

As soon as we got in the room, Pearl said he wanted a bath. He went into the bathroom and the rest of us looked around for something to do. Merle got out the Bible, Axel sprawled out on one of the beds, and I leaned up against the other bed and thought.

It was the third of July and the sound of firecrackers came through the open window. Back home they'd be getting ready for the parade, shining the fire engine, practicing on their band instruments, polishing their speeches, and trying to get into their Spanish-American or Great War uniforms—our town had no Civil War veterans. Ma would be making potato salad, and a watermelon would already be cooling in the root cellar.

"Merle! Merle! Come here!"

Merle went into the bathroom. I thought Pearl's back was bothering him. After a minute Merle stuck his head out.

"What's wrong?" I asked.

"Ticks."

I walked into the bathroom. Pearl was in the tub. When he bent forward, I saw the purple-yellow bruise on his back. Merle pushed aside the hair on the back of Pearl's head, and just on the hairline were two objects that looked like large watermelon seeds. They must have had a lot of blood in them.

"We've got to get 'em out," Merle said.

I looked at them closely. "Let's try matches."

Axel dug in his pocket. "I'm out, but I'll go get some." He left.

"I wonder if I got 'em in that weed patch."

"Naw, they're way too big for that," Merle said. "You got 'em in Minot."

"Then we'd better check ourselves, too," I said.

I stripped one of the beds down to its sheet. If there were any ticks in my clothes, I wanted to know it. I picked up a pair of pants and shook and snapped them over the bed. Nothing showed up on the sheet, but a brown piece of grass and some sand.

Merle stripped the other bed and started shaking his clothes over it, but stopped when Axel came in. Merle took the matches and pulled out his pocket knife. He opened the blade that was an awl, then struck a match and began heating the awl. After three matches he thought it was hot enough and applied it to a tick.

"Don't burn me," Pearl said.

"Don't move then."

The tick moved its legs.

"Don't kill it," I said. "You've got to get the head out. If you don't, it will keep burrowing in, and if it hits the brain, you can die."

Axel looked at me and gave a little snicker.

"Well, it's true." I couldn't recall who told me, but it sounded logical. I'd seen bullheads live for hours out of the water, so a tick's head could probably do the same and keep right on biting and chewing until it got to the hole where the backbone went up into the skull, and then it would start on the brain. Or maybe it could chew right through the skull. Ants could chew wood so maybe ticks could chew bone.

Merle heated the awl again and started stroking the tick.

"How close are we to the Rocky Mountains?" Pearl asked.

"A couple hundred miles," I said. "Why?"

"Quit movin'," Merle said.

"Because ticks can give you Rocky Mountain Spotted Fever, but if I got these here or in Minot, I guess I'm safe."

"It doesn't make any difference where you are," Axel said. "You can still get it, even if you're not in the mountains."

"But it would be worse in the mountains," I said.

"Why?"

"Because that must be where the fever first started out so that's where it would be the worst."

"Why?"

"Because it's like taking a big rock and throwing it in a river. Where it goes in, there's a big splash, but the further the waves go away from the splash, the weaker they are."

"I don't believe it."

"Well, nobody in our town ever died of Rocky Mountain Spotted Fever because it's too weak there, but you can be sure people in the Rocky Mountains have died of it."

"Will you two stop it! I've almost got this one out."

Ten seconds later the tick pulled out and rolled down Pearl's back into the tub.

Merle told Pearl to move forward, then he reached in and picked up the tick. He dropped it in the sink. It was so bloated it could hardly move.

Merle got the awl hot again and went to work on the second tick. Soon it popped out and Merle caught it in his left hand as it dropped. He looked at it closely and then put it in the sink. He picked up and examined the first one and said, "Both the heads are there."

Pearl wrapped a towel around his middle, got out of the tub, and stood by the sink. He took Merle's knife and put the awl on a tick and pressed. Dark, almost black, blood dribbled out. He killed the other tick the same way and ran water to flush them and the blood down the drain.

His bath water was pretty cool, so he drained and refilled the tub while the rest of us checked our clothes for ticks. Merle snapped Pearl's clothes over the bed for him. None of us found any ticks so we brushed the dirt on the floor and made the beds.

When Pearl finished, I went in. I shook out the clothes I had been wearing over the tub, but there were no ticks. I looked all over my body, especially the hairy spots, and used a mirror to check the parts I couldn't see. I searched carefully all over my scalp. I was tick-free.

In the tub I didn't hear any blues, but the water still felt good. I took my time.

Merle took his bath after me and when he had finished, we rested and dozed until suppertime. Axel said he was too tired to take his bath; he'd do it later.

When we went out for supper, Axel said he didn't want to eat with any fat ladies around, so we looked for a different place.

Pearl and I walked on one side of the street, while Merle and Axel went down the other. Pearl and I passed the cafe where Tiny worked and kept going to the end of the block. Standing there, we could see an "EAT" sign two blocks to our right. Pearl whistled and motioned so the other two would know where we were headed. They followed, but stayed a little behind on their side of the street.

One-story, false-front buildings with dirty windows lined both sides of the dusty street. When Pearl and I walked into the place marked "EAT," we saw three bare tables and a small counter with some banged-up wooden stools. No other customers were in the place, but then Merle and Axel arrived.

Out of the kitchen came a large man with an anchor tattooed on his right bicep and a cigarette on his lower lip.

"Whaddya want?"

"T-bone, well-done; cottage fries; and . . . coffee."

I hadn't thought about it, but what Pearl said sounded good, so I said, "Make it two."

"Two chops, American fries, and milk," Merle said.

"Two hamburgs, American fries, and a beer," Axel said.

The large man stuck his unshaven face down close to Axel's and said, "What'd you say, wise guy?"

Axel looked away. "Two hamburgs, American fries, and coffee."

"That's better." The man walked back to the kitchen, then he and a little man with a pink face looked at us through the open window. They were talking low.

Pearl had brought the newspaper. He got it out and began reading about how Harding would be leaving Tacoma on the fifth for Alaska. He looked over at me. "Maybe we should be thinkin' about Alaska."

"To go there?"

"Yeah, it's so big no one could find us."

The large man brought a glass of milk and three cups. He slopped coffee into the cups. I said, "Thank you," and he grunted something back. The coffee was strong. I always put cream in my coffee back home so I asked for some.

"Don't have any."

"No cream?"

"You heard me." He walked into the kitchen and came back with a fly swatter.

"Milk then."

He glanced at me, then pointed at Merle. "That's the last of it. Get some from him."

He began splatting flies on the counter. I forgot about the cream or milk.

I stirred sugar into my coffee. Alaska was too far away. We might never get back home and I knew that someday I was going back. I didn't want to go to Alaska. Pearl returned to the paper.

Our food came. The potatoes were greasy, the chops pink, the hamburgers black, and the steaks ran red with blood.

"Say, mister?" Pearl couldn't abide bloody meat.

The large man came over and pointed his face down at Pearl's.

Pearl looked up at him. "Could I have my steak well-done?"

"And me."

"And do my chops a little more."

Axel crunched into his first hamburger.

"What's wrong wit' 'em? They look O.K. ta me. Hey, Charlie, we got some complaints." The little man came to the kitchen doorway. He was wiping a meat cleaver on a dirty apron.

"These kids want you should cook their meat more." He gathered up the plates and left. Charlie glared at us and started banging things in the kitchen.

"What about the potatoes?" I whispered.

"I'm not sayin' a word about potatoes," Pearl said.

Neither would Merle or Axel, so I decided not to, either.

The large man came back and dropped the plates on the counter, turned, and strode off, looking for flies.

The chops were all right, and the blood was gone from the steaks, but they were reddish inside. Pearl looked at me. I put a piece of steak in my mouth and chewed. It would be O.K. Merle was chewing, too, and Axel was almost finished crunching. Pearl looked at them, cut his steak in half, and studied the red carefully.

"Say, mister?"

The large man swatted a fly and flicked it off the end of the counter. He moved down to us and swatted another at Pearl's elbow. He flicked it onto the floor and stepped on it.

"What?"

"My steak is still too red. Could you have it cooked some more, please?"

The large man went away muttering, carrying the plate.

"Don't these guys ever get lonely?" Merle said to me.

"Why?"

"Nobody's been in here since we came."

The three of us finished eating while Pearl paged through the paper. Finally, the large man came back carrying the plate with a hot pad. Charlie stood in the doorway.

The large man held the plate in front of Pearl. "Here. Take it."

Pearl reached up for it, but before I could really think about what I was doing, I half rose, yelled, "No!" and slapped the plate out of the large man's hands and onto the counter. "It's hot!"

Pearl barely touched the plate with his forefinger and quickly pulled it back. The large man began laughing, and so did Charlie—a deep "Haw! Haw!" and a high cackling "Hee! Hee!"

Pearl stood up and hit the large man as hard as he could with a straight right to the nose. Blood flew away from the man's head. He fell back against a shelf and spread out on the floor. His nose slid down his face.

Charlie screamed and charged with the meat cleaver, but he had to get around the counter, and we were out the door and down the block by the time he hit the sidewalk screaming about bastards and sons of bitches.

CHAPTER XXV

We turned right at the end of the block and then headed for the alley on the other side of the street and ran down it. We had two corners on Charlie or whoever would be after us.

Merle said he'd be the spy so he went left at the end of the alley. The rest of us walked to the hotel in a round-about way, trying to turn a corner every block.

When we passed the front desk, there was a new clerk there, but he looked a lot like the old one. He glanced up from under black hair slicked back and parted in the middle. "You boys in 20?"

"Yeah," I said and went to the desk. Pearl and Axel kept walking.

"You boys got money?"

"We've already paid for the room."

"I know, but are ya lookin' for some fun?"

"Sure."

"Ya goin' out again tonight?"

"What's it to you?"

"Nothin'. I just wondered where ya'd be."

"Why? Someone been askin'?"

"No, but arrangin' fun takes time."

"Well, go ahead and arrange it then."

"Should I double it?"

"O.K."

He turned away. I took the stairs two at a time and knocked on the door. Pearl unlocked and opened it.

"We'd better watch it—the desk clerk acts suspicious. He wanted to know if we'd be in tonight."

"Did ya see any cops?" Axel asked.

"No."

"He couldn't know anything," Pearl said.

"I don't think so," I agreed.

There was a knock at the door and Pearl asked, "Who is it?"

"Me."

Pearl unlocked the door and Merle came in.

"I worked around to the alley of the block across from the café and squeezed between two buildings until I could see the street. Charlie pulled up in a Model T, went inside, and helped the fat guy into the auto. The guy's nose was still bleedin'. The white towel he had on it was soakin' up blood. They took off and I went across the street and tried the door. It was locked. I think they went to a doctor or maybe a hospital."

"Or maybe the cops," Axel said.

"Maybe," Merle said. "But not until the fat man has his nose set. Pearl really broke it."

"He got me mad." Pearl sounded ashamed.

"Served the son of a bitch right." Axel was talking like he had done it.

"Keep the window open. If the cops come to the door, we'll have to go out the window," I said.

Everyone agreed and then Pearl said he was hungry. He was the only one who hadn't eaten, so he walked to the café where Tiny was the waitress.

Axel went in to take his bath.

Merle and I started talking about money. I had quite a bit, and so did Axel because his mother had sent along fifty dollars from Chicago, but the twins were running low.

"Don't worry about it. I've got enough to get us all to the Coast."

"I don't like takin' money from anyone."

"All right, it's a loan then. You and Pearl can pay me back after we get jobs."

Merle thought it over as he looked at his money. "Yeah, we could do that. It wouldn't be charity."

"No, it'll be a loan. Just like a bank. I'll even charge ya interest if ya want."

Merle laughed. "Just the loan'll do. We'll pay ya back from our first paychecks."

Axel was draining the tub and whistling something that sounded vaguely like "Barney Google" when there was a knock, just three light raps.

I walked over to the bathroom door and told Axel that someone was at the door so to hurry up.

Merle said, "Who is it?"

A female voice said, "Just us." I felt relieved—there were no female cops.

Merle unlocked and opened the door. Two women, or really one woman and a girl, stood there.

The woman had red hair that looked dyed. It was short and frizzy. She wore a dark red dress and some beads around her neck. Her face was caked with makeup and her lips were bright red. She was smoking a store-bought cigarette. She could have been thirty or fifty, it was hard to tell.

The girl had on a pink dress and pink stockings. I noticed that there was dust on her shoes and just above them the dust had darkened the stockings. She had black hair and her face had red lips, too. When she looked at me, she smiled, and I saw the spaces between her teeth were black with decay.

The woman took the cigarette out of her mouth and blew the smoke out of her nose. "Lily and me heard that you boys are in the mood for a little fun tonight. Ain't ya gonna invite us in?"

Merle hadn't opened the door all the way. He yelled, "No!" and slammed the door hard. He looked over at me and I started laughing. Then Merle laughed, too.

Axel slowly stuck his head out of the bathroom. "What's goin' on? Are the cops here?"

"No," I said. "No cops."

"What then?"

Merle said, "Just a coupla whores."

"Where?"

"I got rid of 'em."

"What?" Axel came out with just his pants on and ran to the door. He opened it and went down the hallway. Pretty soon he was back. "They're gone. Why didn't ya let 'em in?"

Merle looked at me. I shook my head slowly and made a face. Merle said, "Because they're whores."

"Yeah, but they were women." Axel went back into the bathroom.

Merle and I began laughing and then Pearl came in—Axel hadn't locked the door.

"What's so funny?"

"Axel wanted two whores, but we sent them away," Merle said.

"I think I saw 'em out front. Pee-ewe!"

Merle and I laughed again until Axel came out, then we shut up and began settling down for the night.

I washed, brushed my teeth, and said my prayers.

It was hot, and leaving the window open didn't help until after eleven o'clock when a cool breeze started coming in.

CHAPTER XXVI

When you have to get up at a certain time, you can wake yourself up at that time. It's like your body has a built-in alarm clock.

Everyone was awake early. We cleaned up, dressed, and left the hotel, walking past the sleeping desk clerk or his brother.

We split up and made our separate ways to the depot. I kept a look-out for cops, but didn't see any. I came to the tracks and walked west along them toward the station. I knew that up the tracks Jack Dempsey was waiting.

The others were already on the platform, so I put my suitcase in the waiting room with theirs, and we walked over to a small café. The local wasn't due for half an hour.

The café was crowded with railroad men, most of whom were gabbing about the fight. Gibbons seemed to be the one they liked, though Dempsey was the favorite to win.

A red-faced rail sat down next to me and the waitress came over for his order. The window to the kitchen was right in front of me, and she turned and yelled, "Benny, hot box a-smokin', with headlights and a blind gasket."

She got a cup and poured coffee into it. "Here's your coffin varnish, Hank."

"Thanks, Flo." He pulled a flask and dribbled something into his cup. "Whatcha rubberneckin' for, kid? Ain't ya never seen bust head b'fore."

I looked away. My face turned hot. *Why'd he have to go and say that for?* It had been fun listening to the other rails talk, but then he had to get mean.

Merle's knee touched mine, but I didn't look over. I just went back to eating and pretending I wasn't there. Red Face was talking to the man on his right.

"Them two fairies that run the beanery downtown got beat up last night, at least the big one did."

"You mean the bean queens?"

Several men laughed.

"Yeah, the tall one got a busted nose. I heard about a half a dozen guys came in and tried to roust the place. When one of 'em reached in the till, the tall Mary tried to stop him, and two guys pinned his arms and another one broke his beezer. Then they ran like hell when Shorty chased 'em with a cleaver. They ain't from here—probably on their way to the fight."

His coffee had cooled so to no one in particular he said, "Here's to Rule G," and took a drink.

Flo came over and put down a plate with a steak, two fried eggs, and a pancake on it.

"Hot damn! That looks good enough to eat."

She laughed.

A man came in and walked over. He slapped Red Face on the back. "Hey, Shays, greetings from the DS." He handed a sheaf of papers to Red Face.

Red Face riffled through them. "Hell's Bells." He looked through them again. "Hell's Bells." He turned to the man on his right and showed him the papers. "I'm gonna hang my ashcat's hide on the coal grate today."

"C'mon, Shays, Don't be a rawhider."

"I'm not, Johnson, but just look at this stuff. I've got to get goin'." The food disappeared from his plate and he left.

It was nice being in a hash house and watch the rails and listen to their lingo, but we had a train to catch.

It was early and already the day was hot. At the depot we got our gear and walked across the tracks to wait for the local.

When it stopped, we found an empty boxcar and threw our stuff in. I found a railroad spike, and after I climbed in, I jammed it under the door. Twig had told us that we should always do that in case a sudden stop slammed the doors shut: there were no inside handles. I hadn't jammed the door coming out of our town because it was too dark to find a spike or brake shoe and I was so late.

The whistle jerked the freight to life and we were headed for Shelby. Havre disappeared behind us as we followed the river westward. Soon we clacked over a "frog" which sent a set of rails southwest to Great Falls.

We crossed a small river which came up from the south, and, sitting in the open car door, I watched the big river swing off to the north. We were in wheat country and the fields ran from the railroad up and down hills to both northern and southern horizons, unbroken except by an occasional section line or road.

We rushed through a village with the whistle screaming. Thinking of Dempsey and the fight, I was urging the locomotive on. No stopping, no slowing down, until Shelby. And Dempsey.

But we did stop—twice. The switching was done quickly at both places and we moved on.

At Galata we climbed a low tableland which extended southward from three buttes, and far off to the west, we saw the snow-capped Rockies.

At the last stop we were waiting to attach three more freight cars when a Best tractor came by on a road next to the right-of-way. It must have been only a couple of years old because it had the full-length tracks, and it had the word "BEST" painted both on top and vertically down the sides of its radiator. Black smoke was puffing out of its stack, and dust was kicking up behind it as it ground its way forward. We didn't have many California tractors near our town. We had Case, Oil Pull, Minneapolis, Samson, Twin City, McCormick-Deering, and Allis-Chalmers—all built in Minnesota, Wisconsin, Illinois, or Indiana.

If a farmer could afford to buy a Best and have it shipped to Montana, he was doing all right.

As the Best clanked down the road, it frightened some horses that shied and ran away from the fence where they had been standing. The dirt clods shot up from their hooves as they ran from the Best, which was making a dust of its own.

The sun was heating up our car by the time we were rolling again. I looked for the Best over the next mile or so, but it was gone.

We ran out of wheat country and the Montana plains browned up around us.

Axel was at one door by himself when he exclaimed, "Cripes, they've got big jackrabbits here."

"Where?' Pearl walked over.

"There."

Pearl began laughing so hard he fell against the side of the car.

Merle and I crossed over and looked out. A dozen pronghorns were bounding away and then stopping and then bounding again.

We burst out laughing and left it to Pearl to explain it to Axel, who got sore and sat in the back of the car without saying anything. I didn't care.

The closer we got to Shelby, the more autos we could see on the highway off to the north, with their little tails of dust. "There's gonna be forty thousand people there," Merle said.

"I hope there'll be some seats left," Pearl said.

I motioned Merle over with my head. When he got across the car, I took out my money and counted off some bills for the twins. I handed them to Merle, but he looked doubtful.

"Go on and take it. I've got plenty. Besides, the cheapest tickets are twenty-five dollars, and I don't want to flash this money in a crowd."

He took the money. "Thanks, we'll pay you back."

"I know you will."

He grinned and weaved his way back across the car.

"There's a Hupmobile!" Pearl yelled.

"Where?" Axel asked, getting up.

"Right behind that Model T."

"Which Model T? They're all Model T's."

"No, they're not. One's a Hupmobile." They both continued looking and arguing.

I had just finished drinking from my canteen when Merle asked, "What the heck is that?"

We were in a valley and Merle was on the other side of the car looking forward. I went over and in the distance I saw a lot of dust and in the middle of the dust was a large, dark something. It wasn't so tall, but it was wide.

All of us looked, but no one said anything. Then Pearl said, "Buffalo," and everyone laughed.

As we got closer, we could see dark spots on the hills and then buildings appeared in the valley to the south of the tracks ahead.

"It's Shelby," Pearl said.

I stared. Pearl was right—it had to be Shelby.

"That's the arena, I'll bet," Merle said.

The freight slowed down and as it stopped in the yard, we jumped off and headed for the depot. It was hot and nearly noon; the fight was supposed to start at three.

CHAPTER XXVII

The Shelby station was a plain white frame building with a plank fence extending around one side. We checked the area for cops and, finding none, paid to have our gear sent on to the next division point, a place called Troy, then we headed into town.

The main street was dry and rutted and lined with Model T Fords parked diagonally against the sidewalks. There were plenty of reminders of the oil strike of a couple years before that had made Shelby what it was. We passed the Oil City Drug Store and there was a filling station right across the street.

I wanted to get out to the arena, but the others wanted to eat, so we walked the streets for awhile. I saw a lot of young kids around, but I never heard any firecrackers. They must have banned them.

There were the usual general stores, feed and seed stores, a weather-beaten harness shop, a meat market—stores just like in our town.

What was different were the dance halls, cabarets, and the large number of eating places.

The dance halls were called Cripple Creek Barn, the King Tut, and the Green Lite. We didn't go in.

The cabarets looked more interesting. Axel wanted to go in the Black Cat, but the twins pulled him away. We saw the Days of '49, the Blue Goose, the Shack, the Cave, McBride's Dew Drop Inn, and the Mountain Lion.

We had a large selection of cafes—the Pup, the Turf, the Chicken Shack, the Wayside Inn, Jack and Jill, the Log Cabin, the Mustang, the Gibbons Club, and the Red Onion. Axel wanted to eat at the Gibbons, but I refused. Ever since we had seen its name in the paper, the twins and I had dreamed of eating at the Red Onion and that's where we went.

Most of the cafes were temporary shacks, but they all looked busy, it being noon and everything. It took us awhile to get seats in the Onion and then we had to sit apart.

I kept looking around for cowboys with boots, spurs, chaps, and ten-gallon hats, but I didn't see any. In the Red Onion, at least, the men looked just like they did in our town. They wore dark suits with vests and hats—fedoras, derbies, pork pies, or boaters.

The food tasted good—a thick steak charred just the way I liked it and American fries, a little greasy. Someone nearby said there wasn't a fresh egg to be had within a hundred miles, and fresh vegetables were just a memory. I drank coffee, but I dumped in plenty of sugar since I knew there was no milk.

"Hell, all I know is that two nights ago the fight was off because that bastid Jack Kearns wanted that last hundred thousand guarantee. I'd like to hang that bastid from a tree by the neck until dead." The man who spoke was sitting across from me and down one place. He was talking to a big black fedora over a black vest with a large gold watch chain. Fedora had hung his coat over the back of his chair. The angry man spoke again. "This town's been had, Fred, been had by that bastid Kearns, and we've got to do somethin' about it." He crashed his fist onto the long table, and everyone's plates, cups, and silverware jumped. Some of my coffee spilled. The angry man and I locked eyes, but he didn't apologize. He laid his hand flat on the table and lowered his voice. "We've got to do somethin'."

"But what?"

"Postpone the fight."

"That's crazy."

"Not as crazy as puttin' it on today to an empty house. Just postpone it two days. Even with two days we could still get some special trains lined up from Seattle, Spokane, Denver—three days and I could get St. Paul, maybe even Chicago—and we might even make some money, but if we go today, we'll get nothin'. In fact, we'll lose. I've been out to the arena. That house that Jack built is gonna be rattlin' empty come fight time. The GN built almost sixty miles of side track and how many specials are in? I'll tell you—two or three. Two or three and there should have been two or three dozen and all because of that bastid

Kearns." He raised his hand into a fist, looked over at me, and then put it back down.

I took a drink of coffee. The others were still eating, but I couldn't see what.

"It's not Kearns's fault."

"The hell it's not. He held out for a hundred thousand in June, and when we were a little late, he goes to the press and says the fight's off."

"No, he didn't. He said it might be off."

"The same thing. It scared people. They cancelled the special trains. Now we're sittin' here with an arena we can't fill and I say we got a bum deal. It's Kearns's fault, and I say we go talk to him, make him postpone the fight, get the specials lined up, and make some money. Or else we play rough. Hell, I'll put the rope around his neck myself."

Fedora Fred glanced over at me. "Shut up, Sam." He stood up, swung his coat on, and put his hand on Angry Sam's shoulder. "C'mon. A deal's a deal and we're gonna have to live with it."

Angry Sam got up. "Or die with it." He walked away, a big man with large dark spots around his armpits, muttering about a "bastid."

I got up and paid. I shouldn't have had the coffee. It was blazing outside and roasting in the café, so I was hotter than ever. I bought a sarsaparilla and walked outside.

The two-holer was in back. I don't know why it was a two-holer. Men don't accompany each other when they use such places, and there weren't any women around the Onion to use it.

When I had finished, I dropped the bottle down the hole. The twins and Axel were standing in line so I waited out front. People were beginning to walk and drive to the west.

A few minutes later we were among them. We could see the arena in the distance, surrounded by lines and patches of black that showed through the dust being scuffed up.

We walked beside a wire fence for a ways and passed some tent concessions, then it was thick dust until we got closer to the arena. I was glad Pearl and I had kept our canteens.

The long black lines to the right were extra railroad tracks laid out by the GN for the specials, but there were only a few cars on them. The black patches around the arena were Model T's, concession stands, and hundreds of milling people.

"Look at the cheap ones," Merle said. He was pointing to a small rimland.

"There must be two dozen of 'em," Pearl said.

"But they'll never see anything from there," I said.

Model T's had been driven to the rimland, and spectators were seated on the patchy hillside, waiting for the fight.

"Maybe we should go up there," Axel said. "It's free."

"Not me," I said. "This fight will be worth the price and I want to be absolutely as close as possible."

I edged toward a ticket stand. There was a short line and quite a few of the people in it were women.

"C'mon, you guys," I called from the line.

Pearl looked at me. "We're not goin', Lige."

He nodded at Merle, who said, "You go, Lige. We'll give your money back after the fight. It's just too expensive, but you go."

I looked at my best friends and then up at the scaffolding of the arena.

"What's yours?" the ticket seller asked.

I glanced back at the twins, but they had already moved away. I took out my money. "Fifty dollars. Ringside."

The ticket wasn't much, but I still have it, with part torn off by the ticket taker. It reads "Use Gate 7." There were thirty-two gates.

I found the twins and told them to meet me at Gate 7 after the fight. They didn't say much. Axel had a twenty-two dollar ticket in a different section.

I took a drink of water just before I walked into the arena. It towered above me, not quite as tall as our church back home, but more massive.

The ticket taker notched off a corner and gave my ticket back. Inside, the pine smelled new. Some of the sap was oozing in the heat. I could hear crowd noise above me, but I walked slowly, trying to take in everything.

I came out into the light. The ring was a gray-white square centered in a pine octagon. I tried to get down to it, to touch it, but an usher forced me back into Section G. Most of the ushers wore servicemen's uniform, but mine didn't. I sat down with the sun on the back of my neck.

My first thought was *Where is everyone?* The arena was almost empty. Looking around, I saw mostly boards, but there was Axel, sitting behind me and a ways up. He saw me, but pretended he didn't.

It was getting hotter, but at least more people were filing in. Business for the vendors of green paper eyeshades began to pick up.

Three refreshment stands were up on the rim of the arena and vendors circulated among the fans. Bottled pop was twenty-five cents, but I had my canteen. There were four tall superstructures near the ring, each with a motion picture camera on top. Several uniformed Red Cross nurses were stationed around the ring.

A little after one the ringside sections were about three-fourth's filled, with more fans on my side than on the others.

There was activity around the ring area as they got ready for the preliminaries. A guy started testing the big gong, and another with a megaphone got into the ring and reminded everyone that there was no smoking in the arena, amidst a cascade of "boo's." I looked back at Axel, but he was pretending again.

Every once in awhile I could hear chants outside the arena. One time it was "ten dollars" repeated over and over. Another time it was "Bring on Dempsey." The chants didn't last very long, but they were loud while they did.

Just as the preliminary fighters were coming in, there was a big surge of fans from the upper areas into the remaining ringside seats. The ushers didn't even attempt to stop them. Axel ended up two rows ahead of me.

The first preliminary had Jack McDonald knocking out Ernie Sayles in Round Two. They were light heavies, very awkward, and I was glad it ended early.

More fans began coming in. I learned later that Kearns had cut the ticket prices.

It was a good hour between preliminaries and at first we had entertainment. An Elks' fife and drum corps got into the ring and played. They got a big laugh with "You're In the Army Now." Then they marched around the arena while the crowd applauded.

Some bagpipers from Canada played for awhile, but then the afternoon lengthened. Some guys got restless and began rolling pop bottles down the aisles. A group of Blackfoot Indians, led by their chief, trooped in and stood in the reserved section, decked out in feathered head gear and blankets.

Finally, Gorman and Drake, two heavyweights, dragged each other around the ring to an eight-round decision for Gorman. He deserved it, but the whole fight was an embarrassment.

The third prelim was cancelled.

There was no breeze at all in the arena. I used my canteen a lot.

Three o'clock came, but no fighters appeared. A rumor went around that the fight had been cancelled, and some men near me began cursing Kearns until a distinguished-looking gentleman in a derby quieted them by saying, "Please, men, remember there are ladies present."

I looked around. There were quite a few ladies, all accompanied by men. They sat together in groups with other ladies, none too close to the ring, clumps of color in a black, brown, gray, and white hillside of men.

The guy with the megaphone got up in the ring and, after getting the crowd to quiet down, asked if there was a "Bill Deal" in the house.

"No," someone yelled, "but there's a raw deal!"

The crowd grumbled its agreement.

I recognized the voice: it was Axel's.

A blind veteran—I heard he was from Canada—got up and sang in the ring. We gave him a standing ovation.

It got hotter—it must have been a hundred. A bunch of fans came running up the aisles and began filling in many of the empty seats. They had broken through the fence and no one had tried to stop them. Merle and Pearl got in that way, but I didn't see them. I heard later that Mary Pickford and Douglas Fairbanks were at ringside, but I didn't see them, either.

I fingered my ticket, nervously waiting for Dempsey. I memorized the ticket's face and phrases: "World's Heavyweight Championship," "O'Toole County American Legion," "Jack Dempsey vs Tom Gibbons," "15 rounds to a decision," "July 4th 1923 3 P.M. Mountain Time," "Loy J. Molumby, Promoter." I read them over and over. I recited the words silently, rotating the ticket in my hand. A drop of sweat landed on the ticket and I carefully dried it off.

"It's almost three thirty!" a man off to my left yelled. "Let's fight!" He repeated it louder and a few others helped him, but it died early. I rotated the ticket faster.

I closed my eyes and without warning a cheer went up. I opened them and there he was—Jack Dempsey, the Manassa Mauler, the Heavyweight Champion of the World, Hero of Heroes, god of gods.

He climbed into the ring and took the northwest corner, the one with his back to the sun and the one nearest to me. I was on my feet cheering. He took off his blue sweater coat and stood there, gleaming dark brown in white silk trunks with a ribbon of red, white, and blue tied around them. His face was covered with Vaseline and day-old stubble and his hands were heavily taped.

I was screaming, "Dempsey! Dempsey!" Other fans were yelling, too. Some were booing, while some men were chanting, "Kill Kearns!"

Dempsey stood in his corner and scowled around at the empty seats. He appeared nervous, but he still looked like the picture of a Greek statue that Miss Samuels had showed us in class. The statue looked like it was throwing a spear or trident, so its muscles were flexed, and it was dark just like Dempsey. They didn't know if it was Zeus or Poseidon, but right then I knew who it was.

Dempsey finally sat down, but he kept peering out at the crowd, or the lack of one. A bodyguard held an umbrella over him as he shuffled his feet and played with his hands. The ring was alive with photographers, but he didn't pay any attention to them. I wanted to kick every one of them into the cheap seats. The Champ had to concentrate on the fight.

It seemed to me that Dempsey's welcome was loud, but when Gibbons entered the arena to my right, the noise, the cheers, the stamping were overwhelming. The arena boomed and rocked, and it exploded when Gibbons crossed the ring and shook Dempsey's hand.

It reminded me of the Bible: "Saul has his thousands, but David his ten thousands." But that was wrong. Dempsey was David. Dempsey was the best. It just wasn't right that Gibbons got the cheers.

Gibbons took off his faded brown robe, revealing dark-green trunks. His skin was pale compared to Dempsey's. It was a good thing he had an umbrella man, too. Gibbons walked across the ring and had his bandaged hands inspected by the Champ; then he inspected Dempsey's and went back to his corner. Gibbons' body looked small beside Dempsey.

Kearns stalked around the ring as Dempsey's gloves were adjusted.

Gibbons bounced against the ropes, testing them, then he sat down and his gloves were put on and adjusted. Dempsey was shadow boxing in his corner. Kearns moved to center ring and directed the resin sprinkling.

An announcer tried to get the crowd's attention. He stated that Dempsey's weight was one hundred and eighty-eight pounds and Gibbon weighed one hundred and seventy-five and a half. There was some booing, but I was satisfied.

The referee, a guy named Dougherty, was wearing a checkered pork pie hat, a black bow tie, white silk shirt, and blue trousers. He had been standing impassively in a neutral corner, but after the announcement of the weights, he called the fighters to the center of the ring. The photographers got busy again. After the final instructions, Dempsey and Gibbons clasped gloves, but the Champ barely looked at the challenger. He was too busy surveying the crowd.

I read later that Dempsey told Kearns in the ring, "I'll make this quick, Doc." I never heard it, but I was five rows back.

I took a swig from my canteen and the fight was on. Dempsey charged across the ring—his attack was that of a predator or a god. He hooked a left to Gibbons' jaw and I cheered. They clinched. Gibbons dug three quick lefts into Dempsey's body and threw a short right to his head. The crowd yelled.

Dempsey backed off and then came in again. He swung at Gibbons, who covered up and danced away. The Champ looked puzzled; he couldn't get to Gibbons. Dempsey moved in and shot a right-left combination to the body. The fighters clinched. Gibbons hooked a left to the jaw, followed by a right. They clinched again. Dempsey hit Gibbons with a solid upper cut near the end of the round, and Gibbons' lip started bleeding.

The first four rounds were about the same—Dempsey punching or trying to punch, Gibbons boxing and moving, both of them clinching.

Near the end of the Fourth, Gibbons opened a cut above Dempsey's left eye, and the crowd screamed at the blood. So did I, but the wound wasn't serious.

I noticed between rounds that a few thousand more people had come into the arena and taken up many of the empty seats further back, but the place was still only two-third's full.

Gibbons took Round Five, so Dempsey stepped up his punching in the next round. In the clinches Dempsey had been rough—he got rougher. He tried to bull the smaller man around and he'd rabbit punch him. I couldn't believe it the first time I saw him do it, but he kept it up in just about every clinch. I didn't like it—it wasn't right.

After one exchange Gibbons' head and shoulders went through the ropes, and Dempsey hit him as he was trying to get back in. The crowd booed. Dempsey stepped back and let Gibbons in. Gibbons danced away from a barrage of wild punches. The crowd roared; I was quiet.

The fight kept going in the July sun. I finished the last of my water and I didn't bother to stand up anymore.

Gibbons won a couple more rounds, but he was tiring. During the last few rounds he was just trying to survive. Maybe Dempsey could have finished him off, maybe not. I didn't care anymore. Rabbit punches and hitting outside the ropes soured me.

In Round Fifteen the fans stood and cheered for Gibbons just to hang on. The Blackfoot Indians pounded continuously on their tom-toms. After the final bell, the decision went to Dempsey. The ref raised his hand in victory amidst a lot of boos, but he did it with no hesitation, so he must have been certain.

Gibbons, smiling out of his blood-smeared face, came over and congratulated the champion. I didn't boo or cheer; I only wanted to get out of the sun, but it was hard to because the fans stood and cheered Gibbons for at least ten minutes.

Some of the fans climbed into the ring to be near Gibbons. A woman got in and hugged him. The Blackfoot chief did even better: he put an eagle feather headdress on his head and the crowd went wild. The tom-toms and the chants from the Blackfoot women raised an awful din.

I never saw Dempsey leave the ring, but when I looked over, he was gone.

In the shadow of Gate 7, I waited for the others. It was clouding up in the northwest, but the heat and the dust around the arena were suffocating. We took refuge in a little lunch wagon with a sign saying it was sponsored by a Ladies' Aid Society. I figured they had to be pretty liberal to sell food at a fight.

My stomach wasn't right, so I just bought a couple soda pops and some fruit they had in an icebox there. Then I saw their bread was homemade so I paid for two big thick-crusted slices.

We ate in back of the wagon, in the shade, away from the dust and confusion. The others talked about the fight. The twins laughed over the fact that they'd gotten to see for free what Axel and I had paid good money for. Axel said he was going to demand a refund, but I didn't care.

All of them rubbed it in that Dempsey had to settle for a decision. The razzing didn't bother me. Eating fresh-baked bread and cool grapes in the open air made me feel better.

The crowds were building up, so as soon as we finished, we headed back to town. Shelby was crowded with Model T's and people. We killed some time by walking around, watching folks and the darkening off to the northwest.

Once we walked past the little green-roofed cottage where Gibbons had been staying and saw two little boys shooting off firecrackers (the only ones I heard in Shelby) in the yard. The front door opened and some Indians came out carrying an eagle feather headdress, but we never saw Gibbons.

Back on the main drag Pearl said, "We'd better head for the station; it's gonna be rainin' in a few minutes."

We all agreed, but we had to obey the call of nature, so we went over to the Red Onion's facilities. While I was in line, I heard a man say that the Blackfoot had taken back the headdress they had given Gibbons.

The man behind said, "Indian givers," and everyone laughed.

Two blocks from the station the rain began. By the time we got to the platform, the streets were muck, and our boots were coated with it. We found some sticks and tried to scrape them clean. It would be dangerous enough going "up top" with wet boots, much less muddy ones.

Pearl and I tried to fill our canteens with rain water, but it took too long—the holes were too small—so we used the station's tap.

We bought some peanuts and candy to tide us over to the division point, watched the Model T's lose to the mud, and cursed the rain.

CHAPTER XXVIII

I was getting the shakes, belted to the top of the car in the slashing gray rain. We'd been riding forty minutes or so and the rain hadn't quit. My hands and feet felt like they had chilblains and I was shivering.

Beneath the sound of the rain and the noise of the cars, I heard a deep rumbling, and the top of the car began to move more violently. Across my right shoulder I saw a wide cut, deeper than Gassman Coulee, with high banks and a tiny creek nearer the east side. We careened across the steel bridge, the big drivers on the Mikado engine vibrating the steel trusses and throwing me toward the edge. The shivering got worse.

That evening I could tell we were on an upward grade. After the rain quit just east of Browning, I could see in the dusk the flat prairie and the hummocky buttes, the same as they had appeared in the daytime, but I knew we were climbing. The telegraph poles and fence posts ripped past on the right.

We only stopped in Browning for a few minutes.

I saw the same stars I'd seen coming out of our town, and it was true they were brighter in the mountains. But I also noticed that the dark between the stars was a lot darker.

We careened over a steel bridge. A little stream had gashed the mountains as it ran down into the Flathead. Another small problem for the railroad. I couldn't handle the swaying as easily on my back so I turned over again. The GN was double-tracked west of Summit, and we made good time to the big sweeping left-handed curve at Fielding, where we took on water.

West of Java, I got up on my elbow to look down into the Flathead Valley below. When I lay down again, I saw the four boots in front of me. Merle and Axel looked asleep. Pearl was, too, and soon so was I.

There were five tunnels between Summit and Coram, and I woke up through the longest one, which was maybe the length of two football fields. It was a little tough breathing and you had to watch out for sparks, but it wasn't bad.

I slept past the three water towers at Essex that Twig said were used for the big Mallets and the 2-10-2 pusher engines on the grade. We didn't need any pushers on our way down.

At Belton we turned southwest, away from Glacier National Park, but I was asleep. I woke up as we rumbled over the Flathead River Bridge just outside Coram and again at a stop in Columbia Falls.

Heading southwest out of Columbia Falls was the branch to Kalispell, where Fatty, the man who ran the Eat Shop in our town, had spent a winter cutting ice for the GN on Flathead Lake. He'd met and married his wife there, and after learning how to cook for the section crews, he heard of a café for sale in our town and bought it with a loan from his father-in-law. Fatty and Dorothy worked together in the Eat Shop and built a good business, especially from the rails. Twig knew Fatty and that's how I knew about him. Every summer Fatty and Dorothy spent a couple of weeks in Kalispell. The prairies around our town were just too monotonous for a mountain-bred person like Dorothy.

I drifted off and Dorothy put a hamburger and French-fried potatoes down on the counter and set the ketchup and mustard beside the plate.

"Anything else, Lige?"

"Yes, I'd like a Coca Cola, please."

She opened the icebox and pulled out a bottle. She wiped it off with a towel and pried the cap off. She put it in front of me.

"Is that it?"

"Yes, thank you."

I took off the top half of the bun and spread the mustard on my hamburger. Then I carefully placed the four dill pickle slices equally around the meat and replaced the top. I poured ketchup in a thick puddle on the fry plate and sprinkled salt on the potatoes.

For the first time I was sitting in a café by myself, eating food I'd ordered and would pay for myself. I felt grown up.

Dorothy smiled at me. She reached in the glass bowl, picked out a piece of hard candy, and came over. "Here. This is on the house."

"Thank you."

I took a big bite out of my sandwich and woke up. My coat sleeve and cheek were wet with drool. I raised my head. The moon, going into its last quarter, was up. We were just pulling out of Whitefish, its lighted station drifting behind. I could see the helper engines in the yards, engines to help the heavy drag freights over the Rockies.

I looked back and to the south. It was July and Fatty and Dorothy were probably in Kalispell. I wiped off my cheek and tried to dry my sleeve with my other sleeve, then I put my head down.

It was an empty feeling riding on top of a train half way to the Coast after you'd help kill somebody.

CHAPTER XXIX

Out of Whitefish the High Line swung northwest, looping with the Tobacco River almost to Canada and then dropped straight south following the Kootenai Valley. It went west again through Libby and Troy.

We got off at Troy, but our baggage hadn't arrived yet. There were no bulls around so we walked through the tunnel to a dump. There was a hobo jungle on the edge of the dump and we saw some 'bo's stirring around. We crossed a plank laid across the ditch and entered the jungle.

There seemed to be half a dozen men visible, but how many were in shacks and under canvas we couldn't tell. We passed a 'bo squatting by a fire. He glared at us with one eye. The other one was an empty socket that watered yellow pus down his cheek. He wiped at it with a dirty rag.

Another man was asleep with a bottle in his hand.

A white-haired 'bo was cooking on a grate. "Hi, boys."

"Hello," I replied. The others answered, too.

"Welcome to Troy."

Nobody spoke.

"Sit fer a spell . . . Just git in?"

"Yeah," Pearl said.

"Been to the fight?"

I straightened up. The other three looked wary. Finally, I decided he was all right. "Yeah, it was a wash."

"That's what we heard."

"Heard? Heard from who?" Axel was getting nervous. "It just happened yesterday."

White Hair looked at Axel. "Simmer down, son. Troy's got civilization now. Why, she's even got a telegraph since we kicked all the Injuns out. They kept cuttin' the lines. But I heered tell there's a new invention out called a telyphone, and I'll bet with that invention someone could have called fer the results if they had a mind to. And he tol' Aunt Polly and she tol' cousin Sammy, who tol' Grandpa, who tol' me."

Axel looked down.

"Ol' Sleepy over there won enough off Dempsey's misfortune in missin' a K.O. to earn a good night's sleep."

"Dempsey was a slob," I said.

White Hair turned what was on the grate. "Meybe. Meybe not. He's still the best to come down the pike since Jack Johnson, even if he did git caught wearin' patent leather shoes in that fake war-work photygraph. Dempsey's fought good fights and lousy fights and that makes him human, I guess, flesh and blood, so he'll make his mistakes."

"But he was the champ."

"And still is. There'll be other fights, but boxin' always ends in tragedy. You either lose or have to retire. Bein' champ ain't permanent."

He picked up a tin plate and polished it with his elbow, then he dropped the fish he'd been cooking on it.

"Boys, I've got just enough fer myself here, but if yer hungry, reach over yonder and git my lines and bait. There ain't been a manchild born what can't catch a trout in these here mountains. Walk back through the tunnel and fish under the bridge. Ya can use my fire to cook with."

We thanked him and walked the rails to the bridge. The current beat the water against the pilings. You couldn't see the trout, but all of a sudden one would hit, and then you'd have him, flopping around on the rocks or in the gravelly mud. It was hard to hit them in the head with the piece of tree branch we'd picked up, what with all the moving, but once you did, they were dead. The ones that were on the rocks or grass, we'd throw up on the bank, but the ones that were killed after they'd been in the mud we'd wash first.

A train rumbled by overhead, but it didn't scare away the trout. When we had eight, each of us strung line through the gills and mouths of two of them and returned to the jungle.

"Butcher's block's around back. Be sure to carry those guts to the far side of the dump. We run a clean camp here." White Hair took his lines and bait and we thanked him again.

Behind his shack were a flat rock and a piece of board. A hatchet was hanging from a nail in a tree. I put the trout on the board one at a time and chopped off the heads as carefully as I could. It took several blows to get one off, but I wanted to hit the same spot every time.

Using my knife, I cut off the fins and cut out the anal pore. I split the belly of each fish from the anal pore to the neck and cleaned out the insides with my fingers. I stuck each trout in a bucket of water White Hair had placed there and rubbed it clean, then I put the fish on the other side of the board and whacked off the tail.

Soon there were eight rainbows lined up on a piece of two by four. Pearl took them around to the grill. I told Axel to bury the guts far away. He said he wanted to eat first. I told him he couldn't eat until he'd done his job, so he picked up the can and left. Merle scrubbed the blood off the rock and board with a worn-down brush. I sharpened White Hair's hatchet on an old whetstone he had and put it on the nail.

Pearl and White Hair were talking when I came around the shack. The trout were on the grate, cooking up fine. Their smell was all around.

When White Hair got up and went behind the shanty, Axel came back. "Boy, that smells good."

"Did ya bury the guts?" I asked.

Axel swung around toward me. "What'd ya think?" He was mad.

"I wanted to make sure; this is a clean camp."

He looked at me and then at the fish. "Yeah, I went around to the other side of the dump."

"Good."

White Hair came back. "There's just one bad thing about this here camp. The only water is all the way over to the river."

I turned and walked behind the shack. My face was hot. I felt stupid when I picked up the bucket I'd washed the fish in and walked back to the fire.

"Whoa, there, son. Ya don't have to go now. There's plentya time to eat first."

"No, I'll do it now."

He studied me for a few seconds and then said, "Well, if you're goin', fill this one, too." He went into his shack and brought out an almost brand-new galvanized pail. He dumped about a quart of water from it and gave it to me.

It took me awhile to get the water, especially the walking back without spilling. It's a good thing I didn't mind well-done fish.

CHAPTER XXX

Even in the mountains of Troy, July's can be hot.

After our gear got in, we walked below the bridge and went swimming. I had bought a bar of Ivory Soap in town and we cleaned up. Before we left the jungle, White Hair said that as long as we had soap and water we might as well shave—there was no reason to look like bums. Merle told him we didn't have a razor. White Hair brought out his straight razor and strop, but after we conferred quietly, we told him no thanks. None of us had mastered the intricacies of the straight razor, and, besides, Axel pointed out that even a few whiskers would make a good disguise in case our descriptions had been given out along the line. White Hair looked disgusted as we backed off.

The water was running cold and none of us stayed in too long. We were far enough downstream to stretch out in the sun without fear of girls. We'd seen some in town, but they had gawked and giggled.

I had bought a paper and as I dried off on the riverbank, I read about the fight. I also looked through the paper twice, but there wasn't a word about Pete Wilson and his killers and very little about North Dakota at all except for a lot of rain. I read that the Hardings were sailing for Alaska from Tacoma.

"Trade you," Pearl said.

I looked over. He'd unfolded part of a newspaper that he'd had in his jacket pocket. I took it and gave him mine. "Where'd you get it?"

"In Shelby at the arena before Merle and I got in. It was on the ground."

It was only the second half of the paper, but it had the Funnies. I read them and laughed to myself.

Pearl said, "What d'ya think of that new one?"

"Moonshine Mullins? *Moon Mullins*?"

"Yeah, that one."

"I like it."

"So do I."

"Those big banjo eyes are great. I've never seen it in the papers back home."

"Me, neither. It must really be new."

"Well, it's great."

"Yeah, and ya know who else would like it?"

"Who?"

"Twig."

I waited a second or two and saw Twig reading *Moon Mullins*. "Yeah, yeah, Twig'd like it a lot. It's better than *The Gumps*."

I folded the paper and passed it over to Pearl. I lay on my back and watched a few high clouds. The sky was bright blue, and when the clouds disappeared behind the mountains, there was just the sun, not even a bird. I didn't look at the sun directly. Doing that can hurt your eyes.

The sky was empty. Was it empty over our town? I thought of Twig under an empty sky reading *Moon Mullins* and waiting to read a train. Then I saw Boss reading *Moon Mullins* and laughing and then I saw Bear . . . I had to stop. I went for my clothes where I'd left them on some brush.

When I reached for my pants, I heard a whirring sound in the brush and jumped back.

"What's wrong?" Pearl asked.

"I don't know. Are there rattlesnakes here?"

Pearl came over. "Search me."

Merle and Axel got up. I pointed. "There might be one in there. I heard a noise like one."

"What'd it go like?" Axel asked.

"It whirred."

"Like what?"

I tried to imitate it. Axel picked up a stick and poked it in the brush. A little bird popped out the other side, flew to another thicket, and whirred.

Axel laughed. "There's your rattlesnake, Elijah. It flew away." He threw the stick into the river and began to get dressed.

"Still, it could've been a rattler. I've never heard one."

"Don't cry until you're hit," Axle said, buttoning his shirt. I felt like ripping it off and his head, too.

"Shut up, Axel," Pearl said.

"Why should I? At least I've seen a rattler. Down in Illinois, we've got prairie rattlers, some of 'em six feet long. Once I was campin' out, rolled up in a sleepin' bag under the stars."

He pulled on a boot. My hands were shaking as I buttoned my shirt.

"I woke up the next morning, and when I opened my eyes, not six inches away was the biggest prairie rattler you'd ever want to see, all coiled up. I thought I was a goner, but then I saw it was asleep, so I quiet-like rolled over and got a piece of firewood, then I rolled back and cracked that snake, busted his head clean off. I took his rattles—there were twelve of 'em, so he was twelve years old. I shoulda brought 'em, but they're in Chicago. I took 'em to school once."

I'd had enough. "How'd ya know it was asleep? Was it snorin'?"

"No, stupid, its eyes were shut."

"What?"

"Its eyes were shut, stupid."

"No, Axel, you're the stupid one." I lost my temper. "And you're a damn liar. Snakes don't have eyelids like us. They sleep with their eyes open." I couldn't leave it alone. "Damn liar."

Axel stepped toward me. I put my left foot out, balanced, and waited. He stopped, clenching his fists.

"Don't ever turn your back on me, Elijah." He walked up the bank and headed for the bridge.

We stopped in town and took some food out to the jungle. White Hair baked some bread and later cooked up some pork and beans. We drank coffee out of old soup cans and ate tinned peaches.

Axel ate by himself and smoked a lot of cigarettes.

CHAPTER XXXI

We stayed in the jungle a couple of days, and White Hair showed us how to use bar soap to wash our clothes and how to dry them on bushes and tree branches. Mostly, however, we sat around and listened to the 'bo's, at least the ones that were friends with White Hair, whose real name was George Shirley. Some 'bo's called him Bathhouse George because he was always concerned about being clean.

We were eating mulligan when a 'bo who knew the Coast said we could get jobs as apple knockers at Wenatchee. Another claimed we could work at an amusement park in Spokane—it was easier than apple knocking.

While we were talking, I saw a tall tramp start across the plank toward the jungle. He was followed by a sallow-faced kid of twelve or thirteen carrying the bindles.

White Hair looked at them and got up quickly. "Bricktop, Pickle Bill, c'mon." The two 'bo's went along behind White Hair. They blocked the path of the tall tramp and the kid. White Hair said something and then he and the man began arguing, but not loudly.

Finally, the tall tramp pointed over at us four. White Hair looked back and then turned to the tall tramp and shook his head. He pointed down the tracks.

The tall tramp looked ready to fight White Hair, but Bricktop and Pickle Bill came up close, and the tall tramp turned and pushed the kid, who'd been standing with his head down the whole time, back across the bridge. They walked down track without turning around.

When White Hair and the other two came back, it was pretty quiet until Merle asked, "What'd that father and his son want?"

Pickle Bill got something in his throat and started choking, and White Hair stared at us for a few seconds. He shook his head and said, "Boys, that warn't no father and son. They was a jock and his 'prushan,' and if ya don't know that, then all I can say is you've got a lot to l'arn about this world. We don't 'low no wolves in this here jungle, so I told 'em to go down to the coal dock and punch the wind on the next drag through."

I peeked at the twins and then at Axel, but they didn't look like they knew what White Hair was talking about, either.

Pickle Bill recovered and started describing getting caught in a blizzard riding blind baggage on the Willmar Division of the GN, and if the engineer hadn't let him in the cab, he'd a froze to death for sure.

That started the others talking again—men with what White Hair called "monikeys" like King Tex, Cinders Slim, One-Eyed Dick, Rockin' Chair and two colored 'bo's, Twin Cities Shine and EZ or Easy, I never figured out which.

And they didn't talk Casey Jones' stuff, but about things that they had actually seen and done.

It was great to listen to men who had ridden the rails all over the country talk about wintering on West Madison Street in the Big Junction or on Nicollet Island in the Mill City with the wind cutting you to the bone and you taking it 'cause you weren't a mission tramp or dependent on Sally, which is what they called the Salvation Army.

EZ told about riding the New Orleans & North Eastern through thousands of acres of cotton fields around Meridian, Mississippi, in a voice so soft I could see those fields wavering in the sun, and I'd never been further south than Fargo, North Dakota.

White Hair described rounding the four-tracked Horseshoe Curve on the Pennsy near Altoona. He'd been caught by a cold snap, didn't even have his winter coat yet, and the Allegheny Mountains were dusted white, though the Susquehanna was just icing up near its banks. Running along the rim of the canyon was bad, but when they rounded Kittanning Point and the wind caught him, he said he was so cold he thought his journal bearings were going to freeze, and everyone laughed.

TC Shine said he knew a porter who loved working the Pennsy, but refused to work the Plate, the tips were too poor.

Rockin' Chair told how just before the Great War he got behind the eight-ball in Chi-town and had to blow. "I legged it to the yards and saw an engineer drifting a train for the braky on the Bum's Own and nailed a side-door Pullman with my bindle and only a coupla beagles, a hardboiled cackleberry, and a sinker to eat.

"I rode that rattler through Rubber Town, Little Steel, and all the way to my old stompin' grounds, the Big Smoke. The line followed the north bank of the Allegheny River through the Willow Grove Yard at Millvale, where I got off and caught a 'varnish' which crossed Herr Island and the Allegheny on the Thirty-Third Street Bridge and a viaduct.

"It was night and the steel mills flared red and orange and yellow, burnin' holes in the city and boilin' the river with reflected fire. The moon and stars above were blurred out by the smoke. When I was a boy and Mama told me to behave or I'd end up in the fires of Hell, I knew what they'd be like . . . Well, she's in the bone orchard now.

"Keepin' with Thirty-Third, we soon paralleled the Pennsy line in a large ravine, rolled through an open cut, and rumbled through the Neville Street Tunnel. Goin' downgrade we entered Junction Hollow north of Schenley Park. At the end was Laughlin Junction, just north of the Monongahela River.

"It looked like we were headin' right into the fires of the Jones & Laughlin blast furnaces, but the tracks curved to the right and the train headed to the Water Street Yard and the B&O passenger and freight stations. In the old days we'd've had to back up to 'em. I ditched the train there.

"Lookin' out for cinder dicks, I fell in with a Bohunk, a Flannelmouth, and a Buttermilker. Just outside the yard we met a blinky who shared some Sneaky Pete and then, feeling pretty good, we slept in Resort Alley.

"In the morning we decided to pipe the stem, hit a fishery, and find a flop house, so we cased the main streets—Grant, Wood, Smithfield, Liberty, Penn, and Duquesne—all the way from the Allegheny to Ross Street, from Water Street to Seventh Avenue, everything so fine I couldn't even tell there had been a flood the previous year.

"A harness bull from the police station on Strawberry warned us about stemmin', so we went into a fishery, but it was a dry mission and the bouncer threw us out when the Bohunk dropped a bottle of white mule he'd kept hidden. The Buttermilker took us to a wet mission where we acted as Doughnut Christians, but at least we got a set-down.

"It was a great time. We'd panhandle the hotels, theatres, and clubs. We worked out a circuit, and I did it so many times I still dream it. There was the five-story Monongahela House showin' its white face to the Monongahela River at Smithfield and First. Once it had been the premiere hotel, but even with its white marble floors, black walnut staircases, and a ballroom with velvet curtains and a gilded ceiling, hard times were comin'. Lincoln had stayed there on the trip to his inauguration in Washington, so the help was pretty particular about lettin' 'bo's hang around, so we'd cross Smithfield and hit up the Hotel Wilson and the little St. James a half block north. Up to Second Avenue, take a right, and a half block west of Grant Street was the Oxford Hotel. Backtrack and head up Grant. Go left on Third Avenue and check out the Eagles Club. Across Cherry Way stood the post office, but the cops didn't like us on federal property, so we'd go north on Smithfield, west on Fourth Avenue, cross Wood Street, and pass the Pittsburgh Stock Exchange and keep going 'cause there ain't no money for 'bo's there.

"Hit the Exchange Hotel on Market and Fourth, cross Market and just beyond Filter Alley is the Hotel Regal. Then pass Delray Street, cross Fourth to the south side, and work the 4th Avenue Hotel on the corner of Ferry Street and 4th.

"Head north on Ferry, right on Diamond, and left on Graeme. Opposite the Market House stood a little hotel, but I'd go up Byng Street and left on Drummond to see what I could get at the Arcade there and the other one around the corner on Fifth.

"Walk Fifth, then south on Wood back to Diamond to the Grand Opera House and the Harris Theatre across the street and work the sidewalks.

"North on Smithfield and east on Fifth and there was a ten-story, red-brick building with white letters: HOTEL done horizontal and HENRY vertical. It stuck out like a sore thumb between smaller buildings. When I was a kid, there was what they called the Hump in the street just east of the Henry, but that was gone. The lobby had columns and two large staircases, and the lounge had tables, wooden chairs, padded chairs, rocking chairs, and a piano.

"North on Oliver to the Hotel Duquesne, then back on Fifth to the Hotel Newell, the Hotel Antler, and the Free Mason's Hall. The Antler was a tall building with a tower on one corner with a flag pole on top and a weather vane on the roofline above the front door that showed the wind direction. On the ground floor they had a café and bar with red walls. Behind the bar were three large mirrors. The bar had lots of potted plants and three golden statues of women.

"Sometimes we headed up to Sixth Avenue where the Nixon Theater with its white weddin'-cake front, the Duquesne Club, and six Protestant churches were all packed together, but usually we'd head west to Liberty and maybe to the Victoria Theatre on Ogle Alley, but probably to the Seventh Avenue Hotel with its three large signs and huge flags on top and the Liberty Theatre.

"We'd take Ellsmere from Liberty to Duquesne Way to the Home Hotel, then keep on Duquesne to Sandusky Street and the Hotel Boyer, then south to the Pitt Theater. From there east on Penn brought us to the Lyceum Theater, the Annex Hotel, the Colonial Hotel, and the Hotel Anderson, and from there north on Federal we'd go to the Commercial Hotel, B.F. Keith's New Alvin Theater with its elevated bridge over Federal, and around the corner to the Gayety Theatre.

Back on Penn and we'd hit the New Duquesne Theatre with its little spire on top, cross Fifth Avenue and Stanwyx and try the Pittsburgh Club and the nine-story Hotel Lincoln, where you'd walk up the steps between four lights. The Club was vine-covered and had awnings over the door and all the windows.

"During the day a sob story might work on a lady comin' out of a department store, such as McCreery's, Solomons', the Kaufman Bros. huge store, Joyce's, or Horne's, but in the evenin' the best places were the clubs because the members showed off by helping the less fortunate, and the theatres where the gentlemen would help out a man in need just to impress the ladies. Being outside at just the right time could make you flush for a week.

"I'll tell you, boys, don't ever look for any help outside a bank or a newspaper office. Bankers are rich and they got that way by keepin' their money; newspapermen are always broke. It didn't take me long standin' outside the Bank of Pittsburgh or any of the National Banks—the Columbia, the Peoples, the Exchange, the Diamond, or the First—or the newspapers—the *Gazette-Times*, the *Leader*, or the *Post*—to reach that conclusion.

"And if times got tough, there was always the churches. The Galway at St. Mary's Catholic at Ferry and Third was always good for a buck, but any of 'em—the Reformed Presbyterian and the Second Presbyterian side-by-side on Eighth, the First Presbyterian, the Trinity Episcopal, the German Evangelical, the English Evangelical Lutheran, or the Methodist—were good as gold.

"Sometimes I picked up some change at the Old Block House from Fort Pitt down by the freight yards if the DAR ladies were running a tour.

"When I heard the Pirates had a three-game series with the Reds to end their season—which was terrible: I think they finished seventh—I became a 'trolly tramp' and took the line out Forbes Avenue to Boquet. Forbes Field was a block south and if the Pirates won, the fans were generous. I glommed plenty because they won all three games. I also did some back door bumming at the Oakland Methodist Church, but I had to be careful because it was kitty-corner from a police station. Across Boquet was the First Church of Spiritualists, but they seemed so caught up with the other world that they didn't have much to give to people still active in this one. There was also the ten-story Schenley Hotel with a chef who had a soft spot for 'bo's and a place for us to eat just off the kitchen.

"At night I'd go over to Schenley Park just east of Forbes and sleep under one of the two bridges. In the morning I could go to the Carnegie Public Library and wait for the games to start. At night I had my bedroom of stars, and I could listen to the hot shots comin' through the smoky hole up north.

"After the last game I was workin' the fans, when a guy in a fedora handed me somethin'. When I looked, it was a Honus Wagner baseball card; he played shortstop for the Bucs. What could I ever do with that? I gave it to some kid.

"Between stemmin' and workin' as a pearl diver, I was doin' all right. Sometimes during a rain I'd stand in a doorway and feel like I was in a canyon with the buildings towering over me and the water rushing down the street like a little river. Afterward the brick street would glisten in the light.

"With all the smoke and ash from the steel furnaces, some said Pittsburgh was hell with the lid tamped on, but I never saw such clean streets as they had.

"But then the Flannelmouth brought some skee to the mission and when we got drunk, out we went with two bouncers makin' sure.

"The fall weather wasn't too bad, so I didn't mind bein' covered by the moon. I met an outside 'bo and we put on a Tokay blanket, but I decided that wasn't the life for me, so I endured some mission preacher spoutin' angel food sermons while I prepared to go with the birds.

"Before I made my move, I met a 'bo with some Dago red, and we ended under the Monongahela Bridge span with a hop head, who was drinkin' rubbydub, and a Sally tramp, who was livin' on Third Avenue. The hop head went crazy. He was sick and kept talkin' about not wantin' to go to a hospital where the staff killed off hobos with the 'black bottle.' Then the gink rambled down to the river and punched a hole in the water. After the men from Fire Engine House #30 on Second Street fished out the cabbage head, the cops arrested the Sally and me for murder.

"The city cops and the county cops flipped a coin; the county won and got the collar.

"They took us up in a hustle buggy to the Allegheny County Jail on Diamond with its wall and a round tower. In the morning we walked across the Bridge of Sighs to the Allegheny County Court House. There was a window in the middle and four slit windows, two on each side, and we could see Ross Street below.

"The Court House looked like a castle. It had a tower I heard was almost two hundred and fifty feet high. There were smaller towers, turrets, arches, and columns, and when we went up the stairs we could see a fountain in the courtyard below.

"When the murder rap couldn't be proved, the judge gave us a jolt for vagrancy, and we took the Bridge back to the blue bar hotel.

"It wasn't my first time, and it wasn't so bad. Outside I'd been down to wind pudding and even lowered myself to spearing biscuits, but inside I got three squares and a cot.

"When I got sprung, it was winter and I was in tap city. I fell in with a tramp and we found a large wooden box in Hoag Alley to move into. We lined it with California blankets and piled dirt in the middle of the floor on which we put some wood and lit a fire. As the place warmed up, I looked at the grease ball and thought he was sweatin', but it wasn't sweat: his head was lousy with walkin' dandruff and his clothes with shirt rabbits.

"That tramp was too crummy for me, so even though I didn't have a Benny, it was time to stop eatin' snowballs. I read my shirt and didn't find any crums. I battered the stem, hit a lick by touching hearts at the YMCA at Penn and Sandusky, bought a blanket and some candles, and hid out near a black snake in the hole. When a rattler came by headin' for the mainline of the Dope, I waited until I saw a one-eyed bandit and hopped aboard. The train passed Laughlin Junction and sped up on the double-track. I missed the Glenwood Bridge and powerhouse because I was asleep.

"We crept through downtown McKeesport and powered up for the run down the line. I lit the candle, made a tent out of the blanket, and you'd be surprised how much heat I got sittin' there.

"Sittin' or sleepin' under the blanket, I didn't see too much scenery. I remember headin' up the Youghiogheny River Valley and seein' the two-story station at Connellsville which looked like a country inn and the huge Queen City Station and Hotel at Cumberland with its cupola in the middle. That's where we hooked into the line that went west to Cincy and the Lou, but we went east

"When we got to the District, it was snowin' and blowin' and right then I decided to keep on goin' south, so I got some grub and hitched on the Always Come Late, ridin' her all the way to sunshine and sand.

"I became a beach tramp. At first I had a sand bed, but later I built a little shack. I could get cast-off picnic food or do some fishing in the ocean or a little creek, where I could drink or wash. Soap don't work in salt water. I could throw my feet into town and buzz the housewives or make a gut plunge to the butcher shop.

"But in the spring I got Railroad Fever, made enough to get a road stake, got an old rockin' chair, and found a bob tail goin' on the farm. I threw the chair on board and rode on the plush through the South and Midwest until a hooty cinder dick chased me off, and he and a groundhog smashed my rockin' chair to flinders.

"I hooked up with A No. 1, the famous hobo, and we spread our monikeys on water towers all over God's Creation. After while I got tired of him always tryin' to save me by gettin' me to quit the hobo road and go home, so I cut out. I've been a travelin' man ever since."

It was grand listening to Rockin' Chair, even though I didn't understand a lot of what he said. It was like listening to a man from another country. I imagined myself joining hoboland, writing my monikey, and never settling down.

One-Eyed Dick left to obey a call of nature, saying Rockin' Chair was sure a windy one, and Pickle Bill hunched forward and asked if we'd ever seen a train wreck. None of us had. "Well, Dick has. A staged one."

"What?" Merle asked.

"Back in '96, near Waco, Texas, the Katy put on a train crash, two locomotives each pullin' six coaches started a mile apart and hit head on at sixty miles per hour, a regular prairie meet. They'd advertised it considerable and there was thirty thousand people watchin' ever'where. A bunch of people got hurt and one man was killed. A piece of metal snatched out Dick's blinker. One of the smokestacks landed a quarter mile away."

Pearl whistled low, but I didn't know if it was for the smokestack or Dick's eye.

Dick ambled back and sat down.

The talk continued about riding the Carry-All, the Q, the Dope, the Mop, the Plate, the Soup Line and the Gila Monster, the Katy, the Sally, the Old Woman, and other railroads.

King Tex said he hoped he'd never ride the Gila Monster again. (The Gila Monster was that section of the Southern Pacific that went through Arizona.) Once he had been heading back home in his younger days when he had a home to head back to and was on the Monster east of Tucson. He and another 'bo got to arguing how hot it was, and Tex got mad and said he could fry an egg on top of the boxcar they were in. The other 'bo said he couldn't.

The argument was cooling off when the train stopped at a water tank, and their boxcar ended up opposite a little adobe house with chickens scratching in the yard.

The other 'bo dared King Tex to fill his hand, which made Tex so mad he just had to. He jumped off the train and skirted around to the blind side of the house. He got into the chicken coop and found an egg. The whistle sounded, and he hightailed it back and got on a coupling with the other 'bo.

After they were up to speed, King Tex decided to do things right. He inched his way down and under to the wheels and scraped off some lubricating oil, which had thickened up, with his knife. He put a good glop on a rag, and then he carried the rag and the other 'bo took the egg to the roof.

Tex spread the oil on the roof and let it heat up, then he cracked the egg into it. Almost immediately it began frying.

They had to ride the bumpers to the next stop, which was all the way into Texas, because it was too hot to put their hands on the roof and swing into the car.

Most of the way the sun was scorching overhead and they had no shade. The other 'bo kept crabbing all the way about the sun and about the fact Tex had cheated by using oil.

Tex said, "I woulda throwed him off, 'cept he was my brother."

The talk turned to the hot yards on the UP, and the riding bulls on the Santa Fe, and which yard was the most dangerous—Pocatello, Idaho; Galesburg, Illinois; or Green River, Wyoming. And about the nighthawk in the Portland yard who looked just like a 'bo, and Frisco Pete, "who'd been ridin' the rails for forty years and shoulda know'd better," went up to him on top of a boxcar 'cause he thought he was a fellow travelin' man and caught a brake club across his skull which scrambled his brains, and he had to be put away in some institution. But the nighthawk was still in Portland.

And how it was tough to glom onto a pickle train from New Orleans or the Coast with its cargo of bananas, but it was downright impossible to catch a red hot with California fruit or Idaho potatoes.

"Impossible. I'll tell ya impossible." Cinders Slim joined the conversation. "Ya try hitchin' a Silker on the Big G and those shotgun guards will have ya thinkin' twice."

Eventually, it was time to go. We got our gear and headed for a drag freight stopped in the yard. White Hair walked to the edge of the jungle with us, and an airdale—a tramp that's a real loner—jumped on the freight ahead of us. We'd seen him in the dump, but he never spoke to anyone.

White Hair shook our hands. "Get a good side-door Pullman, boys, one with no splinters. Look out for ridin' bulls and don't forget—on the other side of Troy, Pacific Time begins, so change your watches."

We walked to an open boxcar and climbed in. The floor was fairly new. Pearl jammed part of a brake under the door. The whistle sounded and the freight jerked. We passed the jungle and White Hair waved goodbye. So did we. In a few minutes we were in Pacific Time. We changed our watches for all the good it did.

Pearl had a newspaper, but we still weren't in it. We passed the paper around and followed the adventures of *Moon Mullins*.

The tracks skirted the south bank of the Kootenai, and we raced the water downstream to Bonners Ferry, Idaho, with evergreens covering the valley walls. We passed through Leonia, Idaho, where the east end of the depot platform was in Montana and the west end was in Idaho. At Bonners Ferry the Kootenai kept to the northwest, but the railroad moved southwest to Sand Point and Lake Pend Oreille.

We rounded the western arm of the lake into the Pend Oreille River Valley, with the river off to the south. When we were on the floor of the valley, the grass grew tall along the right-of-way, but sometimes we ran on the shoulder of the valley with blasted rock layers to our right, and sometimes we ripped through deep rock cuts with the sides so close that it seemed if you leaned over, you'd have your head torn off.

At Newport, Washington, the Pend Oreille turned north, heading for the Columbia. We turned south into the Little Spokane River Valley, and shortly after leaving it, we came into Spokane from the north. We crossed over two bridges and the train slowed at the GN station on Havermale Island. When it didn't look like it was going to stop, we jumped off and walked past the three-and-a-half story stone station. The clock on the tower high above the platform read five fifteen.

Looking for bulls, we quickly got off the island. The Spokane River was too fast to swim if we were cornered.

We walked past a night owl lunch counter. I wanted to eat, but the twins said they were broke, and Axel's money was low, so I said I'd pay.

We ordered, and the waitress yelled out to the short order cook, "21, pin a rose on one, take the other through the garden. Put out the lights and cry. All with fried Murphy. Burn the hound with whistle berries. A pair of drawers. And a 5. Stretch one and hold the hail."

One at a time we used the restroom and then we watched the traffic until our food came.

I had a hamburger with a slice of onion, fried potatoes, and coffee. Pearl had the same, except his burger had lettuce and tomatoes without any onion. Merle had liver and onions, fried potatoes, and a large milk. Axel had franks and beans with a large Coke, no ice.

At the till I got a pack of Sen-Sen gum and paid the bill. We didn't leave any tips, and I felt bad about that, but I was worried we wouldn't find jobs.

As we walked out, I heard the waitress who was clearing the dishes call us George Eddies, which I guessed wasn't something to be proud of.

I passed out the gum and we headed for the amusement park.

It was spread out over several acres, with displays, games, and rides. We scouted around and found the owner. He had jobs for hard-working young men.

"Are you?"

"Yes, sir," Merle said.

Pearl repeated it.

Axel and I just said, "Yes." The twins were very anxious to get hired.

"Have you ever worked at an amusement park before?"

"No."

"A carnival?"

"No."

"That's good. My park is nothing like a carnival. A carnival travels around, and if its people take advantage of the local customers, by the next morning it won't matter. However, I have built up a good reputation here. I see to it that my customers are always treated fairly and in a way so they'll want to come back. Especially families."

He looked up at each of us, except Axel, who was the same height. He had bright blue eyes and a neatly trimmed mustache. After looking carefully into our faces, he said, "On this property there is no liquor; no tobacco, either smoking or chewing (Axel shifted his feet); and no cursing or profanity."

He looked at us again. "I will offer you each three dollars a day, six days a week. We open at 11:30 A.M. and close at 10:30 P.M. If you wish, I have sleeping rooms available in some cottages at the back of the park. You can stay there for nothing, just as long as you keep your rooms clean. What do you say?"

The twins agreed right away and shook his hand, followed by Axel and me. I said, "Thank you, Mr. Graham."

He said, "It's settled then. You can start tomorrow and you can move into your rooms tonight. Agreed?"

We agreed.

Mr. Graham raised his right hand with his index finger extended and shook it. "There is one thing more, boys."

"What?" Merle asked.

"Please shave off your facial hair. None of you is quite ready to sport a beard, a style which appears destined to undergo extinction with the demise of Secretary of State Charles Evans Hughes."

CHAPTER XXXII

The cottages weren't big. They were basically king-size bedrooms with a tiny bathroom thrown in. They had electricity, but no stoves. No one lived in them during the winter.

Pearl and I took one cottage because I wouldn't stay with Axel. There were two beds, and even though the Midway was lit up and noisy, after we'd washed and brushed our teeth, we crawled in and went to sleep. My prayers were short and full of thanks for our jobs.

The next morning we both woke up at about the same time.

"Lige?"

"What?"

"I don't have a razor; neither does Merle."

"Neither do I."

"I think we'd better go buy one, but we don't have any money."

"I'll buy one and we'll share it. You go tell Merle that we're goin' uptown."

Pearl put on his pants and went next door. I washed and after Pearl did the same, we set out walking. Spokane was the biggest place either of us had ever been in, and it was interesting to watch the early morning traffic. There wasn't a horse in sight.

We finally found a Rexall store and went in. There were razors like Gillette, Gem, Auto-strop, and Durham Duplex. Each had its own brand of blades, and there was also a cheap package of Keen Kutter blades for thirty-five cents.

I bought a Gem razor for a dollar, a tube of Rexall Shaving Cream for twenty cents, and, after debating about the Keen Kutters, a package of single-edge Gem Damaskene blades for fifty cents.

Because I had bought the razor, I used it first. When I gave it to Pearl, the blade was still ninety-nine percent good. Looking in the mirror before I lathered up, I couldn't see why Mr. Graham had made such a fuss, but if I tilted my head in the light, I could see some growth.

When Merle and Axel had finished scraping, we all went to the dining building for breakfast. Mr. Graham introduced us around to the other workers. The pancake breakfast was good . . . and cheap. I paid.

Mr. Graham showed us through the park and gave us our assignments. The twins were to fill in on the sideshow ticket offices, spelling people off. Axel was to operate a gambling game that had little steam shovels that picked up prizes.

Mr. Graham introduced me to Clyde Hill, a slightly built, slightly bald man who had once played semi-pro baseball in the old Pembina County League in North Dakota. Clyde showed me how to operate the Ferris Wheel, a duty we would share.

The park opened at eleven thirty to catch some hungry people for dinner. Operating on the Midway in the daytime was punk work. It was mostly little kids and their mothers and the lights we turned on didn't show up. The rest of the lights we switched on after eight o'clock, and the next couple hours were the time I liked best, with the music, the bright colored lights, the darkening night above, and the talking, laughing people below, especially the girls.

There seemed to be an awful lot of girls in Spokane and nice-looking, too. Some of them were regulars at the park, and after a few nights, you'd know them well enough to talk and joke with them.

There was a little blonde that attracted me. She was twenty and her name was Annie. She had been playing up to Dan Jenks, a sort of advertising man for the park who went around the Spokane area, drumming up business by giving away tickets to children when accompanied by an adult and things like that. He had a car, a 1922 Big Six Studebaker Speedster, but Clyde said it really belonged to Mr. Graham. In between endless baseball stories, Clyde told me that Jenks had sworn to him that he was going to have Annie in that car if it took all summer.

"But so far they've only been neckin' in the dark places and that's all."

"How do you know?"

"He told me."

"You believe him?"

"Yeah, if it'd gone any further, he'd be braggin' about it. Dan's a real lady-killer, Dan is." Clyde finished oiling a gear and then said, "Lige, leave her be. There's plenty o' nicer ones."

But I couldn't. Whenever I saw her, it was like a little jump near my heart. She wore short dresses, a lot shorter than the girls in our town wore, and I liked the way she looked. I couldn't explain it to anyone because all girls have hair, eyes, skin, breasts, hips, legs, and a laugh, but with Annie all these things, plus the fact that she had been with Jenks, ignited a need in me I'd never felt before. Emily was cute, quiet, and dependable; Annie was like a hot knife stabbing under my rib cage.

Sometimes when I saw her with Jenks, she'd smile at me, and if we were close, she'd wink, if Jenks was looking the other way.

Jenks had gone on one of his trips when Annie and I got together, just talking near the Ferris Wheel at first, but later walking around during my breaks and eating lunch with her knee against mine.

Mr. Graham was gone, too, or we wouldn't have done what we did. When Mr. Graham was around, the park shut down at 10:30, regardless of the crowd because he thought that was late enough for any child up to the age of sixteen to be out. Even when he was away, we closed down at that time, but we'd keep some of the rides going a little later for the customers who'd pay us extra or who were friends.

Sometimes after hot days when the nights refused to cool down and the last customer was gone, Clyde and I would use the Ferris Wheel. One of us would get on and have the other operator stop him at the top to catch any possible breeze.

Annie had been around all day and into the night. It had been hot and the heat stayed in the park even after the sun had set. With Mr. Graham gone, I got Clyde to let Annie and me go "up top."

Most of the park lights had been shut off, and if you turned away from Spokane, you could see a thousand stars beading the dark.

I had my arm around Annie and she was pressed against my side. When I turned my head slightly, I could smell her perfume. She must have carried some with her and sprayed it in her hair.

I was trying to get my bearings so I could tell her the names of the stars and constellations when suddenly she pushed against me so hard that I went back into the corner with her partly on top of me. She kissed me and after we got comfortable, I kissed her.

We kissed a lot and I learned there were many ways to kiss someone. It was all so new and exciting, but it was demanding, too, and after while I wasn't comfortable, so we sat up. I put my left arm around her with my right hand just under her left breast. She whispered, "Yes," and I kissed her, my hand just lifting her breast a little, but that wasn't what she wanted.

She pulled away from me and so quickly I didn't realize what she was doing. She came back to me and her dress was down off her shoulders. Her breasts were bare. I didn't know what to do. I'd never even kissed a girl that wasn't a relative before that night, except for Ruth Randall on the school playground when we were seven, and she told our teacher, so I had to stay after school and write "I will not kiss girls" a hundred times on the blackboard.

Annie snuggled up to me so I kissed her. It was a long kiss and her mouth was exciting. When we finished, she said, "It's O.K."

"What is?"

"To touch me."

I couldn't, so she took my hand and guided it onto her breast. It was the softest, warmest feeling I'd ever had. I squeezed the soft, warm firmness gently and I felt the little bump grow hard.

I kissed her and pushed her down on the seat. The car was moving and she was moving and I was moving and trying to get on top of her. I could barely see her breast, but I kissed it and sucked the nipple.

Annie began thrusting her hips into me and she was making sounds deep in her throat. Her arms were around me and she was scratching my shirt.

"Now! Now!"

"What?"

"Now!"

"What?"

"Damn you!"

She took my hand and pulled it up under her dress. It was all warmth and moistness. I was breathing hard and my face was buried in her perfumed hair and I couldn't see and I started to touch her and she made sounds in her throat and it was wet and dark and I was scared.

"Lige! Lige!"

It was Clyde. I thanked God and sat up. "What?"

"Time to come down."

"O.K."

"No," Annie said. "No, you have to finish."

"I can't."

She sat up. Clyde started the motor far below. "Elijah, you can't leave me like this."

"Well, fix yourself up." I didn't know what she was talking about.

"Are you a real man like you pretend or are you just a sissy boy?" She reached over and touched the front of my pants. "Elijah!" She jerked her hand back.

I felt my pants. They were moist. Clyde started us down. Annie took out a mirror and looked swell by the time we got off.

Clyde asked if we had a good time. I said, "Yeah," but Annie was already flouncing off down the Midway. I took two running steps to catch her and almost fell down. My testicles hurt so bad I could barely move. I tried to walk, but couldn't even do that for the pain.

"Annie!" She kept going.

"Annie! Annie!" Then she was gone.

Clyde shut down. "What's wrong?"

"Nothin'." I was leaning on a post.

"C'mon, then."

"In a little while. I want to think."

"Just 'cause she gave you the brush? You got what you wanted, didn't you? I saw that car rockin'."

I muttered, "Yeah," and Clyde left.

After a minute or so, I thought I was better, but my first step told me I wasn't. I waited, then tried it again, but I couldn't move. I loosened my belt and lowered my pants a little, spread my legs, looked around to make sure no one was there, and duck-walked to the cottage.

Pearl woke up, but I told him to go back to sleep. I undressed in the dark, put on clean underwear, and got into bed without brushing my teeth. I lay there with an ache that wouldn't go away. Every time I thought about Annie, it got worse. I called myself "Dummy" and "Idiot" and "Stupid" because she had wanted it so bad, and I couldn't do it, but I quit after I said "Dummy" out loud and Pearl rolled over.

I prayed to God to ease my suffering. Tears came down my cheeks when I asked Him. I waited, but the ache only seemed to get worse.

Finally, I got up and in my underwear duck-walked out to the trees in back of the cottages. There I did something they say is shameful.

I walked back to the cottage. I washed at the sink and put on clean underwear again. While I was brushing my teeth, Pearl woke up. "You in, Lige?"

"Yeah."

"Have a good time?"

"Yeah."

"Good night."

"Good night."

Good old Pearl. I lay down in bed. I was tired and it felt good. I began to pray, asking God to bless my family, Twig, White Hair, Clyde, and us, but when I got to the place to ask forgiveness for what I'd done in the woods, I fell asleep.

CHAPTER XXXIII

The next day Jenks was back and in the evening he walked around with Annie on his arm. They came over to the Ferris Wheel and I got all hollow when I saw her. The flimsy fabric of her light pink dress caressed her breasts and seeing the roundness of what I had touched the night before made my emptiness turn into an ache of despair.

Jenks climbed in beside her and, not really looking at me, Annie said, "Dan, maybe you can have Mr. Cockburn stop us at the top." She took his hand and rubbed the back of it in her lap.

"Yeah, someday maybe I will." Jenks grinned at me.

I gunned the motor and they shot upward. I jerked them to a halt which rocked the car. Jenks looked over the side of the car and down at me, but Annie pulled him back.

A couple kids and their Dad got on next so I had to settle down. After the ride Annie and Jenks walked arm-in-arm down the Midway. Even above the oil and diesel fumes I caught her perfume when she got out of the car and brushed by me.

They stayed most of the evening, walking by several times, but never stopping at the Wheel again. They ate at the same counter I did during my break, but they never noticed me.

On their last swing by, Jenks was carrying a big pink rabbit he had won. Annie looked at me and said something to him. He looked at me and they both laughed.

Shortly after that I closed down. Merle and Pearl came by. They were going out for something to eat and wanted Axel and me to come. I said I was too tired so they headed for the steam shovel game.

Our cottage was in the middle of the row. No other workers were in yet. I was on the step looking for my key when I noticed an open car parked beyond the last building down by the trees. Beside the car was a big pink rabbit.

I walked down the dark row of cottages and crossed the open space to the car. Annie and Jenks were in the back seat. The light was bad, but I could see them. Then high-sailing clouds uncovered the quarter moon and I could really see them. Jenks was in between her legs, moving up and down. I stood there watching. He had a patch of black hair on the small of his back, and I watched it move up and down. He was panting for breath and I could hear Annie deep in her throat.

It had only been a few seconds, and I was turning to tip-toe back to the cottage when I heard a little cry. I turned back and saw Annie looking at me over Jenks's shoulder. He was so busy he hadn't noticed that her cry wasn't because of him.

When Annie realized who it was, her head went back, and I couldn't see her face, but I saw one hand go up Jenks's spine to his neck. She raised her legs and crossed them behind his thighs, squeezing. Her hand slowly clawed its way down his shoulder, leaving four dark, wet trails behind. Jenks cried out.

Annie's face came back up and she squeezed her arms around Jenks. Looking right at me, she said, "Now, Danny, now!"

Blood was trickling beneath her arm, and I ran away with Jenks going OhOhOhOhOh! and Annie laughingcryingscreaming.

Past the cottages, I stopped running and walked around the Midway a couple times. On the way back I decided to have it out once and for all with both of them, but the car had already gone and there were lights in several cottages.

I was still awake when Pearl came in and stayed awake long after he was snoring.

The next day Jenks was gone on another trip, but Annie never came around, though I kept watching for her. The morning had been warm and the sun made for a hot day. I was pretty well fagged by suppertime, so I just had a sandwich and a couple Green Rivers to kill my thirst.

The late paper talked about the heat wave in the Dakotas over the past several days, with a temperature of one hundred and three in Pembina and one hundred in Minot.

The Yankees and Giants were running away with the pennant races.

There was nothing about any murders or bodies in North Dakota.

After twilight I went back to the Wheel. Clyde asked me to do the lubricating and check the belt. I took my time and some guy in line got on me. He was a sailor with a girl in a yellow dress, and I was thinking about going over the rail and shutting his mouth for him when there was a big commotion down the Midway, and soon Merle came running, knocking into people and breaking through the line at the Wheel.

"Lige!" He was yelling. "We gotta go!"

"Where?"

"Just come on!" He was looking back and another commotion was starting down the Midway. The sailor was showing off with his mouth again, and Yellow Dress was embarrassed, but laughing anyway. Clyde jumped off the operator's seat. Merle looked desperate. In a low voice he said, "C'mon, Lige, the cops'll be comin'. We gotta go."

Pearl and Axel ran by and Merle started after them.

"Why?" I yelled.

"Axel's short!"

I saw crowd movement down the Midway and heard a cry of "Hey, Rube!" Clyde reached under the seat and came out with the sawed-off baseball bat he always kept there "in case of emergency." It looked to be an emergency, but Clyde hesitated like he didn't know whether to go for me, chase the others, or head for the commotion.

I grabbed my jacket and cap, which I never let out of my sight, vaulted the rail, and took off after the others. I dodged around some people and bounced off a few more, but I never looked back. Clyde was too old and his pins were shot.

All I could think was that I already knew Axel was short. It's stupid, but that's what I thought as I ran.

Outside the park we kept running, but either I was speeding up or the others were slowing down. Soon Merle and I were together.

"What's wrong?" My words were choppy.

"Axel's short." So were Merle's.

"What?"

"Axel stole . . . some receipts . . . from the steam shovels."

I ran faster, closing the distance to Axel and Pearl. Merle fell behind. I saw the two turn into an alley and I followed them to the back of an old stable. They leaned against it, winded. Axel was coughing.

I was catching my breath in gulps when Merle came up. I gasped out, "What happened?"

In between breaths he said, "Axel took some of the receipts and Mr. Graham came back unexpectedly. He checked the total and went right up to Axel and accused him of stealin'. Axel hit him in the stomach and he went down. Pearl saw it and got me, and we were tryin' to get Mr. Graham up, but somebody had called the cops, and two of 'em tried to arrest us just as we had him up. We had to fight 'em before they got their guns out, so we let go and Mr. Graham fell down again. We beat the cops up, but they wouldn't quit, so it was a bloody business." He looked at his knuckles. "We were just lookin' after Mr. Graham again when someone yelled that more cops were comin', and we heard sirens. Axel and Pearl went for our jackets and I went to warn you."

I was all right, just mad. I walked over to Axel. He watched me, but couldn't do anything. I grabbed his jacket front and slapped him across the face with my knuckles. It felt good and I did it again. He tried to knee me in the groin, but hit my thigh. I pinned him against the stable with one hand and grinned at him. Then I slapped his face, across and back. Finally, the twins pulled me off, and Axel sat down with a bloody nose and cut lips. He was crying.

"I'll fix you for this, Elijah." His words made the blood bubble.

I looked at my knuckles. His teeth had cut them. Pearl steered me away. "We've got to get out of here."

"I know, but our clothes and our gear are back there."

"We can't get them. We've got to let it go. The place will be crawlin' with cops—I think I broke one of the cop's arms."

"Jeez."

"It was an accident."

Merle pulled Axel up. "We're goin' to the railroad. It's the only way out." Axel had stopped crying, but he was breathing kind of wet-like when they walked by me.

I wasn't so mad then, and I was ready to apologize, but Axel whispered "dumb son of a bitch" as he went past, so I cuffed the back of his head, and he started to blubber and bubble again.

"C'mon, Lige, that's enough," Pearl said. "Let's go."

"O.K., but cousin or no cousin, I'm gonna settle a score with him before this is over."

CHAPTER XXXIV

I felt bad about Mr. Graham, but there wasn't anything I could do, bouncing around a freight car. I thought someday I'd go back and make it up to him, but when I got to thinking about it, I'd end up heading for Axel. Finally, the twins got tired of trying to keep me off him, so we left the freight at Ephrata and went "up top" on a "varnish." At least Pearl and I went "up top." Merle and Axel rode "blind baggage" to put a lot of distance between Axel and me.

Out of Ephrata we headed west to the Columbia River, sailing around a horseshoe curve through Crater Coulee and down the east bank of the river, then north to Rock Island, through a short tunnel and, just past the station, across a steel bridge to the west bank.

It was lightening up in the east when we passed through Appleyard, backed by its deeply gulleyed mountain. The dawn gave a gray appearance to a quiet "warehouse row" a few minutes later in Wenatchee. The fruit season was still a couple months off. The tracks followed the Wenatchee River northwest to Cashmere, and then up we went into the Cascades. At Leavenworth we went into Tumwater Canyon, twisted and turned along its steep and evergreened sides for ten miles, at times rumbling through snowsheds, and then headed west through a gap and up another canyon. Sometimes in the Nason Creek Canyon we were looking straight up sheer rock walls, and sometimes we were looking down on treetops. We went through Berne and on to Cascade Tunnel Station, where the air was a maze of electric wires. In the small yard two B-B electrics coupled onto the Mike, and we started through the large concrete portal marked "CASCADE," the opening to two-and-half miles of tunnel.

Twig had told me about the tunnel. In the old days the smoke and gas built up so bad in the bore that the engineers and firemen were issued gas masks. Temperatures inside the cabs sometimes hit 150 degrees. To avoid suffocating, tramps would try to ride through inside an open boxcar or, better yet, on the pilot or cowcatcher. About ten years after the tunnel opened, the GN put in an electrification system that eliminated a lot of the smoke, gas, and heat.

But not all. The locomotives still worked some steam in back of the electrics and, as soon as we left behind the line of telegraph poles on our right and were in the bore, Pearl and I could smell the gassy smoke. The train was crawling through the tunnel; the engineers were actually holding back since it was a downgrade for westbound trains. My eyes began to smart.

I tried to breathe through my sleeve, but it was no good. Soon Pearl was crying, too. I undid my belt and crawled over to him. "We've got to get water."

He looked at me and understood. Twig had told us how.

Pearl unbuckled his belt. We took deep breaths, ran to the front of the car, and jumped to the next one. We dropped down and tried to get a breath through our shirts. It wasn't very effective and we began coughing as we ran. There were nine passenger cars plus the baggage car. We started from car seven, and it took a lot of coughing before we jumped onto the tender. I looked down and saw Merle and Axel breathing through wet handkerchiefs. Merle waved; he was laughing at us.

We dipped our handkerchiefs in the water tank without the engineer and ashcat seeing us and dropped down with Merle and Axel. Even though they were closer to the engine, the smoke wasn't as bad. We didn't talk, but Merle was still laughing. I looked at Pearl and laughed, too. He had a tear-streaked, grimy face above a sopping, used-to-be-white handkerchief.

Eventually, we popped out of the bore, and on our right was Tye, which Twig had told us about when it was called Wellington. In 1910 it had been destroyed by an avalanche of snow, one of the reasons that there was talk about building a new, longer tunnel and abandon the stretch of track we'd been passing over.

A sign on a false-front building proclaimed "Lager Beer," a hold-over from different days, and the paint was fading. Up the mountainside stood shafts of burned evergreens looking like black and white matchsticks. We passed the station and platform and at the Tye yards the electrics uncoupled. Soon Tye was gone as we entered a half mile of snowsheds built in the old avalanche's path.

We paralleled the Tye River heading southwest and rolled through a series of snowsheds. One long snowshed led directly into a curved, double-tracked tunnel which ended in another long snowshed. We just got out of that shed when the flicker of daylight was cut off by another tunnel. Coming out of that one, we passed Embro, hit two long sheds, a slightly curved tunnel, another shed, and crossed a short steel bridge into the Martin's Creek Tunnel. The tunnel curved us around in a dark semicircle and shot us into daylight that dropped away into a deep canyon as we rattled across a long steel trestle. I was thankful I was still in "blind baggage" instead of "up top."

We had doubled back, and we briefly saw where we'd just been on the upper track, but our view was cut off by another snowshed. We ran two more snowsheds, two tunnels connected by a timber shed, and another long shed before we curved into Scenic with its green, yellow, and brown hotel, its sign reading "SCENIC HOT SPRINGS," and the evergreens carpeting the mountain in back of it.

The train headed west, following the Tye River to the division point at Skykomish, which had six tracks in the yard and where every building on Main Street faced the railroad. The mountains above the town had only a few spindling evergreens on their thin slopes.

Our train stopped and we slid off to get some water and something to eat. We pooled our money, but after the food we were down to our last few dollars. Most of my cash was under a loose board in Mr. Graham's cabin.

Eating didn't take long and we were back on top with time to spare. Merle and Axel went "blind baggage" again.

We headed down the Skykomish River Valley west and northwest to Index, with Mount Index rising up off to the south like a granite monument splitting into three parts.

Goldbar; Sultan, where we left the Skykomish; Monroe; Snohomish; and then the Snohomish River to Everett. We were on the Pacific Ocean, or at least Puget Sound.

As we passed through the switching yards at Everett, I saw dozens of flat cars filled with logs. A switch engine was blowing out a huge cloud of whitish-gray smoke as it tugged at the cars.

Pearl and I were hunkered down on the roof while the passengers were getting on and off at the Everett station, which was built on top of an embankment. Below it there was a second set of tracks, and I could look down on the roof of the platform used by the passengers. Beyond the lower tracks was the Sound. The Everett station itself had a long, roofed platform, and the building was topped by a large, ugly, square watchtower.

We heard some crewmen walk by, and a few minutes later there was the sound of someone coming up the ladder.

"Pearl! Lige! C'mon! It's Axel!"

"What now?" I said, but Merle was already down.

We unbuckled and followed Merle away from the tracks to the weed-broken foundation of some long-abandoned building. Axel lay beside it with a blood-soaked handkerchief over his face. He was moaning in a gurgly sort of way.

I picked up the cloth. Axel had a deep C-shaped gash from the inside of his left eye, down his nose, and into his cheek. Blood was running out and I could see white bone and cartilage.

Pearl went over to the foundation and threw up. I think I would have been all right, except when I heard Pearl my stomach let loose, but it was only the dry heaves.

Merle came over after re-covering Axel's face. "Axel and I had been talkin' about you, Lige, and he said he was mad about what you did to him back in Spokane. He said he was gonna fix you if it was the last thing he ever did. Just then a brakie and an ashcat came by. The brakie saw us and says, 'How ya doin', boys?' Quick-like, Axel says, 'What son of a bitch wants to know?' The brakie had a lantern and he swung it around so hard . . . Axel just fell out. The brakie says 'Get your friend off railroad property,' and the two of 'em left. I carried Axel here."

I went back and carefully lifted the cloth. It wasn't any better. I turned Axel more on his side so the blood could drain out of his mouth.

Merle said over my shoulder, "We've got to get him to a doctor."

"I'll go find one," Pearl said.

"Wait!" I grabbed Pearl's arm.

"What for?"

"We're wanted."

Pearl relaxed.

Axel groaned and Merle knelt down. "He needs a doctor."

"I know, I know." My mind was searching.

The sound of a freight starting up came to us one car at a time as the couplings pulled tight. I could see the tops of the cars moving south. The sky was blue and empty except for the sun.

"My brother works at Letterman General Hospital in San Francisco. We can take Axel there and get him fixed up."

"What if he turns him in?"

"He won't. He's O.K., Pearl. You know Josh. He's O.K."

There was a freight with steam up pointed south. We didn't have much time. "Merle, watch Axel. C'mon, Pearl."

We skittered down the embankment. There weren't any boxcars open that we could see on our side, but it was a long train. Pearl crossed over, and we started pacing down the line of cars. If you get it right, you can see each other at the end of each car, and you're doubling your chances of finding an open one. It took us awhile before Pearl said, "Got one." The door on my side was closed.

I tied my handkerchief to the car and we went to get Axel. He wasn't so heavy that we couldn't carry him easily but awkwardly with Merle going ahead. About halfway to the train, we heard two long whistle blasts and saw the brakies moving and then the train was moving. We couldn't run with Axel and soon the handkerchief fluttered by. We put Axel down and then the train slowed and stopped. The handkerchief was fifty yards away.

We made it to the car and Merle crossed over, but he couldn't get the door open. I thought about rolling Axel under the car, but I imagined him cut in two and dropped that idea. Pearl got on a coupling and I handed Axel up. He was bleeding again. Pearl gave him to Merle on the other side and then I crossed over. I was glad Twig wasn't around to see us do such a crazy thing. It was a good thing Everett wasn't a hot yard or the bulls would have nailed us for sure.

I had just got in the car when the whistle echoed and the train jerked. We were heading south.

The other door wasn't closed tight, but it was jammed. Pearl and I worked on it and it finally came open. We looked around for something to wedge under the doors, but the car was clean.

We rumbled around curve after curve with the gray-green Sound to our right and steep, evergreen-capped banks to our left. After twenty minutes or so the small station at Edmonds went by, and a northbound freight flashed past on the other track.

We slowed down and I saw Merle holding Axel's head in his lap and talking to him. I thought I heard a bell ringing, so I looked out and saw our train rounding a curve and above the trees a tall steel-girdered structure. It was on the south end of a bridge, and as we passed under it, I could see that it was a counterbalance weight for the drawbridge.

We maintained slow speed until the caboose crossed the bridge, and then we built up speed through the Interbay yard. I stood in the doorway and watched the strange-looking bridge disappear. We built up more speed into Seattle. We went through a tunnel for about a mile (it wasn't bad inside the car) and came out into a maze of tracks, switched onto a sidetrack, and stopped.

We waited, but nothing happened. There was the noise of trains pulling in and leaving, switch engines, steam, bells, whistles, and crewmen, but we didn't move. I watched the people at the huge King Street Station, dominated by its tall four-faced clock tower.

Merle came over. "Axel's awful thirsty. He's hungry, too, but mostly thirsty."

I was thirsty, too, so I knew the twins must be. "O.K. Let's get outta here."

We carried Axel behind some old wooden buildings. No one bothered us. We talked it over, with Axel breathing noisily through his mouth, a great C-shaped scab forming on his face.

Merle was to stay with Axel; Pearl would put the bite on somebody and bring back some food; I'd get water and a ride out.

Pearl took off and I wandered around until I found a bottle. It had some brownish liquid in it and the label was gone. I emptied it and hid it under my jacket before I went into the King Street Station.

The inside of the building looked like a church, but it was a lot noisier. The waiting room had long polished wooden benches, just like pews, and the decorations made the interior look Italian. I didn't see any Madonnas, but in the lobby floor I saw a mosaic tile compass, which

I wouldn't step on. I looked at the signs on the walls: "CARRIAGES," "STREET CARS," "RESTAURANT," and finally, "RESTROOMS."

In the restroom I cleaned out the bottle with hot water and filled it with cold. I drank a whole bottle, cleaned the top, and refilled it. I saw myself in the mirror and decided to wash my hands and face and wet down my hair, then I headed back to Merle and Axel.

We didn't let Axel drink too much at one time. Merle also drank. I left, looking for a way south. There were so many tracks and trains I didn't know what to do, so I just walked and looked at the cars until I saw two Negroes sitting in a boxcar.

As I walked by, I looked over and nodded.

One Negro said, "Hey, 'bo."

They both laughed.

I walked a couple steps further, but I had to go over. I kicked a rock and turned. The two men stopped laughing.

"'Hey,' yourself." I stood next to the doorway and leaned against the car. "Sure is a big place."

"Biggerun yuh evah saw," one of them said. He had lost a front tooth. Maybe he was trying to make up for it by playing smart.

I looked far across the yards at a long building with a sign: "OREGON-WASHINGTON RAILROAD AND NAVIGATION CO. FREIGHT HOUSE." Beyond it a street car, looking awfully small, rolled by on a wooden trestle. A big Santa Fe-type went chuffing by on the next track, and when I could be heard, I spoke—I had to get Axel out of there.

"To tell the truth, my friends and I are kind of lost."

The two Negroes cackled.

"I'd be obliged for some directions."

"Directions wheah, 'bo?"

"South. To Frisco."

"To 'Frisco'? Hey, Chahlie, 'bo wants to go to S.F. 'Bo, lemme tell yuh now. Don' nevah call it 'Frisco.' People theah don' like it. It's 'San Francisco', or 'S.F.' is awright, too."

I dropped my eyes and made my shoulders small. He was having a good time.

"Yuh see that OWR&N freight house ovah theah? Well, behind that is the Seattle-Tacoma Interurban. Don' take it." They both laughed. I wondered how much lip I could take. I figured I could handle either guy alone, but with two it could get pretty dirty.

"Those tracks ah the Great Northern, 'Hill's Highway.' Those theah"—he pointed—"ah the NP. Tha's shoht for Niggah Pacific." I looked up at him. "Yeah, tha's right. We built it. Us niggahs. Look it up in the hist'ry books. Then's the Pacific Coas', then's the UP, and then's the Milwaukee, the slowes' ride to the Coas' yuh'd evah want to take. Now, which ones go south to the beautiful San Francisco?" He grinned his gapped grin, then he squatted and said, 'Bo, it jus' so happens that mah frien' Chahlie and I ah about to depaht foh S.F. an' we would be honahed to shaeh this cah with yuh an' yoah frien's, if any." He stood up.

Something was in the air, but I couldn't wait. Charlie was covering his mouth with his hand.

"All right. How much time do we have?"

Gap-Tooth pulled out a dollar watch. "Why, ah'd say this shebang will be on its way within the half houah."

"I'll be back." I took off running.

Pearl wasn't back yet, but I told Merle about the two Negroes, so we got Axel up and headed down the tracks. Axel could at least walk, although he kept his head hanging down.

"Merle!"

I looked around. It was Pearl with a paper bag. I explained the situation as we walked and told the twins to be on their toes.

When we came up to the car, Charlie and Gap-Tooth looked at us and then at each other. Gap-Tooth said, "Wha's a mattah with yoah frien'?"

"Nothin'," I said.

"Is he sick?"

"No."

Gap-Tooth jumped down in front of Axel and lifted his head.

"Lord A'mighty!" He let Axel's head drop and jumped into the car. Charlie had disappeared, but came back with his bindle. Gap-Tooth got his, too. They jumped down and started walking away. Gap-Tooth turned around. "Good luck, in S.F., 'bo."

He smiled his gappy smile.

CHAPTER XXXV

We made Axel as comfortable as we could and tried to get him to eat something, but he wouldn't. He was only thirsty, so Merle went back to the station and filled our bottle with water and almost missed us because a locomotive coupled onto the head end, and we started moving. Pearl stood in the doorway and was yelling for Merle when we slowed, stopped, and backed down another siding to bang into a shorter line of cars with a caboose.

After we pulled out, Pearl and I kept looking for Merle, and soon he came running, saw us, and started jumping tracks to catch up. We were heading for the main line and Merle was running flat out. As he came up to the car, I saw that he had his thumb over the mouth of the bottle. He never spilled a drop. He handed the bottle up to me and Pearl grabbed his hand to help him in.

We hadn't eaten because we wanted to wait for Merle. Pearl opened the bag and pulled out a loaf of bread, a can of Delicia sandwich spread in blue-striped paper wrapping, and four bottles of Brownie's Ginger Ale. He'd panhandled a dollar twenty-five and had some change left. Pearl used his pocket knife on the can and then spread the potted meat on the bread. Afterward, he wiped his knife on his pants.

If you looked closely enough, you could see black flecks of dirt lighting on the sandwiches, and the ginger ale was warm, but riding along with the twins in a freight car, the afternoon sun shining on us, made me feel like a young Twig. I looked over at Pearl and he grinned over his sandwich.

The little stations passed by. I read the names on the depots—Black River, Orilla, Kent, Thomas, Auburn, Puyallup—ate four sandwiches, and finished my ginger ale.

The Union Station in Tacoma looked like it had half an onion stuck on top. They did some car switching in the Tacoma yards, but before they were through, Merle came over. "Axel's got to go."

"What?"

"You know."

"Which?"

"One."

"O.K."

Pearl and I went back with Merle.

"Where?" I asked.

"We can't take him out. We might miss the train. Either in the back or out the door."

"Not in the back. That's not right. Out the door." I said.

We helped Axel to the door. Pearl and I held him while Merle took his pants down. Just as he finished, the car was jolted and all of us went flying. Axel's face began bleeding again. Merle redid Axel's pants and we carried him to the back.

"Do we lay his head on his jacket?" I asked. Pearl looked at Merle.

"We'll have to. He can't ride any other way."

I formed a hollow in the folded-up coat and we put Axel's head there. The bleeding stopped, but he felt warm.

His lips moved. I bent closer. "Cigarette."

"We don't have any."

His eyes opened and he saw who I was. They closed. "Water." Merle got the water and I went back to the door. We had stopped near the onion-topped station.

Merle came over. "He wants more."

Pearl took the bottle and three ginger ale bottles, jumped out of the car, and ran to the station. A couple crewmen came by, but didn't say anything to me.

Two whistles and a jerk and we were moving. Across the tracks, Pearl was trying to run with three bottles pressed against his body by his left arm and one in his right hand. Thirty feet behind him a short man in a white shirt and black bow tie was running and yelling, "Stop!"

Halfway to the train, Pearl jumped a track, stopped, broke the bottle in his right hand on a rail, and turned. He flashed the jagged glass at Bow Tie, who stopped dead. Pearl came loping up to the car with a wet left side. He threw away the broken neck, handed up the three half-empty bottles, and hoisted himself in. Bow Tie was still standing there.

"Guy didn't want me to fill up. I tried to tell him about Axel, but he wouldn't listen."

"Don't worry about it. We'll use the other ginger ale bottle for water later."

Merle was with Axel, but Pearl and I sat by the door, which we had jammed. After we built up speed, the swaying of the car, the rhythm of the wheels clacking on the rail joints, and the four sandwiches made me sleepy. I crawled away from the door and lay down.

It was dark where I was and then it was darker. I was leaning up against something, a wall or a building. The twins were next to me. We were eating garden-fresh peas. We opened the pods with our teeth and thumbnail and ran the peas along our bottom teeth, popping them off the pod and into our mouths, crunching them. They tasted like no cooked or canned peas ever could. We rubbed hot radishes and crisp carrots clean with our hands, but they were still partly covered with dirt that crackled between our teeth, but which only added to the taste and the experience. We skinned green onions first so there was no dirt. We had firm strawberries and mushy raspberries, both slightly tart, and for dessert a watermelon, chosen after dozens of thumpings and soundings, with a knife already in it, poised to split the melon and carve it up for its captors.

In the dark I see someone moving. He almost trips on the melon, but doesn't.

"Boys?"

It's Boss. "Yeah."

"Where've you been? Garden raiding?"

"No, sir, just out walkin'." *Will he believe me?*

"Don't tell me that, Lige."

"Sir?"

"I can smell onions on your breath."

In the dark my face turns hot, but he just walks away. We crack the melon—can't waste it now—but it's not that sweet. North Dakota doesn't grow good melons. We should have known that. So should everyone, but they still try to grow them, and they end up on the manure piles.

It's dark and I'm spitting out tasteless melon and Boss is shaking my shoulder.

"Lige! Lige!"

It's Merle. "Wh—what?"

"Axel's got a bad fever. We've got to get off this freight and onto a varnish and make time.

CHAPTER XXXVI

Southern Washington crawled by. We didn't stop very often, but it was too often. South of Kelso we hit the Columbia, but it was dusking up and we couldn't see it very well.

We slid along the right bank, and it was dark when we hit Vancouver, crossed the bridge, and ran into the lights of Portland. After we stopped in the yards, we got Axel out and put him down in the middle of a weed patch. We huddled around him, trying to figure what to do.

He'd drunk all our water and the ginger ale was gone, too. Merle filled the bottles at the station with no trouble, so we sat in the weeds, drank, went off to relieve ourselves, came back, and figured some more. All the while we were on the lookout for the nighthawk who'd scrambled Frisco Pete's brain, but we never saw him.

Pearl went off to panhandle and I went over to the station to look at a time table. Our best bet was on the SP, which had a varnish that only made a couple of stops between Portland and San Francisco. I got the track and the time and went into the restroom, where I cleaned up.

A colored attendant came in and started sweeping. Soon he was singing "Down Home Blues." I went into a stall and sat down. I began thinking about Bear and Boss, Ma, Twig, and Ted. My eyes were sore and I rested my forehead on the coolness of the stall.

After awhile the attendant left. Feet came in and went out. Finally, I went out. A newspaper lying where someone had left it read, "HARDING DRIVES GOLDEN SPIKE."

I looked around, but no one seemed to want the paper, so I read about Harding completing the Alaskan Railroad by pounding in a gold spike on the Tanana River Bridge in central Alaska. There was nothing in the paper about four killers from North Dakota. I folded the paper, put it down, and left.

Pearl came back to the weeds several minutes after I did. He had bread, canned meat, half a dozen apples, and three bottles of Brownie's Root Beer, which was cold, so we drank it right away. I thought maybe Pearl had gone to Sally, but just then I didn't care.

It was a cloudy night and I couldn't see any stars. We moved Axel close to the SP tracks and waited. The twins and I ate sandwiches and drank water. Axel's cut was festering. We made him drink water, but he wouldn't eat.

The varnish came through behind an old 4-8-4 locomotive that had its headlight slightly below the center of the silver-gray front of the smoke box. That's all I noticed because we had to carry Axel on the opposite side of the train from the station in the dark and get him "up top." Blind baggage was too dangerous with no place to tie him in.

It was tough and dangerous getting Axel up, and we were lucky that we were so big and he was so small.

We strapped in and I was buckling my big belt when we heard the crew checking the trucks below. Merle was near Axel, and I hoped he could move fast and clamp a hand on Axel's mouth if he started calling for cigarettes, but Axel never said a word.

The whistle sounded twice and we jerked ahead. The station lights passed by, the yard lights were gone, and slowly we made our way out of Portland and into a darkened Oregon. On the curves I could see the headlight scouting the tracks and the orange from the firebox glowing in the engine's belly. Other than those lights and the lights of a town or farm, it was black. The clouds must have been thick.

We paralleled the Willamette River a ways, and we made a stop at Salem, but after Salem, I put my head on my arms and got into the rhythm of the train.

I slept a dreamless sleep, waking up twice beside lighted stations whose names I never saw. The second time, a big man on the platform walked just like Bear, kind of stiff. I looked to the northeast and it seemed a little lighter. *Dawn's comin'* and I fell asleep.

Bear was in the lead, walking down the cow path, kind of stiff, but he shouldn't have been stiff because his rheumatism hadn't started yet. Boss was next with a big bundle wrapped up in canvas across his shoulders. Bob Kreutzer and I followed along, watching out for fresh cow pies in the path. We'd left the Model T back on the hill, and Big Sam Lake stretched out bluish-gray to the east and west, but the hills on the north side rose up like buffalo humps, and I couldn't see past them.

It was already too late to hunt the big honkers sitting out in the lake. We hadn't planned to anyway, but we might have gotten a few shots if Boss hadn't buried the "T" up to its hubs trying to get to Chokecherry Lake. It had taken Bear, Boss, and me pushing and Bob grinding gears and steering to get it out, and by then it was too late.

We made camp on the lake shore using the canvas as a tent. Boss had it sewn special so it had door flaps and peg loops. Bob and I cleared away the small rocks where the tent was and arranged the blankets we carried for our bedding. Bear cooked hamburgers and beans, and we ate, sopping up the juice with thick pieces of Ma's bread.

I watched the brown trees in the draws to the north and south turn black. There were no trees close to the lake, which was brackish.

Bob was going to the War in a couple days. He'd graduated from our school in June and worked on the farm through harvest. Now Bear and Boss wanted to give him something to remember in France. Bob was a good wing shot and had his own Iver Johnson doubled-barreled 12-gauge shotgun. I was only twelve, but Boss said it was time to learn a thing or two about hunting geese.

After we ate and washed the dishes, we rinsed our mouths with water and dowsed the campfire. In the tent we listened to the geese out on the lake. The wind came up a little and it rumbled off to the northwest.

Bob asked, "What's that?"

"Thunder," Boss said.

"It's too late in the year for thunder."

"O.K., it's cannon then." All of us laughed.

It came again. Boss listened carefully. "Thunder."

I scrunched down into the blankets and the rain stayed away. I was asleep and then I woke up. The rain was lashing down on the canvas, but we had ditched the tent, so it wasn't coming in. I felt something slimy on my hand and flicked it away.

Something wet touched my ear and cheek. I grabbed it. It had legs and a tail. When I sat up, Boss rolled over next to me. "Throw it out."

I pushed it under the canvas. "What was it?"

"Never mind; it'll be all right." Lightning crackled. "Go to sleep." Thunder went across the top of the tent.

Bob made a noise and sat up. "What the . . . There's somethin' in here."

Bear sat up. Boss said, "Throw it out."

Bob said, "Wait a minute." He moved around and suddenly a light flared from a match and he lit the lantern. I sat up and saw the blankets and the spaces between crawling with dozens, perhaps hundreds, of salamanders. So did Bob.

He started screaming, stood up and tried to run out of the tent, but he went to the closed end, and when he hit it, all the pegs came up, and he ran off, carrying the tent and screaming. He looked like a dying eagle flapping along on the ground. Bear and Boss sat in their blankets howling with laughter above the storm. I was too scared to join in.

Lightning showed the grass alive with scuttling salamanders. Bear grabbed me, Boss grabbed the shotguns and shells, safe in their oilcloth wrap, and we headed for the Model T. It was a half mile away, and we sat in it, soaked and chattering. Water was coming through the windows and roof.

Five minutes later Bob got in, and we all squeezed together for warmth. Bob was next to me. He caught cold and developed pneumonia, which delayed his departure for the Army. After he recovered, he shipped out for France. He was killed a year later in the Argonne, carrying a sawed-off 12-gauge shotgun, the same gauge he would have used at Big Sam if it hadn't rained.

Bob was going to die, but he was warm against me, and the wind was coming in gusts, and the Model T was rocking back and forth in the wind, and Bob was warm and would die in France, but I wouldn't let him. I held on and wouldn't let go, and the wind rocked the car, and I told Boss, "Don't let Bob go."

My hands were clenched tight. We were rocking side-to-side, and I tried to relax my hands. I didn't know where we were. It wasn't a tunnel because there were slats through which I could see daylight. We rocked up and I looked out and saw the sky. Then we dropped down.

"Pearl! Pearl! Wake up! We're on the Pacific Ocean!"

CHAPTER XXXVII

It wasn't the Pacific Ocean, not the real ocean anyway. We were on a train ferry crossing San Francisco Bay. After we landed, we got Axel off the roof and moved onto the Embarcadero. It was a cloudy morning and the early chill made me shiver. Axel was in a lot of pain and his face was pus-swollen. His eyes were blackened and his left eye was almost completely shut from the swelling.

The twins helped him over to a warehouse where he rested against the wall. The gulls called over the Bay. If Axel hadn't been there, I would have enjoyed the sound.

I walked over to the warehouse. "I've got to find Josh."

Merle looked up. "How?"

I stepped to the edge of the building and looked at the city waiting under gray clouds. I had no idea how. Four killers, one wounded, in a big city with a few cents' change.

"I'll walk. The Presidio's to the west. I can make it and bring Josh here."

"Axel's bad," Merle said.

"I know. Be here."

I took off toward the Ferry Building, trying to remember everything Josh had said about San Francisco or written about in his letters. I knew that Market Street was like a Main Street. I could find people there who'd help me get to the Presidio.

At the Ferry Building I turned to go in, but I thought they might have pictures or descriptions of wanted criminals in such a place, so I hurried away. Turning inland, I found myself on Market Street.

I'd never seen so many autos, not where I was standing, but further on up. Dozens of autos, but the street was so wide, it didn't appear crowded. I kept looking for a place to get help without endangering the four of us. Steuart Street. Spear Street. Both led away from Market Street. Then Main Street. That sounded good.

I was about to cross Market to get over to Main when I heard a bell clanging, so I turned to my right instead and ended up on California Street. I saw a cable car rumble to a stop. I went over, checked the fare, and headed back to the Embarcadero on the run.

Axel was feeling cold, and the twins jumped me, saying we should just get him to a doctor and take our chances on going to jail. After they ran out of steam, I told them about the cable car. Pearl had enough coins to get us across the city, so we hoisted Axel up and slowly walked to California.

We had to wait for another car, and when it came, we climbed aboard, paid our fares, and stood around Axel so no one would see his face. Nobody appeared to notice, either his face or the fact we were trying to hide him. We rolled up California, heading west.

At first I watched the autos, the basic black of the Model T's apparent, but not as dominating as I was used to. I saw cars that were familiar in our town—Buicks, Cadillacs, Chevrolets, Dodges, Lincolns, Oldsmobiles, and Pontiacs.

And cars less familiar—Auburns, Essex, Hudsons, Maxwells, Nashes, Oaklands, Overlands, Packards, Studebakers, and Willys-Knights.

And one car I'd only dreamed about—a shiny red Stutz Bearcat.

And I saw the people, too. Dozens, hundreds, maybe thousands, most of them moving, but a few standing still, sometimes talking.

We rolled by a building that was some sixteen stories, with brick from the fourth floor up. The first three floors were of stone and there were some huge Greek columns in front of the doors. They were topped by scrollwork my teacher, Miss Samuels, called Ionic. The words "MERCHANTS EXCHANGE" appeared over the columns. In the short time it took us to go by, dozens of people entered and left by the large doors behind the columns, doors that opened smoothly despite their size.

We had to make a transfer downtown, and what with the crowds and the lack of food, Axel was getting weaker, so each of us took turns holding him up. We skirted around Nob Hill and turned up Russian Hill, where we got off the cable car and transferred to a more conventional street car. When Pearl paid, we were absolutely broke.

On the street car we had to sit inside, but we were on the end, and Axel's head was down, so no one said anything. About fifteen minutes later we got off at the entrance to the Presidio.

Right off the track there was a lunchroom made out of an old-fashioned street car. It had a chimney poking up right in the center of the car, and the word "LUNCH" in big letters on the side. Next to the lunchroom stood a branch of the Post Exchange, looking like a large chicken coop without a front wall.

We led Axel away from the smells of the lunchroom and sat him down on a little bench at the end of the PX, right under a sign that read, "Automobiles Are Not Allowed." A street ran up the hill in back of the sign into the Presidio.

I looked up the hill at the street, the power lines, the buildings, and the trees. Josh was in there somewhere. The twins were sitting with Axel. I could tell the lunchroom smells had bothered them, too. A few soldiers and civilians were walking around the PX, but no one said anything to us.

There was a sentry box with a cupola-shaped roof in the middle of the street, but no one was on duty. I told the twins I'd be back with Josh and started up the hill, expecting to be shot. I passed an American flag snapping on a flag pole. I wondered if I should salute. I didn't and I still wasn't shot.

I walked by residences with perfectly kept green lawns. I saw some large buildings with flags in front. A sign read "LETTERMAN GENERAL HOSPITAL." I went in, breathing the antiseptic air and walked the waxed floor up to the desk where I asked to speak with Josh Cockburn. The woman said it would probably be awhile and I should wait in the lobby.

I sat down with no one else around and riffled through the pages of *Argosy*, *Hearst's*, *Everybody's*, and *American*, and finally picked up the *San Francisco Examiner*. I didn't want to think of what I'd do or say when I saw Josh, so I skimmed the paper for any news of wanted criminals and then read a story about plans to broadcast a speech by Harding when he got back from his Alaska trip. The AT&T lines would carry it from radio station KPO across the country to WEAF in New York.

I was just finishing the story when I heard clipped footsteps on the polished floor. I looked up.

"Lige!"

I didn't know how to act so I put the paper down and stood up. Josh came over and put his arms around me, pulling me close. It was easy to tell he was a grandson of Bear's.

He didn't seem to know that I was a killer.

CHAPTER XXXVIII

After I told Josh about Axel, he took over. The peacetime Army wasn't too rigid with its civilian employees, and he got some time off to go with me to see about Axel.

Josh contacted a friend, an Army doctor, and he cleaned and stitched Axel's face. Josh said it looked worse than it was, but that we'd have to watch out for the infection. He gave us money for a meal and made a call to a boardinghouse over on Haight Street. Axel was supposed to recuperate there.

After supper the twins stayed with Axel while Josh and I went for a drive in his Model T. He asked about Ma, Boss, Bear, Jimmie Pike, and our town as we drove the hills of San Francisco. We stopped just off the Embarcadero and went over to a peanut vendor. Josh bought two bags of hot goobers and two sodas, and we walked out on the wharf and looked at the islands in the Bay and listened to the gulls.

Josh said, "I sent a telegram to Boss this afternoon."

I dropped my goobers on the wharf. The sack hit a piling and fell into the Bay. Josh said, "Oops. Here, you can have some of mine." He dumped some warm peanuts into my hand.

He looked at me close. "I got a telegram back." My heart was pounding. "You shouldn't have done it."

The blood was rushing in my ears and it was hard to breathe. I looked out at a big island in the Bay. My mind flashed back about ten years when our church had a big revival meeting led by an evangelist from Tennessee. With the flares of hellfire and the reek of brimstone filling the nave of the church and the glorious promise of Eternal Salvation being offered from deep in the lungs of the dark-browed stranger in the sanctuary, both Josh and I gave our souls to Jesus Christ.

Josh had his arm around my shoulders as we stood in front of the pulpit with two dozen other lost sheep while the congregation sang "Bringing in the Sheaves."

I looked down at the peanuts bobbing in the water, and I heard myself say in a voice that didn't sound like mine, "I know we shouldn't have." I wiped at the corners of my eyes and in the same voice began telling Josh about Twig and Pete and about Axel and the bat. "So we jumped the train and we've been running ever since."

Josh was staring at me with his mouth open, revealing the perfect teeth Ma said I could have, too, if I brushed mine after every meal and at bedtime.

"I guess you'd better take me to a police station."

Josh shook his head. Then he started laughing, not a lot, but still it was laughter. "All I meant was you shouldn't have left without saying goodbye to Ma. Boss was mad about that." He laughed a little more. "It can't be true."

"It is."

"No, I mean you can't have killed him."

"Why not?" I was defensive because I'd spilled my guts needlessly.

"Because Boss would have mentioned it in his telegram. Somethin's not kosher here."

"He's dead. I saw him. I was there."

"No, it's not right. It can't be right. C'mon."

Josh grabbed at my sleeve, and we headed off the wharf and into the Ford, sodas and peanuts forgotten.

"Where we goin'? The police?"

He looked at me. "No, not even if it were true."

We drove in the dusk off the Embarcadero to a Western Union office, and Josh sent a message to Boss. We walked over to a lunch counter and dunked a couple sinkers in our java and jawed a little, but I was too nervous to say much.

Josh paid and we walked back to the telegraph office. Nothing doing, so we drove over to Market, and Josh started telling me about San Francisco during the War. I was pretty keyed up so I didn't pay much attention. One of the things I did hear was about how the Mooney Case, which happened before Josh came to San Francisco, had split the community over the War itself, and how it had been impossible to remain a neutral, even after our boys went "over there." The only reason I listened to that was that there was a Mooney back in our town.

Josh must have seen how it was with me, so he asked if I would like to see the old Barbary Coast, and I said, "Sure."

We turned off Market and headed up Montgomery. Josh pulled over to the curb at Washington and pointed across to where a street went diagonally up to the northwest. "That's Columbus Avenue. You can't see it tonight, but it runs between Russian and Telegraph hills directly at Mount Tamalpais across the Bay. That building on the corner is the Old Fugazi Bank."

I saw a white building known as a flatiron. It was three stories high, but the third one looked added on, as if the bank was outgrowing itself.

The Columbus Savings Bank stood on the east side of the street, showing off light green carved stonework in the street lights as we drove past.

Halfway up the block, Josh asked, "Have you read 'The Luck of Roaring Camp'?"

"Yeah, we read it in English class and then I read it again in a library book. I liked it, especially Kentuck."

"Harte wrote it in that building." Josh pointed out my window, but it was already past. "It's a fine story."

We went uphill and turned right on Pacific. Down half a block, Josh said, "This is it. This is the Barbary Coast."

I expected to see painted whores, opium-drugged Chinamen, hoodlums, rivers of sailors, but the street didn't look any different than the other streets, and the people were just people. I wanted to see something different, especially if I would be in jail soon. "Show me Chinatown, Josh."

The Model T jerked forward for a second, then it slowed again. We turned and headed back toward Market.

"Yeah, I will, but not tonight. Someday, though."

Josh brought up Bret Harte and his stories. We'd both read "The Luck of Roaring Camp," "The Outcasts of Poker Flat," and "Tennessee's Partner." Josh had also read "The Idyl of Red Gulch" ("Don't waste your time, Lige."), "How Santa Claus Came to Simpson's Bar" ("Lots of action, but sickeningly sentimental.") and a couple others, but he said Harte didn't write that much good stuff. Even the stories we liked had weaknesses.

"But I thought you said 'The Luck of Roaring Camp' was fine."

"It is, as a story, but it has a weak point. Plus, like all of Harte's Western stories, the style in wrong, and his characters seem to lack somethin'."

"What d'ya mean?"

"The West in the Sierra Nevadas was rough, unromantic, and sometimes brutal. It was mud and blood, but Harte uses words like 'rude bunk,' 'tumultuous watercourse,' 'rocky fastness,' and others I don't recall to describe it, and this same style carries over into his description of action and characters. It's ridiculous to use such genteel terms for somethin' wild, crude, and merciless. As to his characters, most just aren't human, the way they talk and act, even those with human possibilities like Tennessee's Partner or Stump or Oakhurst just don't work out."

"Why?"

"We . . . I haven't figured that out yet. All I can say is look at Irving and his memorable creations like Rip Van Winkle, Ichabod Crane, and Tom Walker, and the humanity, good or bad, they show, then compare that with the meager offerings of Harte. I don't think Harte could create flesh and blood characters with human motives, either heroic or not."

"Not even Oakhurst?"

"In 'Poker Flat'?"

"Yeah."

"I guess Harte tried, but Oakhurst is no hero. He appears strong, but he's weak inside. You've got to play out the string to the very end and do it with some dignity, not by blamin' it on bad luck and puttin' a bullet in your heart. Oakhurst is no hero."

"What about Tom Simson? He got through."

"He's too innocent. A human hero has to dirty his hands in life."

"How about Mother Shipton?"

"She might be."

"But she commits suicide, too."

"To gain a noble end, not like Oakhurst. She kills herself to save another. That can be heroic if it's what you want, not what someone else wants or forces you to do, even indirectly. And she doesn't blame it on anyone or to bad luck."

We turned a corner.

"Maybe you can even kill somebody to save someone else, but if you do, you have to accept the consequences." Josh's voice was hard. "And if you do it from your strength, not your fear."

I didn't speak.

"I suppose the character I like most is Miggles, but she's definitely not human, more like a mythic woods creature."

"What about Tennessee's Partner?"

"A victim of misplaced loyalty."

"You said before there was a weak point in 'The Luck.' What is it?"

"Just that they knew the flood was comin', so why didn't they get out and save themselves and Tommy. The story says they were warned, and also Stumpy, who lived closest to the river, knew a flood was gonna hit. Knowin' that, it's hard for me to sympathize with people who insist on bein' victims in spite of their reasoning power."

The man talking wasn't the Josh I'd known. "Where do you come up with these ideas?"

We headed down a hill with Josh riding the brake. "Someone I know, a very intelligent person, a very special . . . well, anyway, we've discussed Harte, and a lot of other authors."

"Here in San Francisco?"

"Yeah."

"I hope I can meet him someday."

He looked over at me and smiled. "So do I."

We drove across some cable car tracks, then Josh said, "My friend has a theory about Oakhurst and Tommy Luck."

"But Oakhurst is barely in that story."

"I know and that's a clue. My friend thinks Oakhurst and Cherokee Sal . . . Oakhurst is Tommy Luck's father."

"What?"

"John Oakhurst was a lady's man, and Sal bein' the only woman in camp, they got together one night after Oakhurst suffered a long run of bad cards. He immediately regretted it and ignored the poor woman even after her pregnancy was revealed. He was too weak to leave her completely, but when she died, he stuck around just long enough for appearance sake, and then hightailed it over to Poker Flat, knowin' his son was in Stumpy's capable hands. He heard news from time to time and that was enough. In the mountains outside Poker Flat, he could only allude to his fatherhood in his self-styled obituary when he wrote about his 'streak of bad luck.' He wasn't man enough to 'fess up'."

"But with Cherokee Sal?"

"She wasn't so bad when she and Oakhurst got together; she only went downhill after he abandoned her. Her secret went with her to the grave."

"Oakhurst and Sal, huh?" I laughed.

"It's only a theory."

"Yeah, but it's fun to think things like that."

"Actually, I don't think Harte will be remembered much for his short stories. I think his reputation will be as a rather minor humorist based on his Truthful James poems and a few others like 'To the Pliocene Skull' and 'The Aged Stranger'."

"I've only read 'That Heathen Chinee'."

"It took awhile, but now my friend finds humor even in that one."

I hadn't noticed, but we were on the Embarcadero; the talk with Josh had completely engulfed me. We turned off, drove a ways, and pulled up to the Western Union office. Josh set the hand brake, then said, "Comin'?"

"No."

He got out and went inside. I sat in the dark and waited. He wasn't coming out. Maybe he was phoning the police. When I thought that, I hated myself for it. I got out of the car—I could make a run for it. Nobody could find me on the lam. We'd proved that until Axel fouled it up. I started down the sidewalk and then went into the office.

Josh was just finishing a telegram; two others were on the desk already read. When I came up, he smiled and handed me a telegram from the desk. It read,

"GLAD BOYS SAFE STOP MA AND MRS POTMAN STILL WORRIED STOP BOTH SEND LOVE STOP WILL WIRE MONEY STOP PETE WILSON ORNERY AS EVER STOP WHY STOP BOSS"

The second one said,

"ENJOY SF STOP BE CAREFUL STOP WILL WIRE MONEY STOP BEAR"

The last one was,

LEG OK STOP BACK HOME STOP HOW WAS DEMPSEY
STOP TWIG"

When I put Twig's telegram down, Josh gave me a hug. "You nutty
kids are the cat's whiskers. Who checked Wilson's pulse anyway?" He
was laughing and the telegraph operator looked over at us.

Josh let go and I folded each telegram carefully and put them back
in their envelopes. There was a small washroom down a short hallway
and I told Josh I needed to use it. He went out to the car.

In the washroom I turned on the light, locked the door, and sat
down. I opened each envelope and re-read the telegrams, Twig's first.

When I finished Boss's telegram, I felt pretty bad. I read it again. It
just wasn't right. I was thinking I'd killed a man, and they hadn't even
known about it, and now I hadn't killed him, and it was like the last
three weeks were the result of nothing. Everyone else's lives were just
like they had been, but our lives were completely different because of
a mistake.

The T-shaped alley in our town went through my mind. Who had
checked Pete? Three of us. Me first, then Merle, then Pearl. All of us,
except Axel, and he had caused everything.

I sat for awhile. Pretty soon I turned the water on in the sink so the
telegraph operator wouldn't hear me crying.

CHAPTER XXXIX

That late July in San Francisco we had plenty of money, and we learned the city by walking it and riding the cable cars, but Axel stayed in bed while his face got better. Josh said that with the stitches out you'd have to look close to see the scar, even though his nose was always going to be bent a little.

Mostly we took Bear's advice and stayed out of trouble.

Josh had said we could go camping over to Mount Tamalpais on one of his days off, so when it came, he picked up Pearl and me in his Ford, with a tent and gear in back. Merle stayed with Axel. He said he wanted to write a letter to Cecilia. He still felt bad about Axel's nose.

Josh told us we could see a little of the city before we went to the ferry. He let out the clutch and drove us south between Buena Vista Park and Twin Peaks, then onto 16th Street.

After a few blocks he said, "This is the Mission District. This is where it all began."

We turned and pulled up in front of two buildings on Dolores Street. Pointing to the smaller one, Josh said, "That's Mission Dolores, the oldest building in San Francisco. The other is the parish church." He got out and we followed.

"The mission was made by Indians out of adobe," he continued. "The walls are about four feet thick and have stood through three major earthquakes."

I saw that the four pillars supporting a wooden balcony were Doric, with some more Doric architecture above the balcony. Three bells hung from the eaves of the tiled roof where a simple cross stood on the peak.

Two women dressed in black with scarfs on their heads came out. As they passed us, I heard words that sounded Spanish, but they spoke so fast I couldn't be sure.

Josh went up the steps. Pearl and I stayed below. He turned and said, "C'mon in. Look inside."

"Is it Catholic?" I asked.

"Yes."

I had only been in a Catholic church once. When the twins and I were nine or ten, our then-preacher gave a sermon on Catholics and Protestants. He said that while many individual Catholics were fine people, their church organization was scripturally unsound, corrupt, and dangerous. I didn't listen to his arguments on doctrine and corruption, but I woke up when he said the Knights of Columbus organization was really a papal army awaiting the Pope's orders to take over the U.S.A., the main bastion of Protestantism in the world. The preacher said that in the basement of each Catholic Church there was a secret room with guns and ammunition which the KC's would use on the Protestants when the orders came from the Vatican.

Boss, Ma, and Josh had a good laugh at home about the Popish plot, especially since we had Catholics living next to us and would probably have our non-fish eating throats cut in our sleep under the orders of Pope Benedictus XV. I didn't laugh.

A few weeks later the twins and I were in the alley behind the Catholic Church on Lamborn when we saw an open side door. I told the twins it would be a great chance to check out the guns so we went inside. There was another door leading into the church itself, and after much whispering and daring, Pearl opened it, and we all filed in.

It was dark, except for the early afternoon sun on the stained-glass windows and the candles flickering on a stand and one candle that glowed red through its container near the altar. The flickering made some of the statues look like they were moving. The building itself creaked every once in awhile.

After we had stood for a few minutes looking, listening, and smelling (it smelled different than our church, not worse, just different), I took a couple steps trying to figure a way to the basement, the floor creaking as I walked.

Suddenly, part of the wall came open and a man in black peered out. "Hello, boys. Have you come to confess?"

We didn't stop running until we were safe in the fort we had built in the twins' backyard.

Later I asked Miss Hall, my Sunday School teacher, if it was a sin to go into a Catholic church. She said it wasn't, but that there was no reason why a good Protestant boy should have to. I'd never gone back.

"C'mon. We don't have all day."

Pearl went up and as I started, a woman passed me and went up. Josh and Pearl waited for me and they let the woman go in first. She dipped her hand in a bowl of water and touched her forehead, chest, and both shoulders. Josh did the same. I couldn't believe it.

The woman got down on one knee and then went into a pew where she crossed herself and kneeled with folded hands on a long board. Josh did the same. Pearl and I stared at each other, but neither of us moved.

Some light came in the windows near the ceiling and the three bigger windows in front, and there were plenty of candles, including the red-glowing one. There were statues, and niches for them. The ceiling and the beams were painted in a chevron design of red, white, and gray. People were coming in, praying, and leaving right along.

Josh finished and came back. He took us close to a wall and pointed up at a beam. In the corner there was a design with the initials "I H S" topped by a cross, some leafy paintings, and the chevrons.

"The Indians painted all this," he whispered.

I looked around for a wall that opened, but I couldn't find one. When we left, Josh dipped in the water bowl and crossed himself.

In the sunshine I asked, "Are you Catholic?"

He looked at me with a little smile. "No."

"Then why?" I nodded my head back at the mission, but he just shrugged his shoulders.

A half dozen kids came laughing by us, went up the steps and in, just as an old man with a cane came out. I turned to go to the larger parish church, but Josh said, "C'mon, Lige. There's nothin' in there." The church's architecture looked interesting, but Josh was the boss—he had the car. We drove around the block and headed north.

At Market Street we took a right and then a left onto Van Ness. After a couple blocks we stopped. "City Hall," Josh said.

We got out, walked along a wrought iron fence, and turned by a hanging lantern to head toward a building that looked like a combination of the Parthenon and St. Peter's, two structures Miss Samuels said she admired a great deal when she was explaining what she referred to as "the nomenclature of architecture."

I looked at the great green dome with a lantern on top. "It's over three hundred feet high," Josh said when he saw where I was looking.

When we got closer, I watched some clouds pass over, and the dome and façade appeared to be coming down on top of us. For a second I pictured us all crushed under the weight of the rubble, but we walked on through the blue and gold doors.

Inside there was a huge four-story rotunda. "It's grand," Pearl whispered.

"It is," I said. "It is grand." I was whispering, too. It was like being in a kind of cathedral or temple with all the arches, vaults, columns, acanthus leaves, and sculptures. Pearl and I pointed them out to each other, and I was glad we had paid attention in Miss Samuels' class.

We went up a sweeping flight of stairs and looked down on the little people below.

As we were going back to the car, Josh said, "The State always likes to appear powerful."

I said, "I thought it was the City Hall. What has the state got to do with it?"

Josh started to say something, but didn't.

We took a left onto Turk Street and drove slowly past a huge church that looked like a French Cathedral. It had two tall steeples, a large round window, and tall arched doorways. From right in front, it looked like a gingerbread church, except for the color. A sign said, "Saint Paulus Lutheran Church."

"Wow," Pearl said.

"Don't be too impressed," Josh said. "It's wood, not stone."

A man and a woman stood very small on the sidewalk, gazing up.

We went north into the city, with Josh pointing out buildings and giving us some history of San Francisco, which he seemed to know pretty well. On Sutter Street we passed a large building with twin spires and an onion on each one.

"Russian Orthodox," I said.

"Jewish," Josh laughed, "but a good guess."

Josh looked at his watch. "One more place. We've got time to make the ferry." He clutched up and over Nob Hill.

A few blocks later, a police barricade forced us to pull over and park. We got out and walked up Stockton Street. Crossing Union, Josh pointed left and said, "Washington Square." It was a park bordered by trees with a lot of grass, some benches, and a monument. On top of the monument stood a statue which I thought was George Washington. I was going to tell Pearl that when Josh said, "The statue's Ben Franklin." I was glad I hadn't spoken: Josh knew too much.

We ran into the outskirts of a crowd halfway up the block and had to push and move through to Filbert. To the left, up Filbert, I saw Russian Hill and the street making a grade I didn't think most cars could conquer. To the right was a nearly completed twin-spired church, with people crowding the sidewalks and the street. A couple blocks away stood Telegraph Hill.

"What's goin' on?" Pearl asked. "Why the crowd?"

"They're makin' a movie," Josh answered.

"A movie! Who's makin' it?" I was excited.

"DeMille."

We wedged closer to the church and I could see a platform a good two hundred feet in the air. Several men and cameras were up there, and then I saw a man lean over and look down. Josh said, "That's DeMille." He was shading his face with his hat and I saw his nearly bald head.

He wasn't my favorite movie director—D.W. Griffith was—and I hadn't seen that many of his films because Ma wouldn't let me. She said they were all bedrooms and bathrooms, at least that's what she had heard. I did see *The Little American*. Its sinking of the *Lusitania* helped reinforce my anti-German feelings when I was twelve. Just the previous year I had seen *Manslaughter* with Leatrice Joy and *Adam's Rib* with Anna Q. Nilsson. I'd liked *Adam's Rib* because of the cavemen, but the twins found it boring.

DeMille seemed to be waiting for something. The crowd ahead of us started moving back and a loud murmuring went up. Hanging from one of the spires was a cable attached to a winch which was pulling it upward and drawing an open platform on which a woman was standing.

Just ahead of me a woman in a velvet hat with pheasant feathers exclaimed, "Leatrice Joy!"

Pearl and I grinned at each other. Not as good as Gloria Swanson or Mary Pickford, but pretty good for our first live movie star.

The platform began to sway back and forth and Miss Joy was holding on. The crowd began to cheer and the noise thundered off the front of the church. DeMille was moving around on the high platform.

The crowd was excited and started pushing back to get a better view. The lady in front of me bumped my chest, turned, and begged my pardon. A man with a toothbrush mustache bumped into Pearl and excused himself. He squeezed behind me.

Miss Joy was almost up. The crowd was applauding. Pearl and I clapped and whistled. The noise died down and I looked for Leatrice Joy's husband John Gilbert, but didn't see him.

Off to my left I heard, "Hey, Rube!"

I looked for Josh, but he wasn't around.

"Hey, Rube!" It was Josh's voice.

"C'mon, Pearl." We moved through the crowd toward the voice. It was about twenty yards. Josh had a grip on the man with the toothbrush mustache and two other men were holding a taller, pale-faced guy. When Josh saw us, he said something to the two men, and all five of them pushed through the crowd, and we followed. They held Toothbrush and Paleface up against the church using armlocks.

"Empty their pockets," Josh said to us. "Pearl, do him. Lige, that one."

I hesitated, not knowing what was going on. "Now," Josh said, not yelling, but forceful.

We pulled stuff out of their pockets and put it on the sidewalk. A lot of people were watching, but didn't say much. I pulled out a billfold, a tan coin purse that smelled of perfume, a billfold with the initials "PP" in the brown pigskin, and another billfold that looked familiar. I felt my hip pocket. Empty. Pearl had an even bigger pile behind Paleface.

"Lousy pickpockets," Josh said.

Word got around, and people came over to claim their wallets, purses, a necklace, and two pocket watches. Some of the men were ready to clean up on the prisoners, but Josh wouldn't let them.

Something happened up on the spire and the crowd "oooooed." Josh told the two men to bring the pickpockets along. He said the woman they were passing the goods to had escaped in the crowd. Josh cleared a path and told Pearl and me to walk behind in case they made a break. At the corner of the church, we turned and went into an alley of some kind. We turned again and were out of anyone's view from the street.

I asked Josh if I should get the cops. There were plenty on the edge of the crowd.

"No. We'll handle this."

He had Pearl and me hold Toothbrush while the other two men held Paleface. Josh came up to Paleface. He looked at the men. "Hold him tight." Josh dug a left into his guts. Paleface bent over, his head dropping. Josh gave him a right cross to the jaw. Toothbrush jumped, but said nothing. "Drop him," Josh said. They did and Paleface lay in the dirt.

Josh put his right hand in his pocket and slapped one man on the shoulder with his left. "Thanks, boys. Thanks for the help. You'd better get back now. You don't want to miss the descent, do you?"

"No, I guess not," one of the men said and moved off. The other one looked at Toothbrush, shrugged, and followed his friend.

After they'd turned the corner, Josh pulled his hand out of his pocket and shook it. "Damn that hurts." He examined his knuckles and flexed his hand. He reached back in his pocket and came out with a roll of coins. He squeezed his hand around the roll a few times. "Damn." He put the roll away.

He walked behind Toothbrush, who tightened up. Josh slipped his right arm around the pickpocket's neck and pulled it tight with his left. Toothbrush started to jerk and tried to kick Josh with his heel, but missed. Josh squeezed tighter; Toothbrush's face reddened, then purpled, then he went limp. Pearl and I let go. He sagged. Josh let go. He crumpled up, his head near a garbage can.

Josh rolled him on his stomach. "What we need is some justice here. Not too much and not too little. Lige?"

"Yeah."

"Kneel down here and hold his hand flat. Yeah, now pick up his little finger." I did and Josh put his boot against it. "Hold his hand tight." He pushed his boot down and the finger went back and snapped. It wasn't loud. It was like the noise when you bite a chicken bone to get to the marrow. Toothbrush groaned, but didn't wake up.

I jerked to my feet. "What'd ya do that for?"

"Justice." He walked over to Paleface. "Let's do it."

"No."

"Pearl?"

"No."

Josh looked at us, then he brought out a jackknife and opened it. He kneeled and put it across Paleface's little finger.

"For God's sake, Josh! No!"

"This way or that way." He nodded at Toothbrush, who was trying to wake up.

I looked into Josh's face. He seemed so detached. He started to press on the knife.

"O.K." I kneeled. The snap came and we left.

No one spoke as Pearl and I walked up Greenwich, down Grant, and up Filbert to Kearny, where there was no crowd. Josh followed.

We stopped at the southwest corner of Filbert and Kearny and sat on the curb.

I said, "We could have had them arrested."

"Yes, but they would have paid their fines and perhaps spent a little time in jail, partly at my expense, and then gone right back to work. This way they won't be working for awhile, unless they're left handed. I forgot to notice."

For a second I was afraid he was going to head back and check. "But you broke their fingers. You mutilated them."

"No, little brother. They assaulted you, Pearl, several other gentlemen, a number of ladies, and tried to assault me. Evidently, they have been doing it quite regularly. The present criminal justice system cannot deter them from their assaults, so we handed out a form of simple justice they'll understand."

Not 'we'."

"All right—I handed it out. It may not deter them from repeating their criminal assaults, though I hope it does, but it will certainly prevent them from doing so for awhile, and if the bones knit improperly, they might have to retire for lack of skill."

"It was cruel."

"You're young. Should we ask the other victims if my justice was too cruel? You know what they'd say. I'm willing to submit to a system of justice where the victim is defended as much as the criminal, but, unfortunately, we don't have that system yet. If our pickpockets had been convicted, their fines would have gone to the government, not to you or Pearl or any of the other victims."

"It wasn't right."

"Perhaps, but it's a case of your values against mine, and there is no way to choose between them. Someday I hope there will be."

Down the hill the crowd was breaking up. DeMille must have come down. We sat quietly in the sun. Finally, Josh looked at his watch. "Do you still want to go camping?"

I stood up. The Bay flashed blue-green and white in the sunshine. There were some ships moving on it. Across the water, Mount Tamalpais swept up.

He was my brother.

I looked at Pearl. He was searching the far side of the Bay.

"Sure."

CHAPTER XL

Josh parked his car just off Jefferson and went to buy tickets for the ferry at the Hyde Street slip. Almost as soon as he came back, it was time to go—we had to hurry to get the camping gear on our backs.

It was a Golden Gate Ferry Company boat and it looked fairly new. It took us across the gray-green waters of the Bay to Sausalito. Josh sat inside, but Pearl and I stood near the bow with the rush of chill air on our faces. The up and down movement didn't bother us, but neither of us said much.

At Sausalito we ate in a little seaside café, but not a big meal because Josh said we had plenty of miles to hike ahead of us. After we ate, we walked to a general store where Josh bought some food and ginger ale. Pearl and I had money, but I figured Josh was trying to make up to us. In a service station restroom he wet some towels and a small piece of canvas he had and wrapped the sodas and meat in them. He put the bundle in his knapsack.

We walked uphill a ways and then sat on a little knoll and looked across the Bay at the city, hazy in the distance.

Pearl and Josh talked a little about Pearl's family, our town, and the trip out. I lay back on the grass, closed my eyes, and wondered if Josh had been bluffing with his knife on Paleface's finger.

Josh got up. "It's time to leave." We adjusted our packs and followed him. We went along a road for awhile with the cars puttering by, some of them sounding their horns. The grass and the brush were brown, but higher up in the draws the trees were green.

After six or seven miles Josh angled us off to the left and we followed him up a trail. We came to the road bed of a railroad which looked either abandoned or not used much, and the walking became easier. After we left the road bed, the climb was steeper and harder and with no rhythm to my steps the straps on my pack started to bite. Josh stopped and we all drank from our canteens and rested.

After several more miles we entered a camping area. My feet ached. "We'll stay here," Josh said. "We can build a fire in one of those pits. They've got a lot of fire restrictions in California, not like back home."

The campsite was in a copse of trees. We took off our packs, and Pearl and I set up the tent, which we had taken turns carrying. We checked for and removed low-hanging twigs and branches.

The further we had walked to the west, the greener things had become. And larger. After the camp was ready, Josh took us over to Muir Woods with its giant redwoods.

The tallest trees seemed to flow right into the sky, but even the largest ones weren't as big around as I had thought they'd be.

It was dark and whispery in Muir Woods, and though I was glad I had seen redwoods, I was just as glad to leave.

Back in camp Josh had Pearl and me sit down as he made supper. We took off our boots and socks and bathed our feet. Josh shaved off some pieces of wood with his hatchet to make tinder. He put the tinder in a pit and carefully placed twigs over it, allowing space for plenty of air. He scratched a match on the pit and put it under a piece of tinder which caught and then put it under a second piece. Quickly, the twigs began to crackle and he added some larger pieces, never too big or too many.

"Watch the fire," Josh said. "Keep it going." He went over to a pipe, turned the handle, and washed his hands.

He came back and took out the two pounds of hamburger he'd bought and wrapped in Sausalito. He formed the meat into six large patties, which he pressed and flattened and sprinkled with salt and pepper from two small envelopes. He placed them in the frying pan he'd been heating and they began to sizzle. He turned them over and opened a can of pork and beans with the opener on his jackknife. He poured the beans in a pot and put the pot on the fire. He poured the grease from the burgers into the fire, which flared briefly. He turned each patty over. Little sizzles of grease spit up and out of the pan. The beans began steaming, and he picked up the pot, swirled the beans around a couple of times, and set the pot down further away from the fire.

"This kind of remind you of Bear?" Josh asked, looking at me. Bear was always camp cook on our hunting trips.

Josh was bigger than Bear, but he squatted beside the fire just like him, with one knee on the ground, so he could move quickly to the different things he was cooking.

"Yeah," I said, then added, "It smells good."

"It sure does," Pearl said.

"Get out the plates and forks."

Josh flopped a burger on each plate and then poured a mess of beans around it so it looked like a dark brown island in a light brown sea.

"Onion?"

"Yeah."

"Yeah."

Josh took out a purple onion—I'd never seen one like it before—and cut the top off and threw it in the fire. He removed a layer of skin and put that in the fire, too. Then he cut a slice and dropped it on Pearl's burger. He did the same for me and for himself. I cut through the onion and burger and forked the combination into my mouth. The onion was sweeter than any I'd ever eaten, but it still had the bite of an onion.

The first burgers and onions were followed by seconds and the rest of the beans. Josh took out a long loaf of unsliced bread, broke it into three big chunks, and gave one to Pearl and one to me. We dipped them in the bean juice and brought them dripping to our mouths. Josh was just as good as Bear; he cooked the same and did the same thing with the bread.

When we had finished sopping up our plates until they were clean, Josh opened the wet canvas and towels and brought out three bottles of Canada Dry Ginger Ale. He opened them and passed them out.

Josh raised his bottle to us. "Here's to Francis Drake and to you two adventurers." We all drank.

Pearl raised his bottle. "Here's to Merle. I wish he was here . . . and Axel." We drank.

I looked at Josh's face, flickering in the firelight. "Here's to my brother, Josh, without whom we wouldn't be here." We finished the ginger ale.

We watched the fire die, and then Josh got out a piece of bar soap and had Pearl and me wash the dishes while he walked up Mount Tamalpais.

When we finished our job, we dumped the water on the embers and headed after Josh.

It was getting toward evening.

CHAPTER XLI

The path up was steep, but easy to follow. There was a regular hiking trail, and periodically there were small rest huts, but most of them were in poor repair.

The day had been clear, and so was the evening, with only some clouds off to the northwest out to sea. As we got close to the top, the sun was an orange-red ball floating on the ocean. It sank quickly.

We saw Josh sitting on a little hummock and he waved us over. We sat down, just below him. I looked around, trying to see things before it got dark. San Francisco started to sparkle off to the southeast.

"Sunsets don't last long here," Josh said. "Not like back home."

He was right. The stars were already appearing here and there. We sat looking for awhile, then Josh asked, "How's Manfred?"

Manfred was a young man in our town who had been born with something wrong. He lived near the river down the hill from our house, where his mother ran a small dairy farm and delivered milk around town herself. Manfred's father was "gone." I never knew where. He was just "gone."

"He's about the same."

Manfred lived in a home-made chair with bicycle wheels on the sides and a tricycle wheel in back for steering. It was made of wood and padded with what looked like fourteen quilts and blankets which were wrapped around Manfred, his face showing at the top.

"Does he get out much?"

"Just in the yard. He likes the sunlight."

"No one pushes him uptown?"

"Up that hill?"

"Suzannah used to."

"I kind of remember," Pearl said. "That was a long time ago."

"Yeah, when Suzannah lived down by the river, too," Josh said. "Just an old lady with not much to do, no husband, no family, and then she started pushin' Manfred around the block. One day he didn't want her to stop, so she decided to take him uptown, and she did, all the way up the hill, pushin' by herself. I must have been five that summer and sometimes I'd see them comin' up that long hill. At first I hid in the lilac bushes near the top because I was afraid of Manfred, afraid of the way he looked, afraid of the way he tried to talk, afraid I'd catch what he had. It took me a couple years to get over that fear, and then I started helpin' Suzannah push. At that time she didn't really need the help, but whenever I was around the hill and saw them, I'd help push. When I was eight, Ma let me go uptown with them. We'd just sit in the park, in the sunshine, and people would come up and talk to Manfred and to Suzannah. On Saturday afternoons there was Market Day, and all the farmers and their families would come to town. Suzannah would buy two bags of popcorn at the theater, and we'd eat one and feed the pigeons with the other. Oh, Manfred loved those pigeons! They lived in the elevators, but they knew Suzannah and Manfred and me on Market Day.

"A couple times I remember the Cornet Band put on evening concerts. Suzannah would pack a lunch, just home-made bread and some cheese or home-made jam, and we'd drink water from the public fountain, but we'd have to bring a cup for Manfred. Then we'd go over to the bandstand and listen. Manfred would grin; he liked music.

"After a few years I grew up and didn't help push anymore, but Suzannah kept goin' up the hill every season but winter. She was quite a lady."

It had gotten dark; the sky was twinkling.

"What happened to her?" Pearl asked.

Josh was quiet. Finally, he said, "She died." Then it was like he was remembering.

I watched some lightning in the clouds over the ocean, but it was much too far away to hear any thunder. A little while later Pearl asked, "How?"

I didn't think Josh was going to answer, but he did.

"I was fifteen. I was the first baseman and heading for practice. Standing at the corner, I could see Suzannah and Manfred starting up the steepest part of the hill. I saw Manfred's red cap with the bill. He always wore a cap."

"He still does," I said.

"Anyway, they were comin' up, but it was so slow I thought I'd better watch. Suddenly, Suzannah just went down. There was no sidewalk like there is now, and she went down on her hands and knees in the middle of the street. Manfred's chair spun around and got away from her. It started rolling down the hill and I took off after it. I caught it before it got to the end of the block, but it took me awhile to stop it. I grabbed the handles and dragged my feet, but Manfred and the chair must have weighed close to two hundred pounds. After I got it stopped, I went around front to check on Manfred. When he saw me, he smiled that toothy smile of his and tried to say my name, which he never could, but just get the 'juh' sound a little. After I saw he was O.K., I turned the chair around and started up the hill. Suzannah was comin' down, or tryin' to, on her hands and knees in the gravel.

"I parked Manfred sideways and ran up to her. She was cryin' and her dress was torn. I helped her up and she clung to me. After a few seconds she got hold of herself, looked at me, and said, 'Joshua, I couldn't push him; I just couldn't push him anymore.'

"I took them both home and the next day Boss told me that Suzannah was in Doc Lee's hospital. She'd had a stroke.

"I went up to see her. She was in a white room in a white bed covered with white. I didn't recognize her at first because she always wore her hair up, but the nurses had it all combed out and spread over her pillow, a little black, but mostly gray. On a night stand they had her false teeth in a glass of water. The top part looked purple, but the teeth-part looked natural enough.

"Suzannah was breathin' with her mouth open, but I thought I heard her say somethin', so I leaned over and she breathed on me. Her breath was foul and right then I realized death. And right then, too, I realized the certainty of heaven."

I could feel Pearl's eyes trying to find mine in the dark. I heard him move a little. When we camped out, we could never tell ghost stories if Pearl was along.

Josh said, "Heaven's the place where God makes it all up to the Manfreds and the Suzannahs. They got a hold on the dirty end of the stick in this world, so there'll be a clean one for them in the next . . . Do you boys believe in heaven?"

"Yes," I said.

"Me, too."

"That's good." Josh stretched back. So did Pearl and I. The stars were there.

CHAPTER XLII

It was getting spooky up there, so I said, "Gee, there must be a million stars out tonight."

"Not really," Josh said. "Maybe two thousand, if we sat here and counted 'em all. There's millions we can't see, of course."

We kept looking up, then Josh said, "Have you read *Huckleberry Finn?*"

We both had.

"Remember the part where Huck and Jim are lyin' on their backs lookin' at the stars and wonderin' if the stars were made or just there?"

"Yeah," Pearl said, "and they thought a giant frog had laid 'em."

"Well, somethin' like that, except I think they agreed that the moon could have laid the stars just like a frog lays eggs."

"Oh, yeah, that was it," Pearl said.

"Jim was right, I think. The stars were made."

"Right," I said. "God made 'em. In Genesis. Our big family Bible says 4004 B.C. at the top of the first page of Genesis."

"That's right, Lige. God did create the stars and the whole universe. See the Milky Way?" Josh's hand arched under the faint white band across the night sky. It really showed up on the mountain. "That's our galaxy."

"Mr. Pomeroy explained that in science class," I said.

"That's good because then you already know that all the stars you see are part of it, part of a huge galaxy of stars."

"Yeah."

"But maybe you don't know that in the dark between those stars, far out in space, are more galaxies or nebulae like ours."

Pearl didn't say anything, so I said, "How do you know? Mr. Pomeroy never told us that."

Josh answered, "I don't *know* know, but I think there are. Astronomers are tryin' to find out."

It was all getting a little much for me. "I suppose you're gonna tell us you know some of these astronomers." I must have said it pretty snotty because Josh waited a few seconds before he answered.

"As a matter of fact, I do. Last summer we . . . I took a vacation and visited two observatories. I drove down to Mount Hamilton to the Lick Observatory. It's over by San Jose." It looked like he pointed southeast, but it was hard to see. "Then I went down to the southern part of the state to Mount Wilson and met Edwin Hubble, an outstanding astronomer. They say that California is hot in the summer, but it's not in those observatories at night. If you ever go, bring a coat."

"You never seemed very interested in the stars at home," I said.

"No, I guess I wasn't. I didn't really understand much, or even want to understand much, about astronomy until three years ago when . . . my friend gave me some write-ups on a debate held in Washington, D.C., on the size of the universe, between two astronomers, Harlow Shapley and Heber Curtis."

I'd never heard of them, but I shut up.

Pearl asked, "Who won?"

"For my money Curtis did, and in doing so he opened my eyes to the fact that other galaxies or nebulae are possibilities, even probabilities, and that they are just like our Milky Way with millions of stars."

"How far away are these other galaxies?" Pearl asked.

"Do either of you know what a light year is?"

Neither of us did.

"A light year is how far light travels in one year. It's about six trillion miles. Shapley argued that our Milky Way is about 300,000 light years across, and that it is basically the universe. Curtis said that other galaxies are a couple of hundred thousand light years away, and that the Milky Way is smaller than 300,000 light years and is certainly not the entire universe. Last summer I saw Curtis, and he said that he was revising his estimate of the size of the universe upward, and that he was more convinced than ever that the universe is made up of hundreds of other galaxies. I talked to Hubble at Mount Wilson, too. He was using both the sixty-inch and the hundred-inch telescopes there to show differences between things he calls nebulae, which he says are gas clouds in our own Milky Way, and the spiral nebulae, which he claims are distant collections of stars. I wrote to him earlier this year, and he's photographing a group of stars with the hundred-inch, and when he's done, he thinks he can prove that it is a separate star group outside our galaxy."

"When?" I asked.

"In another year or two. He's not the only one using the hundred-inch." Josh lay down on his back. His voice sounded far away. "Up there in that blackness is the face of God. Hubble and others are going to throw a little light on it, and then we'll know more about Him. And about ourselves."

Pearl and I lay back, too. I saw the stars all right, and sometimes I could see fainter ones just at the corner of my vision, which disappeared when I looked directly at them, but I couldn't feature God in the dark. Maybe in the visible stars, like Mr. Pomeroy said. That made more sense.

"How long did it take to make all those galaxies, Josh?" Pearl asked. "And how long ago?"

I sat up. I wanted to hear the answers.

"I don't know. Millions of years to make, I guess, and if their light takes hundreds of thousands, or millions, or even billions of years to reach us, that means the galaxies are millions of years old, maybe more. Maybe billions."

"What?" I was upset. "What about the Bible? What about creation in one day? What about 4004 B.C.?"

Josh sat up. He looked dark himself against the stars. "I don't believe the Bible word-for-word anymore."

It got really spooky up there then.

CHAPTER XLIII

"Well, what do you believe, then?" I was ashamed that Pearl was there to hear my brother say such things.

"I believe there is a God. The universe's existence and the life in it demand one. Nothing just happens—there's always a reason, and behind the reason is a cause. The ultimate cause is God. Stars, earth, us—without God we wouldn't be here."

"And that's just what's in the Bible," I said.

"Yeah," Pearl chimed in.

"But you both must understand the Bible for what it is, a record of fallible human beings groping and struggling to realize the existence of a single Being beyond nature. When you dig up a garden plot, you're not digging into God, or when you eat a fish, you're not eating God. God is a spiritual force outside of nature, which is His creation. In history there were attempts to recognize this type of God. Some of the ancient Greeks made excellent tries at it, but it was the Jewish people who hit the nail on the head. The Old Testament is a record of that increasingly vivid attempt. The Christian New Testament extends and expands that record."

I thought he was trying to crawfish out of it. "But you said you didn't believe the Bible anymore."

"No, I said I don't accept certain parts literally."

"You can't pick and choose. When Paul wrote to . . . to . . . I think it was Timothy, he said all Scripture was inspired by God."

"What is 'Scripture'? That book was written before the full Bible was put together and which Bible anyway?"

"What do you mean?" Pearl asked. He'd moved over next to me.

"I mean Protestants and Catholics have different versions of the Bible, and Orthodox Christians have a Bible that is different than the other two."

"The Orthodox don't count," I said. I was feeling surly.

"They think they do. In fact, they think they're more right because they have the most books in their Bible. Protestants have sixty-six books, Catholics have seventy-three, and the Orthodox have maybe five more. Plus the Catholics and the Orthodox have longer versions of some of the books they share with the Protestants. Which version is correct?"

"Ours is," I said.

"Who said so?"

"The Holy Ghost."

"Didn't He tell the Catholics that, too?"

"No."

"Or the Orthodox?"

"No."

"They both think He did."

"Well, smarter men than me have said He didn't."

Josh was silent awhile, then he said, "I don't want to get into a theological debate with you, Lige, or you, Pearl, but I want you to think about a few things. When you get back home, or wherever you're gonna go, I want you to use your own brain and think things out about the Bible. Just look at the first chapter of Genesis, and ask yourself what the logical order for the creation of Man is. Then ask yourself if the order you find was written down under the inspiration of the Holy Ghost."

"You mean there's more than one version? I asked.

"You tell me—someday. But if you see a difference there, maybe you'll realize that perhaps the Bible is not a record carved in stone, but really a groping by men and women sincerely seeking the truth, a searching through the fog for a light in the window. And if you see that, then you'll see that some parts are not as infallible as you've been told."

"Such as what?" Pearl asked.

"Genesis One."

"Somethin' else," I said.

"I don't have my Bible handy, but you can look this up somewhere in the New Testament—Mark, I think. Jesus says that He will be coming back a second time while some of His contemporary followers are still alive. That didn't happen, so what are we to think? Either Jesus lied or made a mistake, both of which are unthinkable of God, or a human being garbled what He said. If that's the case, the Holy Ghost let it stand."

"But the Holy Ghost inspires us with the truth," I replied.

"Yes, but who has the truth. The Catholics, the Methodists, and the Lutherans all claim their churches are inspired in their theology and decisions by the Holy Ghost. Yet all three have different versions of what the bread and wine, or grape juice, at Communion becomes, is, or means. And what has the Holy Ghost been inspiring people to believe about Original Sin, sin itself, infant baptism and damnation, predestination, confession of sins, the number of sacraments, purgatory, Mary's virginity, priestly celibacy, and the infallibility of the Pope?"

Neither Pearl nor I spoke.

"It appears to me that the Holy Ghost has been offering to people the way to the truth, but that some of them have turned onto different paths. The real problem is to determine who's on the right path, who's on a round-about route, and who's going on a completely different trail. The one thing I'm sure of is that you should avoid any religion or religious leader that uses the State to enforce religious doctrines or teachings."

"Why?" I asked.

"Because God doesn't need His words spread by the bayonet, the gun, or even jail sentences. A truly beautiful aspect of our world is that human beings are created by God with free will and free choice. God allows us these things, though He could have created a universe without them. Since He didn't, I assume they are good and that we should and must use them. If a religion wants the State to forbid killing, I will agree with it, not because of the religious dogma, but because killing is a violation of a human right, and also it is a denial to someone of his or her right to choose.

"But if a religion wants the State to enforce Sunday blue laws or anti-gambling laws or prohibition, that religion has revealed its own bankruptcy. Its leadership feels that they cannot convince people to avoid Sunday shopping or gambling or drinking with moral suasion and example, so they have the State step in and forcibly remove someone's freedom of choice, something God created in us and is perfectly willing to allow us to use. Religious teachings enforced by a gun to the head are hypocritical, anti-human, and anti-God."

"But aren't we all sinners?" I asked.

"Yes, but God will be our judge, not the State, not even the religious leaders who clamor for it to use its whips and stakes on freely choosing human beings who are not violating the rights of others."

"Aren't you afraid of Hell?" Pearl asked.

"Yes, if I go there."

"To burn forever," I said.

"No, the God I worship will not roast sinners for all eternity. The wages of sin is death, not everlasting pain. Unrepentant sinners will be cast into a lake of fire, but they won't be burned forever—no loving God would do that to any of His finite creatures. Their bodies, and even their souls, will be consumed, and they will be no more. As to the eternal nature of the fire, that all depends on the meaning you give to the original Greek word—does it mean 'for all eternity' or does it mean 'for a lifetime'? After the Judgment Day, when Time comes to an end, I see no reason why God would keep the stoker going.

"One of the most obscene things I ever read was a description by a medieval theologian who wrote that the joys of the souls in heaven would be increased because they would be able to hear the anguished cries of those souls in hell."

It was getting colder. The constellation Lyra had twisted around to the zenith.

"C'mon, let's get back to camp." Josh got up. We followed him in silence, picking our way down the path in the moonlight. The first quarter was about halfway to full. "Sorry to spoil your camping trip with my palaver."

"Aw, you haven't," Pearl said.

"Naw, it was interesting," I said, but I felt funny inside all the way down to the camp. After we'd gotten ready for sleep, I prayed for a long time in my bag, first about my folks back home, then about the twins and their family and even Axel, and a little bit for myself. I saved Josh for last, and it was rough because I knew he was going to Hell and roast for all eternity. He'd committed the unpardonable sin against the Holy Ghost.

CHAPTER XLIV

Bird calls woke us the next morning. It was gray and wet in the trees, and after we took the tent down, we had to carry it up out of the trees to let it dry off. Breakfast was some donuts and rolls, washed down with water.

We didn't say much while we ate, but when we started to pack, Josh said, "You guys don't have to go back home, you know. California has a lot more opportunities for ya."

"But what about school?" Pearl sounded worried.

"What about it? Education isn't just schoolhousin'. Living and experiencing are education. Stay out here. I'll find you jobs and you can educate yourselves. You already know how to read, write, and talk. What more can you find in a building? What more d'ya want?"

"What kind of a job?" I asked.

"Since you like movies, I thought I'd get you a job with a film company."

"As what?"

"Well, not as a star, but I met a guy last year down near Monterey. He was workin' on *Foolish Wives*."

Pearl grinned at me. Von Stroheim was great.

"Actually, he was there to keep tabs on von Stroheim and report back to the production manager in Hollywood. I went down there because Johnny Aasen and Shorty Buck were up for a few days chasin' a couple of skirts and gettin' nowhere. They wrote me a letter and I went down."

Johnny and Shorty had been friends in our town. Johnny was almost eight feet tall and huge; Shorty was three-and-a-half feet tall. I remembered them shooting pool together at The Corner. Ma wouldn't let me go in, but I could look through the window. Johnny's head would be above the light, then he'd hunch down with a cue that looked like he could pick his teeth with it and send the balls flying. Shorty had to stand on a wooden crate. When he played, he always wore a black derby and chewed a long black cigar. They were about the same ability, and if one of them ever beat the other one in four straight games, I never heard about it, so they remained good friends. About four years before, a carnival had come to our town and signed the two for the sideshow. Johnny was a "sure-nuff" giant, but Shorty wasn't quite small enough to be considered a first-rate midget. When the owner fired Shorty, Johnny quit, too, and they headed for California. Soon we heard they were trying to get into pictures.

"Johnny and Shorty introduced me to this guy, and we chummed around over a weekend, and he told me all about this production manager at Universal, how he didn't look like much, skinny and frail, but that he was on his way up. He told me if I ever wanted to work for him, I had a job. Now earlier this year I read in the papers that the production manager had left Universal and is working for Louis B. Mayer, and my friend went with him. If ya want a job, I can get ya one through him." He hefted his pack onto his shoulders.

It sounded good to me and Pearl looked interested, too. The farther along the trail we went, the better I liked the idea. Just being a carpenter or learning to operate a camera was enough of a start.

We took a short rest after we'd walked along the road a ways. While we had our canteens out, Josh said, "Johnny wrote me earlier this year that he's making a movie with Harold Lloyd down in Los Angeles and Venice Beach. Part of it's about a revolution in Mexico or Chile or one of those Latin American countries and Johnny plays the giant 'Colosso,' who carries a cannon on his back and some cannonballs. Shorty's not in it."

Harold Lloyd—that magic name. We hoisted our packs and started walking. By the time we neared Sausalito, I had raised my career from one of carpenter or assistant cameraman to extra, then to bit player, then to supporting actor. As we walked up the ferry approach, I was co-starring with Harold Lloyd, and as we disembarked at the Hyde Street wharf, I was giving technical and professional advice to the comedian.

In Josh's car, Pearl and I discussed various aspects of our movie careers, and how we could get Merle to join us while excluding Axel, who always gummed up everything.

Josh pointed out some more buildings as he drove us to Haight. On Sutter he showed us a building with a front made completely of glass, with some fire escapes rigged near the two front corners. I'd never seen a glass building before and neither had Pearl.

At Union Square we took a left and passed a huge hotel. Josh pointed and said, "That's where Fatty Arbuckle ended his career."

The St. Francis. Both Pearl and I knew that hotel. Its name had been burned into our minds two years before by the Church Women United for Decency in American Life.

When movie comedian Fatty Arbuckle went on trial for the manslaughter death of starlet Virginia Rappé, his guilt was a forgone conclusion among nearly all the women in our town and the surrounding countryside. The only question was how he committed the homicidal act. One school of thought said that he crushed the poor young thing beneath his great weight and animalistic passion while attempting to complete the sex act on the drunken and/or drugged, but still game, girl. The other school claimed that Fatty was in no condition to do what he wanted to do and had resorted to the use of a whisky bottle, which severely injured the struggling Virginia, who hemorrhaged to death while Fatty nonchalantly returned to the party he was hosting.

Regardless of the school to which any of our ladies belonged, Arbuckle was a blackguard, and no regular method of civilized execution—be it hanging, shooting, or electrocution—was excruciating enough to expiate his crime. Some of the more unrefined women trimmed the borders of indelicacy in their fervent desire to give birth to a commensurate punishment.

When Silas Warner, the owner of the Blackstone Theater, innocently scheduled a Fatty Arbuckle comedy, our town's church women flew into action. The ladies from the Methodist, Nazarene, Baptist, Congregational, Lutheran (all three varieties—German, Norwegian, and Swedish), and German Evangelical Reformed churches fashioned a committee, which called for a meeting. Even the women from the small, but noisy, congregation we called Holy Rollers decided unanimously to join. The only women who did not meet with the others were the

Catholics, and most of them would have if the priest hadn't warned them off.

A couple evenings before Fatty's movie was to start, the ladies met, along with their daughters, in the Methodist Church. They were all dressed in white, just like the suffragettes. Of course, Ma, Mrs. Potman, Elizabeth, Susan, Carrie, Emily, and Cecilia were there, but no men (or boys) were allowed.

Later, Ma told me they listened to speakers, prayed, and sang in the church. At eight o'clock they emerged and began a torchlight parade. I don't know why they did that because it was still light out, but they lit their torches and headed down Villard toward the Blackstone.

The twins and I, plus a lot of other boys, dogs, and curious men, followed along on the sidewalk. The ladies and girls were carrying signs and singing "Onward, Christian Soldiers" and "The Battle Hymn of the Republic."

It was only two blocks to the theater, but they marched slowly enough that they finished both hymns. Some of the Holy Roller women shouted in tongues, threw fits, and fell to the street, foaming at the mouth, but as soon as the last marcher passed them, they would get up and hurry to take their places in line. The Holy Rollers were generally skinny and pale women, with their long hair put up in buns. Their husbands were the quiet, round-shouldered men in the sidewalk crowd, walking together in a humorless knot.

The marchers formed a fiery semi-circle in front of the Blackstone and demanded to see Mr. Warner, who quickly appeared. He was his own projectionist and a movie was on.

After the mayor's wife presented him with a petition signed by all the females present and calling for the immediate cancellation of the Fatty film or the boycott of all future features at the Blackstone, Mr. Warner read it and hastily agreed. His voice quavered as he witnessed to the fact that he approved of the ladies' position and hadn't thought thoroughly enough about the ramifications of his scheduling of the Arbuckle picture. As of that very moment, he pledged, the offending motion picture was cancelled.

Mr. Warner's wispy white hair swirled around in the evening breeze, and the torches lit up the trickles of sweat on his forehead. The white-clad crowd gave him three cheers, some of the men joining in, and marched back to the church for hymns and prayers of thanksgiving.

I was standing in front of Tubby Herfendahl, a ten-year old whose only claim to fame was an uncanny resemblance to the ill-fated comedian, and during the cheers he let loose with a raspberry, but none of the women heard him.

No other Fatty films ever came to our town again, and though he wasn't one of my favorite comedians, the twins and I missed the antics of the round-faced man who appeared so gentle on the screen, but who proved himself to be so vile in real life.

After Josh let us off, we sat on the rooming house steps for awhile, talking about what stardom could do to people, people like Arbuckle, Wally Reid, Mabel Normand, or Mary Miles Minter, all surrounded by scandal.

Pearl started fiddling with his fingers and then said, "Lige, if you want to go to Hollywood and be a star, go ahead, but I don't think I will. I'm not ready for it."

I thought about the St. Francis, parties, booze, drugs, the suicide of Olive Thomas, and the death of director William Desmond Taylor. On the other hand, there were Douglas Fairbanks, Rudolph Valentino, Ramon Navarro, John Gilbert, even Tom Mix, and the way the girls in our town responded to them. That almost convinced me, but a fiery crowd in white flashed in my mind, and I said, "I'm not, either. I think I just want to go back home and finish school. That's enough for right now."

We went inside and never mentioned stardom to Merle . . . or to Axel.

CHAPTER XLV

A few days later I got to go to Chinatown, where Josh lived. Axel was better and had been getting out some, so he and the twins came along after we had eaten supper.

We dropped off the cable car at Powell and Bush and walked east on Bush to Grant Avenue. We took a left at Grant, which narrowed down as we headed north uphill to Pine Street. On the northwest corner of Grant and Pine were two large buildings that didn't look Chinese. On the corner of the next block stood a large Catholic Cathedral.

Pearl said, "I thought this was Chinatown. It don't look any different to me."

"Yes, it does," Merle said, pointing to our left. Two buildings, one on the southwest corner of California and Grant and a yellow brick one on the northwest corner, displayed a pagoda-style, stretching up several stories.

"Now you're talkin'," Pearl said.

"Say, didn't we see them the day we got into San Francisco?" I asked.

"I don't know," Merle said. "I don't remember much about that day."

"Don't remind me," Axel said, touching his nose lightly.

We kept going north, crossing Sacramento. Halfway up the block, across Grant to our right, a street led off to the east, and we could see the Ferry Building. On our left was a building with three balconies and a pagoda-style roof. Josh was standing at an entrance, talking to a Chinaman, who drifted away as we approached.

Josh took us up two flights of stairs and down a short hallway to a door with an orange paper banner that had black Chinese characters on each side. Pearl touched it and looked at the writing. "It says 'May all who enter here have good luck'," Josh said, as he unlocked the door.

He had us remove our boots—"an old Oriental custom"—and leave them by the door. The apartment had low tables, some pictures of pale landscapes with Chinese writing on them, a few pillows with silk pillow cases, and a soft carpet on the floor with some kind of padding under it that made it even softer. There were several hundred books in a large bookcase.

I noticed how clean the place was. Josh had never been one to do much cleaning in our room back home, so it seemed like he'd changed into a new person.

There wasn't a chair in the place, at least in the living room—I never saw the kitchen or the bedroom.

Josh put our jackets and caps in a closet and then sat on the living room carpet, pulled over a couple of pillows, and leaned on them. We did the same. He asked Axel how he was and if we'd eaten. When we said we had, he offered us tea. Everyone accepted, but maybe out of politeness. The twins hated tea.

The tea must have been done already because he was back inside of two minutes. I put the cup to my lips. It smelled like tea, but it tasted a lot milder than the Lipton's Ma brewed at home. I put the cup down on the saucer resting on the low table.

We all said the tea was good, but I noticed that the level of the twins' tea never went down. I figured they were keeping their lips closed when they tipped their cups and only pretended to drink. I didn't care. I would have done the same thing if it had been buttermilk.

We talked a little about how long Josh had lived in Chinatown and about Harding, who was sick in the Palace Hotel. Josh said that both President Wilson and Harding had been sick in San Francisco. Axel told Josh about his family, leaving out the *Eastland*. Soon we were out of things to say so Josh got out the game of Mah Jongg.

I didn't like the game, though Ma and her friends were devoted to it. Josh didn't join in either, so we sat off by ourselves as the twins and Axel drew tiles, looking for the elusive fourteen. Axel had played quite a bit in Chicago and kept up a running commentary on his past successes and present chances. The twins knew the game through their mother.

The tiles clicked as Josh and I sat in silence. Finally, I said, "Back on Mount Tamalpais you said you believed in God, right?"

"Yes."

"But you don't believe the Bible?"

"I believe the Bible is the best expression of Man's attempt to reach out toward an understanding of God, and when the Bible truly gives us insight and knowledge, I believe in it."

"Who's to say when it does and when it doesn't?"

"Ultimately, I do, or you do."

"Then we could have 130 million different religions."

"We could, but we won't. People of similar views will join together in churches and continue their search. And what difference does it make how many religions we have? All you have to do is trust yourself within the bonds of rigorous thinking, and let the others do the same."

"How?"

"By using your rational powers, your logical powers, the God-given faculty that sets you apart from all other animals. God empowered you with a self-conscious mind, and you are responsible for using that mind to form your own beliefs and to base your actions on them, and, when you stand before the throne of God on Judgment Day, you will be judged on those beliefs and those actions. And you won't be able to say you were misled by Rev. Black or Billy Sunday or Luther or Wesley or Pope Pius XI or Moses or Muhammed or Buddha or whoever. God will judge you as an individual with free will to make decisions either good or ill, and you will answer for them."

Josh sipped his tea and the tiles kept clicking, then he continued. "Human nature is such that you have to act and you have to choose, and it's better to rest your choices on your own mental processes than on your emotions, your will power, or someone else's choices. You are the one who is responsible for your own life."

"Yes, but . . ."

"There are no 'but's'. Listen—think a thought, any thought."

I thought.

If you did not exist, you couldn't have a thought. Right?"

"Right."

"But you did think. Right?"

"Right."

"So now you have proven your mind exists. And you can be fairly certain that your mind perceives physical things more-or-less as they are, so you can believe that the world exists, too."

"Well . . ." I hesitated.

Josh reached over and took my cup. My hand automatically went out to stop him. "Hey, that one's mine."

"Right. Now you've proven that I exist, and so does this cup, and so does your hand."

"I guess so."

"Don't guess. Think."

"O.K . . . . Yes, they exist."

"All right, you exist as an individual in a world of real objects that was created by God, who also created other individuals. In this world you must make choices, you're not God's puppet. He lets you choose to do or not to do things. Some of these choices further the cause of evil because in a world of choice, evil must necessarily exist. Choosing evil can cause pain to others or to yourself. You will answer for that pain and that evil. And you won't be able to hide, excuse, explain away, or ignore the evil you choose, so you'd better get control of your life and work on it to the point where, when you stand before God, you won't have to cringe about it."

I saw myself, little and naked, standing in front of a huge chair with a giant sitting in it. The giant had a long white robe, his hair was long and white, and he was yelling at me. I said to Josh, "Explain about Hell again."

"I think there is a place of punishment for those who have deliberately chosen to invoke evil in a repetitious pattern in their lives, but I don't worship a God who would burn a human being for all eternity. I think that after a certain amount of punishment, the body and the soul and the evil therein are destroyed completely, never to exist again."

I wiped some perspiration off my forehead and stood up. I went over to the open window and looked out on Grant Avenue. It was getting late, but there were still dozens of Oriental people hurrying on the sidewalks—old men and women moving slower, younger ones going faster, except for a young woman carrying a small baby on the east side of the street. She was walking north very slowly and seemed to be looking at me.

Josh must have seen me sweating because he went to the kitchen and got us some lemonade. While he was gone, I looked at his books. Most of them dealt with religion, economics, philosophy, history, and political theory. There were a few novels and collections of short stories. The only poets I saw were Homer, Dante, Chaucer, and Milton, but Shakespeare's poems were probably in the two volumes of his *Collected Works*.

When he handed me a lemonade, I said, "I didn't know you could read Chinese."

"I can't."

"Why do you have these books, then?" I pointed to a small group of oversized books in Chinese.

"They belong to a friend. I'm keeping them for awhile."

The game didn't last much longer than the lemonade. While the twins and Axel gathered up the tiles, Josh said to me, "Someday something will happen in your life, Lige, and you'll realize the truth of what I've been telling you, that you own your own life and have to make the ultimate decisions regarding it."

I looked directly at him and he squared up to me and said, "It doesn't have to be a big thing. I'll tell you what mine was. Remember the winter I came home on furlough?"

"Yeah."

"Remember when I took your sled out to the hill? I ran and slammed down on it, and I went sailing down that hill faster and farther than I'd ever done before. It was cold, and the wind was tearing my eyes, when, suddenly, it came to me—that I was an individual as responsible for my own behavior as I was for guiding that sled. Remember when I stopped."

"Yeah, we were cheerin' for you 'cause you'd set a record."

"That's right, but I just got up, gave you the sled, and left. I went back home, polished my boots, and washed and ironed my uniform. I tried to keep busy, but that night I lay in bed and thought about what it means to be an individual who must make moral choices in a world like ours."

"You left the next day."

"Yeah, I cut my stay short. I had to get out of the nest, so to speak. I had to live my own responsibility."

"Like breakin' fingers?"

Josh stared at me, then he reached out and took my glass. "Yeah, like breakin' fingers, if it comes to that." He walked into the kitchen.

A few minutes later we thanked Josh for the evening and went back to the boarding house.

The newspapers said Harding was much improved.

CHAPTER XLVI

I read in the papers how Florence Harding, called "Duchess" by her husband, had become fatigued in Alaska and some changes were made in the President's schedule. The Hardings left Alaska on July 23 and were in Vancouver, British Columbia, on July 25. The presidential ship, the *USS Henderson*, accidentally rammed a destroyer, the *Zeilen*, some forty miles north of Seattle on July 26, but the President and his wife were not hurt.

The President's train sped across Washington and Oregon, heading for Yosemite on July 27, but Harding became ill, and the train was diverted to San Francisco.

The downtown area was awash in flags, bunting, and presidential emblems on the morning of Sunday, July 29, when Harding and his wife entered his sickroom on the eighth floor of the Palace Hotel. All airplane flights over downtown San Francisco were forbidden because the noise might disturb the recovery of the Chief Executive.

No one knew for certain what ailed the President. Some said he was just tired from overwork. A medical release stated that he had bronchial-pneumonia.

Axel commented that it was certainly ptomaine poisoning brought on by eating copper-tainted crab in Alaska. He got that from a girl he had taken up with from the boarding house. Sadie claimed to be a nurse and was very concerned with Axel's damaged nose.

The twins said Sadie hadn't paid much attention to him until Axel showed her some of the money that he had wired to him. Then her sympathies were aroused and the two suddenly became a couple.

She was short, plump, and plain. I could have ignored her easily, but one of her upper front teeth was stunted and looked as if it had a growth of grainy yellow "fur" on it. Seeing that "fur" whenever she talked or smiled made me dislike her.

The twins called her the "Gold Digger" behind her back. I thought of her as "Fur Tooth."

On Wednesday, August 1, the papers announced that the President was on the road to recovery. His temperature was better and his lung condition slightly improved.

The next day his temperature was normal and he was feeling much better.

At 7:32 that evening Warren Gamaliel Harding, twenty-ninth President of the United States, died.

The twins and I were sitting on the boarding house stoop. Pearl, who was upset that the broadcast of the President's address on KPO had been cancelled, was saying that with Harding's improvement maybe he could make the speech before he left the city.

The landlady was playing her phonograph. She loved "Yes, We Have No Bananas" and "Barney Google." Mrs. Byrd reminded me of Ma.

Just as Pearl stopped talking, Axel and Sadie came running across the street.

"The President's dead!"

"We heard it on the street car!"

Mrs. Byrd came out on the porch and so did several boarders. Axel repeated what he'd heard and then all of us ran to the radio. Mrs. Byrd rarely listened to it so it hadn't been playing that evening. She turned it on and got nothing but static out of the big horn-like speaker. She fiddled around with the controls and the static got worse.

Pearl said, "Lemme try." He monkeyed around for a few seconds, and suddenly a voice came on ". . . Mrs. Harding had been reading an article, 'A Calm View of a Calm Man'. She had paused and the President said, 'That's good. Go on. Read some more.' She did so and then looked at him. She thought at first he was asleep, but when he failed to make any response to her, she called the doctor who pronounced the President dead. The cause of death apparently is cerebral apoplexy. Mrs. Harding has withstood the shock well and the funeral train will leave San Francisco at 7 P.M. tomorrow . . ."

"It was ptomaine poisoning," Axel said.

"Shut up, you little rat!" Mr. Cooper, a boarder who had taken a strong dislike to Axel, grabbed him. As Axel twisted away, he knocked the radio and the static returned. By the time Pearl had KPO back, they were playing some mournful music, and Axel and Mr. Cooper were glaring at each other from opposite sides of the room.

Sadie was blubbering on Axel's shoulder.

CHAPTER XLVII

Every one of us went to bed stunned into almost total silence. I prayed for Mrs. Harding and the new President, but for the life of me, I couldn't remember his name.

After a mostly silent breakfast, before which Mrs. Byrd offered up a communal supplication for God's mercy, Axel, Sadie, the twins, and I hurried downtown to Market Street and the Palace Hotel.

Workmen were already busy taking down all the presidential decorations from the streets and buildings and were hanging black drapes and streamers across the building fronts.

We joined the crowd in front of the Palace. It was strange to be with so many people who were so quiet. Here and there were people whispering, and some of the ladies were snuffling into their handkerchiefs, but no one spoke out loud.

The presidential flag that had flown over the entrance to the Palace had been replaced by a large American flag at half-staff.

After we had been there awhile, the news went around that Calvin Coolidge had taken the oath of office from his father in Vermont and was the new president. I thought it strange that earlier I hadn't been able to recall the Vice President-turned-President's name.

At dinner time we ate in shifts. I don't know why, except we didn't want to miss anything, even though there was little to see. Axel and Sadie ate first. They were gone about an hour, which the rest of us thought was too much time.

The twins and I had to eat at a small place near Union Square because of the crowd. All three of us had double hot beef sandwiches, buttered green beans, and milk, and were just finishing when two men sat in a booth next to us. Both were drunk and both wore long coats.

After they settled in and ordered, each one pulled a bottle out of a deep coat pocket and took a snort. The one facing me wiped his mouth with the back of his hand and belched. "Wha' ya said before, Joe, tha's right. I heard it, too. Un'erneath it all, he was a nigger."

"Tha's right. A nigger."

"An' I'll say thiss, Joe. Th' only good nigger is a dead one."

"Tha's right. So he's a good un now." Joe laughed and so did the other man.

"Good an' dead." They laughed louder.

"Bu' at leas' we got us a white man in there now. Coolidge is from Ver . . . Vermont, an' so's my gran'folks an' people don't get no whiter."

"Coolidge, now there's a man. Not a goddam nigger."

The customers around Joe and the other man were listening and so were we.

"Harding's a louse, Joe."

"Tha's right. A louse. Why, when decen' folks can't buy a drink in public, he had all the booze he wanted righ' there in the White House."

"Here's ta crime," the other man said and they toasted each other and drank.

"Crime," Joe said. "I'll tell ya abou' crime. I got connections, p'litical connections, an' I'll tell ya right out, she did it, she kilt him."

A tall man who looked like he was dressed for business stood up and came over. He looked down at Joe and asked, "Whom do you mean by 'she'?"

Joe glared up. He had been trying to light a cigarette without success. He kept Business Suit waiting until he got it, and then, through a puff of smoke, said, "The Duchess, tha's who. The Duchess kilt him to keep . . ." That's all Joe got out before Business Suit grabbed him by the throat and began to choke him.

The man not named Joe picked up a table knife and raised it to stab Business Suit, but Pearl turned quickly and grabbed his wrist. He cursed Pearl and tried to stand up. Merle socked him on the chin and he went back down in the booth, out cold.

A half dozen men took hold of Joe, who was gagging and choking. They carried him outside, with a waiter holding the door, and the owner yelling, "Gid dem oud! Gid dem oud! I don't vant traidors in my plaze!" They dumped Joe in the gutter.

Pearl, Merle, and I followed, carrying the unconscious man. We heaved him on top of Joe. From inside, we watched as they both lay still for several minutes, then got up and staggered off, Joe holding his throat.

We paid for our meals, even though the owner wanted to put them on the house, but we were flush and didn't want to take anything for our patriotism.

We left the café amid cheers, handshakes, and backslaps. We headed down Geary and Market to the Palace. The crowd was larger and it took awhile to find Axel and Sadie. We saw a lot of men in uniform mixing with the civilians.

Working our way through the crowd as people milled around, we gained a good view of the main entrance doors. People went in and out, but no one that meant anything to us and so the afternoon passed.

A little past five we heard a man say the funeral service was being conducted in the Presidential Suite, so the men took off their hats and we took off our caps. A lot of the women were crying.

Those people closest to the doors said there were a lot of military men in the hotel lobby.

Axel and Sadie had gone off somewhere, but they came back and said the Navy Band was forming up at the entrance on New Montgomery Street, and that a hearse and some cars were already lined up there.

We inched our way around the hotel. On the other side of a line of cops, I saw the hearse—a Pierce-Arrow—and several limousines. The line of cops was unnecessary; everyone was quiet and orderly. About 6:30 I saw movement, the doors swung open, and the casket came out, carried by two soldiers, two sailors, two Marines, and two California National Guardsmen. It was accompanied by a general that some man near me said was "Black Jack," but a woman in back of me said, "You mean 'General Pershing'."

The band played "The Star-Spangled Banner" and everyone's hats came off again, then "Lead, Kindly Light," after which every woman I saw and a lot of the men were crying.

The casket looked gray. It was covered by an American flag, topped with a wreath of carnations. As the door of the hearse closed, the chimes of a cathedral tolled "Nearer My God To Thee."

The hearse went down the street, headed for the Southern Pacific station near Third and Townsend. The crowd was so quiet you could hear individuals sniffing into their handkerchiefs. Suddenly, some airplanes buzzed overhead, dropping hundreds of flowers.

Sadie said, "They were going to drop the flowers when the President left for Washington" and burst into tears. After the tears dried, she said, "Oh, poor Laddie Boy," and the tears flooded out again.

Laddie Boy was Harding's Airedale and I got a big lump in my throat because I started thinking about my dog, Ted, back home. After that I didn't think of Sadie as "Fur Tooth" anymore.

The crowd went completely silent when Mrs. Harding came out of the Palace on the arm of a general and got into a limousine, which moved slowly away, followed by other cars, infantry and cavalry units, and the Marine Band playing a slow, sad march.

We followed on foot the half mile to the station. The crowd kept us away from the train, which was covered with flowers and shrubbery, as was the platform.

A few minutes after Mrs. Harding boarded, the locomotive with black and white bunting draped on it chuffed the train into motion, and the cars with all their lights shining pulled away faster and faster. The people on the platform began singing "Lead, Kindly Light."

As the crowd left, a brilliant shaft of sunlight came through the clouds and made the sky above the Golden Gate a bright gold-red.

There was a gasp from the crowd as if we had seen God saying farewell to our President.

I felt that I had to speak to Josh.

CHAPTER XLVIII

The twins offered to go with me to Josh's, but I wanted to go alone, so they went off with Axel and Sadie. I walked over to Grant Avenue and headed up, with the crowd thinning out along the way and the complexion of the people changing until I was one of the few whites on the sidewalk.

I went into Josh's building, up the stairs, and knocked on his door. After I knocked again, he opened it slightly. "Lige? What do you want?" He opened the door a little more, but stood in the doorway.

"I just needed to talk with somebody about the President, I mean the old President. It's so terrible, you know."

"Yes. Say, can you just give me a few minutes to clean up in here? Why don't you go down to the market across the street and get us some cookies and something to drink. I'm fresh out. Then we can talk." He handed me a couple "cartwheels."

I didn't want to go or anything to eat or drink, but he stayed in the doorway so I went. It didn't take me long. The Chinaman in the market spoke enough English to understand, and I hurried back across Grant and up the narrow stairs, excusing myself past several Chinese—an old grandma, a man and his rather large family, a girl and her baby.

Josh met me at the door and let me in. The apartment was neat. He'd cleaned it up real nice and it smelled nice, too. I took off my boots; handed Josh the sack, his change, and the other cartwheel; pulled together some pillows; and sat by a low table. Josh went to the kitchen and brought back some cookies on a plate and the soda in two glasses. He put the plate and two saucers on the low table and the glasses on the saucers. He sat and took a drink.

Without thinking, I just began talking about what I'd seen and done that day, Harding, what a great man he'd been, how we'd all miss him, and how pitiful, but brave, his wife looked. I even told him about Joe and the man not named Joe.

Josh sat there nibbling over a plate and drinking.

When I'd finished, I think there were some tears in my eyes. Josh stood up and got a book from one of the shelves. He handed it to me. It was called *Untimely Papers*, and he showed me a sentence in it that was underlined. "War is the health of the State." I read it and re-read it. "What does it mean?"

"It means simply that we don't need a president, and that Harding's death removed one tyrant just to make room for another."

"What are ya talkin' about? Harding and Coolidge aren't tyrants."

"Anyone who rules me against my will and in violation of my rights is a tyrant."

"But Harding didn't get us into any wars. Wilson did, but it wasn't his fault. And now the Washington Naval Conference agreement will help end war. And Harding wanted us in the World Court."

"War won't end. Either war between nations or war against the people by the State. As long as there are States and leaders in those States who have no conception of human rights, there will be war. As you've just seen, Randolph Bourne wrote that the State thrives on war. War helps the State, strengthens its power, and allows it to crush its critics."

"But you were in the Army and now you're workin' for the Army. Does that mean your actions are immoral?"

Josh laughed. "You're starting to think, Lige. That's good. In a way it is immoral to serve something you don't believe in and to work with things you oppose. But you also have to take into consideration the alternatives. Because I oppose taxes as immoral, should I stop driving the highways, using the post office, or suing in court? Or should I refuse to pay my taxes at all and end up in prison? Maybe I should, and maybe someday I will, but not right now. I have other duties for the cause of freedom. The State's tentacles have wrapped so tightly around us that it is almost impossible to live a completely moral life, except as a hermit or a yardbird, and in each case, to choose that life is to reduce your own humanness. So I have chosen to compromise, if you want to call it that, but next year I'll be working at a different job, away from the Army, maybe away from San Francisco."

"What are ya gonna do?"

"It's not final yet, so I won't say. What I want to do has no connection with the government, so I'll be a little more moral, I guess."

"O.K., but I still don't see what kickin' the Kaiser in the pants did to our freedom."

"You were young—what, maybe twelve or thirteen during the War?"

"Yeah, both."

"Well, I heard Woodrow Wilson's guns at Vera Cruz in 1914, but I was still in junior high school, so I couldn't go. In the spring of 1916, Black Jack Pershing went chasin' Pancho Villa around northern Mexico."

"You mean the Mexican bandit who was killed a coupla weeks back?"

"Yeah, that's the guy. One day Warren Eldridge from just west of town . . ."

"I know him."

". . . and I got to talkin', and one thing led to another, and the next week we were hitchin' a freight to California to join up and fight Villa."

"I remember. Ma cried for a week."

"I'm sorry for that."

"But ya never did go to Mexico, did ya."

"No. Nobody would have believed it to look at tall, lanky Warren, but he couldn't stay on a horse to save his soul. When the cavalry rejected him, we transferred to the infantry and kicked around some posts in California and Texas awhile. Early in 1917 I was sent to the Presidio."

"And you never went to France."

"Nope, and neither did Warren. Some of us in the Old Army had it a little better than the greenhorns. They shipped over pretty fast, but then they were a lot more eager, at least the first few months. Army life for most men is disillusionment and doubly so in wartime. There really isn't anything very patriotic about going into someone else's country to fight a war. What it actually boils down to is a bunch of men being forced by spit, polish, brass, and a flag to bear the burdens of Great Power politics."

"What d'ya mean 'Great Power'?"

"Those powers that can handle any other power head to head. But the 'Great' I disagree with. As historians use it, 'Great' refers to military and economic aggressiveness, the triumph of Force and the victory of violence. To me the greatness of a power lies in its recognition of the human rights of life, liberty, and property, and the determination to base its policies on those rights. The only force necessary for a 'Great Power' is that necessary to defend those rights."

"But isn't that what our government does?"

"No, especially not in this century and especially not since the War. With every crisis, military or economic, the federal government has built up its power, and what is particularly hard to take is the fact that most Americans, heirs to a system of human rights never seen before in history—not in Athens or Rome or England—have accepted the build-up of that government power with little or no resistance. And it is a build-up which will continue until it has reduced individual liberty in this nation to the point where the United States will be indistinguishable from a myriad of other societies throughout history where the individual was subordinate to the State, the person to the Sovereign, the slave to the Master."

"That's not happening here."

"No, not right now. In fact, we seem to be in a period of remission from the Statist infection of the War period. But with the next crisis the power-lust of the State will be back with a vengeance."

"But what happened during the War that was so bad? We won."

"I'm not referring to the outcome on the battlefields of France. I'm more concerned about the lack of opposition to the build-up of governmental domestic power during the War."

"Such as?"

"First of all, and in many ways the most morally reprehensible, was the draft. Do you remember Wilson running for re-election in 1916 on the slogan 'He Kept Us Out of War'?"

"Yeah, it's the first presidential campaign I do remember."

"And five months after he won, Wilson asked Congress for a declaration of war."

"Yeah?"

"What most people don't know is that Wilson approved a draft bill, which was sent to Congress the day before he asked for war, despite the fact that he had always stood for a volunteer Army. A draft is slavery, pure and unadulterated, and most Americans supported it. They were willing to lie in their cozy little beds at night and send their sons or the sons of their friends off to the mud, vermin, agony, and death of the Western Front, as long as the boys went off under a flag, a slogan, and a prayer. And regardless of the denial of liberty involved. Sure, there were some Socialists and the Wobblies who opposed the draft, but only because they weren't running the show. Socialists oppose drafts if they seem to be in defense of capitalism, not the drafts themselves. In fact, many Socialists probably support drafting people, not just to defend a socialist nation, but to fill social-service jobs, once again showing their blindness to human rights."

I thought of Bob Kreutzer and Ray Larkin.

"Then partly to defend the draft and partly to enable the government to control the Socialists, Wobblies, and pacifists, Congress passed the Espionage Act and the Sedition Act—out with the First Amendment and freedom of speech, in with censorship and government control. Citizens who in good conscience spoke out within the limits of human and constitutional rights ended up in prison. Eugene Debs was just the most famous victim. People were jailed for two years, five years, ten years for speaking their minds. A film producer in Los Angeles was given a ten-year sentence because his motion picture showed British soldiers bayonetting Americans during the Revolution, and Britain was an important ally in the War, historical accuracy be hanged. A Eureka, California, man was given five years at hard labor for criticizing Wilson. The Sedition Act gave Postmaster General Burleson power to open anyone's mail and to revoke the second-class mailing permits of any newspaper or magazine. Not many Socialist periodicals outlasted the War. And do you know what is just as bad?"

"What?"

The Supreme Court has upheld those laws and the power of the government to impose slavery on a select minority and to suppress freedom of speech and press during times of crisis, as declared by the government itself. What legal safeguards do we have left to protect those vital freedoms during government-defined crises?"

I couldn't think of any, but then I'd never realized the extent to which the government had expanded its powers during the War. Boss and Bear hadn't talked about it. Only Twig was mad about the railroads, so I said, "What about the railroad take-over?"

"Yes, that. One part of a larger picture. During the War the federal government empowered itself to dominate the economy and eliminate or severely restrict free choice, and the people who did it now present it as a record to be proud of."

He went to his bookcase and got two books. He handed them to me—one, about government control and operation of industry in both Great Britain and the United States during the War, written by Charles Baker; the other was *Industrial America in The World War* by Grosvenor Clark. I put them on the table.

"During the War the federal government regulated shipping rates for waterborne carriers; constructed and operated ships; controlled food, feed, and fuel production, distribution, and use, as well as prices; supervised, browbeat, strong armed, and had the legal right to confiscate all major American industries; set industrial commodity prices; solved labor-management disputes with cost-price contracts which increased the economic burden on the average citizens; took over and ran the railroads, which were in a period of decline as a direct result of government policies; and raised taxes. Woodrow Wilson became our political and economic king, confirmed by the Overman Act in 1918, and Bernard Baruch became his prime minister. Or maybe I should say his 'crime' minister. The then Assistant Secretary of the Navy, that Roosevelt who ran for vice president with Cox in 1920, said that during the War years, he broke so many laws he could have gone to jail for nine hundred years. Just think if people like that ever got into positions of real power."

"They won't. We won't let 'em."

"But if they do get power, the Supreme Court has made it easy for them because it has upheld the government position in every case questioning the powers assumed by the federal government over the economy during the War. Freedom is sitting on a time bomb, waiting for a crisis to set it off."

"And then what?"

"America isn't immune from demagogues, and if Americans look to the State for more so-called solutions, the time is coming for an

American Lenin, or, more likely, an American Fascisti, someone like Mussolini."

"The government, the State, can't solve problems?"

"Not without violating basic human rights, making the solution worse than the condition."

"Josh, are you . . . are you an anarchist?"

"Yes, any logical person devoted to individual freedom has to be just by pursuing his own rational thought."

CHAPTER XLIX

I had seen certain cartoon drawings of anarchists in one of Bear's books. They were Russians with long hair and beards that stuck out, and they carried bombs with the fuses lit in their hands. They were dangerous and people were supposed to report them. I sat in silence.

"Look," Josh said, "when we were talking here the other night, I thought you agreed that you exist as an individual, that other individuals exist independent of you, and that physical objects also exist."

"Yes, I do."

"All right, in this world nothing is guaranteed to you except death. Birth is a one-way ticket to death. All of the living you do is based on action, on choosing. Every human being because they are human must make choices since we don't have instincts to the extent other animals do, and our best guide for making choices is our ability to reason, to think logically, to realize that 'A is A' and act on that knowledge. Unless you are feebleminded or senile or not yet mature, you have this ability, if you work at it. It's what makes you human. Emotions don't. Even dogs can love and be loyal."

I thought of Ted and Laddie Boy.

"So we're all born equal to the extent that we can reason. If we truly believe that, then each person should be able to run his or her own life on the basis of the choices made by reasoning, as long as force is not used to violate the right of other people to run their own lives. Do you see that?"

It made sense to me so I answered, "Yes."

"There are only two alternatives to being responsible for your own life. One is that everyone reasons for everyone else in the entire world. That isn't a true alternative because it is physically impossible for me or you to reason for Mussolini or Leonard Wood or they for us. The only real alternative is to have a select group of individuals reason for the rest of us. What that means is that the reasoning group allows itself to become truly human by making choices based on their own thinking, but they deny the rest of us our humanness because we have to obey them instead of relying on our own ability to reason and make choices. And this is precisely what any government, any State does. Its leaders fulfill their human nature by choosing, but deny the rest of us our right to choose for ourselves under penalty of arrest, fine, and imprisonment."

"So you have become an anarchist."

"Only in anarchy can we be human because only in anarchy are we free to choose."

"But anarchy means the end of everything—no schools, no libraries, no highways, no police, no civilization."

"Only if you subscribe to a peculiarly Russian variation. I don't see why all these things would disappear under my form of anarchy."

"Because who would pay for them?"

"The people who want them would. Aren't schools, highways, and police important to people?"

"Yes, of course."

"More important than soap or bicycles or motion pictures, and yet those things are all produced without government control. Why not things that most people value highly?"

"Maybe some people wouldn't pay for schools."

"And if they didn't want to, why should you make them? In doing so, aren't you destroying their right to choose, their liberty, as well their right to control their own property, their money?"

"But what if some people spend their money on bootleg booze instead of supporting their local schools?"

"What if they do? It's their right, even though you and I may think they are wrong."

"What makes it their right?"

"Because they are human and humans have three rights. Each of us has the right to own his or her life; each of us has the right to control and order his or her own life, under any value system, as long as it doesn't destroy someone else's right to do the same; and all of us can use our lives to labor in the production of a previously unowned good and make it our property, and then destroy, keep, sell, barter, or give it away without fear of outside interference. That's all the rights we have, but they are morally inviolate. If a human being produces a good or service without infringing on someone else's rights, and exchanges it, he or she has the right to the ownership of the money obtained, and not you nor I nor the government has any moral right to take it away or to divert part of it, even for a high-minded purpose. You can't reduce anyone else's three basic human rights in order to provide someone else with a so-called 'human right' and leave yourself any claim to moral integrity."

I drank some soda and tried to mull over what he had said, but there was so much, and it was so new to me, that the silence in the room began playing on me. Finally, I said, "Where do you get your ideas?"

"Oh, from my books and from discussions."

"I don't think I could come up with ideas like these."

"Maybe, maybe not, but you could learn to challenge yourself and sharpen your thinking on the ideas of great thinkers. Wait here." He got out a pencil and paper and went over to one section of his bookcase. "There's one here in French by Etienne de La Boetie which my friend reads to me, but I won't put it on this list."

When he came back, he handed me a list of authors, each with at least one and many with several book titles behind their names: Plato, Aristotle, St. Augustine, St. Thomas Aquinas, Descartes, Thomas Hobbes, Spinoza, John Locke, Adam Smith, Thomas Paine, J.B. Say, Thomas Jefferson, Richard Cobden, Frederic Bastiat, Emerson, Thoreau, Darwin, Lysander Spooner, Benjamin Tucker, Herbert Spencer, Lord Acton, W. Stanley Jevons, William Smart, Albert Jay Nock, and H.L. Mencken.

"The last two are fairly recent authors, but they show promise. You might find Spooner, Tucker, and Smart hard to locate, but the rest are all available, and I'll mail you some addresses where you can order them after you get home."

"Thanks. Do you believe everything in those books?"

"Of course not. In fact, some of them contradict each other, but they have all influenced me in some way or another."

"But what you have accepted from them tells you that without a government, people will pay for an army, a policeman, a street, and a high school."

"They will pay if that's what they want. And if it's not what they will pay for, then the leaders of the government who tax those who do not want those things are acting immorally, without any ethical sanction except their own value system. In doing so, they are destroying humanity. The truth is that political action is always the enforcement of value judgments at the point of a gun."

"What if someone hasn't paid for a policeman and the policeman sees him being robbed?"

"Those who hired the policeman will stipulate in their contracts with him what his action should be in that circumstance. He will know what to do in advance, dependent on his contract."

"What if a man won't pay to support an army or navy, but lives in an area protected by them."

"That's a tough one which I haven't worked out yet. Right now, I would say that unless there is an invasion, not a whole lot can be done about him. He will just have to benefit, and others will have to make that a part of their value system in determining how much they will pay to support their armed forces. In the case of invasion, the man will have to put up or lose everything."

I felt good that I finally found something Josh didn't have an answer for. I was almost ready to leave, but I needed to find out one more thing.

"Didn't you feel anything for Harding?"

"I was glad when he pardoned Debs, and he didn't involve us in any wars. He also steered us out of the post-war depression quickly by doing nothing, but the presidency is the single-most immoral office in the United States, and the man who occupies it acts immorally just in carrying out his duties. To that extent, I felt nothing but contempt for Mr. Harding as president. As a human being, Harding was luckier than many in that he didn't suffer much in death. I was happy for that. But from what I know, Harding was about as far removed from the life of the mind as you can get. Because of that, he was a failed person and I'm sorry for him." He picked up the two books and put them back in their places.

I stood up. "Aren't there any presidents you liked?"

Josh turned. "William Henry Harrison. He only served thirty days and was busy dying through most of them, so he did less than any other president to destroy human rights. I appreciate that."

I didn't have anything else to say. Josh was my brother, but he thought a lot differently about things than I did. He walked me to the door and we said good night.

I put on my boots and opened the door, then Josh said, "Lige, before you go, I've said a lot of things about reason and rational thought determining your actions, and that is important."

"O.K."

But I don't want you to leave here believing that the thought processes of one or even a small group of individuals are complex and powerful enough to infuse and correctly control an entire economic or social system."

"What d'ya mean?"

"I don't think a dictator-genius can run an economic/social system in a way that will protect human rights, administer justice based on the inviolability of those rights, and provide efficiency and material prosperity in production. And if he or he and his advisors try it, the system will fail."

"What will work then?"

"The only system that can simultaneously produce goods efficiently and protect human rights is laissez-faire capitalism built on a foundation of liberal political and human rights theory pushed by logic to anarchy."

There it was again—anarchy. I was with him all the way to the end. I knew something about Smith and Locke and I could read more when I got back home, but I always lost him when he plunged into anarchy. I shook my head and said good night.

I was two blocks down Grant when I remembered that I was going to tell Josh that I'd be leaving with the twins and Axel on Monday. I hurried back up Grant to his building, took the stairs two at a time, and went to his apartment. I didn't think I needed to knock so I just opened the door.

A Chinese girl was standing with her back to me, her long hair ebony on green and gold, a combination I'd seen earlier in the evening on the lower stairs. Josh was on the floor playing with the baby and they were all laughing. I could see it was a boy; it was naked on the blanket.

I almost spoke, but then I realized that the baby was Josh's. He was my nephew. The girl was my sister-in-law, if they were married. Did Josh have a wedding ring? I hadn't noticed. I felt funny looking at Josh and two people he hadn't introduced me to, for whatever reason, so I backed out and started to close the door when Josh's eyes came up and locked into mine.

I shut the door and left.

No one came after me.

CHAPTER L

I called Josh the next day and he said he'd try to see me before we left. Neither of us mentioned the girl or the baby.

Axel waited until the night before we were to leave to tell Sadie, and when he did, she went nuts. She said she loved him and wanted to get married. Axel said he was sorry, and she began to yell so loudly that Mrs. Byrd had to come up and settle her down. The twins and I just sat there.

After Mrs. Byrd left, Sadie was crying on the bed. I wanted to go to my own room, but as I got up, Sadie said, "Ax, we have to get married."

"Wh—what?"

"We *have* to get married. You know what I mean."

I hadn't seen too many guys blush, but Axel turned red. He lit a cigarette and walked to the window. Everything was quiet, except Sadie's sniffles.

After the cigarette was half gone, Axel turned and said, "O.K. O.K. We'll get married."

Sadie vaulted off the bed toward Axel, but Merle grabbed her arm and held her back.

Axel got mad. "Damnit, Merle. Leave her be!"

"Listen," Merle said, pushing Axel back. "She's not pregnant. There's no way she can be pregnant or no way she'd know it yet. You've only known her two-and-a-half weeks. How could she know . . . if it's yours, that is."

I was glad Mrs. Potman had taught the twins something about sex.

Sadie shrieked and tried to rake her nails across Merle's face. He caught her wrist and she started bawling. She pulled free and flung herself on the bed.

Merle came over and said in a low voice that it was his duty to get Axel home safe, then he'd break every bone in his body and ship him to Chicago in an orange crate.

An idea came to me and I left. As I closed the door, the bed squeaked and Sadie said, "If we don't get married, I'll do away with myself. I don't care."

I walked over to Cooper's room and knocked. I heard him move away from the door and then call, "Come in." He was pretending he'd dozed off in his chair. I let him pretend.

I explained how if Axel left that he could have Sadie all to himself again, so he should help us leave.

"How?"

"Get us some booze."

"It's Sunday night. Where would I get booze?"

"Don't kid me. Do ya want Sadie or not?"

"How's booze gonna help?"

"It will. Just get it." I held out a wad of bills. He hesitated and then took them.

"How long?" I asked.

"A half hour."

"Make it quicker."

"I'll try."

He was back in twenty minutes. I had him help me doctor the booze so some of it was full strength, some of it was cut in half by water, and some of it was water colored with booze. Then I went to Axel's room.

Sadie was trying to get at the window, but Pearl had her blocked off. It was only a second-story window, so the fall probably wouldn't have killed her, but Pearl wasn't taking any chances. Sadie was spouting rat poison, razors, pistols, hanging, drowning, gas. She didn't need a window. Axel was sitting beside an ashtray buried under ash and butts.

I put Cooper's glasses and the bottles on a table and nodded Merle over. "Go along with me on this."

He looked hard at me, and I said, "Hold it, hold it. If both Axel and Sadie want to get married, I don't think we should say no."

"What?" Pearl was surprised, but then shut up when Merle gave him the high sign.

I proposed toasting the lucky couple and passed around the well-watered stuff to the twins and kept one for myself, the fifty percent to Axel, and the real red-eye to Sadie, who at first refused.

Axel drank, but he must have thought everything was watered because he never said anything, just motioned for another hit. He sat on the bed with Sadie, and soon they were drinking and hugging, then drinking and talking, then drinking and laughing.

Sadie kept draining hers into an apparently hollow leg because I had to send Cooper out for more hooch. After he rapped on the door and passed it in, it wasn't long before both Axel and Sadie were sprawled out snoring. Sadie's was louder because of a peculiar resonance the gap around her stunted tooth added to the noise. The twins and I didn't feel a thing, except my bladder was aching.

The twins lifted Sadie by the armpits and knees and I opened the door. Out into the hallway we went, down to her room with Cooper's eyes peering out from behind his door. We placed her on the bed. The thought of undressing her fled my mind like dirty water out of a bathtub.

We packed our clothes and gear into some new suitcases we'd purchased and did the same for Axel. We already had our train tickets.

I was too keyed up to sleep so I asked Pearl if he wanted to take a walk. He told Merle, who said he'd stand watch.

We walked west on Haight, with the lights of the city dimmed by a cold fog. At the end of Haight, we went north a couple blocks and entered Golden Gate Park.

We passed a stone building on our right; the fog seemed to be swirling around it. We had come to the park before, but hadn't stayed too long, and though we knew the stone building, we were soon in uncharted territory.

We came to a cross looming up out of the fog and found that it was on a bluff. We walked up to it. Fog was moistening it and dripping off the crossbar like gray blood. The moon in its last quarter was above the cross and to the west. Sometimes the fog blotted it out.

"Hadn't we better pray?" Pearl asked.

"Yeah."

We both kneeled in the fog. I prayed for a safe trip home and forgiveness for getting Sadie drunk. I could have prayed for Josh and his family, but maybe he wouldn't have appreciated it.

We got up and decided to go further. The chilly air was keeping us awake. We passed a small lake on our right, and a little while later there was a large lake, again on our right.

"Maybe we should go back," I said.

"O.K."

"Shhh. What was that?"

"I don't know."

We walked forward and came to a fence. The sound came again. The fog swirled and lightened a bit.

I said, "It sounded like Sadie snoring."

"Yeah, you don't think . . ."

I grabbed the fence and it rattled against the steel fence post. Suddenly, a dark horned head came out of the fog and hooked at the fence. The sound came low out of its mouth.

Pearl and I jumped back. My heart was pounding. Pearl said, "It's a buffalo! It's a goddang buffalo!"

We took off the way we'd come, but it didn't take us half as long to reach Haight. On the way out of the park, I thought *A buffalo in the middle of San Francisco—now I know it's time to go home.*

CHAPTER LI

We were going home, but first we'd have to head north the way we'd come before we could make the final long run east on the GN.

Josh came to the boarding house early because he had to work that day. We stood out on the porch while the others were still sleeping.

"Well, kid, I can still get ya into the movies if ya want."

"No, I think I'd better go home. Finish school. Then I don't know."

"O.K., it's your life." He stuck out his hand and I took it. "Tell Bear he's still the best wing shot I've ever seen. Give Boss and Ma my love and surprise her with a hug and kiss from me. You can tell 'em I'm fine . . . and anything else you've a mind to." Our eyes met. We were the same height.

I didn't know what to say, so I just said, "Yeah."

He turned and stepped down, then came back up. "I almost forgot—a little going away present." He held out a leather sheath with a knife inside.

"Thanks, thanks a lot."

"Here. Ya hook this over your boot top and it hangs inside your boot. Most guys wouldn't think to check there."

I took the knife out and tried to pry open the blade. It had only one.

"No, not like that." He took the knife. "Hold it like this . . . so your fingers are out of the way. Then push this."

SNICK! The blade snapped open and locked into place.

"Then ya push this again and it releases the blade like this."

He watched me operate it and then said, "Remember this, Lige. Don't ever pull a knife on a man unless you're prepared to use it, unless you're prepared to kill him. Threats are bull shit." He walked lightly down the steps and got into his car without looking at me. As he drove away, he waved once.

I went inside and got the twins up, then we got Axel dressed. He was hung over and we practically had to carry him to the taxi. He was coming around by the time we got to the station, but he never said a word about Sadie. He did open his suitcase and got out a bag of jawbreakers, which he'd bought after we decided it was time to go home. Merle thought there was something funny about them because Axel had borrowed a couple old lamps from Mrs. Byrd and took them and the candy to the basement for an hour or so behind locked doors, but when we checked the bag before we packed it, there were just a bunch of black jawbreakers in there, nothing else.

The trip through northern California and into Oregon dragged on and on.

At first the twins and I talked baseball. The papers said Rogers Hornsby of the Cards was batting .408 and Detroit's Harry Heilmann .392. The Babe was at .390 with twenty-five home runs, but Cy Williams of the Phils had twenty-seven. The Giants were up by five games on the Bucs in the National, and I felt confident of a World Series berth for the Yanks, who led the American by thirteen-and-a-half over Cleveland.

With neither the Cubs nor the "Black Sox" doing much, Axel wandered off.

We talked the fight game to death. Criqui had been beaten already by Johnny Dundee, so there was a new featherweight champ. None of us mentioned the jawbone. Gene Tunney (which we pronounced "Toon-ee") had decisioned Dan O'Dowd in twelve rounds, but we knew that light-heavies never amounted to much. Benny Leonard had retained his lightweight crown by decision over Lew Tendler, showing that Jews could fight. And the world flyweight champ, Pancho Villa—the boxer, not the bandit—had won two fights in eleven days, proving it could be done and not much else. It was all dry stuff and I exited the conversation.

The twins kept going awhile longer. Pearl said that Eddie Kane, Tommy Gibbons' manager, wouldn't allow Gibbons to fight Siki or any other Negro because both the fighter and Kane were opposed to mixed matches. The twins debated whether or not that would affect a fight between Gibbons and Luis Firpo, who had KO'd Jess Willard at Boyles' Thirty Acres. They asked me if I thought Firpo was white enough, but I pretended to be asleep. All the talk was of a Dempsey-Firpo match, not one between Gibbons and Firpo—and I didn't have anything to say about Dempsey.

The fight game talk died.

Merle said Harding's body was in Iowa. No one responded.

The mountains, valleys, trees, roads, and towns came and went outside the windows and were replaced by more of the same. The inside of the car was crowded with the noise of children laughing, talking, and occasionally yelling or crying. Axel talked with most of the kids, but the twins and I tried to ignore them.

Adults looked after children, conversed, knitted, read, stared out the windows, or slept.

The clack-clack of the wheels on the rail joints, the deeper noise of the "frogs," and the rumble of the bridges were the only connections I had between what I was doing inside and the way I had been "up top" or in blind baggage.

After I made a rather expensive trip to the dining car, I bought a paper and read the Funnies. There were the familiar ones from back home—*Bringing Up Father, Freckles and His Friends*, and *The Gumps*—and some I'd read occasionally in strange newspapers—*Mutt and Jeff, The Katzenjammer Kids*, and one that looked almost like it called *The Captain and the Kids*, a dream-like *Krazy Kat, Gasoline Alley, Thimble Theater, Harold Teen, Winnie Winkle*, and *Smitty*.

I didn't see *Moon Mullins* and I fell asleep.

I awoke to the sounds of crying and yelling. I sat up and heard the conductor lecturing Axel, who was surrounded by five or six mothers and a couple of fathers.

The children were on the outskirts of the group howling to beat the band. The twins had been sleeping, too, and as I walked down the aisle, they got up and followed me. As we got closer, several children turned to look at us with reddened eyes above blackened mouths.

I realized that Axel had gotten all the children into his confidence and then given each one a jawbreaker coated with lamp black.

The suggestion that Axel be thrown off the train at high speed was rejected by the conductor just as I arrived.

"Are you with him?" the conductor asked.

"Unfortunately," I answered. Axel's eyes glared.

"Then take him back with you and keep him tied up if you have to until you switch trains, but don't let him wander around this car again."

"All right." I reached out to guide Axel down the aisle, but he jerked away and accidentally clipped a little boy alongside the head. A blood-curdling wail went up, so to shield my embarrassment and to help keep us homeward bound, I grabbed Axel and forced his arm behind his back. Walking him to our seats, I pushed the arm lock up until he was practically on tip toes.

When he sat down, he stretched out his arm carefully and said, "I'll fix you yet, Elijah." He turned and stared out the window at nothing, rubbing his arm.

By the time the mothers had gotten their children's mouths pink again, the twins and I had decided we'd had enough civilized travel. When we stopped at Salem, we asked the conductor to get our suitcases off, which he was only too happy to do once we told him Axel would be coming with us.

CHAPTER LII

At Salem we threw our suitcases into an open boxcar and rode a freight to Portland. Axel sulked off by himself, but the twins and I sat by the doors, jammed open, and settled into the rhythm of the train.

We found that the rhythm didn't last too long, however, because the train was a local, making every pitiful tank town stop between Portland and Seattle.

At Kelso we debated whether to wait and catch a fast freight, decided against it, jumped off, drank some water at the station, and then hopped on the local again. It was getting dark, so I rolled up my jacket for a pillow and went to sleep. I had no dreams.

Pearl was shaking me in the dark.

"Wh—what?"

"Bulls. On both sides," he whispered.

I put on my jacket and looked out. We were in a yard, and there were lights coming toward us from both ends of the train. I went to the other door and saw lights in both directions again. The pale illumination of the depot was three hundred yards away.

Merle and Axel were looking out, too.

"What'll we do?" Merle asked.

"Run for it or hide in here," I said.

Axel said, "I'm runnin," and he jumped off, kicking up rocks as he hit. He went down on one knee and then sprang up, running directly away from our car.

Somebody yelled just as I was ready to jump, and then a sparkle of light off to my left and the sound of a shot made me change my mind.

It wasn't much of a moon, but I saw Axel freeze in his tracks, then the twins and I gathered our gear and crept to the back of the car.

Soon we heard voices.

"This car's open. He came from here."

"Lemme look."

A light hit the other end of the car, revealing nothing. We ducked behind our suitcases. The light came to our end.

"Well, lookee here."

Another light followed and a different voice said, "All right, you fellas, come out from behind there and get over here."

We waited.

"Come out or we'll come in."

I heard a lot of voices in support, so I whispered, "Let's get it over with," and stood up.

"That's right," the voice said.

I picked up my suitcase and put on my cap. The twins did the same, with Merle grabbing Axel's case. We walked to the light.

As we got to the doors, light sprayed us from both sides. We turned to the door with the voice and a semicircle of lights hit our faces.

"Leave those cases and get down here."

We jumped down. I slipped on the ballast and went to my knees. As I started to get up, someone said, "Goddam Red," and something smashed across my back and head.

The next thing I knew I was being dragged somewhere along a track by two men, one of whom had extremely bad breath. He kept calling me a Wobbly and a Red, but what was worse, he turned his face to mine every time he said something.

My arms were around their shoulders and my feet were trailing behind. When I recovered a little more, my feet started moving and the men adjusted their hold on me so that I could walk on my own. We came to an auto and the men stopped me. I turned around and saw the twins and Axel walking inside small rings of men. They acted like they'd been thumped, too.

When we were formed into a group with two men grabbing each of us, the voice said, "Empty their pockets." A little later, it asked, "Find anything?"

"No, no cards."

"Ditched 'em, huh?"

None of us spoke.

"They've got plenty of money, though. Let's keep it."

"No. If we're goin' after Reds and Wobblies, we're not gonna act like Reds ourselves. Not in my county. Give 'em back their wallets, but keep those knives. Thanks for your help tonight, Pete. We'll take it from here."

A group of men detached itself from the larger group and went back to the yard. The voice questioned us, but wouldn't believe our answers. The four of us were handcuffed and forced into different cars with our guards. There were maybe a dozen autos altogether.

The car started, and I was on the floorboards in back with Bad Breath sticking me in the ribs off and on with what felt like a pickax handle. He said, "We've had enough from Reds like you."

"We're not Reds."

"Wobblies, then. We know what to do with 'em, too. Right, Bill?"

"Right."

"Maybe we should do just that. It's about time for another lesson. Damned Wobblies. Maybe we should go over to the Chehalis River Bridge and do another cuttin' and stretchin' like Everest. Got a knife, Bill? These Wobblies cut easy."

"Shut up, you knucklehead," Bill said.

"What'd I say?" Bad Breath sounded hurt.

"Just shut up about that."

"All right, but we still got to teach these Reds a lesson."

"We will. Just shut up."

Bad Breath had been punctuating his remarks with the end of his club in my ribs. When he said "Everest," he gave me an extra something that took the wind out of me for awhile.

It was just as well. The whole car reeked of his breath and for those few seconds I didn't have to smell it.

We went over a chuckhole and Bad Breath said, "3-7-77."

I said nothing.

He repeated, "3-7-77."

Another man laughed and said, "Ain't you curious, kid?"

I didn't say anything, so Bad Breath prodded me. I said, "Yeah."

Bad Breath said, "Them's the dimensions of a grave—three feet wide, seven feet long, and seventy-seven inches deep. Wanna try one on for size?"

Most of the men laughed, but I could tell Bill didn't.

Bad Breath's gas warfare and aerial bombardment continued until the cars stopped and we were dragged out. We were in a river valley and I heard a train whistle not too far off.

Someone removed my handcuffs, not too gently.

The voice said, "Now you're out of my jurisdiction. Just keep headin' north and you'll be all right. But Reds, Wobblies, and just plain tramps aren't welcome in Lewis County, and, boys, whichever you are, we're gonna give you somethin' to remember so you won't come back. O.K., men."

Bill pinned my arms back, and Bad Breath hit me in the guts with his right, then he hit me again. I bent over and I could tell the others were getting the same treatment.

Bill let go and I was down on my hands and knees with lights shining on me. I saw Bad Breath's boots close in front of me. The toes were worn and a lighter color. I couldn't resist it. With all the force I had, I butted my head upward, smashing my skull into his groin.

Bad Breath went down, but I was up. Bill and some others had jerked me to my feet.

While Bad Breath was crying, holding himself, and making dust, the voice came up to me and said to his men, "Spread him." My legs were grabbed and held apart, then the voice took a step to the side and swung his club in an upward arc that sent me off into darkness.

CHAPTER LIII

"**S**ure they left us our billfolds, but our suitcases must be halfway to Seattle by now, and I had five letters from Cecilia in mine. If I could catch some monkey reading one, I'd . . ." Merle's voice faded out as I came to. I was on my back with my head on Merle's lap. We were beside a railroad right-of-way and he was swabbing my head with a wet rag. My right testicle was shooting pain. I touched it through my pants and decided I didn't want to do that again.

Merle asked, "You O.K.?"

I thought for a second and said, "Yeah, but I didn't think a hit to the groin could knock you out."

"It didn't. Another guy belted ya with a club behind the head at the same time. It looked as if they'd done it before. Ya got a cut and lump on your head."

I felt. The egg told me Merle was right.

Pearl came over. "Can ya stand up?"

I stood up. My head didn't want me to.

"Can ya walk? We had to carry ya this far."

I walked. My groin didn't want me to.

"Where to?" I asked.

"North. We gotta make a town sooner or later."

We started out, the others overcoming their poundings remarkably well. All three of them were moving swiftly on the ballast. I tried, but I ached too much. I moved off onto the dirt-and-weeds shoulder. It was slow going and Axel moved out far ahead, then the twins, then me acting as caboose. Night things kept running off into the woods to my right and I noticed the moon was still rising.

I kept plodding. Once a freight came up behind and blew past us, its fire box ablaze.

After what seemed hours, but which, according to the moon, wasn't, I had to stop. I felt myself, tender and swollen, and I sat down on a rail.

Eventually, Pearl came back. "Lige, ya gonna make it?"

"I don't know. I'm hurtin'."

"Yeah, I know." He sat with me.

Merle came back. "Axel says there's a town up ahead. He saw lights. He wouldn't wait; he's makin' for it right now."

Pearl got up. "C'mon, Lige. We'll catch a freight there."

I stood up. I felt better, but I still had to walk off the ballast. With the moon at my back, a few lights showed ahead.

Axel came back. "There's a freight in the yard pickin' up some cars. Hurry up and we can make it."

I tried to hurry and then quit. They could leave me if they wanted to. I watched the lights come a little closer, then closer, then I was in the yard. The train was on a siding, but it was moving toward the mainline. Axel found a car and jumped on, followed by the twins. I had to run and it hurt like holy hell. I got my hands on the floor of the car. The twins grabbed me under the shoulders and pulled me aboard. I had to crawl away from the door and lie down in darkness, my groin on fire. I couldn't move until it was time to get out in Seattle.

We ate breakfast in a little eat shop, and then Axel and Merle went to a surplus store and bought us canteens. While they were gone, I had the waitress bring me a pitcher of milk, which I finished. I was still thirsty so I drank two glasses of water.

When Axel and Merle got back, we each used the washroom, left a healthy tip, and walked to the King Street Station. Near the southern part of the harbor, I noticed a skyscraper that looked taller than anything we'd seen in San Francisco.

At first I wanted to get a ticket and ride a varnish home, but after I sat around awhile, I thought I felt well enough to go home uncivilized. Pearl went to dope out a train that would take the High Line east.

In the station I read a newspaper about Harding's funeral train in Chicago and about the huge crowd. The body was heading for Pittsburgh. I was reading about a guy from Massachusetts swimming the English Channel in twenty-seven hours and forty-five minutes when Pearl came back and said he had us a freight.

We left the station and started crossing the tracks until we got to the freight. We were walking down to an open car Pearl had seen when two bulls with clubs jumped off the caboose and began yelling. We ran back the way we had come. At the end of the freight, Axel and I took a sharp right around the locomotive and headed for some buildings. The twins kept going straight.

I checked to see about the twins and turned back in time to see Axel disappear in the darkness between two long sheds. I hit the darkness a few seconds later with a glance back at one of the bulls and his club, the canteen weighing in my hand, and a ton of lead in my pants.

Despite my groin I jumped a mud puddle at the end of the sheds and wheeled right. Axel was crouched just around the corner, and when I put out my arms to prevent a collision, he grabbed them and kneed me in the groin.

I heard him say, "Now we're even, you son of a bitch." Then he was running. I didn't care. My face was near the mud and my mind was elsewhere.

A strong hand grabbed my jacket. There was movement, followed by a thudding noise. The hand let go. There was more movement, and a pair of hands turned me over and, grabbing my jacket, pulled me up. The nails on the thumbs were perfect circles.

"We've got to get out of here," the man said. "His friends will most likely be around."

We stepped over the bull, out cold, in the mud.

CHAPTER LIV

The dark path we walked had weeds on both sides, except when we crossed a rotting wooden bridge over an oil-choked ditch. At first the man helped me along. I didn't feel too good, but I noticed two things about him besides his strength. His hands, when they occasionally touched my skin, were soft like a woman's and he smelled faintly of lilacs.

As we walked, I got stronger and he wasn't helping me when we came to the jungle.

It was the trashiest, smelliest jungle I'd ever seen. Cans, bottles, broken boards, boxes, pieces of paper, and garbage were littered like wind-fallen apples. There were apples, too—cores, both fresh and rotten, with coats of flies. Someone must have gotten lucky in a chicken coop—near a stump there were feathers, claws, and several chicken heads, again with flies. There was also a pile of something that pulsated with maggots, but my stomach could only stand one glance.

We were halfway through the jungle when a big Negro with a derby hat and a dark coat called out, "Uh, huh. The ol' Duke o' King Street done got hisself another chicken."

Laughter erupted from all the tramps lying around, but I noticed one especially. He was a bald old man with a sparse growth of gray whiskers on a toothless face. His skin had patches of red on top of his head, his nose, and a loose flap on his neck. When I walked by, his laughter sounded just like a turkey gobbler.

The man hurried me through more weeds and junk, then between some sheds, and finally up to a sidewalk.

"You can call me 'Duke'," the strong man said, sticking out his hand.

I shook it. It was very soft and looked white against mine. "Lige," I said, and thanked him for the help. I looked around, trying to get my bearings.

"Don't mention it and don't worry. There aren't any bulls comin'. I kept a lookout."

"I'm not worried about bulls. I was with some friends when we got jumped."

"You mean that little runt was a friend of yours?"

"No, not him. Two others."

"I never saw 'em . . . Are you hungry?"

"No. I've got to find 'em." I turned to go back to the yard, but his hand caught my shoulder.

"You can't go back yet. The bull I laid out is up by now and sore as hell. You go in there and you'll get your skull busted sure as you're standin' here."

"What should I do?"

"I got a place off King Street. An apartment. We can go there, and you can wash up and rest for a few hours,'til things cool down in the yard, then we'll go back for your friends. They won't leave without you."

He didn't look like any bum I'd ever seen before—for one thing his shoes were nicely polished, except for the fringe of mud at the edges of the soles—so I asked, "Won't your wife mind?"

He looked at me and then started up the sidewalk, saying, "I'm not married."

I caught up to him. "I didn't mean anything. I'm sorry."

"I just could never find the right girl."

He didn't say much on the way, only asking about where I lived and how I got there. I saw an Interurban line that reminded me a little of San Francisco, but Seattle sure wasn't "S.F." or maybe it was, with most of the big hills ironed out.

Duke's place was up an enclosed flight of wooden stairs hanging on the outside of a yellow brick building with a faded green and yellow sign reading "New and Used Furniture." The cloudy windows displayed furniture in various stages of life.

A hallway ran away from the stairs, showing six doors. Halfway down to Duke's door, we passed #3 where two girls were coming out. They both had short hair and short skirts, one of which was pink, and their skin looked nice, even in the dim hallway. For a split second I thought the pink one was Annie. The other one bumped into me and I said, "Excuse me." The girls looked at me and then at Duke, then back at me and began giggling. They kept it up all the way to the stairs.

Duke said, "Uncouth peasants," before he unlocked the door to #6. He had three rooms. The largest was a living room-bedroom, the next was a dining room-kitchen, and the smallest was a bathroom.

The place was clean. Everything seemed carefully arranged. There were slipcovers on the chairs, flowers by the windows, and dozens of paintings on the walls. I looked at the paintings. Some had sailors and trainmen and lumberjacks in the front and things like docks, ships, trains, or trees in the background.

"Do you like them? I painted them myself."

"Yeah." I looked at one with the King Street Station in the background. "Yeah, I do." Actually, I didn't because while the men all had big muscular bodies, their faces were finely featured like those of women, and in many of the paintings there were figures of young, slightly built boys. Things just didn't fit together right.

Only one painting didn't follow the pattern. It was of an old, tired man wearing a top hat, with his head bent forward and shoulders slumped beside a woman with dark hair in the back of an open car. There was a driver or maybe a chauffeur in front, and two motorcycles with policemen beside the car. In the background there were large buildings and the car was in the middle of a parade. Along the sides of the street stood tall, gaunt working men with their arms folded. The ones up close were solemn, so I guessed that the ones whose faces were blurred were the same. On the cap of a close one, I read "RELEASE POLIT" and on the cap of a man directly across the street were "ITICAL PRISONERS."

The Duke came over. "Oh, yes. That one."

"Who is it?"

"That's President Wilson and his wife. In 1919 they were here in Seattle trying to gain support for the Treaty and for the League of Nations. I went down to see them, but I only got so far before a man told me to go back to the last block and watch. There were many other men there, so I did. They were Wobblies and they lined up, filling six blocks of the President's route. When the Wilsons' car drove those six blocks, not one man cheered. Every man stood silent, staring straight ahead. A few children had gotten in among the Wobblies next to where I was, and I heard their little cheers, but that was all. Poor President Wilson. To have to go through that. I followed along a ways, and he looked like he'd been poleaxed. And it wasn't long, you know, before he had his stroke, right on that same trip. He wasn't even here about labor or unions or arrests or anything like that, just peace, which would help the Wobblies, too. But they just stood there, mute. They acted like brutes that day and when I got home, I painted it right away. I didn't want to forget."

I looked at the bowed President, but my admiration was for the genius of the silence.

The Duke said, "The bathroom's in there. Feel free to use the tub. I'm goin' out and get a few things to eat. We can have an early supper here . . . after we find your friends, I mean."

After he left, I went in the bathroom and locked the door. While the tub was filling, I took off my clothes. Gingerly, I touched my testicle. It was still swollen a little, but it didn't hurt as bad, except for a lump at the bottom. The back of my head had a scab on it and the hair around it was matted.

The bath almost put me to sleep. As the tub was draining, I saw why Duke's hands were the way they were. He had a bottle of Hind's Honey and Almond Cream on the shelf. He also had a manicure set and some lilac toilet water, as well as his shaving kit and a comb and brush set. I almost opened his medicine cabinet, but then I thought that was snooping too much.

He wasn't back yet and I was tired. My pants were dirty, so I dressed in my underwear, pulled down the Murphy bed, and went to sleep on top of the covers.

I woke up when I felt something rubbing my cheek. I heard a movement and looked around. Duke was sitting in a chair right next to me.

"I didn't mean to wake you. You looked so peaceful."

I sat up. "What time is it?"

"Just about three."

"Three!" I jumped out of bed and pulled on my pants. "I should have been to the yard hours ago." I got dressed and left. Duke followed me, apologizing for not getting me up. I didn't care. I had to find Pearl and Merle.

We didn't. Duke and I looked all over the yard, avoiding the bulls. No twins. The jungle dwellers didn't know anything. No one we talked to had seen them, either, or Axel, for that matter.

A little past six we were back at Duke's place. He said he'd make supper and went into the kitchen. I sat in a chair with a black hole in my stomach, not knowing what to do.

Duke was a cook. As he prepared each thing, he kept up a commentary for my benefit or he whistled softly. When he called me in, the table was perfect. For supper there was fish—haddock, with little onions he called shallots, mushrooms, parsley, and a sauce of butter, flour, water, egg yolks, whipped cream, and crabmeat. The sauce was on the fish and baked to a glaze. Duke had topped each plate of fish with a shrimp and a slice of black olive.

There was a kind of mashed potatoes with egg yolks and nutmeg, and an oyster stew. Duke seemed very disappointed when I wouldn't even try the oyster stew.

For dessert he had prepared a thick chocolate pudding that he called something like "Moose."

I hated to admit it, but Duke cooked almost better than Ma.

After supper I helped with the dishes. It was the least I could do. When we had finished, he asked if I wanted another bath. I'd worked up a sweat looking for the twins so I took one. He said he had an extra toothbrush and got it for me, along with some Klenzo Toothpaste. After I had finished, Duke went into the bathroom. I heard water running.

I was in my underwear. I folded my clothes and put them on a chair next to the bed. I dropped my socks into my boots and put them by the bed with the canteen between them. Then I crawled under the covers.

I prayed that God was with the twins wherever they were. After I prayed for everyone back home, I prayed for Josh and his family—they were part of my family, too. While I was praying, I tried to remember if Josh had a wedding ring when we were on the boarding house porch. Then I realized it didn't make any difference. I debated whether or not I should pray for Axel. I was still debating when Duke came out of the bathroom.

He had on a silk robe. On the back was either a dragon or a rearing stallion. I couldn't quite make it out before he had both the robe and the light off.

What I did make out was that he had a big chest and large arm muscles and that he was stark naked.

I rolled over on my right side. He moved a little and then was still. A minute or so later he cleared his throat like he wanted to say something, but he didn't. He moved again.

So did I. I was right on the edge of the bed. He moved and turned. He was on his side, right behind me, and I could feel him, hard, up against me.

His left hand came up to my cheek, that soft hand, and he said, "Well, how about it, kid?"

I drove my elbow back into what I hoped was his solar plexus and then reached down for my boot. Kicking the covers free, I was out on the floor, facing him when he turned on the lamp.

He was holding his belly and trying to get a good breath, but he lunged across the bed with his left arm.

SNICK!

His eyes popped and he went back.

I kept the knife pointed at his heart. I got my stuff and edged around the bed, trying not to drop anything. Halfway around, Duke began to chuckle. He lay back against the pillow, chuckling, then he said, "Kid, I haven't ever begged for it or raped for it, so you're safe. Now, get the hell out!"

I backed up to the door, switched the knife to my left hand, unlocked and opened the door with my right, and slammed it shut just as I took off running down the hall and then the stairs, two at a time.

I was in my underwear in downtown Seattle with a knife in my hand.

I was an idiot.

CHAPTER LV

I ducked under the stairs and listened while I got dressed. I didn't hear anyone on the steps, so I put the canteen around my neck, held the knife at my side, and headed for the King Street Station. Each step away from Duke's place was like another "thank you" to Josh.

There were several trains in the yard and people milling around on the platform, which was well-lit, and cursing a derailment. Before I got too close, I stopped and put the knife back in my boot.

I was going to buy a ticket and ride the High Iron in a varnish, but I changed my mind when I saw an open boxcar in a train of boxcars and reefers. I jumped off the platform and headed across the tracks. My train was the second to the last one over. In the dark on the last track stood a shorter train, eight baggage cars and coaches, and it looked ready to roll as soon as the derailment was cleared.

As I climbed into the doorway of my boxcar, a bull came out from behind the door and brained me with a club. My cap took some of the blow, but I still went out into the night with my back hitting the ground. The bull started laughing above me, but I couldn't see him. I crawled in the dark under the train to the other side where I could hear the bull calling for "Jake."

I wobble-crawled across to the other tracks, trying not to throw up. The short train began to move. I looked back and two lights appeared. I touched the back of my head; the fingers came away with blood.

The short train stopped; the whistle sounded in the dark. I heard men on the other side of the cars. The two lights were coming. I was bleeding. I didn't want the night to grab me. I crawled under the short train and found a place.

The car jolted and began moving. The two lights went searching by in a hurry. The train picked up speed and passed the two lights standing still.

I worked myself around between a steel I-beam and a long rod with a flat projection on one end that supported my weight more-or-less comfortably. I got my belt loose and tied myself in a couple feet from the ground. If Twig had seen me, he'd have kicked me in the butt with his good leg. I was pulling the dumbest stunt a traveling man could pull—I was riding the rods. In my case, there was only one rod and it wasn't on a boxcar, but I knew Twig would be angry anyway.

About that time, I didn't care. I went into a dark place.

When I came to, Seattle was gone, but I figured we hadn't passed Everett yet because when I loosened my belt and leaned down, the Sound was off to my left. I tried to get settled as best I could and not think about falling off. Every once in awhile I'd feel gorge coming up, but it never came out. My head hurt worse than my groin, but I didn't think that was necessarily better.

After we passed Everett, I began going in and out of sleep. Once I woke with a start because I dreamed I was falling, but I wasn't. I lay there awhile and thought that riding the rods didn't seem that dangerous if you were belted in.

Another time I woke up and it was raining. It was a little damp where I was because of the water kicked up by the train itself, but if I had been "up top" or in blind baggage, I'd have been soaked.

Even taking tunnels was better on the rods. The air was a lot easier to breathe.

It was daylight by the time we were in the Big Bend country and working toward Spokane. I discovered two flattened sandwiches wrapped in wax paper in my jacket. I'd bought them after breakfast the day before. The fried egg sandwich didn't smell so bad, so I ate half of it. I thought I should ration myself because the short train was really making time. It hardly ever stopped and then not for long.

We crossed the five railroad bridges in Spokane, and I had a good view of the Falls from the second and longest bridge, but I never ducked down to see the amusement park.

My head was bothering me quite a bit after Spokane, and I was either sleeping or blacking out a lot for the rest of Washington and Idaho.

Coming into Montana, I figured out that we only stopped to change crews and power and to take on water, and that we did mostly at division points. That meant a quick trip home. I smelled half my summer sausage and cheese sandwich—it passed—and ate it. I drank some water from the canteen, which I had been doing right along.

I didn't see White Hair in the Troy jungle or anyone else I recognized.

All through the mountains, whenever I burped, it smelled of summer sausage and cheese. My digestion wasn't too good, what with lying down and also looking right over the edges of canyons at white water hundreds of feet below.

Daylight turned to dusk and dusk to dark, but Montana was still there.

After we shook loose of the helper engines and got onto the plains, the engineer really opened it up. I felt like we were hitting sixty miles per hour, but the swaying didn't bother me like it would have up above.

I deliberately hadn't thought of the twins since Seattle, but out on the plains I couldn't help it. The small towns we flashed through were just like our town. After thinking of all the ways they could be dead or hurt or arrested, or how Duke might "rescue" them, and of all the inadequate things I would have to say to their mother, I forced them out of my mind. They were driving me crazy.

The short train kept driving eastward. Along the way I noticed several times other trains had pulled off onto sidings, so that we could highball through.

At our stops the train was inspected more than any train I had ever seen. In daylight I saw dozens of feet, and at night I watched dozens of lights at every stop, but no one saw me in my burrow.

Just before we got to Shelby, we ran through some new ballast, went over a crossing, and a rock bounced up and caught me in the back. When we stopped, I undid my belt as soon as the inspection was done and used the shadow to get "up top" before we pulled out.

It felt good getting into the rhythm of a train again from the top of the car. I caught myself looking over for Pearl, but then I forced my mind to think of good things. I looked at the stars—Vega still so bright—and thought about talking with Twig and eating Ma's pie and hunting with Bear and Boss and then I started to think about my little black-haired nephew.

I took out the other two halves of my sandwiches and ate the summer sausage and cheese. The fried egg was too far gone so I threw it for a coyote.

It was yellowing in the east when we pulled into Havre. They switched on a new locomotive and were just finishing the inspection when someone on the platform yelled, "Hey, there's somebody on that car!"

I looked over and a guy was pointing right at me.

I didn't even have time to undo my belt before I knew someone was standing over me. When I did look up, I was staring down the barrel of a pistol with a star behind it.

"Son," the Star said, "you're under arrest. Now climb down real careful and come with me."

I peered over the edge of the car, and there were twenty or so men waiting, at least half with guns.

When I was on the ground, another Star checked me for weapons, but didn't look inside my boot. The first Star came over to me and I asked, "What's wrong? What did I do?"

"It looks to me like you were gettin' ready to sabotage the Silk Train."

The Silk Train! My mind flashed. *Of course! What a horse's ass you are!*

CHAPTER LVI

The cell had a bunk bed. Both the beds were made of metal with no springs or mattresses. An Indian snored on the bottom one. The top bunk was covered with something sticky so I lay on the floor.

The Indian woke up when they brought us breakfast, which we ate in silence. After the jailer took our dishes, the Indian sat on his bed, leaned against the wall, and stared straight ahead. He seemed in a trance.

About mid-morning they came in and hosed out the cell, but the Indian didn't move. They cleaned off the top bunk so I stayed up there until dinner.

The smell of food brought the Indian around and he ate quietly. They told me I'd be going to court soon, so after I passed my dishes through the slot, I washed as best I could. When I finished, the Indian was staring at me. I stared back and his hand came up. He put a finger to his lips so I would be quiet. Then he motioned me over.

I tiptoed to his bunk. He indicated I should put my ear to his mouth, but after Duke that was nothing doing. I stood in front of him, ready to go to fists or knife (their quick search hadn't found mine). Again he indicated he wanted me closer so finally I bent over a little. He looked at the door and then at me. He whispered, "I'm not here."

I straightened up and he leaned against the wall. When they came to get me a few minutes later, the Indian was in his trance again.

"What's wrong with him?" I asked the jailer.

"Who? Charlie Crow Flies High?"

"If that's him, yeah."

"Livin' lonely, I guess. He and his kid brother, Tommy, volunteered together in '17 and served in the same unit in France. Tommy didn't come back. Three, four years later a fire burned down the family's shack. Charlie couldn't get anyone out—his parents, grandmother, two sisters, and a baby brother all died. Now he goes on a toot, gets arrested, does ten days. He don't seem to mind it. Gettin' so we don't even notice him anymore."

When the judge came into the courtroom, the thirty or so of us in there all stood up, but he motioned us down right away.

"Sorry to be so late, gentlemen and lady." He smiled at the woman who was poised to take notes. "We had a birth this mornin' at the ranch"—I felt that maybe I should say congratulations—"and it's a male, big and strong"—I felt good—"but he wore his poor mother plumb out, and we almost lost her"—I felt sorry for the judge and his wife—"and I'da been sorry for that. She's the best damned—excuse me, Shirley—breedin' quarterhorse in the county." I didn't know what I felt.

He studied a piece of paper in front of him and then looked over the top of it at me. "Well, son, it looks like you got two meals on the county instead of one, thanks to my new foal. Let's hope the handouts stop there."

After he read the charges, but before he had me plead, two men asked to approach the bench. The three men had a whispering conference, after which the judge announced that all charges would be dropped, except for trespassing. The men behind the railing in back of me began buzzing, but the judge rapped them into silence.

The judge ran his hand through his pompadour and said, "Son, you've caused quite a stir, quite a stir, in our community, and I'd like to hear your explanation."

The judge listened to my story, chewing off the ends of his mustache hairs. I didn't see him spit out any. When I finished, he said, "Son, that's the damndest—excuse me, Shirley—story I've heard in three months." He looked at the paper in front of him. "Like I said, all charges have been dropped at the request of the railroad and the state's attorney, except for trespassin', and I don't think attempted robbery could have been proven anyway, seein' you don't even have a weapon."

I felt the knife in my boot and a cold sweat afflicted my armpits and back.

He squeaked back in his chair and said, "I'll tell you what. I'll drop this trespassin' charge—just wipe it clean off the slate—if you'll buy yourself a passenger ticket down at our little station and ride home on the inside. Will you do that?"

"Yessir."

The buzzing began again, but the gavel whacked it dead.

"Well, that's good. That's the right choice. I'll have one of our policemen there to help you find the station, and maybe he'll look in on you at train time. You can go now. I don't hold with too much formality in my court so goodbye and good luck." He reached over the bench and shook my hand with a firm, leathery grip.

"Thank you, sir. Goodbye, sir."

Mine had been the only case, so the policeman and I walked out in a crowd of men resentful of the disappointing outcome of the Case of the Silk Train Saboteur.

The policeman took me to the jail where I picked up my few valuables and then gave me a ride to the station where he watched over my shoulder as I bought my ticket. After I got my change, he left.

It would be a long wait, so I walked over to a beancry and ordered a hamburger, American fries, and large glass of milk. It sure beat jail food. I had the waitress put two sandwiches in waxed paper—one trip to a railroad dining car was expensive enough for me. In the restroom I filled my canteen with cold water. I bought a newspaper and hiked back to the station to wait.

I had forgotten all about Harding until I read that his funeral was in Washington that day. The sports page said that Babe Ruth was the first player to score a hundred runs in 1923, but in the game he scored his hundredth, the St. Louis Browns outlasted the Yanks 12-10. Even so, the Brownies were sixteen games out of first, and their manager, Lee Fohl, was out of a job.

I finished the paper before the train pulled in, so I looked at the other men in the waiting room and gave names to each one, trying to figure what they did for a living. I guessed "cowboy" for most of them, followed by "salesman."

I got ready to board the train, but on the first step, I turned and waved at the newly returned policeman, who just stared at me. I heard "Silk Train" whispered by some of the lady passengers, none of whom would sit near me, nor allow their children to, either.

I didn't care.

Riding a varnish across northern Montana in August was ten times worse than the trip up California and Oregon, and Axel wasn't around to break up the monotony. At the first stop, I got off.

The train winked off in the heavy evening and I waited around for a freight. When a long one stopped, I checked out a boxcar for riding bulls, hopped aboard, jammed the door, and watched Vega blinking on the high dome of the night sky.

The quarter moon, which was thinner than it had been in Washington, let me see the stars pretty well. I looked for my favorites—Deneb and Altair completing the triangle with Vega, red Antares off to the south, and reddish Arcturus at my back.

After the freight got moving, the engineer opened up the throttle and really began "walking the dog." Even though the car was straining violently side-to-side, I rolled up my jacket, moved away from the door, and lay down. Seeing the stars and the darkness between them made me feel safe.

I said a prayer for each member of my family, for Twig, and for the twins. I fell asleep watching Antares bound along with the freight over the Montana plains.

CHAPTER LVII

When I woke up, the sun was shining, but it was still cool. Either we hadn't made many stops, or I had slept through them. I put on my jacket and sat in the doorway, letting the sunlight warm me. I took out one of the sandwiches, had breakfast, and tried to figure out where we were. The ripening fields, the browned-up grass with patches of still-green weeds, and the fence rows could have been anywhere on the northern plains. I couldn't see any landmarks.

A station went by and I looked back at the sign, Hoff. We were in North Dakota. We whistled through Grenada and off to the east I saw a low range of blue-gray hills. Wallace, and we were in the hills. Walther, and down into a valley. Becker, and then we clattered over the Gassman Coulee trestle. Three miles and we slowed down for Minot.

When we did switching in Minot, I caught sight of some fire-blackened rubble near the Leland Hotel. A lot of it was in the street and workmen were trying to clear it.

After the switching was completed and the crew was changed, we were off.

East of the round house, I saw a little smoke coming from a huge pile of burned wood. It looked like the car barns had gone up in flames a few days earlier. I saw the trucks of some of the burned-out freight cars and cabooses still sitting on the tracks. We went by slowly. The burned building had been over a hundred yards long.

The Minot Fire Department must have been busy since I was last there.

Near the east edge of the city, the engineer gave two short toots on the whistle. I looked out. There was no crossing; there was nothing on the tracks. Sitting on a small embankment were a pretty, dark-haired girl about ten, a little boy, and a younger girl, maybe two. They were all waving. On the sidewalk beyond the embankment stood a tall, dark woman with a wicker baby carriage. Even though they weren't waving at me, I waved back.

At Carver I got lucky. The freight took the Cut-off and I was only a hundred miles and change from home. I peeled an eye for Wobblies, but the bulls must have cleaned them out.

We didn't switch at all on the Cut-off so we passed Hamlein at mid-afternoon. The train went over a little trickle of water that became a river just west of the res, whose dusky humps I could see blocking off the light and dark patterns of our town as it spread north of the tracks a couple miles away.

There were gray wooden snow fences to the north of the tracks, then the yard with its various switches and sidings, then the west track of the wye, the car barns, the roundhouse, and then I was dropping off the train. I hoped Twig hadn't seen me do it; I should have waited for it to stop.

Twig wasn't in either of his Spots so I went over to his house. He was in his chair, listening to some blues. When he saw me, he hopped up and got his crutches under him. I came over and he put out his hand, which I shook.

"It's good to see ya, Lige."

"It's good seein' you, too, Twig."

"Ya just get in?"

"Yeah."

"Ya don't know about Pearl, then?"

"No, what's wrong?"

"He's in the hospital here. Just got put in a couple hours ago."

"What's wrong?"

"He just about chilled and suffocated to death."

"What?"

"It's true, but he's gonna live."

"I'd better go up there."

"Wait. I'll get my hat and come, too."

While we walked toward the hospital, Twig filled me in with stuff he got from Merle. When the bulls started after us in the Seattle yards, the twins headed down a track with a train made up mostly of reefers. Pearl climbed on top of a reefer and got down inside through a trap door on the roof. Before he could get out, someone shut and locked the trap door and the train started up.

Merle had seen Pearl go into the car, but, shaking the bulls and all, he couldn't remember which one. He doubled back and hopped the reefer train as it was leaving. It was a high-priority train with its fruit so it didn't stop much. Even when it did for crew and power changes and to fill the lees with ice, Merle couldn't get Pearl out. He still didn't know which car he was in and all the "reefs" were locked, so Merle figured if he got arrested pounding on a car, and no one believed him, Pearl would suffocate if the train went all the way to St. Paul.

So Merle rode the reefer to our town with his canteen of water and the two sandwiches he had ordered with me in the Seattle eat shop.

When the train pulled up at the water tower, Merle jumped off and started yelling that his brother was trapped inside one of the cars. Mr. Hedman, the station agent, knew Merle, so he made the crew check until they found Pearl, twenty-five or so banana skins, and an empty canteen on the floor. Pearl was pretty low. He looked blue and the air inside was almost used up so they rushed him to the hospital.

When Twig and I walked by the bank, I saw Bear sitting in the big chair he still kept for when he wanted to visit his former business. He saw us, too, and waved with a mile-wide smile. I smiled and waved back. A block-and-a-half later, he pulled up in his Pierce-Arrow and gave us a lift to the hospital.

Pearl was still bluish and his lips were dark purple. Merle and Mrs. Potman were there. She hugged me and whispered that Pearl was going to be all right.

I walked over to Pearl so he could see who it was. He put out his hand and I took it. His skin was a little cold. We didn't speak.

Merle and I went into the hall and he told me what Twig already had, but I let him talk anyway. Neither of us could remember if Pearl bought sandwiches in Seattle, but we didn't think he had, wanting to grab something fresh down the line.

Merle said that Axel had sent a wire to Mrs. Potman asking her to send his clothes and things he'd left to Chicago, which she had done. He said the twins and I were still in Seattle without any explanation, but that he was on the Oriental Limited, heading home.

For one mad moment I thought of charging down to the main line, derailing the Limited, searching the debris for Axel, and beating him to a bloody pulp. However, the moment passed.

I told Pearl I'd be back to see him, but he was still kind of groggy. In the car again, I told Bear and Twig a little about the trip, but no details. I promised I'd give each of them the low down as soon as I could. Bear dropped me off at my house and continued down Lamborn to take Twig home. I hesitated on the curb, wondering what to do because I remembered that when Odysseus finally got home, his dog saw him and died. I didn't want that to happen to Ted.

The yard and house looked the same, and as I went through the gate, Ted came barking around the corner, stopped dead, and then leaped into my arms. I held him tight and he was giving out little whimpers. I put him down and scratched his ears and petted him awhile. When I got up, he wound himself around and through my legs and beat my knees with his tail. I petted him some more and then told him to "stay."

He didn't want to, but he did.

I left the canteen and my jacket with the other sandwich in the pocket in the garage and went into the house. I smelled pie. Blueberry. No, apple. No, blueberry and apple. Ma was at the stove and two pies were already cooling on the window sill. She had on her baking apron and when she heard me, she turned and her mouth got big.

She had a streak of flour on her forehead and another alongside her nose. I walked over and gave her a hug. She held me tight and then gave me a kiss on my cheek. I kissed her on the cheek twice and I could tell she was crying. We stood there, kind of rocking.

The kitchen smelled fine.

CHAPTER LVIII

Pearl got better and went back to his radio. Merle started seeing Cecilia a lot. Boss wasn't upset about my going, but he complained, "Jumped up seven Marias, Lige! Goin' off without telling your Ma was a fine kettle of fish."

We must have told half the people in town about our adventures, but we never told anyone why we really left. We only said we wanted to see the Dempsey-Gibbons fight and the West Coast.

We were going to tell Twig the truth, but decided against it because we thought he'd probably blame himself for what happened to Pearl in the reefer and for the beatings we'd gotten.

As for Josh's family, I figured it was up to him to tell Ma and Boss.

For a week we were the heroes of all our friends and acquaintances, except for David Dailey, and I even took Emily to a movie. She wouldn't let me kiss her good night. The excitement wore off, however, and things returned to normal. The sound of threshing machines soon gave way to the sound of the school bell.

The Dempsey-Gibbons fight films came to our town, but neither the twins nor I went.

I did take some paint and a brush and spent part of a Saturday morning giving a second coat to my job down by the river, but mostly I just felt empty inside.

Even school didn't help. Our football team had another mediocre season, with a lot of size and no speed. We were grateful for at least being average when we read that in the southern part of the state Maple beat Ellingson 130-0.

Miss Davies, our old Sunday School teacher, had moved away, her place taken by Mr. Walter J. Burnside, a man of definite ideas whose correctness could only be challenged by fools, heretics, or benighted souls misled by the Old Serpent.

After two sessions it seemed to me that Burnside's ideas contradicted those of Mr. Pomeroy and Josh, so I rushed to the defense.

During the third meeting of the class, I pointed out a difference between what Burnside had presented and what Mr. Pomeroy had told us on the same subject. Burnside spent the rest of the class lecturing us on the mistaken theory, even the sinfulness, of evolution.

Despite what I saw as a weakness in scientific attitude, Burnside was a whiz on the Bible, and he began reading passages to bolster his arguments. Over the next six weeks our Sunday School class became more and more a debate between Burnside and Pomeroy/Josh, with me acting as proxy. At first it was quiet and fun, a real exchanging of ideas, but it eventually became personal and heated on both sides.

It came to a head in October.

For the third straight year it was the Yankees and Giants in the World Series, and the Yankees took their first World Championship four games to two. I felt lousy after the first game. The Giants won 5-4 when some has-been named Casey Stengel hit a 3-2 count for an inside-the-park home run. I felt better after a 4-2 Yankee victory in game two with the Babe belting two out of the Polo Grounds. There was only one run in game three—a home run by Casey Stengel again. I told myself that no true Yankee fan would ever like that man.

The Yanks swept the last three games, with the Babe hitting another one out. Considering how great I felt over the Yankees' win, it was surprising that I locked horns with Burnside like I did. Maybe I was upset because the week before, Pearl, fed up with the school's lack of response to "wireless telegraphy," quit and went to Fargo to try and work his way into radio at WDAY. Or perhaps, given the gulf between our ideas, the clash between Burnside and me was inevitable.

Through the early part of the class, Burnside had been sticking pins into many of Mr. Pomeroy's ideas—that a great lake had once covered the eastern part of North Dakota, that the hills near Big Sam Lake were glacial in origin, that Java Man was a human ancestor, that Adam and Eve were really symbolic figures—and I couldn't come up with much to say in Mr. Pomeroy's defense, which made me angry. I knew that one of the text books he used, Elhoff's *General Science*, said the Earth, moon, and sun were millions of years old and that the Rocky Mountains were three million years old. I also remembered that another of his books, Hunter's *Civic Biology*, had classified humans with vertebrates, mammals, and primates. Monkeys were also classified as primates, the book said, but humans were far above them intellectually. When we went through general science and biology class, most of the material presented on evolution came directly from Mr. Pomeroy.

My anger got the better of me when Burnside made some remark that while many men had made monkeys out of themselves, the reverse was not the case. Amid the laughter, I raised my hand and responded that I subscribed to the Darwinian theory of evolution and would accept the evidence in its support over any Hebrew fairy tales in the Bible or anywhere else.

I said it as loudly as I could without actually yelling, and I thought Burnside was going to have apoplexy. He turned red and had to loosen his tie and collar. "Mr. Cockburn." (I was the only student he addressed by other than a Christian name.) "You will apologize for your blasphemy this instant."

"I will not apologize for what I believe to be the truth."

He must have seen himself being challenged in front of nineteen younger people he was supposed to be teaching. "Either apologize or get out. I will not have a dirty little atheist in my class, polluting minds."

I stood up. "Wrong on all three counts. I'm neither dirty, little, nor an atheist, but I will leave before you embarrass yourself any further."

I walked out of the room and down the stairs. Once outside I headed for the alley to avoid any church goers that were coming early to pray or gossip.

The more I walked, the angrier I got. I kicked a rock and it hurt my toe. That made me madder.

Boss and Ma were at Adult Sunday School. When Ted barked up at me, I asked him what he wanted to do. He barked again. "Oh, hunting, huh? O.K."

I went inside and got my hunting jacket and gear. I took Boss's 1897 twelve-gauge Winchester Pump Action Repeater and a box of shells. I packed my knapsack with a couple pieces of bread and cheese and a jar of peaches Ma had put up. I filled my canteen and was just starting out the door when I saw Ma's Bible on the kitchen table. I put it in my knapsack and, calling to Ted, headed for the river.

CHAPTER LIX

Winslow's pasture had been hayed so it was easy walking. The hay stacks humped up here and there along the bottom land with Ted smelling around their bases as we went by.

A half mile east of our house we passed the point of land off which Bear said the Sullivan sisters—Mary, Martha, and Margaret—drowned on July 4, 1897. They had gone wading (none of them could swim) farther east than any of the other picnickers along the river. The oldest, Mary, went first, then Martha, and little Margaret—red-haired like her mother—was last. They came to the point and joined hands, according to some boys who saw them from several hundred yards away. Mary led the way into the water off the tip of the point, her sisters following. She stepped into a hole and pulled the other two with her. They all must have sucked a lungful of water right away.

The boys ran and got some men, including Bear. They reached the point, but couldn't see anything, so they took off their shoes, socks, and outer clothing and formed a human chain in their underwear. Jonas Williamson was the tallest so he went first. He was still in his red long handles, even thought it was July Fourth and hotter than blazes. Bear was anchoring the chain, and he never got over Jonas wading out from the point in his red union suit.

Jonas kept trying to reach down with his hand and feel the bottom, but when he came to the hole, it was too deep, so he waded into the hole with the other men holding tight, and pretty soon he said, "I think I stepped on one of 'em." He held his breath and went under. He came up with little Margaret by the ankle. She was passed from man to man to the river bank, her red hair hanging down, dripping water set on fire by the sun. Bear never forgot that, either.

The other two girls were recovered the same way. The men worked their arms and whacked their backs and rolled them around on the ground, but they were too dead to come back.

Mrs. Sullivan had a fit at the funeral and grabbed hold of Margaret's coffin and screamed about not letting her baby go into the dirt. Bear said when the priest motioned some men to pull her away, her fingernails left scratches across the wood. She had always been a hard worker, and she had short, strong nails.

Her red hair slowly faded and turned gray, then white. Her mind slowly faded and then snapped. She would sit in her rocker most of the time, holding Margaret's doll and singing lullabies as she rocked.

Five years to the day, Mrs. Sullivan got up early and started walking north with some flowers she'd picked. The Grayson family, coming to town in a wagon from their farm up on the Divide, saw a woman walking on the NP tracks, and old man Grayson told the sheriff at the Independence Day Picnic.

Sheriff McDonald, Bear, Boss, Mr. Sullivan, his two sons John and Michael, and some other men had been looking for her, so they took a couple of buggies and headed north. On the Divide they found her face down in a pothole with so little water in it that Bear said later, "You'd think she had to try and drown herself in it."

On the hillside above the pothole, the men saw three neat little piles of wilted flowers.

They buried Mrs. Sullivan beside her three girls. Mr. Sullivan and his two sons sold out and moved back to Iowa shortly after the funeral.

A quarter mile beyond the point was a low reed-covered island and just past that the river fell down a small series of rapids into a steep-sided channel. It was there I began to hunt.

I stepped across the rocks that caused what Boss called "riffles," moving from south of the river to the north bank. Ted splashed beside me; he knew we were hunting.

The channel swung north, and we moved away from the river and then curved back on it where it turned to the east. I moved slowly through the buckbrush, trying to follow the cowpaths and standing upright every eight or ten feet to reconnoiter the river below.

The wind was out of the northwest, so I knew the ducks would be hugging the calmer north shore. I stretched up slowly and saw two, three, four; marked their location in line with the big rock sticking out of the middle of the river; and backed off to my left. Ted followed.

We got out of the buckbrush and walked a cowpath along the edge of a round depression where I had trapped some ermine the previous winter. We crossed some flat land and went down into a gully, keeping low because the river was in sight. I checked the stretch of water off to my right, but I could only see the south shore and the middle, and no self-respecting duck would be there with a northwest wind.

We climbed the east side of the gully, still on the cowpath, and then turned right and headed toward the river. A few steps later and I could see the big rock a little to my left, so I adjusted my approach. In the summer turtles would have been all over the rock sunning themselves, but it was too late for turtles.

I took off my knapsack, loaded the '97, and moved forward, avoiding the lichen-covered gray rocks sticking out of the prairie.

Most of the river was visible, but still no ducks. I bent low for a ways and then got down and bellycrawled, being careful not to jam the shotgun's muzzle into the ground.

At the crest of the bank, I released the safety and pushed forward, but saw nothing except the water, the rock, and the reeds. Keeping the '97 pointed at the river, I got my feet under me, stood up, and walked slowly down the bank, my eyes everywhere watching for movement.

Then to my left there were splashing and quacking, and I brought the muzzle up as a canvasback broke out of the reeds, already exploded into flight. Boom! It was down in the water, but another was rising off to the right. I pumped and swung. Boom! Another "can" splashed into the water. I pumped, the exploded shell forming a red arch to the ground, and two more birds left the reeds directly in front of me. Boom! They were both down together.

I ejected and had three shells left in the gun. I waited, tense. Nothing moved but the wind driving the reeds and the water, so I sent Ted in. Five minutes later he had three "cans" at my feet. The other one had only been winged and was hiding in the reeds. I told Ted to get it and he hit the water. A minute later I heard quacking and splashing, then heavy splashing, then Ted came out with the "can" in his mouth.

I praised him, took the bird, still alive, and grasping it by the head, twirled its body around a few times, breaking its neck. I put all four ducks in the deep, rubber-lined pockets of my hunting coat, slung on my knapsack, and headed east.

When Ted trotted up beside me, I scratched and petted him between the ears. He was a good dog.

CHAPTER LX

Some people will tell you a hunter becomes his gun. When he pulls it up, sights, and shoots, the pulling, sighting, and shooting is he, the man: he has become the pulling, the sighting, the shooting.

I don't see it that way. I've never felt myself become a gun. What it is, I think, is that my gun is a substitute for me, but it is separate. It takes my place by doing what I would do if I were twenty or thirty or however many yards away. The '97 was my substitute when I shot the four "cans" because if I had been at the edge of the reeds with a club, I would have used it to kill each one. Instead, I was on the bank and the shotgun did my work thirty or thirty-five yards away.

Shooting takes more skill than clubbing or knifing or snaring and in that respect I prefer it. I could hunt ducks the way the Indians did sometimes by going out in the water with a bunch of reeds and twigs around my head, floating up to a duck, grabbing its legs, and drowning it. That would take a certain skill. Bringing a club and using it in the water would require another skill. My four birds with three shots called for the skill I preferred.

Ted and I moved back, away from the river. The north bank was higher along the next stretch and didn't allow a very good shot.

On the far shore, I saw some Russian olives and, higher up, patches of thick buckbrush. On our side the bank began leveling out and ran flat into a point that in high water was an island. It was surrounded on three sides by cattails. Some days you got some nice pass shooting from the tip of the point, but nothing was flying in the wind that day.

Two ducks flew out of the cove made by the point and the north bank, which wasn't much of a bank anymore. They went quacking down the river.

We came to a springy area dug full of holes by cows as their hooves sank in the muddy earth. I moved from hummock to hummock, passing some small willows growing at the shoreline and three ancient willows, one of which had a large limestone rock with fossils at its base. The twins and I had discovered it when we had camped out just to the north of the springy area during a summer of low water. We had shown Mr. Pomeroy and he was very grateful.

Crossing a narrow trickle of water coming from the north, I looked down the length of the river which was swinging south, but saw nothing. I moved up and onto level ground, which quickly became springy again, and reached my first fence.

I made certain the safety was on and went over to a fence post. I put the shotgun over and leaned it solidly against the post. Then I moved down two posts, crawled between two strands of barb wire—being careful not to snag my coat—and walked down to my gun.

I headed for Long Pond, a cutoff ox-bow, circling some to the east. Ted followed easily, even though cows had been there earlier that morning, and the soft ground was a honeycomb of muddy holes, flavored with an occasional cow pie. The cows were off to the northeast and I checked to see if there was a bull in the herd. Satisfied there wasn't, I moved down to Long Pond.

It was shaped like a large, extra-curved kidney bean, and I wanted to come up in the middle of the curve to get a clear view of both ends of the pond.

Slowly, I worked out of the springy ground and up onto some grassy higher land. I took off my gear, got down, and crawled forward, checking each end. Nothing. I crawled some more. Checked. Again nothing.

I got up on one knee and looked. Still nothing. I stood up and there was movement on the water in front of me. The '97 came up, but it was a mudhen beating the water with its wings and walking on the water until it settled down at the far east end. Keeping the shotgun ready, I walked forward and saw two birds to my right. I swung over and they disappeared beneath the surface—helldivers.

Ted came up. I snapped on the safety, looked at the passive cows, and heard a shotgun go off one-two-three times far to the southeast. I got my gear and decided to try Cliff Pond, a part of the river just to the south.

There was a thicket of buckbrush between Long Pond and Cliff Pond, too thick to go through quietly, so I steered off to the west of it on solid prairie. I moved forward toward the eroded cliff jutting straight up from the river. To my left the river slowly showed itself, but there weren't any ducks on it. I kept moving south toward a "narrows" filled with rocks and running water.

By the narrows I straightened up and looked the full length of Cliff Pond, but didn't see anything. The river widened into Cliff Pond just beyond the narrows, so I went over and sat on the bank with some snakeberry bushes at my back. Ted drank at the narrows and then came and lay beside me.

I took off the knapsack, dug out the canteen, and drank. I noticed some buffalo berries growing near a deeply grooved cowpath. They looked like large red grapes on the dry grass.

Suddenly, there was a swishing sound. I looked up and saw a large "can" fly past so close I could see its eye. It flew like a feathery arrow, following the river. I figured the hunter whose shots I had heard must have scared it, and it might have cousins, so I dropped off the bank onto the firm mud shoulder behind some rushes and waited, looking east.

Soon, zigging and sagging up the river, four "cans" came flying low and fast. (For my money "cans" and blue wing teal are the fastest ducks there are. Teal are smaller, so they're harder to hit, but "cans" take a lot of skill to bring down in full flight, too.) I put a good lead on the head "can." Boom! It crumpled into the narrows. Boom! A miss. I swung more to my right. Boom! A tough going-away shot, and Ted was after the "can" as it splashed down in the river beyond the narrows.

I left the '97, crossed the fence, and reached for the bird in the narrows. Ted already had the other bird in his mouth.

Woosh! Five "cans" divided right over my head as they caught sight of me, then closed up after they passed and traced the river west.

I felt stupid, getting caught out like that. I grabbed the duck and went back to my natural blind. Ted loped up, dropped his "can," and lay down near the rushes.

Usually the ducks would be down, hugging the shore at that time of day, but the hunter to the southeast had them flying. Six more flights of ducks came over—some more "cans," some redheads (which I didn't like because they sometimes laid their eggs in canvasback nests, just like cowbirds, and the "can" parents raised the redhead ducklings, while their own died), and some bluebills. I didn't eat redhead or bluebill. They're diving ducks, not tippers like mallards and teal which I loved to eat, but which seemed to have migrated by then. Divers didn't taste very good, almost muddy.

Every one of the redheads and bluebills was flying with its legs straight back. They had no intentions of setting down until they were a long way to the west.

I shot two more "cans," then the flights stopped.

I didn't want to carry eight birds in my coat so I lined them up in a row in a cowpath. The six males with their reddish-chestnut heads, black breasts, and white-gray bodies were to the east, and the two pale brown females were to the west. All of them had that distinctive wedged-shaped head.

I brushed the feathers of the "can" on the end. It was the largest one at maybe three pounds. A duck louse scooted out. I pinched it between the nails of my thumb and middle finger and dropped it in the grass. Ant food, if there were any still around.

I got up to hunt the river where it wound back and forth like a crawling snake just beyond Cliff Pond. I walked down the cowpath a few steps and then looked back at my ducks. They appeared warm and fine. Not one had any blood mark showing, and I had folded all the broken wings so everything looked nice.

Working the curves of the little river took a lot of time compared to the amount of ground I covered. I wanted to do it right, so I walked slowly, stopping often to stretch up and see what was on the water as it curved around the next bend. Then I'd move forward, stop and check the base of the next loop, move forward watching the two sides of the loop as they became more visible with each step, cross to the base of the next loop, and do it all again until the river straightened itself out and wandered more or less straight to the southeast.

At the end of the loops, I came to a small pond with a muskrat lodge in the middle. I jerked the '97 up as a dark object swam away from the shore, but it was just a muskrat. I squatted and rested until it climbed up on its tiny island, dragging its ratty tail.

Ted drank, but I'd left my canteen in the knapsack by Cliff Pond, and I wasn't too keen on drinking water where cows had been earlier, so I started back. If any ducks had landed there since I'd been gone, I decided not to shoot them. Eight was plenty for awhile. I cradled Boss's shotgun with the safety on as I walked the path, thinking of Bear out hunting when the daily bag limit had been fifty.

I'd been away thirty minutes or so, but the ducks were where I'd left them. I came up to the biggest "can" and stared. There was a hole in its chest and half its right side had been torn open and eaten.

The next "can" had the same chest hole and its side was ripped open, too, but not eaten. A length of gut had been pulled out of the rip and trailed in the dirt.

The rest of the ducks had not been eaten, but each one had the same bloody chest hole.

"Goddang weasel," I said aloud.

Ted came running over and sniffed. He backed off and whined, but I didn't know if it was because of the blood or the weasel smell.

"Goddang bloodsucker," I said. "I'm glad I got your cousins last winter. This winter I'm comin' after you."

From a few steps away the ducks looked pretty much the same as before. The bodies hadn't been moved any, except for the big "can" which had been pulled a couple inches away from the rest, but I couldn't look at them anymore with those dark, bloody holes that ruined everything.

I left them where they lay, picked up my gear, and headed downriver with Ted at my heels.

CHAPTER LXI

I didn't hunt; I just moved away from where I didn't want to be. I went past the Johnson place, across the section road, and into Hepburn's pasture, the river to my right.

I walked under the GN bridge, built on steel supports because of the high river banks. I walked fast and despite the cool wind, I was sweating. On the other side of the bridge, I stopped and drank, but then kept moving. The miles went by—one, two, three, four—until I was on a length of river I'd never hunted before.

The river curved in a lazy bend a mile long with the same high cliff to the south and a broad sloping approach from the north. The river was still a series of ponds, but they were bigger, with lots of reeds. One pond was like a small lake.

Ted and I skirted the bend by cutting a tangent. I could see water most of the time, and there were ducks on it.

We came to a fence line. On the other side was a farm Bear had bought through the bank. I'd driven down with him to look it over. The farm yard was a little to the north. Beyond the yard stood another fence and beyond that there was a stubble field.

To the south the river narrowed. Ponds were on either side of the "narrows" which were flush with reeds, making it a natural pass. Ted and I walked down to the narrows. I found a flat rock to sit on and ate what I'd packed.

Ted was hungry, too, so I tossed him some pieces of sandwich, but he looked disappointed. After we ate, I went through the fence the safe way (the second fence didn't extend to the river) and walked along the edge of the reeds. I couldn't go too far into them because of the soft mud, but it was solid along the edge, so I hunched over and kept going until I saw a lone duck.

I raised up, but instead of flying, it dove under. I got down and waited. It came up further away and when I raised up, it dove again. I could tell by the shape it wasn't a helldiver. I thought it might be wounded and couldn't fly, but it was strong enough to be getting away, so when it came up again, I put a spread on the water and "potted" it. Shot raindropped all around the little duck.

I sent Ted in and he brought it back, all reddish-chestnut with a black-white head and a bright blue bill. It was a Ruddy, my first one.

Back at the pass I got out my knife and split the Ruddy open on the flat rock. I pulled out its insides and threw them to Ted, who caught them in the air. The guts were hanging from each side of his muzzle when he began chewing. I ripped back the skin and feathers over the breast and sliced off that meat. I threw it to Ted while he was still wolfing down the entrails.

The sandwiches and peaches made me feel a little better, so I walked down to the water and washed. Then I crossed over some rocks and stood below the cliff where it had been worn down by cows. I climbed up onto the prairie and sat down, scouting what I could see of the river. There were plenty of ducks, but every one I saw was a "diver," not a "tipper": bluebills with dark heads and breasts and a faint purple luster on the head; redheads with dirty white bellies and short puffy heads of red; their chests were black. No good eating there.

I was just getting up to move out of the wind when I saw something at the edge of the cliff. I crawled over and saw it was a buffalo horn core. I pulled it out of the earth, but there was no skull. I searched around and in a little hole I found a tooth.

It was the size of the first joint of my thumb. Part of the root was broken off and what remained was dark gray. The enamel was mostly white, but dark in the two grooves at the back of the tooth. The grinding surface was gray and sunken away from the ridge of enamel like a twisted valley.

I rubbed some dirt off and put the tooth in my pocket. I planned to polish it and be just like Bear and Boss, who carried an elk's tooth on their watch chains.

I went down the cliff and crossed the river that the buffalo whose tooth I carried had drunk from. Not really, of course. Mr. Pomeroy had said a Greek philosopher, Heraclitus, claimed you couldn't step into the same river twice, so my river was different than the buffalo's river.

The wind was dying and it wasn't as cold. The fall afternoon was quiet and the ducks would stay on the water diving for food until it was time for some of them to fly over to stands of sedges, wild rice, foxtail, and other grasses, or, as more and more had begun to do, land in a stubble field for leftover grain. All except the redheads who seemed content to remain diving ducks.

I took off my coat and lay down on it. Ted put his head on his paws and rested, too.

Running along the fence was a line of telephone poles. The man who owned the farm before Bear had put in a telephone when wheat was high, even though he had to run the line several miles south to tie into a company line. And he had to pay for it himself. Maybe making decisions like that was a reason why he had lost his farm.

I dozed off for a few minutes and when I woke up, the first thing I saw was the sky and the second was a kingfisher, sitting on the telephone line directly above the river. I'd never seen a live one before, but it looked exactly like the pictures in an Audubon book Boss had given me for my eleventh birthday—blue back and wings, white belly with a brown belt across the chest, and that long bill and spikey crest.

I didn't move. The kingfisher kept watching the river. Without warning, it launched itself downward, wings tucked close, crest down. Four feet from the surface it stopped and hung suspended, its wings beating rapidly. It did that for twenty or so seconds, then a splash, and up it went with a small, pale fish in its beak. The kingfisher flew off to the south and was gone.

After that a carload of hunters pulled up north of where I was, and the men who got out started circling to the west. I knew what would happen, so I picked up the '97 and walked to the pass. I found some solid footing in the reeds and got ready. The reeds that broke where I walked smelled a little like peppermint, but the mud smelled of rot.

Soon, five shotguns began blasting to the northwest, and hundreds of ducks lifted from the ponds, many of them heading right for me. The shotguns kept going off and the first of the ducks flew over the pass.

I raised up out of the reeds, pointed the '97 at a flock, and drew it ahead. Boom! A "can" fell. Boom! Another went down.

More ducks entered the pass, but higher. I shot and missed. Another flock came in, but sheared off to the south because I raised up too soon. More ducks came over, sky high, but I tried it anyway. Boom! Boom! Boom! Three misses, but the last shot raised a duck up even though the pellets didn't have enough force to do any real damage.

Two ducks came toward me, hugging the north bank. I stood and they veered further north, but not out of range. Boom! Boom! Two redheads fell out of the sky and lay quiet in two wagon tracks that came from the farmyard.

The acrid smell of burned powder was everywhere. I reloaded and hunkered down. I let a small flock of bluebills fly over, unmolested, then another. Some "cans" came over, low. I raised up. Boom! The force of the blast tore one out of the sky.

The guns to the northwest were silent and only straggler ducks were coming by. I raised up and a male "can" tried to veer off. Too late. Boom! He splashed down.

The ducks were gone. I sent Ted into the water, and he began bringing in my kill while I went looking for my last duck. He was swimming with an oddly angled wing, and when he saw me, he dove. I walked along the bank to get closer.

The "can" popped up and I fired, the pattern lifting water all around him. He dove again near some reeds and stayed down. I waited and worried because sometimes ducks bite onto an underwater reed and hold on until they drown. Finally, he came up and I shot him. His head flopped over and he began drifting to shore.

When he got close, I reached in and picked him up. His right eye had been shot out. I carried him to the pass where Ted had recovered two birds and was swimming in with another.

The five men and their dogs were walking back to their car. I saw a couple ducks dangling, but maybe they had more in their coats.

I looked at my four "cans." One was bloody and broken, and I saw the gore seeping from the last "can's" sightless eye.

Suddenly, I was tired of hunting.

CHAPTER LXII

I put the "cans" in my hunting coat, but I left the redheads. Two less to pester "cans." Plus, weasels and worms had to eat, too. I walked away from the river up to Bear's new farmstead. The sun was trying to shine and it was warm on the porch where I sat.

Ted headed toward the faded-red barn. Halfway there, he turned and looked at me. When I didn't call him back, he trotted off to do some exploring.

October days can be chilly, but out of the wind and with a sun, even October days can be too much for a hunting coat. I took it off, got Ma's Bible out of my knapsack, and leaned back against the house.

Ma's Bible was leather-bound and smooth from years of reading. Her maiden name had been printed in gold on the lower right-hand corner, but it had completely worn off.

I opened the pages to the old familiar words, "In the beginning God created the heaven and the earth." They were good words and I felt good reading them.

I read about the light and the darkness; the waters and the firmament; the land and the plants; the sun, the moon, and the stars. I had to glance back to verse five. How could there have been Day and Night making a first day when God didn't create the sun and the moon until the fourth day, and how could plants live without a sun? It wasn't right, but the first light could have been a miraculous light so I went on. It bothered me, though, that I'd never noticed the apparent contradiction before.

The fish, birds, and whales came next, then the land animals, and finally men and women. Except for the displacement of the sun, moon, and stars, everything else in Chapter One appeared to be O.K.

In Chapter Two God rested. That didn't make any sense at all. My God didn't get tired.

I looked around the corner of the house and saw Ted sniffing through an old garden plot that had come up from seed and was choked with weeds. In the middle of some year-old corn stalks stood a cross with tattered rags moving slightly in the wind, the remains of an old scarecrow.

I turned back to the Bible and re-read, ". . . and he rested on the seventh day from all his work which he had made." When we had studied the Greek gods and goddesses in Mrs. Kelley's class, she had called them anthropomorphic because they acted just like humans. I saw that was what had happened in Genesis Two, the author had anthropomorphized his God.

In verse four there was a mark like it was a new paragraph, and the story began again. God created the heavens and the earth, and then He worked on the plants. I could see that the writer was summarizing in that part because he was including the sun, moon, stars, and firmament in the word "heavens."

I started verse seven and stopped. I began again slowly. "And the Lord God formed man of the dust of the ground . . ." Something was out of whack. I skimmed down through the garden, the trees, and the rivers, and on the next page God made the animals and birds and later on the woman.

I looked back to Chapter One and figured out the order: heaven and earth, plants, fish, birds, whales, land animals, men and women.

In Chapter Two it plainly put the order as heavens and earth, plants, man, animals and birds, and woman.

It didn't make sense. I closed the book and put it away. You couldn't have it both ways. There was only one Truth, and I'd found a definite contradiction which couldn't be explained away by a miracle. I knew I'd have to think about what I'd read, but I already knew then that it would be impossible to accept it literally and still maintain a belief in logic and reason.

The sun was gone again and I got up and called for Ted. He came out of the old tree claim carrying a dead cottontail in his mouth. He dropped it at my feet. I patted his head. "Good dog." He picked it up and went over by a crab apple tree. He began worrying it.

I realized I was hungry again, but there was nothing left to eat in my pack.

CHAPTER LXIII

I tried the front door, but it was locked. There wouldn't have been food in the house anyway, but I rattled the knob just the same.

In the lined pockets of my coat, I had eight pounds of "can." If I got some wood, I could eat roast duck. "Cans" tasted pretty fair.

I hung my coat on a rusty nail and crossed the fence, heading for the tree claim where I thought there'd be plenty of deadfall. The stubble crackled underfoot, and I could see occasional feathers and droppings, showing that ducks had been feeding there.

There wasn't as much downed wood among the trees as I had thought, so when I saw a big limb that had broken off and blown ten feet into the field to the east, I went after it.

As I broke off a branch, it snapped with a sharp crack and immediately several birds rose out of the stubble thirty yards away and flew south to the river, quacking.

I saw that unmistakable glossy green head, yellow bill, and purplish-blue wing patch on at least three of them. Male mallards—greenheads.

They were marvelous, but it was hard to fathom. It was late in the season for mallards and it was early in the afternoon for them to be feeding. What had happened to them in Canada?

The half dozen or so birds circled a pond and settled. I marked the spot. Mallard was even better tasting than "can." I went around the trees, dragging the branch. I threw it over the fence and climbed the strands at a post.

Halfway over I saw my coat and stopped. The bag limit on ducks and coots was fifteen. I counted—eight "cans," a Ruddy, four "cans," and two redheads—I already had my limit set by the government.

I looked to the river where the mallards were. I stared, trying to see them, but the river was invisible under its bank. I was up there with one foot balancing on the top wire when suddenly it came to me. Who owned those ducks? Certainly not the government. It did not create, control, or buy them and did not provide for them. Who did provide for them? In a way, they provided for themselves when they ate wild, but more-and-more the farmers did. Bear did. And I was Bear's grandson and heir. If his wheat fed ducks all fall, that gave him—us—ownership of some of the ducks. Those mallards were mine. One, anyway.

I jumped off the fence and ran over to the '97. I spooked Ted, who barked and I quieted him.

Fifteen minutes later I had worked and bellycrawled my way to where I could see the mallards riding the water. I picked out a greenhead, snapped off the safety, gathered myself, and rose up.

The mallards flashed off the water. The '97's stock was smooth on my cheek as I sighted and led my greenhead. I squeezed the trigger and he splashed down, and Ted was another splash.

CHAPTER LXIV

Ted and I came up the fence line and I unloaded Boss's shotgun and put the shells in my coat.

I found a bare spot of dirt near the old well and kicked some grass clumps out with my heel to widen it. I broke off some small branches and twigs from the large branch and shaved some of the twigs with my knife. I put the shavings in the center of the dirt circle with a few twigs on top.

I cleaned the knife on my pants, picked up the mallard, and carried it to the porch. I found the joint on the lower part of a leg and sliced around it, then I broke the leg off. I did the same to the other leg. I put them side-by-side on the porch, orange against the weathered wood.

I cut through the wing joint next to the body and pulled the wing off. I cut off the other wing and put the wings together on the porch.

The head lay at an angle against the wood. I pressed the knife against the neck and worked it back and forth between two bones. I placed the head near the wings. The various pieces looked like a blueprint for building a duck. A tiny puddle was forming on the porch, as a trickle of blood came out of the stump of the neck.

The feathers were soft as I probed for the crop. I punctured it with my knife, cutting a slit through the skin. I put the knife down and tore the skin loose from the muscle beneath it. It came away from the neck and chest, and I pulled it away smoothly until I had to work it around the muscle of the legs, and then it was off. I smoothed the skin and feathers out on the porch. My blueprint duck was complete. The neck blood had coagulated and was drying out.

I slit the belly and reached inside, the smell of the violated guts wrinkling my nose. I worked my fingers up past the heart and pulled out the insides. They were still warm. I dropped them in a pile off the porch and called to Ted. He sniffed them and walked away.

The duck was dark red in its nakedness, and the hemorrhages where the pellets had hit were turning black.

Some chokecherries grew in back of the house. Their branches were long and straight and would have made good spits, but the sap was gone, and I had to walk to a Russian olive and cut a couple of crooked, thorny, but still green, spits.

I walked back and kneeled by the dirt circle and wood. I dumped some water on my hands from the canteen, rubbed them together, and dried them on the brown grass and then on my pants.

From a small box in my knapsack, I got a farmer's match. I used my body to break what wind there was and struck the match. The tinder caught and I released the breath I had been holding. I added more wood and the fire took off.

I walked to the porch, sliced off two large chunks of breast meat and the two thighs, and threw the rest of the carcass to Ted. He seemed mildly interested and carried it to the crab apple tree. I spitted a breast and held it over the flame.

Everything I did, I had done many times before, just like Bear and Boss had taught me. Everything in a certain order and done just so. I had done it, and it was right, even though it had never been my sixteenth duck before.

The breast meat tasted fine, gamey and smoky and fine. I ate it while I roasted the other breast. When I finished that one, I drank some cold water from the canteen. I spitted the two thighs together and they were fine, too. Once or twice while I was eating, I found a piece of shot, which I spit into the fire.

I let the fire die down, washed and dried my hands again, and cleaned my knife. I thanked God for the duck and the fire and got out the Bible.

Over the cliff to the south, I saw a hawk, but I'd never seen a hawk fly the way that one was flying. It wasn't hunting any field or pasture, gliding on its wings. It was rising and swooping and rising again. It looked like pure enjoyment.

I opened the Bible to the Concordance and thumbed to near the back. I wanted to look up "Stars," but I went too far, into the "T's." The word "turtle" caught my eye, so I turned to the Song of Solomon 2:12 and read ". . . and the voice of the turtle is heard in our land."

I'd been around snappers (Bear had kept one for a summer that was as big as a washtub) and painteds, and I knew turtles had no voice. That verse was bunk.

I looked around. The hawk was still there, and way off to the southeast I saw a flight of ducks coming upriver.

"Stars" had quite a few entries. I always liked the Psalms so I read Psalms 8:3. "When I consider thy heavens, the work of thy fingers, the moon and the stars, which thou hast ordained." Then I turned to Psalms 147:4. "He tellest the number of the stars; he calleth them all by their names."

The hawk went after the ducks, gaining altitude on the last one. They flew like bluebills. Swiftly the hawk hurtled down on the bluebill, slamming it with its outstretched talons. The bluebill folded up and fell like a feathered stone. The hawk followed it to the ground, picked it up in its talons, and flapped off to the south.

I flipped over to Job 22:12, "Is not God in the height of heaven? And behold the height of the stars, how high are they?"

Suddenly, it all began to make sense. The ideas of Josh and the astronomers plus Mr. Pomeroy's ideas (those I truly thought through, not just parroted with no real understanding as I had done with Burnside) could be a tool of explanation. If I could read enough and study enough and think enough, and if I could avoid the emotional reactions I had thrown against Josh and Burnside, I could grasp a little piece of God's Mind.

I got down on my knees, and in one of the most honest and shortest prayers I ever said I thanked God for the human brain.

It was late afternoon and I had to get moving. I found a rusty spade and dug a hole near the well. I put the duck parts and carcass in the hole and scraped the ashes and charred wood over them. I poured some water over everything and covered it with dirt.

I thought that if Josh was right about astronomical and biological things, maybe he was right about political things, too.

I dug through the wet dirt and ashes until I found the green head. I picked it up and cleaned it off as best I could. I covered the hole again, carried the head over to the porch, took down my coat, and hung the head on the rusty nail.

I took out my knife and carved "#16" under the head.

I put on my coat, gathered my gear and gun, and headed for home. Ted ranged ahead.

CHAPTER LXV

The ducks were flying through the later afternoon. Hunters were keeping them moving, shooting from bluff, blind, and bank. I'd had my fill of that for awhile, so at the railroad bridge, I climbed the embankment and started walking the tracks toward our town.

The sun was going down through gray clouds that crimsoned and pinked the horizon and made me feel good despite the chill growing in the air.

A couple miles from town I kicked up two white tails from some brush just off the right-of-way. I'd heard that a deer never makes a sound, but as I watched the two flags move off toward a tree claim, I could hear a distinct high-pitched wheeze coming from the bounding deer.

Ten minutes later Ted and I took to the ditch as a train rumbled by, throwing smoke and soot behind it. Up on the tracks again, the smell brought out feelings both good and bad. I picked up my pace and soon our town showed itself speckled beside the tail light of the train. The twilight began to blind me.

At the first crossing I turned north off the right-of-way and onto Salem Street. Five blocks and a right turn and I was quieting Ted and easing open the door of the garage.

Through the living room window I had seen Boss reading the paper, and I could smell the supper Ma was making, but I wasn't hungry, and I wasn't ready to go in yet. I put the ducks down on the shelf to be cleaned later. I unloaded my gear. I was especially careful with Ma's Bible and Boss's '97, which I checked once more to be certain it was harmless. I'd clean the shotgun later, too, or Boss would skin me.

I had Ted lie down on his rug and I went out, shutting the door quietly. I walked the alley and passed the houses with lights warming them.

At the NP I walked the tracks north. I took the buffalo tooth out of my pocket. It had broken into three pieces. Crossing the railroad bridge, I tossed the pieces into the river.

I headed west on the river road, stirring up the dogs. The moon was almost full and slow-moving clouds crossed its face. Miss Hoar's house stood out in white.

The river was trickling over the rocks leading out of the ice house pond as I passed. I crossed the West End Bridge and tramped through the pasture east of the res. Slowly, I climbed the east side embankment and watched the moon reflect off the water as I walked around the north side.

Most of the clouds were gone and the stars were cold and winking. I saw the dark space between them, but with the moon it wasn't as inky black as I had seen it, and I knew it would never be that dark again.

I walked west and saw the swimming places off the far shore, and I saw the deep water which some day I'd swim, too. Next summer. Across and back.

I continued around the narrow west bank, climbed over the sluice gate, and went up the south bank, moving higher and higher.

At the top of the south bank, I was on the highest point of land in our town, whose buildings, streets, and lights were to the southeast, but whose people I couldn't see.

It was just me and the moon, the stars, and the dark, a dark that would reveal its secrets slowly, but still reveal them.

I looked down at the black water and pulled my coat tighter. My breath came out in puffs of whitish-gray. I heard a dog bark somewhere and then moved off the hill toward the wye.

I climbed up onto the ballast and heard music coming from Twig's place, carrying so cleanly through the night that I thought the singer was right there.

It was Bessie Smith, the blues singer I'd first heard in Minot. Twig was playing some records the twins and I had bought for him.

"If I should take a notion
To jump into the ocean.
'Tain't nobody's bizness if I do, do, do, do.

If I go to church on Sunday,
Then just shimmy down on Monday,
'Tain't nobody's bizness if I do, if I do.
If my friend ain't got no money,
And I say, 'Take all mine, honey,'
'Tain't nobody's bizness if I do, do, do, do."

I crossed the plank bridge. I hoped Twig had a Bible, so we could read Genesis together. I already knew he hated both the Republicans and the Democrats.

He was bundled up on his porch changing records.

"Hi, Twig."

"Evenin', Lige. Out for a stroll?"

"Yeah."

"Kinda chilly, ain't it?"

"Yeah."

"Pull up a chair."

A long freight was heading west, following its headlight.

"Lige, it's the darndest thing. I was out back today and part of my grave had sunk in. Ya know what I found?"

"No. What?"

"Somebody had buried a baseball bat with my leg."